Bound for the Promise-Land

by

Troy D. Smith

I0634085

Best Paperback Original, 2001

Bound for the Promise-Land

Published by *Cane Hollow Press*

Copyright © 2000 by Troy D. Smith
Cover Art Copyright © 2016 by Laura Shinn

Cover image: Sgt. Tom Harris

Writers' Club Press edition: 2000
Western Trail Blazer edition: 2011
Cane Hollow Press edition: 2016

Licensing Notes

No part of this book may be reproduced in any form or by any electronic or mechanical means including information storage and retrieval systems, without permission in writing from the author. The only exception is by a reviewer, who may quote short excerpts in a review.

This book is a work of fiction. Names, characters, places and incidents are either products of the author's imagination or are used in a fictional manner.

Reviews for *Bound for the Promise-Land*

An illuminating book ... believably drawn and complex ... a book that everyone should read. – *The Shootist, January 2001*

Smith creates a classic from the first chapter ... a magnificent novel that I predict will become a classic. – *Roundup Magazine, June 2001*

Other works by this author:

Good Rebel Soil: The Champ Ferguson Story
Cross Road Blues
The Trail Brothers
Brothers in Arms
Riding to Sundown
Caleb's Price
All That We See or Seem
The Stealing Moon
The Blackwell Chronicles

Dedication

For my friends, First Sgt. Tom Harris and Robert Shockley — never forgotten.

Foreword

"The pursuit of truth, not of facts, is the business of fiction."These words were penned many years ago by Oakley Hall, author of the Western classic *Warlock*, and I agree with them whole-heartedly. I have taken some liberties in this book with *when* certain things happened, and I have intermingled the history of the Ninth and Tenth Cavalry — both black regiments. I have done this with a view toward more concisely showing the *how's* and *why's* of the black experience in Nineteenth Century America.

In a more technical vein, I have made mention of a couple of military medals in a time before they existed under those names. I apologize to those readers with the specialized knowledge to be aware of this if it is a distraction; my reasoning is that 99% or more of readers would immediately understand those medals' significance with a more moden nomenclature, preventing the need to slow the story down with a history of military awards.

Part I: The Slave

Chapter One

I was born on the old Moss plantation, outside of Hawkin's Point, not far from Charleston. Best I can figure it, that was in 1839. My daddy was the blacksmith. He was a big, powerful man, name of Billy—his daddy was from Africa. I remember his huge roughened hands, how they gripped that hammer as he pounded and shaped iron.

And I remember how he stared at the birds. He would pause in his labors to watch them wheel up there among the clouds, a faraway look on his face. Though he looked peaceful then, he was really a hot-tempered man. He had done been sold three times when he came to the Moss place and took up with my mama. He had tried to run away from every master that bought him.

One day, when I was eight years old, Daddy was leaning on his anvil and watching them birds. The overseer happened to come by, and gave him a good cussing for not working hard enough. He fetched him a lick with the little quirt he always carried around.

Quick as you could tell about it, Daddy took that big old hammer and stove the overseer's brains in. The poor man fell back moaning and dying in the dust, the thick blood spreading from under his head, his fat fingers twitching that quirt a little like, without any brains to guide them, that's all they knowed how to do.

Daddy put those rough hands briefly on my shoulders.

"Goodbye, son," he said, and took off running. It was actually more of a jog – he seemed to be in no hurry, as if the act of running was just a necessary rule that had to be carried out.

They caught him and hanged him, right in town. Folks came from all over, some bringing their slaves so they could learn a lesson. Doctor Moss brought all the young boys from his plantation, including me.

Daddy stood there on that scaffold like he was ignoring them all. Then he dropped, and his powerful neck struggled against the rope. His legs kicked wildly – kicking and kicking like he was trying to launch himself into the sky with them birds.

That just left Mama and me—I'm Alfred—and my little brother, Roby. We had a sister once. Jenny, four years younger than me and as cute and sassy as a button. Doctor Moss give her to his nephew in Virginia one year, as a Christmas present. I never seen her again.

Daddy killing that overseer didn't help us much – the next one was just as mean. All of us little boys used to run around barefooted and bare-bottomed, all we ever wore was a long-tailed shirt. That new overseer had a game he played with his snakeskin whip. He used to lash it out at us when we'd come close by to see if he could flip up that shirt-tail without touching the black behind that was underneath. More often than not, the trick didn't work.

He whipped my mama one time. It was the first time I'd ever seen her get whipped. I forget what it was for, but it couldn't have been much 'cause mama always walked around white folks like she was walking on eggs.

The overseer made her pull her dress down around her waist—with everybody looking on—and took out that whip. He called it his "blacksnake." He didn't tie her to the whipping post set into the back yard, which was usually used. Instead he tied her hands to a tree limb up over her head. She was left unable to hide her nakedness, and she shrilly cried out to Jesus and the overseer for mercy. The whip bit into her back. It broke apart her flesh, including many old scars – even our scars was not our own, they could be broken apart and added to and changed at the whim of the overseer.

I remember standing by, my young eyes popping at the spectacle – and how my mama trembled and moaned even before the whipping began. Once the overseer had got to going good, and warmed to his task, she screamed and sobbed pitifully.

I felt angry and helpless. And somewhere in the back of my childish mind, I thought that my mama must have done something awful bad to deserve such punishment.

When I growed older I began to understand better. It usually wasn't our masters who mistreated us so, it was the overseers and the pattyrollers – that is, the road patrollers. Unlike the masters, them people could not afford a single slave and probably never would. While slave-owners lived in luxury, rednecks ate dirt – many of them ate and lived less comfortably than slaves. The only way they could strike out at the high classes was through their property. Which was us.

And they did strike out. I seen not just that overseer but later ones whip pregnant women. They would dig a hole in the ground for the woman's belly, and then lay her across it and start in.

Not the masters, though. They seen to it that we was well-fed and healthy, that nearly all our needs was taken care of. That was so's we could work. When we was whipped, and couldn't work, they wasn't getting their money's worth out of us.

Doctor Moss was like most other plantation owners I knowed of. His main concerns was always business and money – we didn't even exist to him, at least not as people. We hated them overseers with all our hearts, but at least they knowed us by name.

The Missus was different. It seemed like that to me, anyways, though my recollections of her have dimmed with time. I do recall that she always wore a smile. I know now that she probably wasn't smiling at me, just smiling in general. That was still something to set store by, though, for the smiles of most white people melted when they seen us.

But she must have taken some liking to me. She arranged for me to work in the big house during the summer time, shooing flies away from her with a feather-duster. I was a little shaver then, maybe five years old. And one day she had me help her plant a magnolia tree in back of the house. We clawed through the soil with our fingers, wordless, planting that tree which she had said would watch over her family for decades to come and give her young'uns shade to play in.

Doctor Moss was upset at her, or pretended to be. He claimed that the very reason they owned slaves was so she wouldn't have to do that sort of thing. She just laughed, and so did he – I was tempted to let out a peep or two myself, but I didn't know how it might be taken so I kept my mouth shut.

The Missus died several months after that, while giving birth to the Doctor's only child, Phillip. Her tree managed to grow up to a pretty good size, but one day it died too. Some kind of tree disease, is what they said. The leaves all curled up and fell off, right in the middle of summer. They blowed away – skittering and bouncing down the road like they had gone looking for her. I watched them go. Looking at them empty branches reminded me of how lonesome and empty my own life was. Mine and everybody else's, I reckon.

I growed up to be a year-long field hand; I didn't get no more summers off to shoo flies at the big house. Every day was pretty much the same as the one before. The overseer would wake us up blowing that big old horn of his, and we would file out of our shacks and head for the fields. We would bake all day in the hot sun, ever' once in a while managing to get the waterboy's attention. Then we'd trudge back – making sure our hoes was stacked nice and neat – eat our supper, lay down on our straw-filled pallets, and rest up for more of the same.

The only day that was different was Sunday. We didn't have to work, and the master encouraged all his niggers to go to church. One of the slaves was a preacher, or claimed to be, and they would congregate in a field to hear him repeat what he had been told was in the Bible, or maybe just what he thought ought to be in it. Most masters didn't like that kind of goings-on, for a crowd of niggers would spell rebellion to them even if the crowd in question was all cripples. The slaves had a harder time on them plantations. They had to meet in secret, and would usually leave a pot turned upside down outside their meeting-place. The pot would be tipped over a little, so that there was just enough of an opening at the mouth to catch the noise of their praying and singing and keep it from reaching the master's ears. At least that's what they said. It seemed a little far-fetched to me – I sure wouldn't want my life counting on such precautions.

I was never a real religious-minded man, so Sunday didn't mean nothing more to me than getting some rest. Mama and Roby always went, though, and shook their heads at my sinfulness. I preferred the peace and quiet of the mostly-abandoned slave row over all the singing and hollering I knowed was going on at church. I could do fine without company.

All that changed one Saturday night after work. I had just ate, then stepped outside in the moonlight for a breath of fresh air, when I heard a hissing noise. Looking around cautiously, I seen that it was a couple of other field hands – Sid and Topaz – trying to get my attention. I stepped around the corner to see what they wanted.

"What you fools doin' loafin' 'round my house, dis time of day?"

They shushed at me. "Listen up," Sid whispered. "You wanna have some good fun tonight?"

"I sholy hope dis ain't it."

"We could of went without you, but we didn't," Sid said, but his smile was as broad as before. "But de mo' de better. Come on."

I followed them into the darkness. "Where we goin'?"

"You'll see," Sid said cheerfully. Sid worked as hard as anybody, at least when he thought someone was looking. I could never understand, then, where he got all his energy.

That boy was always into something. Sometimes he would start one mess before he got all the way out of the last one.

"Say, Alfred," whispered Topaz. "I seen a ole tomcat pitterin' around back yonder. You ought to th'ow him some scraps, see if he'll stay around. Stray cat stay at yo' house, it's always a sign of good luck."

I peered at Topaz's leg in the moonlight; sure enough, I seen a flashing. He had his usual silver dime tied to his leg with a piece of string to ward off spells. Everybody believed in spells and conjuring, even me back then, but Topaz believed enough for everybody. His whole life was a series of omens and spells and jinx-breakers.

We half-ran through the grassy hills behind slave row. As we neared the slave graveyard, Sid turned around. He was more serious than I was used to seeing him.

"We got to run from here on out," he said. "An' I mean run hard. They's ha'nts all around here. Ha'nts, and will-o'-the-wispses, and worser."

I snorted. "I been out this way huntin' plenty of times," I said. "I ain't never seen no boogers."

"They out here, sho' enough," Topaz said. "I seen 'em. White folks cain't do nothin' but hear ha'nts, they ain't got the eyes to see 'em. Only us darkies."

Sid chuckled softly. "Alfred cain't see 'em. Maybe he got some cracker blood."

The anger in my eyes must have showed through even in the dark, 'cause Sid fell back a couple of steps like he thought I was fixing to hit him.

"Come on," he said then. "We gonna git left out!"

There was a big old gulley past the graveyard, and I could tell that was where we was going. I could hear whispers as we drawed near, as well as muted laughter, and I could detect a faint smoky smell. We stepped down into the gulley and right into six other slaves.

"Awright, we here," Sid announced. "Let's start the festivities."

"They done started," one man informed him.

And they had, at that. There was several bottles of whiskey being passed around, and a pig was roasting over a small fire. I looked all around – down in that gulley, we was completely hidden from view.

"Where'd we get the pig?" I asked.

"Where do we always get pigs?" the first man said. I recognized him now as the carpenter. He had big pouches under his eyes that made him look like a bloodhound. "Outen de barn."

I laughed out loud, amazed at their audacity. "You mean we roastin' up de massa's pig? Lawdamighty!" I fell to the ground, trying not to laugh myself into a fit. "You better cook dat pig up good, boy, so's we can remember how good it tasted while dey whippin' our hide off!"

"Ain't nothin' to worry about, Alfred," said Topaz. "Ole Doc here, he done put a spell on massa so he'll believe whatever we say. We gon' stay out here all night, eatin' and drinkin' and not go home until noon. We'll tell de massa we got a early start at church."

A fat little silhouette that I recognized as Doc nodded. "It's guaranteed," he said.

"Awright den," I said. "Where'd we get dis liquor? We charm it out of somebody?"

Sid said, "Raymond is de best carpenter in Jefferson County." Baggy-eyes nodded humbly at the compliment. "De massa hires him out, and he gets to keep some of de money. He's been savin' up for dis for months."

If that was the case, I decided that the only polite thing to do was to sit back and enjoy it. I nipped at the whiskey when it came my way. I savored the harsh bite of it.

"We should have brung Uncle Wiley," Topaz said. "He's always real good company. Maybe he could tell us one of dem stories of his."

A couple of the men sneered at him. I doubt if Topaz seen it, 'cause it was so dark and he wasn't looking that way anyhow, but I did. The men was bought off another plantation, and must not have understood a grown man's affection for Uncle Wiley's tales. The fact is, Uncle Wiley was a master story-teller. He was also a master whittler, jester, and listener – and the years had turned him into a pretty good gardener. All of the men and women on Moss's place who was less than forty years old had grown up sitting on Uncle Wiley's knee, listening to his musical voice. That included young Philip Moss.

"You crazy," Sid said. "Dis ain't Uncle Wiley's kind of fun. If he was here right now, he'd prob'ly lay dat whiskey bottle upside yo' head."

We all laughed at the image Sid's words raised. It was hard to imagine the old man doing such a thing, especially to a great big man like Topaz, but we could picture him trying.

One of the new hands—the ones who had sneered at Topaz—was staring at me. I started to feel uncomfortable. I hoped he would get bored with it, but he never let up. So I said, "What you starin' at, anyway?"

"How old are you?" he said, ignoring my question.

"I don't know. About eighteen."

He shook his head. "I thought I knowed you, but I reckon not. Seems like I seen you years ago, when I was at Old Man Trent's plantation."

"Might have been his daddy," Raymond said. "He looked just like the boy, only with a beard. Used to be our blacksmith."

"Yeah, that's it! Massa Moss's overseer brung him to Massa Trent's to straighten out some metal fence-railin's. The two overseers got to braggin' 'bout how strong each one's nigger was. They finally made a bet, and made dat blacksmith fight with one of our field-hands – a real big man. Blacksmith near about killed him. Den our overseer got mad because he lost his money, and he killed dat boy his self."

When informed that Daddy had took a hammer to an overseer, the man – whose name, I had picked up, was Bill – took a long drink in tribute.

We sat there in the grass all through the night, gnawing on the massa's pork and getting drunk. I thought back on tales my daddy had told me, passed down from his own father. His African father had told him about being the son of a village chief. He told about having his own goats and of walking through the jungle to suit his fancy – no passes, no overseer, just doing what you wanted whenever the urge struck you.

I looked at my friends. In the bright daylight we shuffled and bowed before our masters, said yassuh and kept our eyes glued to our own dusty toes. But here, sprawled in the moonlit grass with nothing over us but the sky, we was all African kings.

After being woken by the midday sun, we all stumbled home. A couple of fellows remained behind to dispose of the evidence. Since Simon the tanner had some money saved up too, we decided to do it again the next week.

Slave row was still deserted. It would be awhile before the church-goers returned, which was fine with me. I crawled onto my bed to get a little extra shuteye.

I was awoken this time, not by the warm sun, but by the voice of my mother.

"Out drunk, I see," she said. Roby was standing behind her, grinning like an idiot. "Not surprised. Got too much of your daddy's hot blood. Probably wind up hanged, or worse."

It was as close as she had come to anger in years. For the previous decade she had become more and more withdrawn. Even her frenzied singing at the church meetings had slowed down until it was barely more than a mumble.

Roby, I could tell, really was mad. He was mad because I didn't take him with me. I considered offering to take him next time, but I was not sure how well the others would take to a kid's presence. I wasn't sure if he would come anyway. That would mean missing church, something he hated to do – not that he was especially pious. He just couldn't bear the thought of not being seen.

No more was said about it, though, by neither one of them. Mama clattered through her regular Sunday routine – sweeping things that had already been swept, straightening things that wasn't crooked. It was all done with a vacant look on her face, like she no more cared about what she was doing than the rain cared if it watered the crops or flooded them.

Then Roby took out a old jew's-harp he had traded for somewheres. He thought he could play it and his ignorance was harder on the rest of us than it was on him. That tinny, unbalanced music filled the little cabin. Mama's body swayed a little as she pursued her duties, like it was remembering something from long ago that her eyes had forgotten.

Not able to put up with the racket no more, especially with my head in such a delicate condition, I staggered outside.

Breathing the fresh air was nice, but the sunlight felt like it was burning a hole right through my eyeballs. I dropped roughly to the ground I was sitting there in the dust, rubbing my head, when I heard Uncle Wiley.

"Lawd, boy. You look like you done stepped on somethin'."

"Somethin' like that." I tried to ignore him, but it was more than I could do. He just stared at me in the special disapproving way he did sometimes. I felt like a little young'un again, caught in meanness.

"You want somethin'?" I asked after what seemed like a long time. The words didn't come out as strong as I had intended.

"Want a lot of things. Want a softer bed for my achin' back. Want a quiet woman with a big behind. Ever' once in a while I want a hot slab of fresh-roasted pig meat, but I got sense enough to be careful where I gets it from." He emphasized the last part by spitting in the dust.

My head jerked up, an action I regretted as soon as I did it. Trying to see through the stars, I said, "What are you talkin' about?"

Uncle Wiley snorted. "I ain't stupid, Alfred. And neither is Massa Moss. It just so happens that I work my own truck garden at night. I might be old, but I can still hear drunks squawkin', no matter how far off it is. And I can still smell pigs roastin' where no pigs is supposed to be."

I stared at him, unable to deny his charge. Behind his stern face a faint little smile was starting to crack through.

"Don't worry," he said. "I ain't gonna tell on ya, or nothing like that. Won't have to, the way you fools announce yourselves. You listen to a word of advice from Uncle Wiley. You run around with heathens like that Sid, you'll come to a bad end. You need to straighten up and find Jesus."

I scowled. I wanted to tell him what I really thought of his old-time religion. Near as I could tell, if Jesus was as all-powerful as everybody always said, he could set us all free in a heartbeat. He hadn't done it yet, so either he didn't exist or he didn't care about us. If that was so, he was just like another massa. I figured I had massas enough without volunteering for more.

"Uncle Wiley!"

A little girl was running toward us, wearing a smile so big she practically fell over it. She still wore her church-going brogans. I recognized her, or I thought I did – I believe she was the daughter of Burl, Doctor Moss's driver. As closed as our little slave community was, I didn't know everybody by name. I didn't even know how many of us there was – just that it was more than I could count. For that matter, I didn't know where the Moss plantation was in relation to the rest of the United States. I doubt if any of the slaves did.

"Come here, missy," Uncle Wiley said as he took the girl in his arms and swung her high into the air. All complaints about his tired old back were forgotten; he had grown a smile big enough to match hers.

"Tell me a story, Uncle Wiley," she said.

"Why sho'," the old man answered. He winked at me over his shoulder, and then the two oddly-matched friends was walking hand-in-hand toward Uncle Wiley's rickety front porch. I watched them, too far away to hear their words but close enough to see their happy faces.

How many times, I wondered, had I sat on that porch and listened to his gentle words? The innocent and meek seemed to be drawn to him. When had his gaze started making me uncomfortable instead of content?

I decided to see what Sid and Topaz was up to. I couldn't wake Sid up, but Topaz I found sitting outside just as I had been.

"I reckon you couldn't sleep, neither," I said.

Topaz shook his head. His big eyes was wide with worry. "No," he said. "I slept a little, but I had a bad dream an' it woke me up. It was about snakes. An' then, when my sister Rosie was eatin' dinner, she sneezed with her mouth full."

I stared at him, expectant. "Yeah?" I said.

"Yeah," he repeated. "Them's all signs of death. I'm not sure if it's mine or somebody else's."

I shrugged. "Somebody's always dyin' somewhere."

"This'un will be close."

"Maybe Massa Moss is gonna have us all skinned for that little barbecue we had."

Topaz smiled. The very mention of the event seemed to cheer him up. "Ole Conjurin' Doc's hoodoo is guaranteed," he said. "'Sides, the massa wouldn't kill a body over somethin' like that. He's a good massa, not like some of the others around here."

It never ceased to amaze me how slaves spoke about their masters, even me, before I got older and my anger ripened. We spoke reverently of them, almost lovingly. Slaves from different plantations would argue about which had the better master, as if we owned the masters instead of the other way around. Everyone's hatred was saved for the overseers.

The masters did not personally beat us, and that was enough to make some slaves love them.

And yet at other times we would all make fun of them, mimicking their words and actions. We would laugh at them to make them human, to show that they was as flawed as we was. It was like we couldn't make up our minds how to feel about them. We was torn between loyalty to our self-proclaimed "benefactor"—a word I heard used many times before I figured out what it was supposed to mean—and our own need for dignity.

The next Saturday night we was back in that gulley, drinking and eating away. We was a little louder this time, for we had been encouraged by our past success, and had gotten a little cocky.

Sid leaned toward me and spoke, his speech slurred. "You too stiff, Alfred. Know what you need? You need a woman to loosen you up, that's what."

I stumbled forward to stoke the fire. "I ain't seen no girl around here that strikes my fancy." I tried to return to my seat, but found that I couldn't control my legs. I fell heavily into the grass.

"You de stubbornest man I ever knowed," Sid said. "Even yo' legs is stubborn. You go one way and dey go another."

"I ain't stubborn."

"Dat proves it. You so stubborn you won't even admit to it."

Ignoring him, I passed out.

This time when we stumbled home it was to an unpleasant surprise. Doctor Moss and the overseer was waiting on us. It seems like Conjurin' Doc's spell to cloud the massa's mind was working fine—till the massa counted his pigs.

The overseer was massaging that whip of his. He was a fat, sweaty man, name of Felts. He reminded me a lot of that pig we had roasted. He was always itching to beat on

15

somebody, and he probably thought he had the perfect opportunity, but he was disappointed.

"Put that away, Felts," Doctor Felts said. "You won't be needing it."

Felts was dumbfounded. "But Doctor, we caught 'em red-handed! Thievin' off you like they think they own the place. If you let them get away with that, every uppity nigger on this plantation will be seein' how far they can push us."

Moss smiled. "Oh, I don't intend to let them get away with anything. First let me say, you boys, if I ever catch you at anything like this again, I'll sell you away with no questions asked.

"So far as this time is concerned, well, there are still several hours of daylight remaining. Get your hoes and start working those fields."

I didn't look forward to having the hot sun bake my brains while I had a hangover, but it was better than Felts' blacksnake. It was the next part that I really didn't like.

"There shall be no whipping," Moss announced. I was surprised, for he had never been the easy-going type before.

"A whipping is over too soon. I think I know something that these niggers will hate even worse. From now on, every Sunday come rain or shine, I expect all nine of you boys to spend the day at church. If I hear that you've been laying out, I'll send you to the auction block with some fresh stripes on your backs. Now, get to work."

I was going to get religion anyway, only now it was going to be as a punishment. That didn't exactly put me in a receptive frame-of-mind about the whole thing.

We sweated and struggled in that field, knowing that our friends and family was relaxing in the shade. I didn't mind, though. It was worth it.

Out there, in a gulley just past the graveyard, I had my first taste of freedom.

Chapter Two

I worked in them fields all week long, just like always, but with an attitude I had never took before. I had never really been scared of work, although I had never run to it, neither – but that week I kind of savored every minute, hoping it would last forever. I didn't want Sunday to come. I would gladly have worked seven days a week, sunup to sunset, if only it would save me from the awful fate that Massa Moss had decided for me.

But I couldn't avoid my punishment forever. Come Sunday I walked with Mama and Roby down that dusty road to church. It was my first time going since I was a little fellow, but I knowed exactly what kinds of hollering and goings-on to expect. That preacher used to scare me half to death.

When we got there I learned that some things had changed, but not much. It was still held out in a field in the open air. The preacher wasn't the same one I remembered, neither – the first one's master had decided that if he was so good at stirring niggers up for Jesus, he might be just as good at stirring them up against white folks. He got sold.

There was more people there than I remembered, too, though me and Sid and the others counted for part of that. Mostly, though, it was folks from neighboring plantations. A couple of the masters had come to agree with Doctor Moss about the value of having Christian niggers, and allowed their slaves to attend. Most masters did not, not only out of a fear of slaves conspiring but because it was considered a waste of time. I know of one man on our place who was bought from one of them masters – he was tickled half to death to be able to attend them meetings once he belonged to Doctor Moss. He told me he had begged his old master to let him come, but had been brushed off.

"Don't waste your time," his master had told him. "I'm goin' to heaven. I'll make sure you're there with me."

Like a lot of white folks, he thought his slaves would still be his slaves in heaven. He couldn't conceive how the Lord could send a man to heaven and not let him have slaves; it just wouldn't be paradise. I don't know why they expected us to be happy to go there, if that's how it was going to be. Another thing different was the white overseer standing in the back, wearing a whip and a revolver. I soon learned that the overseers from all three of the plantations involved took turns standing watch at the proceedings. They was there to make sure that nothing was said which might incite the passions of us "easily-swayed" Negroes.

I took a liking to that little preacher right off, 'cause he acted just like the overseer wasn't there.

"One day, brothers and sisters!" he shouted, as he pranced back and forth in the grass before his audience. "One of dese days, we ain't gonna have but one Massa - God Almighty!"

"Amen!" a dozen voices cried out from the crowd.

"God's chillun de Israelites was slaves in Egypt!"

"Hallelujah!"

"Dey wandered aroun' in dat wilderness fo'ty years, as a punishment fo' dey sins!"

"Yessuh, dey did!"

"But one sweet day de Lawd led 'em into dat Promise-Land! De Promise-Land of milk and honey!"

I glanced back, fearful that the overseer would be getting agitated. To my surprise, he looked half-asleep - overcome with boredom. He was probably daydreaming about all the better ways he could have been spending his Sunday. All other eyes seemed to be on the fiery little preacher.

All eyes except mine and one other pair. A pretty young girl about my age was sitting close by, and she was smiling at me with sort of a wistful little smile. When she seen that I had caught her she looked away real fast, but I seen her look back several times before the service was over.

Everybody was on their feet before long, singing. I remembered this from my childhood, but I never listened to the words back then. I just knowed they was delivered with an intense, gut-wrenching emotion.

> *My latest sun is sinkin' fast*
> *My race is nearly run. My strongest trial now is past*
> *My triumph just begun.*

I closed my eyes, swaying with the rhythm, and listened close. Before I knowed it I was singing along.

> *I am bound for the Promise-Land!*
> *Oh, who will arise and go with me?*
> *I am bound for the Promise-Land!*
> *I've got a mother in the Promise-Land,*
> *My mother calls me and I must go*
> *To meet her in the Promise-Land!*

When the preaching and singing was done, the eating started. Cloths was spread out and what food the people could carry was laid on them. Cold cornbread and molasses, pork – some buttermilk. They was all things we wasn't allowed through the week.

I sat off by myself. Mama and Roby had their own circle of friends to move around in. I wasn't alone for long, for Sid and Topaz soon found me.

"How'd you like it, Topaz?" I said.

"I don't like it a'tall. I heared some crows a-cawin' back yonder somewheres, and dats always a bad omen."

"I mean how did you like church."

"Oh, it was all right, I reckon." He tore into a piece of pork. With his mouth half-stuffed, he said, "I do like dis pig-meat."

Sid chuckled "It ain't as good as de pig-meat we been a-havin'."

"It's more done, if you ax' me," Topaz said.

"I don't care. It ain't near half as good."

I stopped listening to them. A few yards away that girl was staring at me, and smiling. I made to get up and she ran away.

Sid shook his head, "Dat gal is sho' 'nuff took to you," he said. "Which just goes to show dat purty gals is sometimes not too bright."

"You crazy," I told him. "If she liked me she wouldn't keep runnin' off and lookin' away and such."

"Don't you know nothin' but cotton fields, boy?" Sid said. "Does ever'thing dat you know'bout mother nature have to do wit' mealy bugs?"

"I don't know what you're talkin' about," I insisted. "I would like to know her name, though, at least."

Topaz looked up from his food, his mouth circled by a curious mixture of molasses and buttermilk.

"I can get Conjurin' Doc to mix you up a love potion," he said. "Dey's guaranteed."

I snorted, "What, like dat pig-spell on de Massa was guaranteed? She'd prob'ly wind up stabbin' me in my sleep."

To my surprise – and panic – Sid leaped to his feet. "I'll be right back," he said, and I knowed I was in trouble. Sid walked right over to where that girl was sitting with a bunch of her friends. He spoke to them awhile, his face beaming and his hands waving. Me and Topaz couldn't hear the words, but we heard the gals laughing. They all stared at me, and I pounded on my leg in angry frustration. Sid took his time coming back, even stopping to offer greetings to several people he hardly knew. When he did return it was all I could do not to strangle him.

"Dis gal of your'n–" he began.

"She ain't no gal of mine. And you ain't my friend, neither, makin' a fool out of me like dat."

"Dis gal of your'n," he continued, "is named Frankie an' she's a house slave over on the LaRue plantation. I told her about you."

"What did you tell her?" I asked, almost afraid to hear the answer.

"I said you're stubborn. I left it at dat, 'cause I figured I had purty well covered it."

I sighed. "I swear, Sid, you drive me crazy sometimes."

"Maybe I do, Alfred, maybe I do. But you don't know what crazy is 'til a gal gets ahold of you."

I waved the comment away, because I knowed better. I decided to change the subject, so I prodded Topaz about what kind of signs he had seen that day. While he listed off all the terrible omens, I went back to eating. Then I seen her. She was staring again, and somehow my appetite just melted away.

Any time a slave was off his plantation, he had to have a traveling pass. It was a piece of paper, signed by his master, explaining the slave's business. The only exception was church on Sunday. No master would want to sign passes for every last one of his slaves. The patty-rollers did not make allowances for this oversight – any slave caught on the road without a pass was to be beaten, Sunday or not. They didn't enforce it much on Sunday morning, but by Sunday afternoon they was rested up and had eaten their breakfast, and was looking for some sport.

And so every Sunday we had to run home from church. Men, women, children, old folk – we all had to run as fast as we was able. They wouldn't grab you if you was running – unless they was in a bad temper – but a walking, "lolly-gaggin'" nigger was probably up to no good. If you slowed down before you got home, you'd be sorry.

On that particular Sunday, as I was running down the road toward the Moss plantation, I couldn't think of nothing but that gal Frankie's big brown eyes. That, and how much I looked forward to the next Sunday. I found the next week to be just as long as the one before – only this time it dragged by 'cause I was so anxious for church-day, not 'cause I dreaded it. The field work didn't seem nearly so hard, though. I attacked the weeds around every cotton plant like they was the days that separated me from Sunday.

When the long-awaited day finally arrived, I sat listening to that preacher with something close to pleasure. I didn't have the first idea what the little fellow was talking about, but I sat there smiling just the same. Every once in awhile I'd even throw in a "amen" or a "hallelujah".

Gradually, though, I realized that no one was staring at me this time. Nobody but Sid, anyway, and it looked like it was all he could do not to bust out laughing. My face burned – I had a feeling that I had been took, somehow.

The preaching ended and the singing began, and if anyone wondered why I stopped singing so lively, they never said anything.

Then the meeting was over and I stood up to leave. I figured I'd rather go on home hungry than try to choke down Mama's dry cornbread, with nothing to wash it down with except for a big dose of my own shame.

And then she was there. It was Frankie, smiling as sweet and pretty as before, and holding out a skillet of bread.

"I made this special," she said. It was the first time that I had heard her voice, "A big fella like you, I figured it would take a lot to fill you up."

I thanked her, at least I think I did – I know I intended to, anyway. But she was already bouncing away like a young deer. I sank back to the grass.

"I'll be right back," she called. "I brung you some sweet milk. Miz LaRue lets me have some, ever' now an den."

I felt a hand on my shoulder after she disappeared.

"Lawd-a-mercy, boy," Sid was saying to me. "I reckon dat gal gon' find out just how much sweet milk it takes to fill up a big boy like you."

"Hush up Sid. We're at church."

"Yessuh. Where de righteous, dey say, will rise up."

He was almost choking himself trying not to laugh. I leaped roughly to my feet and grabbed the front of his shirt. "Sid, by God, I'm fixin' knock you flat on yo' black ass!"

Someone cleared their throat behind me. I turned, and to my horror it was the little preacher. Uncle Wiley was beside him, looking almost as tickled as Sid.

"Dis ain't no place for profanity, boy," the preacher said, "an' he dat takes de Lawd's name in vain is playin' wid his own soul."

"He didn't mean nothin' by it," Sid said. "He just used to playin' rough, ain't you, Alfred?"

I couldn't speak. The way things was going, I figured I'd be better off that way anyhow.

Frankie returned and sat across from me. She handed me a glass jar, laughing softly as I took it, and said, "Go on, Alfred. Eat up."

I wanted to say something impressive-or at least polite-but I had forgotten every word I ever knowed. Instead I started shoveling cornbread into my mouth as she looked on, admiring. I chased it all down with that milk. Lord knows how she done it, but it was ice-cold. I realized when I looked at the empty skillet that I probably should have offered Frankie some, since she made it. I felt like slapping myself in the face.

Sid must have caught my embarrassed look and figured out the cause, for he snickered behind his hand. I gave him the most threatening look I could muster.

Sid stood up. "You folks'll have to excuse me," he said. "The sight of that fine sweet-milk has done made me thirsty. Sholy a fella like me could find his self a jug or two around somewheres."

Sid swaggered off. As soon as he was out of sight I realized what a fool I was - now I was alone with her, and *I'd* have to do the talking.

I sort of mumbled a little, and she bent her head to catch the words. "I - um. Thanks," I said.

"Did you like it?"

"Oh, yeah. Yeah, I liked it real good. It was mighty-mighty fine." My voice broke like a young boy's on the last couple of words, because she was touching my hand.

"I think you're nice," she said. "Do you think I'm nice, Alfred?"

"I ain't never seen nobody like you, Frankie."

She laughed. "Well, that could mean all kinds of things."

"I mean, well, you know. I ain't never seen nobody as pretty."

She thought for a moment. "Good," she said, with a toss of her head.

That was the start of something good. Me and Frankie would sit next to each other every Sunday. She would slip her fingers between mine, and I would lift my head up and feel the sunshine on my face – and sometimes the cool rain – and think that maybe the little preacher knowed what he was talking about after all.

One evening after work, while I sat on my doorstep and enjoyed what little breeze there was, Uncle Wiley shuffled up to me. He took a spot right next to mine, groaning with effort as his skinny body settled into place.

"Wish't I could borry some of yo' energy," he said. "Time was, I could plow twelve hours straight and not think nothin' of it. Now all I do is pull a few weeds and squish a few bugs, and I'm so wo' out my bones creak when I even think about movin' 'em."

I didn't say nothing. Uncle Wiley didn't need no acknowledgment; he'd probably make the same complaints if all the rest of us was laid out dead. He set down his walking stick and fumbled in his pockets. Uncle Wiley took out his old pocket knife, and in the gnarled fingers of his other hand he held a smoothed-out piece of wood. I closed my eyes while the old man whittled. The scraping of the blade, the smell of the fresh shavings-they was comforting things. They was a quiet, gently familiar part of the world I had grown up in, like the birds singing and the taste of molasses. Peaceful things like those was such a small portion of our harsh lives, whenever I came across one I had to lean back and savor it. Maybe if I breathed in enough of them little things, and ignored enough of the big ones, it would all balance out.

"Looks like you an' dat LaRue house-girl is all wrapped up in each other, boy."

I shrugged. "I reckon."

Uncle Wiley nodded and gave out a grunt. "Wouldn't surprise me none if y'all was thinkin' bout gettin' married up."

"Ain't nothin' been said 'bout it."

"Things like dat don't need to be said." He grew silent, and turned his full attention to his whittling. I waited patiently.

Uncle Wiley sucked on his teeth, and I found the peculiar noise irritating. Then he spoke again. "I 'member what it was like to be a young man, an' get all heated up 'bout gettin' married. Fact is, I was married my own self fo' a long time. My Emmie died when you was no more'n a baby."

"I never knowed."

"Dat ain't what we talkin' 'bout, nohow."

"What we talkin' 'bout, den?" I said.

Uncle Wiley's face became stern. "What we talkin' 'bout, Alfred, is you runnin' after a gal from another plantation. Have you give any thought to how dat's gonna work?"

"It's worked for other people," I said.

"Maybe so, maybe so. I ain't tryin' to tell you what to do, or even to talk you out of nothin'. I just wanna make sho' you thinkin' wid yo' *brains*. Now you know dat if you marry dis Frankie girl you ain't never gonna live together."

"Maybe we—"

"Hush up, now," Uncle Wiley said. "I'm tryin' to tell you how it is, not how it *may* be. 'Maybe Massa Moss gonna buy her', you was gonna say.'Or maybe Massa LaRue gonna buy me'. Well git it outen yo' haid, chile. You just 'bout de biggest, strongest hand Massa Moss have. He ain't gonna sell you lessen he has to.

25

"An dat Frankie? She's a house-girl, Alfred. You know how long it takes to train up a house-girl just de way dey wants 'em? Don't look for her to be sold over here, neither. Dat means you gots to live here, she gots to live over yonder, and you gets to see her once't, maybe twice't a week."

"Awright den," I said. "If dat's how it gots to be, I can live wid dat."

Uncle Wiley's face moved closer to my own. "Can you, boy? You think wid all dat young-man energy you got, once yo' passion is all stoked up, one or two times a week seein' yo' own wife is gonna be enough for you? And what about when de young'uns come? You gonna be content to see yo' own chile a few hours a week?"

"Well, good Lawd, Uncle Wiley!" I exploded. "What you want me to say? What you expect me to do?"

He laid a restraining hand on my arm. "Now, now, Alfred, take it easy. I ain't tryin' to work you up, I'm just helpin' you figure out what to expect. Den maybe it won't hit you so hard when it comes. You still little mo' dan a boy, an you ain't got no daddy nor even a step-daddy, so somebody gots to do it.

"See, I done seen all dis stuff befo'. Mo' times dan I care to think about, an' it always comes out de same. Young man has to have a pass to go see his own fambly, an dat one or two times a week. Fo' long he start wantin' to see 'em three times, or fo' times. So he starts sneakin' out at night, sneakin' home in de mornin' – slippin' down dat road widout no pass.

"Only problem wid dat is de patty-rollers is out dere. Dey catch a nigger at night, wid no pass, dey figure dey can do whatever dey wants. *An dey can.* Even if yo' massa don't want you hurt, if'n you gets caught off de plantation ain't a thing he can do or say 'bout what happens to you.

"Dey'll whip you half to death, boy. Dey'll say you run off. An' sometimes dey do worser'n dat. As long as you can work in de fields, what do it matter to dem wh'er you can see outen bofe eyes, or hear outen bofe ears? Or wh'er you can have chilluns? Do you understand what it is I'm sayin to you, son?"

I nodded. "I understand, Uncle Wiley. But I can handle it."

"I hope you can. I hope you can."

No more was said between us, though we sat there another two hours.

Despite the silence, I was full of turmoil inside –but I knew, as only the very young can know, that Uncle Wiley was wrong in my case.

Me and Frankie got married on a Sunday afternoon. It made sense to do it that way, what with the preacher being handy and all our friends and family from both plantations being present.

We was laughing like little kids when we locked arms and jumped over that broomstick – jumped out of the land of singleness and into the world of matrimony. Folks was clapping and singing just like it was the first time they had ever witnessed such an event.

Even my mama was wearing a little smile. Roby was half-smothered with joy, maybe because he had just caught on to a real good way to get a whole lot of attention all at once. Uncle Wiley was grinning as well, but he gave me a knowing nod and wagged a long finger at me – a concerned warning.

Doctor Moss had given me a pass that day, and informed me that the words written on it guaranteed me safe passage to the LaRue plantation and back. I was still required to be at work in the fields at first light on Monday morning. That in itself was pretty exciting, for I had never spent the night anywhere other than Doctor Moss's property.

Me and Frankie walked back to her home. I was sweating like a stuck pig, and I thought my heart was going to jump right out of my throat. Frankie smiled at my discomfort, but she didn't say anything – she just squeezed my hand tight, and walked a little faster. At least we didn't have to worry about the patty-rollers that day. Even they had enough manners not to bother a wedding party.

The LaRue place was a little different from what I was used to. The slaves wore clothes that was a little more threadbare, for one thing. And our little cabins was like mansions compared to the shacks those folks was given. I didn't notice it right then – I didn't notice much of anything, to tell the truth – but later I realized that their attitude was different, too. They was a lot quieter than the slaves at home.

Of course, I was going to have to start thinking of this place as home, now. Frankie's was one of a half-a-dozen cabins that was nicer than the others. It was on the end of slave row, close to the big house. The social order was the same on every plantation – the closer you lived to the big house, and the closer you actually worked to the master himself, the higher up you was. A lot of those house-slaves really *believed* they was special – "I don't act like no nigger," I would hear them say sometimes. "I act decent, like white folks."

Frankie had that cabin all to herself, for her mama had passed away a couple of years before. It had two big rooms and a real bed. It wasn't much of a bed, by white folks' standards, but since it was the first off-the-floor bed I had ever seen, I was in awe of it.

"I was always Miss Peggy's favorite," Frankie explained. "Sometimes, befo' she went away to boardin' school, she used to give me some of her things when they got too wo' out for her to use."

"Won't dat bed break if'n I set on it?"

"Don't you worry none, Alfred, it'll hold up. That bed is stronger dan it looks." She pressed up close, arms circling my waist. "It's like me," she said. I turned around, and she looked up at me – smiling, just like she smiled that first day. "I'm yo' woman now, Alfred. I've been in love wid you since the first day I laid eyes on you, and now you're finally mine."

"And we gonna be together forever," I said.

She held me tight, her cheek pressed firm against my chest. "Don't know about forever," she said. "Don't never know about forever." She looked back up. "But we together now."

We sank to the bed, and I knew that no two people had ever been together in quite the same way we was. Other men might have felt the way I did, I reckon, but it was still fresh and new and alive. It's still alive even now, when I look back on it through all these years my heart still wants to bust with joyful agony. It was the agony of feeling a moment of bliss, and holding on to it with your every muscle for fear it would slip away somehow.

She touched me, and I marveled at it. I had never really known that a man could be touched in a way meant only to bring him pleasure, not to punish him or to teach him fear. For the first time, I *felt* like a man. Not just a growed-up nigger, but a real live human man – someone who was capable of being loved and respected and adored. Someone who a woman trusted; trusted enough to open herself up to him and receive all that he was, and all he was going to be, and cling tightly to it – crying out her approval.

I slipped quietly out of our bed when the roosters started crowing. I kissed her cheek, making her sigh gently in her sleep, and tiptoed out the door. I ran most of the way back to the Mosses', because I was alive and I felt it, and that's what people who are alive do.

Wednesdays was hard. I got to see Frankie on Wednesdays, but the visit was always too short. It seemed that I had no sooner got there than it was time to go. We didn't have much time for talking then, or for setting on the doorstep holding hands. There was only time to fall into each other, like starving people at a banquet who knowed they would not eat again soon.

Saturdays was my favorite. We quit work at noon and I got my pass and was on that road. We had enough time together to feel like we was a family; we got to wake up together on Sunday morning and go to church together, and I didn't have to leave until nearly dark.

It was on my first Saturday with her that Frankie showed me her special place among the corn. I got to her cabin in the early afternoon, and we made love on Miss Peggy's cast-off bed. Afterwards we lay in each others' arms for a long while. Then Frankie got up and started getting dressed, and she throwed my clothes at me.

"Come on," she said, excited. "I've got somethin' to show you."

"I'm lookin' at everything I want to see right now."

"Put yo' britches on, fool, or I'll go widout you."

I followed her outside. We walked down slave row, and I waved at the familiar faces. I hadn't taken time to learn anyone's name yet. Soon we had left them behind, and was in a cornfield.

"Good Lawd!" I said. "What is dese peculiar-lookin' plants? I ain't never seen nothin' like it! Honey, I sho' am glad you showed me dis. Wait'll I tell dem other ignorant niggers back home!"

Frankie laughed. "Quit actin' a fool. Here it is."

We had come to a hollowed-out place among the cornstalks. Frankie sank to her knees; she was out of sight to the rest of the world other than me. I knowed what it was then, for I had heard many folks talk about them. It was a prayer-site. A lot of slaves decided at some point that they needed privacy for their worship, and little cornfield hideaways like Frankie's was common.

"Dis where you come to pray, honey?" I asked her.

"Sometimes dat's what I do. Sometimes I think. And sometimes I just remember – remember everything about the last time I seen you. All de words you said, all de things you done. I save 'em all up an' live 'em again in here, where nobody else can't come bargin' in. Where I don't have to share 'em wid nobody else."

I knelt beside her and pulled her close. We kneeled down that way for a long time, and it gave me pleasure to know that she was saving up that very moment itself, to feed off the echoes of it when her heart got hungry.

It was a couple of nights after that when I broke. I was laying on my straw pallet listening to Roby snore, but all I could think about was my Frankie. Straws poked me in the face, and I thought of her warm body. I pulled my flimsy blanket to me, but it didn't hug me back. I was drenched in a nervous sweat. My heart felt like it was being squeezed.

I couldn't stand it no more. I left the cabin, then I left the plantation. I followed the road, keeping to the bushes, sometimes tripping in the dim light. Once I heard a mounted patrol pass by.

Finally I reached the LaRue place. I crawled on my hands and knees until I reached Frankie's cabin. The door opened easily, and without effort I walked through the darkness to our bed. I slipped under the covers, feeling the warm flesh I had been yearning for.

"Alfred," she whispered. "You gonna git caught!"

"Hush."

"Dey gonna sell you away, you keep pullin' crazy stunts like dis!"

"Never you mind about dat," I told her. "Tomorrow don't matter. We together right now."

Chapter Three

The biggest day of the year on the Moss plantation – and on most of the others, for that matter – was corn-shucking day. It usually came on the first part of November, so that corn-shucking day was nestled in-between the next two biggest events: Christmas and hog-killing time.

Shucking the whole corn crop was actually a big chunk of work, but it was presented to us as a holiday and that's how we took it. Along about dark – after a half-a-days work – we would get divided into two teams and set to husking. It was a serious competition. The shucking race would go on until far into the night, each team trying to do more than the others. There was no prizes at stake other than pride. It was sort of a spooky sight, in a way: all that corn, piled as high as a house, and all around you the sweating black faces. The faces sang as they glistened in the flickering light of the burning pine knots that had been dipped in pitch. They sang with a deep rhythm which coursed through me, and I would join in without deciding to.

And above it all, there was the Master. While young Phillip danced and sang along with the black folks his own age, his daddy stood on a little hill overlooking the whole thing. The flame-shadows danced on his white suit, and a contented smile rested on his face. He was a father watching the frolics of his playful, helpless, ignorant children. He was a god looking over the happy little world he had made – and his carefree subjects, their every need attended to, and he knowed that it was good. There might be some beatings every once in a while, some sellings, even some mutilation – but the niggers can still dance and sing, so they must be truly happy after all.

I watched him out of the corner of my eye. He looked so content. We was acting out his fantasy for him; the graceful darkies, playing happily, proving that the master was a kind benefactor. He needed to have it proved to him every so often, I reckon. The way of life he defended so loudly, him and his kind, never existed except in his own eyes – and that only a couple of times a year when he bothered to look our way as we celebrated the fact that we had a few hours with not much threat of a whipping. It's funny, really, now that I think back on it. A white man watching as black men did his work for him, harvesting a crop introduced to him by red men just before he stole their land – and the white man was proud of all his good works.

As always, Doctor Moss seen to it we had plenty to eat that day. There was huge pots of rice cooked out in the open, and just about everything you could think of to go with it. He even had a few kegs of whiskey and brandy brought down from the big house. Then, his works of charity done for the year, he took Phillip and headed back up to his mansion – allowing us a few hours of private celebration. Once them big front doors closed, the only reminder he would have that we even existed would be the faint sound of our singing.

Once the corn was all shucked and the master was gone, things really started cracking. Corn-cobs was traded in for fiddles and harmonicas. We had us a cake-walk, and then a chalk-line dance. The chalk-line dance was a contest – again, with no prize other than the rewards of vanity – in which each dancer wore a pail of water on his head. They would dance their way down that chalk-line, moving only from the hips down, trying not to spill any of the water. Further, each contestant would try to use fancier moves than the one before him.

Our tongues was loosened by that time, not just by the alcohol but by the fact that Doctor Moss was making a deliberate effort to ignore us, even more than usual. As the dancers snaked their way down the line, the onlookers sang words which had rattled around in our souls and hearts and now poured out into the fresh air.

Mule fell in a ditch
Got it out Monday
Had I been a white man
Got it out Sunday.

Sid, clapping fervently, made his own variation:

I fell down a well
Dey'll get me out in May
If I'd a been a white man
Dey'd get me out today.

Several lively young men danced their way into a circle around Sid, and one ambled gracefully forward. "Buggy horse r'ared,' he sang. "Buggy horse pitched! Th'owed de massa in a muddy ditch!" The man did an exaggerated pantomime of Doctor Moss falling out of his buggy, an event that had occurred a few weeks before. No one had dared to openly snigger or laugh then, when the doctor came dragging home all wet and muddy.

Rising to the other man's challenge, Sid - a smile wrapped all the way around his head - sang a reply.

"Buggy horse is muddy,
Massa is wuss -
Damn if dat massa
Ain't blacker'n us!"

We all laughed loudly, our laughter bringing us to tears as the two singers tried to out-do each other. Each man would build on the closing words of his opponent. To the crowd's delight, Sid performed a hulking swagger which they immediately recognized as Felts.

"Overseer whip us,

He think he slick –
But at least we ain't been beat
Wid no ugly stick!"

I shook my head, chuckling, and walked away from the group to where it was quiet. Sid and his friends was entertaining, sure enough, but not sufficient to take my mind off my troubles.

My trouble was that it was two days before I was due to see Frankie, and I was being driven half out of my mind by the desire to see her now. So I walked, not even thinking, until I had passed right by the graveyard without knowing it and found myself in our grassy gully.

I wasn't alone. A dark figure sat a few yards away, staring dreamily into the night sky. He did not seem to notice me, even when I walked closer to see who he was.

"Hi'dy, Topaz," I said. "Whatchu doin', lookin' for signs in de stars?"

"Don't know much 'bout de stars," he said in a distracted tone. "I know dat when I was little a bunch of 'em fell, an' ever'body said it meant de Judgment Day was come. But it didn't."

"I 'member dat," I said. "We was all scared out of our heads."

"An' I know dat's de Nawth Star right yonder." He pointed into the sky.

"So why you out here, den?" I asked.

Topaz shrugged. "I dunno. Jes' didn't feel like dancin' no mo', I reckon. I was feelin' sort of quiet."

I nodded my understanding and he continued. "I wish't I did know what de stars mean," he said. "Dey say dat de Nawth Star points de way up Nawth. It sho' looks a long ways off, though, don't it? Hundreds of miles, maybe, or even mo'. Reckon how far it is up Nawth, Alfred? Do you know?"

"No," I said, puzzling over the question. I was sort of surprised by it. For as much as I had heard about up North I

35

had no idea where it was. "If you go far enough dat way you hits Fayette County. I reckon Nawth is somewhere on de other side of dat."

I sat down beside him, and for a long time we studied the sky together in silence. It was not total silence, though, for we could clearly hear the music and the voices.

"Do you reckon," Topaz said, "dat up Nawth is close enough dat de people there can hear us singin'?"

"I ain't sho'. Dat music an' stuff does carry quite a ways. But I doubt if it carries even so far as Fayette County."

"Maybe if we sung louder," he said. His eyes glistened in the starlight, and I thought I seen a tear.

"What's wrong wid you, Topaz?"

He shook his head sadly. "I dunno, Alfred. Have you ever ached for somethin', and didn't know what it was?"

I scratched my head. "Well, no. I've ached for something, all right, but I always knowed just what it was I was achin' for."

"You a lucky man, den. You know how to fill dat ache up. You might not can do it whenever you want to, but at least you know how to go about it when you got de chance."

This kind of talk made me uncomfortable, so I decided to change the subject.

"You seen any bad signs lately?"

Topaz, chuckled softly and it sounded hollow, there in that gully. "I see bad signs everywhere I look."

I looked at the stars some more, and their twinkling reminded me of the slitters and flashes in Frankie's eyes sometimes when they looked up at me in the dim light of our bedroom. I decided that there was no sense in both of us sitting there aching, not when my cure lay just a couple of miles away.

I stood and walked off; Topaz did not seem to notice. "See you directly," I told him.

He turned his head toward me and smiled lazily, waving. "Good night, Alfred," he said. "I'll be seein' you."

With that I jogged away toward the LaRue plantation. The aching need which ruled over my body and soul was about to be soothed, at least for a little while. I glanced once over my shoulder and saw that Topaz had not moved. He still scanned the dark sky, eyes narrowed as if even he did not know what he hoped to find.

Over the weeks I had developed quite a bit of pride in my ability to avoid the night patrols. They did not seem to be as fearsome as I had been led to believe; after all, they was made up of nothing more than ignorant white trash. Their patrols was so irregular and unplanned that it didn't take much to stay out of their sight.

That was the kind of thinking I had fallen into. It was just like our secret barbecues in the gully; a little bit of success went to my head and I let my guard down. I made it to Frankie's cabin easy enough that night, but it was on my way back home that I run into trouble.

It was still an hour or so before daylight, and I kind of half-figured that the pattyrollers had all gone home. I was exhausted too, what with no sleep, drinking the master's whiskey, and satisfying my needs with that young woman of mine. What it comes down to is that I was too tired to go scrambling through the bushes, and I wound up taking to the main road.

The horsemen was upon me before I knowed it. I had thought I would hear any approaching riders in time, but I reckon my senses was dulled. There was four of them, and I could see their happy sneers in the moonlight. They reminded me of a bunch of drunk hunters who had stumbled onto a wounded raccoon on the side of the road – they hadn't really counted on catching anything, and now they had a helpless critter practically handed to them.

"Well, well – what have we here?" said their leader. He was a big burly man, and he looked like his eating was done on a better than regular schedule. He was the only one of them that gave me that impression; the others was lean and rangy, like wild dogs,

"Where's your pass, boy?" one of them demanded. As much as it pained me to do so, I went into my shuffling, stuttering field slave routine. That kind of behavior burned me inside under ordinary conditions, but especially before men such as these – men who even white society regarded as little better than me. I bit my tongue, though, and acted servile.

"Oh, Lawdy, massa, I don't know! I must of lost it on the road somewhere. But Doctor Moss, he always give me a pass on Monday night to see my fambly on the LaRue place, you can ax' anybody."

The leader trotted his big bay closer to me; his friends dismounted. "Don't you be tellin' me what to do, nigger," he snarled. "I don't care if Jesus Christ hisself wrote you out a pass on a stone tablet, if you ain't got it with you, your black ass is mine, do you understand me?"

"Yassuh," I said, forcing myself to fake a cringe. I knew that men like these wanted nothing more than to feel important and powerful, like the slave-owners they hated and envied so much. I was willing to indulge them in their fantasy in hopes they would be satisfied and leave me alone.

"He looks like a prime hand, don't he?" one of the other men said. "I could shore use a strong buck like him over at my place."

The leader snorted. "This nigger's probably worth more than your whole miserable dirt farm, Charlie. I bet Doctor Moss sets a lot of store by him."

Charlie snickered. "Ain't that just too bad."

"It shore is," the leader said. "Tie him to that tree yonder, boys."

They hurried me over to the side of the road and lashed my arms around an elm tree. I felt my shirt being ripped from my back, and had a twinge of regret; shirts was mighty hard to come by.

The leader walked around in front of me, to where I could see the long leather strap in his hand. It had big holes placed all along it, designed to raise blisters.

"I reckon this'll learn you to hold on to your pass better next time, boy," he said, and stepped out of sight. I knowed right where he was, though, for a moment later the strap bit into my flesh. I steeled myself, determined not to cry out. The pattyrollers laughed, calling out encouragement to their leader.

"Lay into him, Grady!"

"Ain't that strap gettin' heavy, Grady? I bet the nigger can hold out longer than you can!"

Grady grunted with the effort of delivering the stinging blows. His breathing was heavy. The more he struck me, however, the more energy he seemed to get – all his hatred was being poured out on me, and each blow made it stronger, not weaker. He unleashed his hatred for Doctor Moss, his better, and his hatred for me, his inferior – and for a system which gave us both some things which he believed he deserved instead.

As for me, my resolve weakened. The pain became unbearable. I whimpered once, then cried out. The man's laughter increased. I hated them for laughing, and I hated myself for giving them something to laugh at.

I don't know how many lashes there was. I wasn't there for all of them, for I passed out. The beating continued anyway; my awareness was no longer needed. They had got all the fear and pain out of me that they could, the rest was just to relieve their frustration. Like the masters and overseers, they didn't care if I was aware of anything – so long as my black body was present to serve their needs.

I was dimly aware of being trussed up and draped over the back of Grady's horse, like a killed deer. They carried me the half-mile to the Moss plantation. Strong black hands carried to my cabin. I opened my eyes as I was being taken off the horse, and saw Grady laughing and joking with Felts, the overseer. They spoke as easy and comfortable as brothers, which they might have been for all I know. They was surely brothers in spirit.

I was laid face-down on my cot. My mama was there, just getting ready to go to the fields. She spoke nary a word, though I know she must surely have seen that I was awake. She walked past me like I was nothing more than a lump in the mattress.

She was gone, and in her place stood Felts. He was accompanied by a slave named Aaron, a man that was hated by the other slaves almost as much as Felts was. Aaron was the overseer's helper – sometimes he even gave the whippings. Felts treated him like a dog, but the big slave still seemed to enjoy his position.

Aaron's rough hands ran over my back, making me moan in pain. He whistled.

"Dese here some bad lookin' stripes." Aaron said. "Dey done worked him over purty good."

Felts grinned. "Fine with me. The big monkey deserved it. That's what comes of Doctor Moss's fancy ways – throwin' 'em parties and givin' 'em liquor, sendin' 'em to church like real people and lettin' 'em mix with property from other plantations. What does it get him? Two runaway niggers. Don't you doubt for a minute, Aaron, that they'll catch the other'n too. And he won't come back in as good a shape."

"Yassuh."

"Runaway niggers is thieves, that's all there is to it. They try to steal good property from their betters." Felts sighed. "I don't reckon this'un will be workin' much today. Neither will them others if I don't get out there and ride 'em. Thing I'll never understand about you niggers, Aaron – you quit workin' and start playin' as soon as a white man's back is turned. Worser'n kids."

"Yassuh"

I had never heard Aaron talk much to Felts – probably a sign of his good sense, for talkative niggers would get in trouble. That never stopped Felts from talking to him. Aaron was the only person I ever seen the overseer talk to at any length, and even then he was really just talking to himself and using Aaron as a prop. He would frequently voice his opinions about Negroes; whenever he did, a barely noticeable fire would smolder in Aaron's eyes.

"We ain't got all day, then," Felts was saying. "Fix him up and let's get back to work."

Aaron took a little bag from his pocket, and I winced. I knowed what was about to happen, but no amount of knowledge could have prepared me for it. Aaron rubbed salt in my wounds, to clean them; it hurt like the devil but it was nothing I couldn't handle. It was the next part that had me screaming in agony.

First he took an iron file and ran it up and down my back, filing away the blisters; then he rubbed red pepper in the wounds. This was a favorite trick of overseers everywhere. It served no medical purpose, it just made injured slaves return to work sooner. They would be in such unbearable pain that they couldn't stand to sit still-they would go back to work immediately just to have something to take their mind off the terrible torture.

The two men went back to their tasks, leaving me to suffer in lonely silence. I was so sleepy and tired I was about out of my head, but the fresh pain on my back kept sleep just out of my reach.

Later in the day Uncle Wiley came by. I recognized his tired old gait long before I heard his voice.

"Lawd-a-mighty. You in bad shape, boy. 'Course, I reckon you don't need me to tell you that."

He pulled Mama's single rickety chair up to the head of my pallet. He sat down with a grunt and looked at me with his eyes filled with compassion. I was waiting for the words of rebuke, for things had turned out just as he had said. They never came.

"I brung you a new shirt, Alfred," he said, holding the article out for me to see. "Ax'd Massa Moss 'bout it. He allowed as you oughta have one, 'cause if you don't cover that back of your'n it's liables'ta git wuss."

I didn't thank him. Bandages would have done a whole lot better. Massa Moss was a doctor, he'd know that – and he had plenty on hand. For that matter he could have tended to me himself, instead of sending his heartless, inexperienced overseer to do it. The only problem with that, I knowed, was that such an action would require him to touch my inferior black flesh.

Uncle Wiley helped me put the shirt on. I settled back onto my pallet, trying to ignore the pain.

"I heard 'em talkin'," I said. "They was sayin' somethin' 'bout two runaway slaves. I reckon one of 'em is me, though how they can call me a runaway when they caught me comin' back I don't understand. Who would the other one be?"

Wiley's face became grim. "Heard about dat, did you? Well." He fumbled around, looking uncomfortable. "Fact is, Topaz is gone."

"Topaz?" I repeated. "Run away?"

"Yeah, an' dat ain't de wust of it. Seems like late last night de fool boy crawled in a window of de big house. He stole some of Miss Maggie's necklaces an' rings an' stuff, things dat Massa Moss has kept aroun' for years, ever since she died, as a remembrance. I never would of 'spected such a thing from dat boy, an' dats fo' sho'."

I wouldn't have suspected it either. Before that previous night in the gully, I had never seen anything which would even indicate forbidden desires in Topaz. That in itself disturbed me. Our desires for freedom had been pushed down so far, and hidden so well for so long, that a terrible thing had happened. They were hidden not just from the masters but from each other, sometimes, maybe, even from ourselves. I could not look into the eyes of one of my best friends and see his secret yearning – not until I came across him in a gully, unguarded and unawares.

Wiley said, "I reckon he plans on usin' dat joolery to pay his way Nawth." He shook his head. "I sho' hope he makes it. It's gonna go mighty bad for him if he gits caught."

I don't know when Uncle Wiley left. He had lapsed into thoughtful silence, and I had finally slipped into a half-delirious sleep. At one point I opened my eyes and looked up – the old chair was empty, and a small pile of wood shavings lay at its feet.

Topaz didn't get away. The next day I was back in the fields, hobbling up and down the cotton rows with a hoe in my hand. Every vibration sent shivers of pain up my back; the shirt Uncle Wiley got me was plastered to my oozing skin, and would probably remain like that for quite a spell. I was trying to keep up with the other workers, and one step ahead of the overseer's quirt, when word came to us to assemble at slave row. Topaz was back.

Every slave on the plantation was gathered there, crowded together nervously, when Topaz was dragged in by the pattyrollers. His bloody face hung down, like he neither knowed nor cared what was happening to him. I scanned the faces of my companions; no one spoke or made a sound, but their straining eyes showed that they wanted to say something. It was either fear or wisdom that stopped them. Maybe it was both. Topaz was dumped roughly into his cabin, and the pattyrollers stationed themselves outside the door. They flashed their taunting grins at us. My face burned with helpless fury, and my fists was clenched behind my back.

Doctor Moss walked into our midst and stood before us. His lips was drawn tight, and his eyes was sort of empty. He paced back and forth, like he was working up the nerve to speak his mind. Felts was behind him, carrying that quirt of his like it was his one true love. I don't know if his attitude was contagious, or if it just made me pay more attention, 'cause I seen that his pattyroller friends had their hands resting on their knives in the exact same way.

"I am a forgiving man," Doctor Moss said, in a voice that told us forgiveness was the last thing on his mind. "I forgave when two of my pigs were stolen. I can forgive a strong hand for running away once, although I will see to it that he regrets his action completely."

The way he said it made me believe that if a weak hand ran away, he'd be sunk the first time. Doctor Moss's forgiveness ran mostly towards folks strong enough to turn him a good profit in the future.

"But this," he continued, "this I cannot forgive. For a nigger that was raised on my generosity to steal out of my house. To put his dirty fingers on the treasures of my dear Maggie!" The doctor's voice broke. As he tried to compose himself, the pattyrollers sighed impatiently.

"I'll not put up with it!" the doctor said. "Selling won't be enough – there's a lesson to be taught. This boy's blood is on his own foolish head." He turned to Felts. "You gentlemen may do with him what you will."

Felts smiled broadly. "Yes sir! We'll make him squeal. Doctor Moss, I guarantee it."

Doctor Moss did not acknowledge Felts' zeal. He acknowledged nothing at all, merely walked back to the big house.

"You niggers stand right there," Felts roared. "Stand there and don't move 'till I say. Doctor Moss wants you black-assed monkey bastards to learn a lesson, and I intend to see that you learn it good. Come on, boys."

We stood there a long time. Accustomed as I was to moving constantly through the fields, just standing there was harder for me than working would have been. The sound of the beating didn't make it any easier. It started with a strap, but the sickening thuds indicated that the white men had moved on to fists.

After awhile the beating stopped, and for the first time we heard Topaz scream. The screams went on and on, flavored with pleas for mercy – directed not to his torturers, but to God, who was more likely to listen.

It was a couple of hours before the screaming stopped. Felts stepped outside, drenched in sweat, and covered with blood.

"Burn this shack down," he ordered. "It ain't fit to live in no more, even for niggers. And a couple of you monkeys bury that boy – ain't gonna be no funeral."

Killing a slave was still considered to be murder by the authorities. We all knowed, though, that there would be no inquiries.

The pattyrollers wandered off, fatigued by their hard day's work, but apparently very satisfied by it. Felts walked away as well. "A couple of you niggers do like I said. The rest of you, get back to work."

No one stepped forward. Ignoring my back, I did – I walked toward the cabin, and someone followed behind me. It was Raymond the carpenter. Once inside, we both almost gagged. The whole room was covered with blood and vomit. Topaz – or what little was left of him-lay in the middle of the room. He had been horribly mutilated, and the pieces lay scattered about.

"We gonna need a sack fo' dis job," Raymond said. "A box would do better, but I doubts if dey would spare us de wood."

"Good Lawd," I said, choking.

"Topaz was a good man," Raymond said. "I reckon he just had too many big notions for a nigger. Look what it got him."

"He free," I said.

Raymond snorted. "I reckon bein' a live slave is better'n dis kind of freedom."

I wasn't so sure anymore.

We loaded the remains of Topaz into a heavy sack and carried it to the graveyard. Raymond only brought one shovel, and he did all the digging. I nodded in his direction and thanked him, but he ignored me.

"Sho' is cool an' shady out here," he said. "Dat's one good thing. At least we get a cool shady spot to rest in when we're gone."

I looked ruefully at the sack. Blood had started soaking through it. "If he couldn't see ha'nts afore, he sho' enough ought to be able to see 'em now," I said without humor.

"We ought to say somethin'," the carpenter said. I stared at him, confused. "Over Topaz," he continued. "We ought to say somethin' over his grave. Massa say we cain't have no funeral, but at least we can send de man off right. If'n we don't, his spirit might become restless an' get to wanderin' around here."

That was something to consider. Topaz was always mortally scared of ghosts; I certainly didn't want to be responsible for making him into one. Besides, it was one small dignity – everything else had been taken away from him, he deserved something.

"Let's put him down in the hole first," Raymond said. We lowered the sack down into the moist ground. Topaz's short life was finished after only twenty years – we gently placed him back into the dark womb of the earth that had spawned him. He had accomplished nothing in those two decades, except to look up at the stars and sense that there was a better place somewhere, a better life, and spent his last hours in a desperate gamble trying to find it. It was more than most of us would ever do.

"You do de sayin'," Raymond told me. "You was his friend."

I stood over the open grave, wringing my hands as I searched for the right way to do the task set before me.

"Oh, Lawd," I said, in little more than a whisper.

"Speak up," the carpenter said.

"I reckon He can hear me plain enough," I said sharply. "Oh, Lawd, we have before you today de remains of a young Christian man. His body might be bloody an' stove-up, but we know dat his spirit is alive in Heb'm wid you."

"Amen," Raymond said softly.

"We pray, Oh Lawd, dat you receive his soul and set it free. If you can take de time, Lawd, show him some of dem stars up yonder and 'splain 'em to him. He'd like dat. Anyway, Lawd, take good care of him – and take care of yo' other chillun down here too, 'cause You all de help we ever likely to get. Amen."

"Amen," said the carpenter, and then quickly turned away – but not before I seen the tears streaming down his face.

"You awright?"

He cleared his throat. "Sorry about dat. It's just dat I ain't never seen nobody have nothin' done to 'em like what dey done to Topaz. An' it could just as easy of been you or me, if'n dey took a notion. You go on back to work, boy, I'll take care of dis. Ain't no use in you standin' here watchin' me"

I did like he said. I was haunted for a long time, though, by what I heard as I walked away. It was the shucking sound of the shovel as it covered over Topaz, taking him out of human sight forever – mixed in with the choked-back sobs of the carpenter.

"Damn nigger," I heard him saying under his breath, his voice cracking. "Why you have to get such big notions?"

Being as it was Wednesday, that evening I collected my pass and made my way painfully down the road to Frankie. She didn't seem surprised by my condition; she must've known it was coming one day. Like Uncle Wiley, she had no words of rebuke for me.

I didn't have to tell her what happened to me, but I wanted to tell her about Topaz. I tried, but I didn't know the words to give the full impact of it. My description was clumsy and halting.

"I know he was yo' friend," she said, "but I gots to say dis. It takes a real fool to run off somewhere an' not know where he's goin'. I hope you don't never get no crazy idea like dat."

"Long as I got you, why would I want to run off?" I said. But I knowed that – if I hadn't had Frankie to consider – I might well do the same thing. Topaz had woke something up in me that had been inside for years, but I had never tried to put my finger on it.

That night I sat alone on the front step – after Frankie fell asleep – and looked at the bright stars and thought of my friend. I tried to imagine what it was like to come and go as you please, to be a human being instead of a piece of property.

While I watched, one flaming star fell into the horizon. I wished Topaz was there, so he could tell me whether or not it was a good sign.

Chapter Four

"How come you ain't got no young'uns yet?"

"Good Lawd, Uncle Wiley," I said. "What kinda question is dat?"

The old man shrugged. "Jes' wonderin', dat's all. You been married long enough – dat little girl of your'n ought to have dropped one by now, sholy."

"Well shoot, I dunno. Dem things takes time, I reckon."

"Maybe she's dried up." He raised his hand when I tried to protest. "Now, boy! Ain't nothin' to be ashamed of. I was married to my Emmie fo' twenty years, and we never had no chilluns. Maybe it was all fo' de best, really – we never had to live wid de fear of havin' our own young'uns sold off from us. Dat'd be a terrible burden, an' dat's a fact. Still, sometimes I wished I had somethin' to remember her by."

He saw me staring at him, and realized that he had been talking to himself instead of to me. Uncle Wiley cleared his throat and continued.

"Anyways, dis here's jes' my roundabout way of sayin' dat if dat's how it is wid yo' woman, don't take it too hard. It's happened to a-plenty."

I thanked him, though I wasn't sure why,

"You're prob'ly thinkin' it ain't none of my bidness," Uncle Wiley said. "And you'd be right. But if'n I didn't tell you, who would?"

Wiley wandered off to his garden, leaving me alone with my thoughts. They wasn't thoughts, really, just the familiar yearning for my wife's touch. My back was pretty well healed up, and the painful memories still stung me, but I knowed I couldn't hold out forever. One Monday, or Thursday, or some other night I would slip off down that road again. I couldn't help it. Two days a week was not enough to be in love, especially not when the pure misery of living each day weighed on a man like a rock caught up in his throat. Not when, in the back of your mind, you can't help but wonder if – by next Saturday – you might be beat to death, or sold off to Cuba.

I don't know how long I sat there on the doorstep before Sid approached, but the moon was high up in the sky. He dropped down in the dirt beside my mama's door – his back against the wall, one leg sprawled out and the other bent so that his knee served to prop up his hands. He didn't face me, just stared into the distance like I did.

"You seen Topaz," he said, and I grunted. "Was it as bad as dey say?"

I resisted the urge to close my eyes and blot out the vision that had haunted me for so many days. "I don't know what it is dey say," I finally replied. "But ain't nothin' nobody could say dat's as bad as what happened to pore Topaz. We had to carry him to the graveyard in a damn sack."

"Lawdamighty."

"Is that all you wanted to know?" I asked, a little mad at having the whole thing brung up again.

"Yeah," he said. "I don't know – I just wondered, dat's all. 'Bout how bad it was."

"Why? You thinkin' on runnin away?"

Sid snorted. "Shoot no, boy. You crazy? I'm too scared to even run down de road an get myself some puddin', de way you do. Dem rednecks has done took enough of my hide, widout me handin 'em all of it at one time."

I couldn't help laughing, which made his tone even more mock-serious.

"Don't think I ain't got no backbone, now," he said, "I'm thinkin' about de good of ever'body. Why, the womens around here would lay down an' never do a lick of work again – all out of grief, if somethin' was to happen to me. Runnin' off just wouldn't be worth it."

"Besides," I added, "as long as you're on dis here plantation, de gals ain't got no choice but to put up wid you."

"Say, I never thought of it like dat," Sid said, his eyes gleaming. "Dat's a idea worth goin' over."

We sat in the lengthening shadow, laughing and talking as we always had before. Both our moods was considerably lightened. Whenever there was a lull in the conversation, though, Topaz's ghost was there – reminding us that our circle was broken forever.

Pretty soon my back was healed up enough that I could run if I had to – so naturally I lit out one moonlit Monday night for the LaRue place and an extra evening with Frankie.

I creeped around behind them shacks, mindful of dogs, heading for that sweet cabin. I was surprised to see that the lights was on inside. I almost walked right up to the place, but just before I turned the corner Frankie's door opened. She stepped out, stifling a giggle, and so did a white man. He walked away, not even trying to be quiet, headed for the big house.

When he was gone I opened the door and stepped inside. "Frankie?" I said softly.

She appeared from the next room. "Alfred? Good Lawd, man, what you doin' here?"

"What do you think?"

She puffed up, angry. "Dey done caught you sneakin' off once – and you seen what happened to dat thief friend of your'n. You want de same thing to happen to you? Ain't you got sense enough to keep your britches drawed shut ever' once in a while?"

That hurt—hurt *deep,* and it must have showed in my eyes 'cause she turned her head in shame.

"Dat ain't de only thing dat brings me here, an' you know it." I wanted to tell her exactly what it was that did set my feet toward her shack, but I didn't know the right words.

"I know it," Frankie whispered, the anger gone from her race now. "I just worry about you, Alfred - afraid you'll get yo'self sold, or worse."

"Who was dat white man, and what was he doin' here?"

She smiled. "Dat's just Massa Jesse. We been friends since we was little. He was bringin' me his washin' to do."

"Why should you have to do his washin'?"

"Why should you have to pick Doctor Moss's cotton?"

I winced - she had a good point there. I had asked a pretty stupid question.

"Let's just go to bed and forget about it," Frankie said. "Forget about ever'thing."

We lay there in the dark, me holding her close. We didn't do no loving or nothing. She never made no moves in that direction, and after the things she had said I sure wasn't going to be the first to start it. Besides, as much as my body ached for her, my heart was aching more - holding her there didn't make the ache go away, exactly, but it added a kind of sweetness to it. I drifted off to sleep with my face nuzzled into her neck, and her heart beating beneath my hand. I dreamed of falling stars, and birds wheeling in a cloudless sky.

It got to where I seen a good bit of Master Jesse, and of his two brothers, Fred and Jake, too. Seems like they always had washing to get done, or something another. Frankie naturally had to drop everything when they came around. Every once in a while they would even show up with their little chores on Saturday night and Sunday afternoon, eating into the only time me and my wife had together. I started getting a little jealous - not jealous like a man gets, worried about someone else eyeing his woman, but jealous like a little boy gets - begrudging every scrap of attention. I never said nothing about it, though, and I tried hard not to dwell on it.

The more I seen of them LaRue boys, the more I yearned to sneak out to Frankie's cabin when I wasn't supposed to. She gave up on complaining about them dangerous visits after a little bit; maybe she could sense the heat kindling up in my soul, which I had to throw a little water on whenever I could.

Whatever it was, everything went along good and smooth for a spell, until I let them ignorant patty rollers get ahold of me again. Once more it was pure carelessness that got me caught. Me and Frankie had been in that big old bed of hers, right in the middle of our marital business – along toward the end, actually – when that pasty-faced Jesse LaRue come knocking on Frankie's window. I had to hide myself – to keep from being caught with my own wife – while he called Frankie outside. She wound up spending most of the night at the big house, polishing walls. Them LaRues took some mighty funny notions, it seemed like, and at some pretty peculiar times.

While I was walking home, confused and distracted by all of that, the pattyrollers slipped right up on me. I recognized their fat leader, Grady – with all the small bands which crawled over the country, I figured it was just my luck to run into him twice in a row. He didn't remember me though; in fact, he was about to administer the same punishment to me as before when one of his men spoke up.

"Say Grady, ain't that the Moss nigger? The one we already whupped a few weeks back?"

Grady snorted like a horse. "Damned if it ain't." He moved around in front of me – they had me tied to a tree again – and grinned. "You might be strong as an ox, boy," he said, "but you surely ain't very bright. I thought we had taught you the lesson of a lifetime, and here you've done forgot it." He turned to his cronies. "Tell me boys, is niggers borned with shortened memories?"

"I reckon," said one with a laugh. "Most of 'em can't remember who their daddies was!"

Another man waved a knife. "Maybe we ought to shorten something else, you reckon?"

Grady shook his shaggy gray head. That, added to the evil glint in his eye, made him look like a wolf – a wolf that was well-fed but still hungry.

"No, fellers," he said. "Not this time, anyways. A cut like that might keep the good doctor's precious boy out of the fields for too long. We sure wouldn't want that, no sir." He said the words in a mocking tone, but that did not hide the fact that he was afraid to cross the doctor unless he was sure he could get away with it. None of his companions made fun of his attitude, for they was probably more scared of the idea than he was.

"Lem," he said, "hand me one of them grease lamps." The lamp was placed in his hand. It was a crude thing, with a long neck like a swan and a rag wick sticking out the top. It was filled with grease.

Grady walked behind me again and leaned over so that his mouth was almost touching my ear. The heat from the grease-lamp warmed my skin.

"You think that damn hide of yours is somethin' precious, don't you boy?" he said softly. "You think that just because you belong to a big-shot doctor, that means you can act like you own the roads. Well, you're wrong. I'll show you what I think your hide is worth."

Grady tipped the lamp forward, and the hot burning grease spilled onto my back. It ran all down my spine, and I could hear my flesh hissing and sizzling. And I screamed—I screamed every last bit of air right out of my lungs.

"Do you like that?" Grady shouted. "Here, have some more!"

He emptied the contents of the lamp onto my skin. I screamed again.

"Make 'im squeal louder," the one called Lem said. "I know he's got it in 'im." He waved his knife again. "That nigger thief of Moss's squealed a whole lot louder once we started cuttin' on 'im."

Grady laughed. It was the most obscene noise I had ever heard. "We've got to save somethin' for later," he said. "If this coon is fool enough to wander off again, nobody won't begrudge us the right to do whatever we want to with him. Cut him loose."

Lem did as he was commanded, taking the time to wave the knife under my nose with a flourish. I collapsed into a heap on the ground. Lem kicked me in the ribs.

"Get up! You've walked this far, I reckon you can walk the rest of way home. Now get movin'."

I marched down the road ahead of the loud horsemen, who made jokes at my expense and fetched me a blow to the head whenever I slowed down. I smelled something like meat left too long in the cook-stove. It was my own flesh.

The next day, as usual, I was back out working in the fields. That was my last time sneaking off to the LaRue place. Frankie was madder than a hornet at me – she said to come home to her only on the nights I was supposed to, or not to bother coming home at all. It wasn't easy; in fact, it tore me up inside worser than the paddyrollers had tore up my outside, but I done it.

Something new got added to the mixture not long after that. My Frankie was with child. That little unborn child was like a string, cinched up tight and drawing both of us closer together than ever. Our love wasn't as desperate as it was before – it started to be light and cheerful, like everything was turning out all right after all. Frankie wasn't even called up to the big house to do the washing no more, not after she swelled up real big. Even Mama smiled sometimes, when she seen us together at church on Sunday.

The only time I wasn't happy was when I felt of the scars on my back, or passed by Topaz's grave. At those times my secure feeling faded like morning fog; when they was stripped away they left only an angry, bitter feeling which I could not put a name to.

Them days and nights away from Frankie became a different kind of hardship as the months wore on. I lay awake on my pallet worrying, wondering if my baby might be coming into the world at that very moment without me knowing it.

I got to wondering, too, about being a father. It seemed like a tough chore under normal circumstances – how was I going to manage, having only two days a week to work with?

I had no real model to go by. I tried to wring memories of my own father out of my mind – specific ones, like what he used to say and how he used to teach me about basic things. All I could remember was the stories he told, and the feeling of his hands on my shoulders that last day, and that I loved him.

I asked Sid about his pa. Sid's father had keeled over dead in the fields one day a few years ago – no one knew why, exactly, it just looked like somebody had knocked his legs out from under him with a hoe. Sid was near about full-growed then.

"Ain't much to tell," Sid said. "He was just a ole man. He'd holler at us young'uns when we made too much racket, and whup us sometimes, and set us to fetch him things. Folks say that if he'd lived longer I might be of some account, but I doubt it."

"Didn't he never talk to you or nothin'?"

Sid shook his head. "Not much. He never talked to nobody much. He did used to hold me up in his lap, though, when I was little. We'd set out on the front step when the sun was goin' down, and he'd hold on to me so tight that it mite-near hurt, and he'd hum them ole songs to hisself. I remember that."

I shrugged, a little disappointed. Sid hadn't been much help either. "I reckon I can handle dat much," I said.

Sid grinned. "Is dat what you worried about, Alfred? Is you gonna be a good daddy or not? Shoot, dat ain't no reason to set around here lookin' horse-faced. Any young'un you ever bring into de world can't be no worser an' no uglier dan you."

Since I couldn't find my own memories, and since Sid's hadn't done me much good, I decided to ask Mama to help me put my finger on what Daddy had been like. For the first time in longer than I could remember she got honest-to-goodness mad. She whirled around, put her face up next to mine, and stamped her foot. Tears welled up in her eyes.

"Don't you never even think about bein' like dat Billy," she said with a sob. "Dat man run off an' left me to raise three young'uns all by myself. He never give no thought to what we was gonna do!"

"But Mama, he lost his temper when dat overseer took to beatin' him." I could understand now, as I could not when I was a boy, how such a fury could come over a man.

"He never lost his temper," Mama argued. "He give his temper up a long time afore dat happened, an' he was waitin' for an excuse. All de time dreamin' an' whisperin' low in de middle of de night about his pride – whispered when he thought nobody but me was listenin' but de Lawd heard him! Dat man knowed he wasn't comin' back."

"Mama, dey hanged him!" I shouted, getting angry myself. "He couldn't help it!"

Mama slapped me, and the pop stuck in my ears like a gunshot. "Yo' daddy was a selfish, prideful man," she said, "an' he's burnin' in Hell. Do you think Doctor Moss would've took any notice of us if it hadn't of been for him? Do you think Felts an' dem others would of got it in their heads we was all troublemakers?" Her shrill voice was breaking. "Do you think dey would've took any notice of my little Jenny?"

I ran outside. Before I half-knowed my own intentions I was sitting on Uncle Wiley's stoop, telling the old man about my mother's outburst.

"Don't you go too hard on her," Uncle Wiley said, "Most folks has got to find somebody to blame when somethin' bad happens. Some things, you see, just is, and there ain't nobody de cause of it. Dat's hard to face up to. It's easier for some folks to make up somebody to blame, even if it's somebody dey love. It's easier dat way."

I shook my head. "Dat don't make no sense. Why not just blame Doctor Moss? He's de one dat done it all."

Wiley shook his head. "You know dat wouldn't do no good, Alfred."

"It's de truth. De truth always does some good, don't it?"

"You'll understand some day. You still young."

I never did understand thinking like that, and I'm happy of it.

One Saturday evening I walked – pass in hand – onto the LaRue plantation and had a strange welcome. All the slaves stared at me, wearing odd expressions – it was like someone had just died, and nobody knowed how to tell me. My heart started to pound.

"Frankie," I said. "Is somethin' wrong with her?"

One old man, who was named Gus, shook his head. "Dat gal fine," he said.

"De baby?"

"She done had it," a woman named Nan told me. "A little girl." No one seemed happy about the news. "Is somethin' de matter wid de baby, den?"

"Dat gal fine," Gus repeated. I rushed to our cabin and went inside. Frankie was laying in bed, holding a bundle up to her breast. She looked drawn and tired, and she didn't smile when she seen me.

"Frankie," I said. "Is dat our little girl? Is she healthy? Let me see." I held out my arms but Frankie made no move to give me the child. I pulled back the blanket; the infant was suckling at her mother's breast.

The child was yellow.

At first I was scared, thinking that maybe the odd complexion was due to some disease. Then my heart fell as I realized the real reason for it. It was kind of like being on one of those real high, swinging bridges and having it fall out from under you; that moment when you're hanging out in space and everything looks real clear for miles around, and then your stomach and your guts start falling, and you realize you are going with them.

"Good God," I whispered, Frankie said nothing. "Good God, girl," I repeated. My face was on fire - the flames seemed to crackle in my ears. "Dammit, Frankie! What have you done?

"Which one of dem' childhood playmates' was it - or was it all of 'em? You had the nerve to leave me alone on our nights together so you could carry laundry up to the big house, an' hop in bed wid de white folks?"

Frankie covered the baby's ear with a gently cupped hand, "What was I supposed to do, Alfred?" she demanded. "We is their property, dey own us. We gots to do whatever dey say."

I could hardly see through the tears. "No! No, *dammit to hell,* no! You didn't have to, you didn't!"

"Have you done forgot what we is, Alfred? Property don't say no! Dey could've sold me, or got Doctor Moss to sell you - or even killed one of us. We'd never see each other no more. We'd never be together again! Sholy dis is better dan dat?"

I could no longer speak, only shake my head and clench my fists. "No," I managed to sob. I fought for breath until I could talk again. "You all I got, Frankie, you all I got. All I ever had. Onliest thing dat was mine, an' nobody else's. An' still dey can come an' take you any damn time dey want!"

She reached out and took my hand, trying to pull me close, but I wouldn't move. I longed to bury my face in her bosom and sob until my eyes dried up, sob straight into her heart until she made it all right, but I could not place my head next to the mulatto bastard who sucked the sweet milk that should have been for my child.

"You still my man, Alfred. You always gonna be my man."

I shook my head again. "I ain't no man at all!" I said with a ragged breath. "I ain't man enough to make you a chile, an' I ain't man enough to keep nobody else from doin' it either!"

"I love you, Alfred..."

"I'm gonna kill 'em. I'm gonna kill 'em all, by God!"

Frankie was crying as hard as me now. She put her fingers delicately on my lips. "Shush! Shush, honey, shush – don't say dat! Somebody might hear, an' think you mean it, and do you like dey done Topaz."

"I do mean it! I don't care if dey kill me, I hope dey do, but I'll git me one first!"

"No, you won't, honey," she said. "You wouldn't never even get close to em. And den who would I have? How do you think I feel, Alfred – carryin' dis little girl in my belly, not knowin' whose she would be, knowin' she might be a part of one a' dem? A part of one a' dem, an still their property, just like us?"

I had sunk to my knees beside the bed. "I'm gonna kill de son-of-a-bitches," I said absently, trying to convince myself and at least take comfort in the possibility. I let her take my hand this time.

"Don't leave me alone," Frankie said. "I can't live in dis kind of a world if you ain't wid me, Alfred. Please, don't leave me all alone."

I thought of my mother's words earlier about my father, and the anger in her face. My own anger was ebbing away, leaving me weak and numb –and helpless. I slumped against the bed, still holding Frankie's hand; I listened to the distant gurgling and playing of the white man's child that my wife held to her breast.

I made my way home slowly the next day. Uncle Wiley spotted me at once – he was anxious for news about the new baby – and he made a beeline straight for me.

Wiley's customary little smile melted away when he seen how agitated I was. I was stumbling through the dirt, not hardly knowing or caring where my feet fell, just like one of them voodoo zombies you hear tell about sometimes.

"Why, good Lawd, boy," Wiley said, putting a feeble hand on my shoulder to steady me. "What's de matter wid you? Has somethin' bad happened to yo' fambly?" His eyes widened. "Is it de baby?" Even through my own agony I could see the fear in the old man's eyes.

I shook my head. "It's a yaller baby."

"What you mean? Is it got de jaunders?"

"I mean what I say. It's a yaller baby, Uncle Wiley – a little yaller gal."

"Oh," Wiley said, nodding and staring at the ground for a moment. Then he looked back up, his dark eyes eager. "Is she awright, though?"

"I reckon." I moved to walk off – I didn't much want to talk about the subject at all, much less out in the open – but the old man restrained me.

"Listen, Alfred," he said softly. "I know you hurtin'. But a yaller chile is better dan no chile at all. I'd just about trade my soul for a chile to raise as my own, wh'er it really was or not – an' be it yaller, brown, or black."

"Fine, old man. You can have de damn little bastard." Tears of fury welled up in my friend's eyes.

"Don't you talk like dat in my presence, boy." He struck my chest – weakly, but with passion.

I looked away, a little ashamed at my outburst. "I'm sorry," I told him. "But no matter what you call it, de chile is still a damn bastard."

"You wrong, Alfred. No chile is damned, not when dey dat little – not by God. Some of 'em grows up an' damns dey own self, I reckon, but dey all comes into dis world pure and innocent. After dat, it's mostly a matter of what dey mama and daddy turns 'em into.

"You de onliest daddy dat little girl ever gonna have. She needs you. You think dem LaRues is gonna give a care what happens to her? She ain't never gonna be much more dan a dog to dem."

I stared at him, resentful and silent. Wiley had lost some of his fire. He had gone back to being a half-crippled, old man with a face that was somehow happy and sad at the same time. "You love dat Frankie gal, don't you?"

I nodded. "Yeah," I said. "I love her."

"Dat yaller baby is her young'un. You can't love a woman and hate her young'un, it plain won't work. She's just a chile, and chiles comes from God. Dat's what she is—she a gift to you from out of Heb'm. You don't th'ow presents back in de Lawd's face, just 'cause you don't like de way dey come wrapped."

He shuffled away. I was left standing in the hot sun, feeling like one of those lost souls in perdition that the preacher was always talking about.

That Wednesday I got permission to take Mama and Roby with me to the LaRue place to see the new baby. Mama came along without a word, like she wasn't real sure where we was goin' or why - even though I told her. Roby was real excited, but not because of his new niece. It was his first time off the Moss plantation. Once we got to walking down the LaRue slave row, though, he started looking a little scared - here was a whole other world of folks, and none of them knowed the boy from Adam or cared. Pretty soon he got over his bashfulness and got to mixing it up with the young folks, doing his best to charm them all. It was a good while before he even stuck his head in the cabin to look at the baby.

Me and Mama went on in. Frankie was setting on the edge of our bed, rocking the child. She looked up when I entered, her face neutral.

"Howdy, Alfred."

"Howdy, honey," I said. I went down to my knees on the dusty floor beside her. Mama was wondering around the room, staring at every little item with wonder, like she was the newborn babe.

"I come home, baby," I said. I reached out and took the baby's tiny hand –all her fingers wrapped around my thumb. Frankie was biting her own mouth, trying not to cry. She leaned her head against mine.

I picked the baby up – Frankie had to show me how – and held her out to my own mother. "Look here, Mama. Look what I got."

Mama's jaw dropped and here eyes teared up. She made a funny moaning sound in the back of her throat as she took the child.

"Aaaahh," she said. "Oh Lawd-a-mercy. Oh Lawd-a-mercy. After all dis time, Sweet Jesus, after all dis time an' I done thought she was lost forever."

"What are you talkin' about, Mama?" From the corner of my eye I could see that Frankie was growing concerned.

"My little Jenny," Mama said. "It's my little Jenny. Where'd you find her at, boy? I been lookin' all dis time, an' here I about give up hope. Sweet Jesus."

She held the baby close. Mama was sobbing deep sobs of joy and her face was all lit up with a smile like I had never seen on her in my whole life. "Baby Jenny," she crooned. "Baby Jenny..."

"Dat ain't Jenny, Mama. Dat's—" With a start I realized that I didn't know her name. I turned to Frankie, embarrassed, and said, "What's her name?"

Frankie was smiling now, too. "I didn't think it was right to name her. Not 'till her daddy come back." She got up off the bed and embraced my mother. "Dat's Jenny, Mama," Frankie said. "Dat's Jenny."

"Why, I know it's Jenny." Mama said. "How'd she get so pale? She needs her some sun, is what she needs. Ain't dat right, baby Jenny?"

Mama walked outside with the baby. I heaved myself up on my feet and watched them out the front door. We had, in fact, found Jenny after all those years, and found more besides.

But a part of me still felt like a hog at castrating time. I had felt the knife; I was being held tight, and there wasn't a thing in the world I could do about it.

Another yellow baby came in the spring. We called him Billy.

Chapter Five

I was trudging home from the fields when the war started. Leastways that was when we all got word of it for the first time. Old Man Weeks – who owned the Pine Gate plantation down the road a little ways – came tearing onto the place in his carriage. While his Negro driver was drawing up them horses, Weeks was already hopping out onto the ground. He stumbled a little, regained his balance in mid-stride, and took to running right up the front steps of the big house.

"George!" he yelled. "George, get out here! They've gone and done it!" Doctor Moss came to the front door and motioned his friend inside.

"For goodness sake," the doctor said. "What's gotten into you, Jonathan?" The big door closed behind them, and the rest of their words was lost to us. Weeks' driver, Danson, looked around slyly and then motioned me and Sid closer to him.

"What's goin' on?" I asked him. Danson's eyes was wide with excitement. "War! War is what's goin' on, nigger! I heared 'em talkin' about it in town. Dem boys has done opened fire on de Yankees in Fort Sumter. Dat ain't far off from here, you know!"

I didn't know. "What boys?" I said.

"De Rebs," said Danson.

Sid jabbed me in the ribs. "Dat's right you fool, de Rebs," he said. "Don't you know nothin'?"

I shrugged, and suspected I probably knowed about as much of the situation as Sid did. "Reckon why come 'em to do dat," I said.

"Because dey's Rebs," Sid replied, indignant. "An' dem others is Yankees." He looked to Danson for verification, and the driver nodded.

"I reckon we gonna run dem Yankees clean outen de country," Danson said.

Everybody was all worked up over that war, let me tell you. I still didn't know for sure what it was all about – the Up-North white people was getting into it with the Down-South ones, that's all I was able to decipher. None of the other slaves knowed any more than that, either; when you got down to it, I doubt if many of the white folks did.

Young Phillip Moss joined up to the infantry, with his father's blessing. The doctor came up with him a uniform somewhere. Phillip looked slick in it, with his boots polished and a feather bobbing in his hat bigger than he was. The Reb soldiers came marching down the dusty road one day, right past the plantation, and Phillip fell in right behind them. They was all local boys, and at first I thought those two dozen or so was the whole Reb army. I told Sid later that the whole thing was being exaggerated some. He laughed, and told me that them boys was on their way to join up with the real army. I felt pretty ignorant.

"Good luck, son," Doctor Moss called out. "Honor our name!" Phillip looked back, smiling. "I'll be back in a month, Pa – soon as we whip the Yankees. Goodbye, Pa! Goodbye, Uncle Wiley!"

Wiley waved to the boy. From the proud tears running down Uncle Wiley's face you would think he was bidding farewell to a child he had brought into the world himself, instead of to someone who stood to inherit him someday.

"You be careful, Massa Phillip!" Uncle Wiley shouted to the now distant line of soldiers. "Lawd! Dat boy ain't but seb'nteen, an' look at how he carries hisself. Ain't he a fine-lookin' soj'er, tho'!"

Doctor Moss stood beside the old gardener, so close they actually touched, and stared at his son's ever-smaller back. "A fine soldier indeed, Wiley." The two old men shared something silent and timeless, something which almost made them equals. Then Doctor Moss turned away, and the spell was broken.

"You niggers go on back to work now," he said.

Phillip marched off on a Friday. The next day I went to my other home on the LaRue place, only to find more war-talk. All three of the LaRue sons was getting ready to join up with the Reb army come Monday. They already had their "commissions" – a word which meant they got to be masters over the poor-white soldiers, even though nary a one of them had ever been on the inside of a uniform before.

There was a lot more commotion over the army-joining over there than there was at the Mosses'. Old Man LaRue was about to bust out of his shirt with pride – his own little brother had risen to the rank of first lieutenant with the engineers down in Mexico, so he knew a thing or two about combat hisself. Or so he said.

And Miss LaRue, Lord how she took on. She was sniffing one minute and giggling the next, searching the eyes of all to make sure they had grabbed hold of the notion that she was sending three handsome young men to defend the state of South Carolina.

There was a big party. It started Saturday afternoon and lasted 'til well into Sunday. Folks came from all around – even Doctor Moss was there for a little while. He left quick. Either he thought the whole thing a waste of time, or he felt guilty he hadn't done the same for his own son.

The famous Miss Peggy came back from boarding school to take part in the celebration – her and Frankie fell all over each other. For a minute they did, anyway. Then Miss Peggy's eyes widened like she suddenly recognized who she was, and that she was growed up, and she drawed away. It was just Frankie doing the falling-over then, and seeing the look on her face was a sad, shameful thing.

Me, I spent most of the night in our cabin looking after the young'uns. I half-expected Miss Peggy to come looking for her old bed back. Part of the time a field-hand named Ben came over and sat with me. His wife had been called over to the big house to help with the serving of so many guests. Ben gave me the feeling he understood a little about my family problems – he'd had another family once, back in Virginia. A wife and four young'uns. Then the folks started running a little low on cash, and they sold Ben away. He sat there with me, neither one of us saying a word for two hours. Then he got up and walked back to his tiny shack. I felt a little guilty – our cabin was a much more comfortable place to wait.

After the children went to sleep, I sat outside on the doorstep. I could see the lighted windows of the big house, and the music and laughter floated back to me on the spring air. I stared at them windows, imagining what kind of celebrating might be going on in some of them this late at night. I wished I could will the strength and power into some Yankee soldier to blast holes in a LaRue hide. Some folks said that Yankees had tails and ate children, but I doubted that they was anything more than human. Looking at them lights I hoped I was wrong – I hoped they was the worst kind of monsters.

Frankie didn't come home the next morning. We went on to church without her, me thinking she would show up late, but she never did. Instead Nan came up to me after the services, saying that Frankie had instructed her to bring the children back. Frankie had stayed late at the big house, cleaning up. I handed little Billy to Nan.

Jenny was with my mama. The little girl was walking now, and the two of them was always hand-in-hand on Sundays. Three people put together couldn't love a child like Mama loved Jenny, and the little girl could tell it. Mama came alive when Jenny was near – she almost acted like normal folks, but for the fact that no one else existed to her. Mama and Jenny, and that's all there was in the world. Once Frankie took the child back to the LaRues', Mama would melt away. Me or Roby would have to take her by the arm and lead her back home.

Once we got there she would set in her chair, not speaking or moving unless it was to go back to work, or to rock back and forth and whisper to her Jenny. She stumbled through her work like a wind-up toy that's almost run down. Felts threatened to whip her, but Doctor Moss forbade it. He eventually let the "demented woman" help Uncle Wiley with his gardening. The old man took her under his arm and babied her just like she did on those few Sunday hours when she had little Jenny and was alive.

Frankie was home when I got there Wednesday. She was nursing Billy, singing to him in a low, sweet voice. Jenny was nowhere in sight.

"Where's Jenny at?"

"She's up at the big house. Miss Peggy has taken a shine to her – she likes to have her around to play with."

"Miss Peggy is a growed-up woman," I said. "Besides, ain't she got dat boardin' school to go back to?"

"She don't have to go back for a few days."

I put it out of my mind. Besides, whether she knowed it or not, Miss Peggy had more right to see the child than I did – they had the same blood running in their veins. But most likely the young white woman viewed Jenny as an amusement, like a new kitten.

"'Well, it's been two days," I said, sitting in the bed beside Frankie and Billy. "Reckon dem LaRue boys has whupped de Yankees yet?"

"I hope so," Frankie said.

"Why?" I asked, shocked at the comment.

"Why not?" she said, equally surprised by my reaction.

"Shoot honey, it ain't gonna matter none to us wh'er dey whup de Yankees or not. We still gonna be slaves – worse dat can happen is we be slaves to somebody new."

"Worse dat can happen, Alfred, is dat a lot of folks could get kilt."

"Like de LaRues."

"Dem, or Phillip Moss, or all kinds of other folks."

"You worried 'bout dem LaRues, ain't you?" I said sharply.

"Folks is goin' to get shot at, it ain't nothin' but natural to worry about 'em. It's Christian."

"Nothin' but natural," I repeated. "Dey ain't nothin' natural 'bout what kinda things dem boys has done."

Her eyes narrowed. "I've knowed people dat's done worser. You don't know nothin' 'bout what folks can do, if dey gots de power to do it."

"Seem like maybe dey gots more power over you dan you been lettin' on, woman."

She turned away. "I ain't in no mood to put up wid such foolishness, Alfred. Go away an' leave me alone."

Her voice broke on the last part, and she cried. Everything seemed to be swimming around in front of my eyes, making me dizzy. The hard part was not knowing what made her cry - that I hurt her with my bull-headed stubbornness, or that I was right.

Next Saturday, Jenny wasn't there again. "Where is dat gal?" I asked, a little harsher than I had intended.

"She wid Miss Peggy again," Frankie said. "Miss Peggy say she thinks Jenny is adorable, and cain't get enough of her."

My jaw dropped open like a stunned fish on a riverbank. "Are you plumb out of yo' head, woman?"

"What?" Frankie said, and it was clear to me that she didn't have the first notion what I was talking about.

"Don't you know how dangerous it is to let some white woman start gettin' attached to yo' chile?"

Frankie's brow furrowed. "Miss Peggy and me is friends. Yo' friends has got de right to be aroun' yo' chillun."

I sat on the floor, shaking my head and almost laughing from shock and anger. "She ain't yo' friend, Frankie. Maybe she was once, when you was kids, but things change when folks grow up. I seen how she looks at you – like you was an old, used-up play-purty from when she was nine year old. She might be sort of fond of it, but it still ain't nothin' but a play-purty. A thing, Frankie, and so is Jenny."

Frankie straightened her dress. "Well, it don't matter noway. She leavin' Monday mawnin'."

I nodded. "Yeah – and if she's as took wid Jenny as you say, she just might take dat gal wid her."

Frankie's eyes widened. "No. No, Miss Peggy wouldn't do dat."

I stood up and grabbed her by the shoulders. "You ain't learned nothin', have you? De day dat Jenny was born you told me dat you an' her would never be nothin' but property to dem LaRues. An' yet here you still are, carryin' on like you think dey gonna make you part of dey fambly or somethin'. You know better. An' you know better dan to send Jenny up to dat big house so much!"

"What am I supposed to do, Alfred? Hide de fact dat I got any young'uns? How am I supposed to do dat?"

"We have to hide de fact dat we got souls," I said. "I don't know how we did dat, neither. We do it 'cause we got to."

"Miss Peggy ax'd for her."

"You shoulda tole Miss Peggy she cain't come. Dat you need her help wid chores an' sich."

"Have you forgot what we is again, Alfred?"

I gnashed my teeth, feeling the hot tears trying to break free from my eyes. "Dey ain't a day goes by dat I don't know what I am, woman. An' dey never will be. Just make sure you don't go forgettin' it, neither."

"She leavin' Monday," Frankie repeated. "Goin' back to dat boardin' school."

"Den I reckon we just has to wait an' see."

The way we both lay in bed that night, all chilly and stiff in spite of the heat, told me that Frankie was just as worried as I was. She knowed I was right, though she never said so in words – being in the right for a change didn't make me feel any better.

We had to go to church without Jenny that next day, and it tore Mama up when she found out. She started rocking back and forth faster than ever, moaning, "Where's my Jenny? I'se s'posed to have her here – have you seen where I laid her?" We tried to give her little Billy, but she wouldn't have none of that.

Me and Frankie sat in the grass – off from everybody else – and ate our cold, dry cornbread in silence. Mama's moaning had gone down to a whimper, but it still made dinner hard on the whole congregation.

"I cain't believe you let dat chile go," I muttered under my breath, and was sorry I'd said it even before I seen the hurt in Frankie's face.

"I don't see where it ought to matter to you anyways. You as much as say out loud ever' day dat you don't love dat chile. She may be little, but she catches on to things. At least she laughs aroun' Miss Peggy."

I had nothing to say to them words. They surprised me, and they cut me to the quick because they was true. Before I could find a way to answer, Frankie spoke again. Her face showed nothing but anger.

"Miss Peggy ain't de real problem nohow. If anybody's a danger to little Jenny it's dat crazy mama of your'n. I swear, de way she takes on, she's liable to smother my baby someday an' never even know she's doin' it."

I looked away, down into the grass. The ants was scurrying around and picking up crumbs. Frankie laid a hand on my arm.

"I'm sorry," she said. "I didn't mean dat. Yo' mama an' Jenny is good fo' each other. I'm just worried, dat's all."

"I know, baby."

Frankie sniffed. Forcing a smile, she pointed at Sid – he was makin' the rounds, flirting with all the young girls.

"You reckon he's ever gonna grow up?" she said.

"I hope not. Place'd get awful borin' if he did."

"I never seen him widout a smile. Sure must be nice, not havin' a care in de world."

"Hey Frankie, you 'member dat time he told you 'bout me? What did he say, anyways?"

"He said, 'if you ain't got sense enough to give me no sugar, I know a mule-headed nigger settin' over yonder dat's almost as sweet as me an' a whole sight easier to hold onto'."

I laughed and shook my head. "An den you brung me some sweet milk."

"Yeah, I brung you sweet milk."

Them next few days was torture. I'd get up in the morning and go the fields, not knowing if little Jenny was home waiting for me or sent away to some whole other state. I was burning to head down the road Monday night and see for myself – but I couldn't risk getting my own self sold, not with my family needing me like they did. So I settled in and waited for Wednesday.

When the day finally came, I hesitated a little before I started off – I was almost too scared to find out. I walked a lot slower than I'd expected I would.

LaRue slave row was quiet, and so was our cabin. There was no sign of movement inside. My hands trembling and my heart heavy as lead, I opened the door and went on inside. Frankie stood over a pot of greens, little Billy on her hip – but there was no sign of the girl. Even before Frankie could say a word to greet me I was casting my eyes into every corner, growing more and more desperate.

"Lawdamighty," I said, my voice breaking. "Jenny."

Frankie was shaking her head roughly. "No, Alfred, wait."

"Jenny! Jenny!"

I heard a noise behind me. I turned to see Jenny toddling through the front door, a big smile on her muddy face. "Howdy, Daddy."

I swept her up in my arms and shouted in triumph. "Howdy darling!" I said, squeezing her close so that my tears wet her cheek. "I love you, little girl! Lawd, how I love you!" Frankie had come over; I grabbed her and Billy and hugged them too.

"And I love dis feller!" I pinched the fat baby cheeks, and I kissed my woman. "I love you, little girl," I told her, and we all fell to the floor and laughed and tickled and listened to the pot boil over.

Of course, me and Frankie both had it in the back of our minds that Miss Peggy couldn't stay at boarding school forever. She might yet remember the little darky child she had been stuck on, and ask her daddy for a present. It was one more thing to worry about, one more rock setting on our chest while we slept.

Phillip Moss and all them other young fellers was wrong. The war wasn't over in a month; it dragged on and on. Some of them same boys started coming home, all right, but not in a parade – they hobbled in on one leg, or with one arm. Or they was carried home in boxes. Many didn't come home at all, the only thing that returned was their names and the name of the site where they fell.

One night me and Uncle Wiley was setting on his front step, him whittling and me watching, just enjoying the stillness of the evening. Some dogs was barking off in the distance – most likely Felts' hounds was smelling a critter, and was anxious to set off after it.

The stillness was broken by a whisper. It seemed to come from around the corner.

"Uncle Wiley!"

We both looked up. I had to stare hard into the shadows before I made out the figure that leaned forward from around

74

the edge of a nearby shack. It was a small, nimble form. The person's features was shadowed, but they seemed familiar.

"Uncle Wiley!"

The old man dropped his whittling stick and stood, absently folding his knife. His face had grown slack with shock. He had already recognized the visitor – the gardener took a small step forward.

"Come on out here, boy," he said softly.

Phillip Moss stepped out of the shadows. The boy's face was pale and dirty, and his fancy uniform was ragged. The big slouch hat with its bright feather was gone; in its place was a little cap, what they call a *kepi*. "What you doin' here, Massa Phillip?" Wiley said.

Phillip's mouth worked a couple of times before he could manage to get any sound out. "I–I don't know."

"Did dey let you come home for a visit?"

The boy looked down. His fingers nervously toyed with the outside seam of his britches. "No. No, they didn't. We was passin' by, on our way to reinforce somebody or other, and I snuck off."

"You snuck..." Wiley's voice trailed off. He continued in a whisper. "Get in dis house, boy, quick! Afore somebody sees you!"

Phillip hurried across the clearing and disappeared into Wiley's door, with the old man close behind him. I followed them inside. No one had invited me, but no one had forbidden me either.

Wiley gestured for the boy to sit down in the big rocking chair, which Doctor Moss had directed Raymond to build for his gardener. Uncle Wiley kneeled in the dust at Phillip's feet. "Tell me 'bout it, boy," he said.

Phillip shrugged. The boy looked confused about the whole thing himself. "I don't know, Uncle Wiley. I never planned on runnin' away. But we passed so close to home, and I was so tore up about everything – before I hardly knew I was doin' it I stepped into the bushes. I crawled past the pickets on my belly. It was done too late then, I couldn't go back. If those pickets would of seen me, no matter which way I was goin', they would of kilt me as a deserter. So I kept goin', and I wound up here - but I don't know what I'm gonna do next."

I nodded. I was more familiar with the boy's predicament than he could ever have guessed. A part of me—a real strong part of me—wanted to enjoy the irony of it. Now the pampered child knowed what it was to be a runaway.

But I couldn't. Young Phillip was so scared, and so harmless, that I could feel nothing but compassion for him. He was wide-eyed and panting like a young deer running from the hunters.

"It ain't like I thought," he said. "It ain't like I thought."

"What ain't, chile?" Wiley said.

"Soldierin'. It ain't fun at all, Uncle Wiley. Bullets whinin' all over an' makin' wet smackin' sounds when they hit people, and poor Jimmy Marshall walkin' right next to me and gettin' hit in the belly with a shell, and this long greasy gut squirts out right at my feet, and the blood—"

He buried his face in his hands, sobbing, his little frame heaving with the effort. "I was scared, Uncle Wiley!" he said, and I had to strain to understand the words through his weeping. "I was scared to go back."

Wiley took the boy in his arms. Phillip's face was pressed against the old man's shoulder, wetting his shirt, and gnarled fingers caressed the boy's back.

"There now, chile," Wiley whispered. "It's awright, now. You just cry it out. Ain't nothin' wrong wid dat. It's awright - it's awright."

The gardener's smooth, soft voice calmed the boy down just like a man whispering in the ear of a skittish horse. After awhile, Phillip sat back in the rocking chair, still sniffling and red-eyed.

"I don't know what to do now," he said. "I can't see my pa. I just can't."

Wiley nodded. "I know, chile. I reckon you has to go back."

Phillip's face blanched even more. "I can't. I can't do it."

Wiley laid a hand on the boy's shoulder. "If'n you don't, boy, dey'll get you fo' sho'. I know it's skeery, but de Lawd gonna be wid you."

It occurred to me that the Lord's company had been no great comfort to Jimmy Marshall. I barely bit back from saying it out loud.

"But the pickets," Phillip said. "They'll shoot me. It's a miracle I got past 'em the first time."

Wiley shook his head. "Dey'll shoot you here, Massa Phillip. Or hang you. So come on, we gots to move quick – maybe dey ain't missed you yet."

Phillip was frozen in the chair. Wiley stood up. "I'm fixin' to take a quick look aroun', an' make sho' t'ain't nobody in sight. I be right back."

Uncle Wiley left, and I said, "How's dem LaRue brothers, Massa Phillip?"

Phillip's voice was weak and hopeless. "I don't know. Not about all of 'em. Captain Jesse LaRue, I heard he took a cannonball not long ago. Tore his head clean off. I reckon his family will be gettin' word any time."

I nodded, and even managed to look sad. I walked to the door and looked out – Uncle Wiley was nowhere in sight. The two of us waited for him in silence.

"Come on, chile," Wiley said when he returned. He stood on the doorstep. Phillip rose, his knees shaky.

"Massa Phillip," I said.

He half-turned to me; Wiley gave me a stern look.

"What is dis war about, Massa Phillip? What dey fightin' for?"

"I don't understand it all myself, Alfred. I know it all started 'cause the Yankees didn't want to allow any slaves in the new states out West."

"Dat's fine wid me," Wiley said. "I ain't plannin' to go out West nohow. Now come on, Massa Phillip, we gots to go."

"What do you mean, Uncle Wiley?"

Wiley sighed. "I'm goin' wid you, chile, to be sure you makes it awright."

"But I've got to crawl through the lines."

"Den I'll crawl wid you." He took his young charge by the hand and led him back into the shadows.

I stayed through the night at Wiley's cabin. He came limping home in the gray dawn, his face grim. He had indeed crawled through the lines with Phillip, delivering him safely to his place, and then crawled back through alone. He refused to let Phillip write him a pass, which would have ensured his safety, because he did not want to risk Doctor Moss finding out about his son's lapse of nerve.

"Dis here is a mean world sometime," Wiley muttered. "A mean world."

I was still having trouble getting a handle on that war Phillip was fighting in. What the boy told me didn't really help; in fact, it muddied things up worse than before. Why would all these folks be shooting at each other because they couldn't agree on whether there should be slaves out West? Of course, the words I heard from all white folks on the matter was "pride" and "honor". I could see where those things might play a part, but I had very little experience with them. Them was words that I was not exactly encouraged to understand.

The person that cleared the picture up for me the most, oddly enough, was Felts. One day Felts' friend, Bill Jardine, rode over to share the latest news with our overseer. I happened to be passing by Felts on the way to my shack, and he ordered me to stable Jardine's horse. They stood at the stable door talking. I brushed the horse slowly, listening to their every word.

Jardine spoke of battles at places I had never heard of, and generals and colonels whose names was unfamiliar to me.

Felts spat in disgust. "I reckon them damn Yankees will learn sooner or later not to meddle in our business," Felts said. "Tellin' us how to live, like our state guv'mints wasn't for nothin' but show. And over somethin' as stupid as niggers."

"You ain't heard the worst of it," Jardine said. "Lincoln has made some new law freein' the slaves."

"What?" Felts thundered. "He cain't do that!"

Jardine nodded. "Only he didn't free 'em in all the border states – just the 'states in rebellion.' In other words, a slave is still a slave in Louisville or St. Louis, but free here! Can you imagine that?"

Felts laughed. "Let that big monkey Lincoln come down here his own self, by God, and tell my damn niggers they're free. I'll free his ugly head from his shoulders! I thought he promised when he was runnin' for office that he wouldn't never meddle with our institution. Turns out we was right not to trust him, after all."

"Newspapers say he's tryin' to get support from Europe. Says they won't come out in the open and help any country that has slaves."

"So he frees our niggers."

"It don't mean nothin', 'less'n the Yankees occupy us here, and you know how likely that is. Yankees is almost as stupid as niggers."

The two men walked away, then – Felts told his friend he had some bourbon at his house, and they went off to sample it. I went on home, myself, trying to wade through what I had heard and see if I could make sense of it.

Phillip and me – the one that would someday own slaves and the one that was owned, the one that was doing the fighting and the one that was being fought over – neither one of us had known much about the reasons behind the war. But them two rednecks – the ones who had the least stake in the whole operation – was the ones that knowed the most about it. They was also the ones that got the maddest over it. It was odd, too – Felts nor Jardine either one had done any fighting or owned any slaves.

I decided to wait and see what else happened before I chose to believe Jardine. His story was a little too fantastic. Still, it was an interesting idea; it seemed like there was people somewhere besides me – and white people, for goodness sake – who thought I should be free.

Chapter Six

Phillip was right when he said word would come to the LaRues soon about their dead son. On the very next night, which was a Wednesday, I went for my regular visit to my second home and was greeted by weeping and wailing. It wasn't just the LaRues doing it, either; most of the slaves was just as grieved, and was a lot more vocal about it.

Frankie was not much different. She didn't take on like the others, out of respect to me, but her eyes kept filling with tears that she couldn't blink back. We didn't talk much. I moved to hold her, but she turned away – then apologized with her eyes. My soul ached to know that she was reserving the day entirely to the memory of the man who had mishandled her.

As far as I had seen during my stay at the LaRues, Jesse wasn't even that good as masters went. He was more arrogant than most, with a quick temper and a spoiled streak. I couldn't figure out why the slaves was so tore up. They reminded me of how some of them Bible pagans acted when they found out their wooden god had been knocked over.

I didn't feel comfortable in the cabin with my weeping wife, so I went out for a little walk. A group of folks had built a big fire a little ways off, and was setting around it with long faces. Some spoke lowly of the war, and of other white folks gone forever; most stared grimly into the flames.

Another, smaller group was gathered in a field barely within earshot of the fire. The wind carried me a few notes of laughter, and some snatches of conversation. I was glad to know I wasn't the only Negro on the place not crippled by grief. I decided to join them.

I found several men gathered around Marcus, the LaRues' carriage-driver. He was delivering a lively account, which his audience greeted with friendly disbelief.

"Here come Alfred," said a field hand named Eddie. "Alfred, you gots to hear dis! You ain't gonna believe what dis fool is tryin' to put over on us as de news."

I cocked my head and looked at Marcus, smiling at his frustration. "What is it dis time?" I said. I wasn't really skeptical of the driver as a rule, for his reports almost always came out right. He must have tried to pass on a real whopper for the normally eager crowd to have turned on him.

"I know dis is hard to believe," Marcus said, "but it's all over Charleston and I swear it's de trufe!"

"Well, what is it?" I said. "Has de Lawd started whiskin' folks away in broad daylight?"

"No, my friend, it's even stranger dan dat. De Yankee army is puttin' out de word – dey recruitin' runaway slaves, fo' de army!"

"Dey gonna let 'em be slaves fo' de Yankee army?" one hand asked.

"No, you ninny! Dey gonna let 'em be sojers!"

"Yankee sojers?"

"Yes, Yankee sojers."

"Wid guns an' ever'thing?"

"Yes, Lige, wid guns an' ever'thing. Good God, cain't you niggers hear?"

Lige shook his head. "Marcus, you crazy."

"Maybe so, maybe not, but facts is facts. Nigger sojers is free sojers, an' dey gonna fight like men."

"Is dey gonna be nigger reb sojers, too?" Eddie asked.

"Like Hell."

"If dey ain't no nigger Rebs, den who is de nigger Yanks s'posed to shoot at? Lawd knows, if a nigger sojer shoots a white man, Rebs an' Yanks bofe is gonna be lined up to hang him."

The crowd laughed, but I didn't. I buried Marcus' news away, deep in my mind, to mull over later.

Not long after that, there was a big change at the Moss plantation. The old doctor started acting agitated – word was he had been deeply moved by his young son's heroism – and started expressing to visitors his wish for youth and vigor so he could serve "in a martial capacity". Since the war had drug on a whole lot longer than the month or two everybody expected, the need for skilled doctors was on the rise. Doctor Moss decided to volunteer his services.

He left the care of the plantation to his nephew, Rupert, a spindly-looking man with a gimpy leg. Felts was still there, of course – he deferred military service in order to "keep the niggers in line", which I guess counted as a matter of national security. Doctor Moss wasn't about to leave Felts in charge of the whole operation, though. The overseer was as likely to kill the slaves as to get a good day's work out of them. No white cracker overseer in creation is going to cake care of a plantation as well as a man who might stand to inherit it.

Doctor Moss gathered us all together to bid us farewell. He sure seemed to enjoy having us for an audience when he had important speeches to make. He told us to be good and behave ourselves for our new master, Rupert. He told us to remember the sacrifices all the brave young men like Phillip was making on our behalf, in order that the damn Yankees not get ahold of us and steal us – maybe even sell us away to Cuba to help pay for Mister Lincoln's war. A little shiver of fear seemed to pass over some of the other slaves when he came to that part.

Things wasn't really different with Rupert Moss there, not in any way a man could put his finger on. There was just a feeling – the way Rupert looked at us, little things he said in our presence – which showed that he was anxious to make use of some of his new authority over human life. He took Felts's favorite description of us, monkeys, and changed it to make it his own.

We became his "gorillas."

It was neither more nor less of a compliment in my eyes as "monkey" or a dozen other words, including "nigger". They all meant the same thing when they came from a white man.

Sid came over to the shack one evening; we sat outside and talked in the cool air.

"Whatchu think 'bout dese tales folks is tellin', Sid?"

"What tales is dat? You mean 'bout ole man Starkey havin' a treasure buried in de swamp an' how his ghost stands guard over it?"

"No, I don't mean dat. I ain't talkin 'bout nonsense."

"Ain't no nonsense, Alfred. I know a feller seen it once't."

"The ghost, or the treasure?"

"I mean de ghost, 'course. Once't dis feller seen de ghost he knowed de treasure must be somewheres close by – but dat ole ghost was hooin' an booin' an makin' such an awful racket dat de feller couldn't hardly concentrate on findin' de treasure, so he went home an' went to bed."

"I mean de tales from out of town – 'bout how de Yankees is lettin' runaways be sojers, an' how de Yankees is tryin' to set us all free."

Sid laughed. "Dat's mo' fantastical dan de one 'bout ole man Starkey's gold."

"You don't believe it?"

Sid frowned in thought. "De fust part might be right, 'bout de sojers. I can see where white folks would naturally want to round up a few niggers if dey's any gettin' shot at to be done. Things might get a little rough around here sometimes, but at least dey ain't gonna send me off to be shot at when dey's work to be done."

"But dese fellers – dese colored sojers – dey fightin' fo' dey own freedom."

Sid shook his head. "Ain't no such thing as Freedom, Alfred. Not fo' you an' me. Only freedom we ever gonna get is what little mischief an' fun we can get ourselfs into when dey ain't nobody lookin.'"

"Dey's gotta be more'n dat. Dey's got to be."

"You startin' to think like pore ole Topaz now, Alfred. We don't want to wind up like him, no suh. Mischief an' fun." He nudged me in the ribs. "Dat's why I come lookin' for you dis evenin'. 'Course I ain't brung you no sweet milk or nothin', but I reckon you got plenty of dat at de LaRue place."

"What you got in mind?"

"Raymond has done earned enough off of extry carpenterin' dat he been able to buy some mo' of dat lightnin'-in-a-bottle. Me an' him figured a few of us could go over to de holler - we could use us a little of dat kinda freedom 'long 'bout now. It's been a dry spell."

I shook my head. "Doctor Moss got awful mad de last time, Sid."

"Ain't no' Doctor Moss 'round here no more, boy. 'Sides, reason he got all tore up was 'cause we stole his hogs. Ain't gonna be no stealin' dis time - jest drinkin'."

"I don't know, Sid."

"Shoot! Don't you never wanna get a little livin' done, Alfred? You done been down dat road to de LaRues too many times for me to believe you don't know what I'm sayin'. We alive - let's make de most of it."

"Awright, den," I said. "But it don't feel right."

Sid grinned. "Jest wait'll we get halfway through dat first bottle. It'll feel plenty right den!"

My friend put a hand on my knee and pushed himself to his feet. "I'll see you at de holler Saturday night, 'long 'bout midnight," he said. "I'd stay around an' shoot de breeze some mo', but I got me a few ladies to pester." He winked. "Might be one of 'em'll pester me back."

Sid walked into the darkness. I could hear his cheerful whistling long after his form was no longer visible.

"Guess what, Alfred! I'm goin' to de big house!"

I stared at Roby a moment, trying to figure out what the boy was talking about. Now sure, the big house is an exciting place – what with all the silks and the statues and all – but Roby had seen it all three or four times. I saw no reason for him to get so worked up about seeing it again.

"Dat's nice, Roby," I said, trying to share his enthusiasm. "Are you deliverin' somethin' to de kitchen?"

"Onliest thing I'm deliverin' is myself," Roby said. "I don't mean I'm goin' to visit – I mean I'm goin' to work there. From now on! I'm gonna be Massa Rupert's personal servant." My brother throwed his chest way out as he said the last two words. "Massa Rupert says I look classical."

"What does dat mean?"

"Shoot, Alfred, you don't know nothin'." He punched at me playfully, something he had not done since he was very little. "I reckon I'll still be seein' you around, big brother – but not in no fields, nossirree! I might even be movin'. A personal servant ought to live a little closer to de massa." He grinned wider.

"Lawd-a-mighty!" Roby said with a pleased squeal. "I might even live in de house! You reckon, Alfred? You reckon I'll live in de house?"

"You might jest do it," I said. "What does Mama say 'bout all of dis?"

Roby's smile faded for a moment, but then regained its luster. "I tried 'splainin' it to her, but I don't think she heared a single word. All she ever talks about is dat young'un of your'n. Mama ain't hardly dere no more." His face bunched up, like he was actually thinking. "Maybe I can get her a place in de big house one of dese days. Dat'll make her feel better."

"I reckon it will."

"I gotta go, Alfred. I gotta go tell de other fellers and watch 'em all squirm. Better yet, I need to tell all de girls!"

Roby scampered off without another word to me. It was just as well, because I didn't know what to say to him. Was working in the big house cause for congratulations? It meant that Roby was one step closer to being a white man. That was like saying that a dog was one step closer to being human because it lived in the house. All that really means for the dog is losing its natural senses and getting kicked more often.

Roby's status change started right away. He moved his few possessions out of our shack that night and took up residence at the other end of slave row – living with two other houseboys. It was just me and Mama then, for the first time ever. I laid awake watching her form as it rocked gently and she whispered the name of her lost daughter. If Mama had her mind she would have known that her son Roby was lost to her now as much as that long-ago Jenny was. I squeezed my eyes tight and imagined I could see another form on the pallet across the room – my father. The world seemed so secure when he was with us. If I had been looking through his eyes it might well have looked as shaky as it did now through mine.

I seen Roby the next day. He was walking with Master Rupert to the carriage, carrying an umbrella for him – it was drizzling rain. My brother fawned and scraped. I was disgusted. Roby's umbrella wavered a moment, allowing a couple of raindrops to splash on Master Rupert's cheek. Rupert slapped Roby so hard across the face that Roby stumbled and almost fell – my brother's sickly smile remained attached. I went back into the fields and resumed smashing mealy bugs beneath my bare feet.

I was not sure how to bring up the subject of Sid's Saturday night plans to Frankie when I got to the LaRues' on Wednesday night. I did not really want to accompany Sid into that holler, but neither did I want to appear hen-pecked to him. I was about to pay the price for my pride; I knowed my wife would be furious. I was wrong. She was not even angry. I would not go so far as to say she approved – even though I had not told her of the bottle Sid and Raymond would provide, she acted cold toward me. I wondered what had happened to us – one day our love had been as hot as the sun.

A cloud had passed between me and that sun, I reckon, named LaRue. It only allowed an occasional ray to sparkle through. I felt my soul shriveling up on account of it, like them leaves that blowed down the road after Miz Moss when I was a child.

So I sat in that dark holler with Sid and Raymond and the others. We passed the bottle around and whispered crude jokes to one another, squeezing our own cheeks together to keep from busting up with the giggles.

I couldn't keep from ever' once in awhile peeking over the grassy ridge to see if Felts or Massa Rupert was coming down the road. Everyone else done the same, between laughs and exclamations of manly conversation. When one of us got the bottle he'd look over his shoulder before he took a swig.

Everybody done them things, that is, excepting Sid. He never once looked back toward the big house. Sid never checked a laugh, or a word, or done anything that showed he was not entertaining on his own lands, with his own self-owned person.

I figured out that night that Sid did not care. He liked to act like freedom was the last thing on his mind, but he wasn't being straight-out honest about that. If he got caught drinking in that gulley, and he got beat half to death for it, he'd be right back doing it again before long. Sid's freedom was in his laughter and his mischief, and I knowed he would never give it up.

We all got blind drunk and didn't get caught. It didn't matter, though, whether we was caught or not – or whether we got beat or not. What mattered was that we done it.

I seen Uncle Wiley next day, same as always – but this was one of them Sundays when my eyes clearly showed what my gullet had been up to on Saturday night. Uncle Wiley didn't scold me or nothing. He was distracted, like somebody quietly fretting about sick kinfolk.

"I'll sho'ly be glad when Massa Moss and Massa Phillip comes back," he whispered, more to himself than to me.

So that's what was wrong. I grinned. "Massa Rupert gettin' under yo' skin too, is he," I said, "wid his white trash ways?"

Wiley's head snapped up. "Hush up. You better watch yo' mouf, boy, else it's gonna get you in mo' hurt dan dem legs of your'n has already walked you into."

I shrugged. The old man shook his head and said, "Ain't got nothin' agin no particular white folks. I jest wish things could stay de same, is all. I'm done too old to start follerin' changes."

"Even I'm old enough to know dat things keeps on changin'," I told him. "An' dey ain't gonna stop."

I walked off – still a little unsteady after the previous night's reveling – toward the church meeting. I heard Uncle Wiley struggling to his feet behind me, still mumbling. "I'm too old to start follerin' changes. I declare I am."

Me and Frankie sat together at the sermon. I held the children who had none of my blood flowing through them, but who sometimes felt like they was more mine than their mother was. Mama fidgeted for a chance to hold Jenny, not even noticing that her own Roby was absent – off fetching for his master on the Lord's day.

After my work was done Wednesday I started for the road, like I had been doing for years. This rime, though, I heard Rupert Moss's high-pitched voice hollering at me.

"Hold it right where you are, nigger!" I stopped, but did not turn around immediately.

"Turn around when I'm talking to you, damn it!" As I was turning he waved for his overseer to come closer. "Felts. Where does this gorilla think he's going?"

Felts directed a greasy smile at me. "Alfred here has got a wife an' some young' uns over at the LaRue place. He gets a pass to visit with 'em twice a week. The stupid monkey used to try an' slip over yonder plumb near ever' night, 'till my cousin Grady learned him to behave."

Rupert stared at me without really comprehending, like I was a bug that had somehow crawled into his taters.

"Do you mean to tell me that niggers has been coming and going through this main gate like it was a damn train depot or somethin'?"

"Just this 'un and about a half-a-dozen more," Felts said.

"Not no more they ain't," announced Rupert. "The damn Yankees is just over the river – I don't want my slaves running away and getting stolen by 'em. The bluebellies have been trying their best to stir the darkies up, you know.

"From now on my niggers stay on my place, and that's all there is to it. And no more of this ridiculous church-going, either. If niggers had souls, I reckon they'd be white." He rapped his cane on the ground. "See to it now, Felts."

"Be happy to, sir," Felts said. Then he waved a fist at me. "You heard the master, monkey! Get on back here, you ain't goin' nowhere for a good spell."

My hands was clenched almost tight enough to draw blood, but I did as I was directed. My feet responded like they was made out of lead.

Felts laughed so hard that his gut bounced up and down. "I reckon that by the time you get out to the LaRues again, you'll have two or three more yeller bastards to bounce on your knee!"

I came to within a hair of grabbing Felts by the throat right then and there. I figured I might as well, I had nothing left to lose. But an idea flashed in my head. I knowed what I had to do, and I forced the red mists back from my eyes.

I had to bide my time. I couldn't risk ending everything right then, after all.

"Yassuh," I said humbly to Felts, and I trudged back toward slave row. "Yassuh, I reckon you right."

"'Course I am," Felts said, putting his hands on his hips. Then he seemed to forget all about me, like my very life was just of passing interest to him.

My path was clear. It was finally time to take it.

I slipped away and headed toward the LaRue plantation. I had no pass. I wasn't being cocky this time, though – I kept to the bushes and moved slowly, listening for patty-rollers.

Frankie looked up when I came into the house. "You late," she said. I nodded. She said, "I was startin' to wonder if you was comin'. I done put de young'uns down to bed."

I stared at her, my heart aching. Her brow furrowed. "Somethin's de matter," she said. "What is it, Alfred?" I swept her up in my arms and held her so close to me it felt like we was being pressed into one.

"Ain't got no pass," I whispered.

"Did you lose it?"

"Yeah," I said. "I lost it."

"You shouldn't of risked comin', den," said Frankie. "Come Saturday you can have 'em make you up a new pass."

"Ain't gonna be no mo' passes," I said, and I told her about Rupert Moss's new rules.

"Oh, Alfred," she said. "Alfred!" She squeezed my neck and cried – big tears, pure tears, tears just for me – and she was mine again.

"It won't be for long, Alfred," she said, her voice breaking. "Dem awful Yankees will be whupped soon an' de War gonna be over, an' ever'thing's gonna be the way it was."

I shook my head. "No honey. Everything ain't never gonna be back de way it was, not ever again. I don't want it to be."

I held her face in my hands. "I'm runnin' away, Frankie."

Her eyes bulged and her breath went away. She jerked her head back.

"Is you crazy, Alfred? Don't you remember Topaz? Up Nawth is a long way - they'll catch you afore you get halfway dere!"

"Ain't runnin' all de way Nawth. All I got to do is make it to de other side of de river. De Yankee sojers is dere, an' dey lookin' for runaways to join up wid 'em."

"Join de Yankees?"

"Dat's right. I'll be a sojer den, my own self."

Frankie pounded my chest with her fists. "Join de Yankees! Agin yo' own people!"

I grabbed the flailing hands. "Ain't you got good sense, woman? De Yankees is tryin' to set us free! Dese folks around here want to keep on usin' us like their animals!"

"I don't care if you run up Nawth, or clean up to Canada," she said, showing that she knew more about maps than me or anyone else I knowed at the time. "But don't you dare be no Yankee sojer! I won't never speak to you again if you do."

I pushed her away from me. "You don't care what de fightin' is about," I whispered hoarsely. "You jest afraid I might fight agin one of dem damn LaRue boys."

"Dat's a lie," she said, but I done knowed it wasn't.

"I love you more dan I ever thought a man could love somebody," I said, softer than before. "Why can't dat be good enough for you? Does it make you better somehow, lovin' a white man?"

Frankie was shaken - as shaken as if I had struck her. "I love you, Alfred," she said. "Why can't dat be enough for you?"

"I reckon it ought to be," I said. "But I share your body wid dem folks. You shouldn't ask me to share your heart, too, it ain't right. It's just too much."

"Yo' pride," Frankie said. "Yo' selfish—"

"Daddy, why you cryin?"

I turned around and seen little Jenny standing in the doorway. I dropped to my knees and held out my arms – she ran into them. I gently rubbed her head.

"I ain't cryin', chile – I been laughin'. What you doin' awake at dis time of de night?"

"I heared hollerin'."

"Well. I'm sorry 'bout dat." I stood and scooped her up. "We'll try to be quieter from now on, so's my little girl can get her rest."

I carried her to the bed she shared with her brother Billy. I held her hand and sang to her, songs my father's father had sung to him, whose words I did not understand. When she was asleep once more, I kissed her and her brother and walked slowly away, pausing twice to stare at their sleeping forms.

Frankie was standing in the corner.

"You right about one thing," I told her. "Dis war gonna be over. When it is, I'm comin' back fo' you."

We kissed—halting, uncomfortable. I walked out the door and slipped once more into the darkness.

I headed north, for the river, moving with an ease which surprised me. I had never been so far from the Moss place in my life.

I seen the river shining in the moonlight, and I hesitated. I seen no signs of human life there. What if Rupert Moss had been wrong, and I had gambled my life away for nothing? I edged closer to the water, leaving the cover of the woods.

Then I heard a voice holler out from the trees, somewhere behind me. "It's a runaway! Get him!"

I didn't hesitate no more, but ran straight into the water. Guns was going off in the woods and I heard the bullets slapping water all around me. The river itself was almost as scary as the guns – it was nothing like swimming in the pond back home.

I managed to make it across unhurt, and set off for the woods – they was a match for the ones I had come out of on the opposite side. Even the gunfire was a match – someone was in these woods, shooting back across the river.

"Come on!" several voices urged over the racket. "Hurry!"

I was among the trees. Smoke rose from behind a fallen log, and long, wicked rifle barrels poked out from it. I dived over the log. Strong hands pulled me over.

I was surrounded by men, most of them firing at the river. They wore uniforms similar to ones I had seen before, but all of blue.

"You're free now, boy!" one of them yelled.

A man with a drooping mustache, who seemed to be their leader, knelt beside me.

"When daylight comes," he said – and it was only an hour or so away – "we'll send you back behind the lines to be relocated."

"I didn't come here to get relocated, suh. I come here to fight."

The man smiled. The smile was grim in the faint light. "Well," he said. "I'm sure we can arrange for that, too."

And they did.

Part II: The War

Chapter Seven

I had thought they'd hand me a gun and dress me up in one of their blue suits, right then and there, and point me toward some Rebs. I was wrong. Them white soldiers kept right on shooting at the Rebs near the river, but they sent me on back behind the lines. Everywhere I went I found somebody that would send me back a little further. Finally, I had got shuffled plumb out of the woods and into a clearing.

Half-a-dozen other Negroes was there, standing around in a bunch. I went and joined them. After awhile a soldier with yellow stripes on his sleeve ordered us to get into a wagon – once we did, it started rolling. The wagon traveled away from the woods; I reckoned that meant we was still going north. That seemed kind of odd to me at the time – so far as I knowed, there wasn't any Rebs in the north – but I was still new at soldiering and figured that army ways might take a little getting used to.

A couple of the other fellows was scared. One, a skinny man with a twisted lip, said, "Dey's fixin' to sell us, boys, I just knows it." His misshaped mouth quivered a little. "Ever'thing dem white folks said back home is true!" The man whispered, just enough to hear him over the creaking wheels. "De Yankees was jest tryin' to steal us, an' sell us to dem Cubans!"

"Lawdy, Tom," said another one, not much more than a boy. "You really think so?"

"Hush up, Tom." The speaker sat next to me, and was about my age. He was short, but powerful-looking. "Don't go scarin' dis chile wid yo' foolishness."

"I ain't tryin' to scare nobody," Tom said. "It's jest dat ever'time a white man loads a bunch of niggers into a wagon like dis here, ain't no good comes of it. I thought we was s'posed to be fightin'. Ain't no fightin' goin' on in no cart."

"We run away once," I told them. "If'n we have to, we can run away again."

The boy looked at me with widened eyes. "You run away?"

I shrugged. "Hell, yeah. Didn't y'all do de same thing?"

Several of them shook their heads. The man beside me did not.

"I run away," he said, with a hint of pride. "Ran away three times – third time it took." He turned to me and said, in the tone that proud men reserve for members of their own class, "My name is Chamas."

"Alfred," I told him. "If you an' me is de only runaways, how'd dese other fellers get here?"

"We got freed," one of them said. "De Yankees came and took de plantation, tole us if any of us wanted to join up we be free – mebbe even make enough money to buy our families. So we come wif 'em."

"I freed my own damn self," Chamas said.

The white soldier who was driving the wagon looked over his shoulder at us. "Did anybody tell you boys where it is you're goin'?" His voice sounded funny – even funnier than the other Yanks. I would learn to identify that kind of talking as being Irish. There was a whole bunch of them in our army, and several more dressed in gray.

We all shook our heads. "No suh," one of my companions said. "Where we goin'?"

"You're on your way to camp to get inducted, lads."

We stared at him, not comprehending. Tom looked uncomfortable, as if the soldier's words confirmed his own worst suspicions.

"All that means," the soldier continued, "is that you're going to be signed up into this man's army, official-like. Learn how to drill, and march, and shoot, and get equipped, and such."

"Oh, and you'll have to tell 'em your last names – if you ain't got one, now's the time to be comin' up with somethin'. Most freedmen use their old master's name, but you're free to use whatever you like – it's gonna stick with you from now on, though, whatever it is."

There was a lot of talking about names for the rest of the ride. My comrades was excited about it – imagine, free to choose your own name, which you would possess from then on out. Four of the freed slaves agreed to use the same one, Layton –after their master, who they was still fond of – and swore to stick together. Another one chose the last name Moses, for the Lord had delivered him from the lash. Chamas became Chamas North. He decided his name ought to match the direction he had always looked.

I couldn't make up my mind just yet. I said nothing, even when pressed.

We reached our destination and piled out. We was in a big messy field – the mud came up to our ankles. Everywhere you looked there was little tents, and Negroes bustling around to and fro. Most of them was every bit as ragged as us. The noise was so great it pounded into your skull like a sledgehammer, instead of trickling in. Rattling pots, hundreds of chattering voices –they all pressed together.

"Welcome to the U.S. Army," our driver said, and then he flipped the reins and rolled off. We was left to stand there like lost children.

"This way, if you're new recruits," a soldier said. We followed him through the crowd until we reached a small table. An officer sat behind it, jotting in a notebook with a little pencil. We lined up and he took us one at a time – asking each man's name, then writing it down and telling the man to make a mark beside it. He explained that, by making that mark, we was agreeing to serve Mister Lincoln for three years, after which we would be free to go wherever we liked and do whatever we wanted.

My turn came, and I stepped up to the table.

"Name."

"Alfred, suh."

"Last name, please."

"Mann, suh. Alfred Mann."

When I learned how to read I found out they'd put an extra n at the end of my name, making it a little different from the word "man." But "man" is what I meant. I was a man, not a boy, and I was my own man. Missus Garvey, who taught me to read, told me that "Mann" means the exact same thing, only in German. Which is all right, I guess – I met some Germans after the war, and they was pretty decent folk. It don't really matter how nobody spells my name, or what they call me. I know what I am.

"Put your mark here, Private Mann."

I drawed a crude 'x' just as the men before me had done. Then I followed the others as the first soldier led them deeper into the camp. My chest was swelled a little; I noticed that the others, too, stood a little straighter. It was like that big millstone of slavery – so heavy it even crippled the spirit of Samson in the Bible – had been lifted right off our backs and we immediately started to buoy up like a woodchip that had been held under the water. My daddy was born a slave and he died a slave, but I was not a slave anymore.

I was Alfred Mann, and I was a soldier in the United States Army.

I felt like a soldier that first day. At least I supposed I did – not knowing what it was supposed to feel like. The uniformed white men called me soldier, and the word felt right.

But it wore off quick. We was all piled into them muddy tents, with little food and no blankets, and there was no soldiering in sight – at least not for us.

One of the men in my tent was named Lonnie Blake. Lonnie was real tall – he seemed to be all arms and legs – and tended to move and speak slowly. He had a light complexion, which was unusual in our camp; most of our recruits was slaves abandoned by their fleeing masters, who usually took the "more valuable" mulattoes with them. Lonnie must have only been a few years older than I was, but he always gave you the impression he was much more worldly than you. Whatever odd thing might occur, Lonnie acted like he had seen it all before.

"How much longer you reckon it's gonna be," Chamas said one day. "We come to fight Yankees. I done been here a week, and I ain't even seen one colored man in a blue outfit. I ain't even seen no blankets - we're liable to all catch cold and die."

Lonnie shook his head, "Dat ain't nothin'. I was in another camp for five weeks. Dey just picked me up and moved me here, to wait some more."

"I'm gettin' tired of waitin'," Chamas said.

"Go with what you know," Lonnie said.

That was Lonnie's favorite saying. He used a lot of different ones, but that was the one he said the most - and probably the one that said the most about him. No one knowed what it meant, you see, maybe not even Lonnie himself. He could find a way to use it on almost any occasion, and would say it in such a way it left no doubt that it was a very important proverb. Sometimes I felt that if I could figure out what Lonnie was talking about, I would understand everything.

I believe that Lonnie was far wiser than the rest of us, and had trouble finding the right words to convey that wisdom. At least he was confident enough to make it seem that way, and maybe that's enough.

"What I want," Chamas said, "is to see one nigger in a blue outfit."

"Don't use dat word," Lonnie scolded. "You ain't no nigger."

"What I know is, I'm a soldier without no outfit, without no gun, and without nothin' to patch up the seat of my britches – which I am wearin' out sittin' here."

"Go with what you know, my brother."

Chamas got his wish soon after – at least part of it. We got something to do. We was all excited at the news that our camp was finally going to get outfitted. Which did not mean that we would get outfits, at least not yet. What we did get was blankets, rations – and guns.

Along with the guns came more white soldiers. They was drill instructors. We was all called out into the field – which had dried out some since I first got there – and learned things like falling in, and forming ranks. Our commanding officer stood in front of us and gave a speech.

"I understand that you men are anxious to begin your duties," he said. "There has been a necessary delay in getting equipped, and now you must learn to be soldiers – but believe me when I say that the Fourth South Carolina Volunteer Colored Infantry will soon be ready for action!"

After the cheers died down, he continued. "I am Colonel George Wentworth, and I am your commander. Standing behind me is Major Peter Nelson. You will become familiar with your other officers soon. Some of you will be chosen to serve as non-commissioned officers, but for now we will make use of these borrowed sergeants from other units. They are all trainers of men – obey their every word and you will do well. The sooner you learn to be soldiers, the sooner you can fight to free your families and friends. Begin."

Them sergeants marched us up and down that field all day long, and for many days after. All the while they went up and down the line, screaming and hollering at the top of their lungs and sometimes hitting men who fell out of step. They had a manner of cussing which withered your heart away right inside your chest.

Tom Layton was still not convinced that we wasn't all bound for Cuba. These sergeants, he pointed out, was an awful lot like slave-handlers. Lonnie assured him that he had seen such men training white troops, and the treatment was exactly the same. Drill instructors hated everyone equally.

One of our men who had an especially rough time was Asa Ledbetter. No one used his real name; we all called him Congo, because he was only five or six years out of Africa. He could still barely speak English, which made it hard to follow commands. After he received a little personal attention from Sergeant Macke, Congo's language improved almost at once.

Colonel Wentworth made quite a fuss over Congo. He seemed to be real angry that Congo was African, and at first Congo thought the colonel was mad at him.

"This young man," Wentworth fumed. "A native-born African! After all these years, it's still happening. We've always known that the African slave-trade did not stop just because it has been banned for fifty-five years. But to see the living proof!"

The colonel, it turned out, was a Boston abolitionist. He had been preaching for years about the evils of a system he had never even laid eyes on. Now he was seeing it close up, and finding it just as bad or worse than he had been told.

Colonel Wentworth got another shock one day when several of us was doing "fatigue work" – a fancy way of saying they was working us to keep us busy. It got to be real hot, so we took off our shirts. The colonel passed by and saw our bare backs – he approached us, and we all stood at attention.

"What is your name, soldier?"

"Private Mann, suh."

"Private Mann – good God, man, what happened to your back?"

"I got whipped, suh."

He peered at my back – I could feel his eyes. "Those don't look like lash marks."

"I got hot oil poured on me, too."

"Merciful Christ. What did you do to deserve this?"

"Dey caught me sneakin' to another plantation to visit my wife an' young'uns."

Wentworth moved on to the next man, Herman Watley.

"Yours are even worse," the colonel said. "I've never seen scars like that before – how did you get them?"

"De nigger dogs, suh."

"The what?"

"De nigger dogs, colonel. I tried to run away, an' dey set de dogs loose on me."

Wentworth shook his head. "Go back to work, men," he said. "Go back to work." He walked away very slowly.

I didn't know quite what to make of Colonel Wentworth, not for a long time. He was moved almost to tears at the sight of our scars, and had been speaking out for years against slavery. And yet, at the same time, he seemed to regard us as little more than ignorant children. I once overheard him talking to an officer from another regiment – a white regiment – about us. I was passing by his tent, and he could not see me.

He was bragging to this other officer about his "little barbarians" and how quickly we was learning to drill. "'Young Sambo' is more pliant and childlike than the white man," he said. "He takes orders and discipline better, and seldom complains."

I had a hard time making such words fit in with the kindnesses the colonel had showed us. I thought back to the way many slaves on the plantation couldn't seem to make up their minds whether to love their masters or hate them, trust or fear them – they kept swinging back and forth from one feeling to another. I seen now that many white folks was the same way.

Colonel Wentworth would stand, arms folded, before the regimental line while sergeants called out commands and we marched like cogs in a well-oiled machine. The Colonel stood there and smiled – I found myself wondering whether he was proud of our achievements or just content with his own kind treatment of Young Sambo, who was too backward to care for himself. Him and Doctor Moss would be opposites in the eyes of most people, especially each other, but they was alike in some ways too.

The drilling eventually became routine, which I guess is a sign that we was getting it down. We got to where we could get through them without thinking about it – even Congo. The rest of our days was spent doing fatigue work: digging trenches then filling them back up.

At night I would often think of Frankie. I would close my eyes tightly and try to squeeze out the sound of the snoring men – I would imagine I could hear her whispering, hear the babies' soft breathing.

Our last meeting played out in my mind time after time, and I wished we had parted with more love and less stubborn pride and anger.

I prayed, hard as I knowed how, that they were thinking of me, too. I prayed that they tossed and turned and wept. Selfish as such a thing was, I prayed for it anyway – and hoped that the knowledge I had of my wrongness did not anger the Lord enough to make him refuse my prayer.

One morning Bullfrog ran into the tent all excited. This was not an unusual state for him, so we all thought little of it. The Mississippi-born runaway was really named William Robbins, but no one called him that. He was always busting with energy – more so even than my friend Sid back home – and was known to bust into song without warning.

The ditty which he sang most often was the one which gave him his nickname. We all assumed he made it up, but it is possible he heard the tune somewhere and twisted it around until it suited him.

It went:
"I was down – by the river—
Lawd, what I seen, what I seen!
It was a ole green bullfrog,
Sewin' on his britches green.
I said 'Mister Bullfrog, how come you work so hard?'

He said, 'I'm just hangin' on by a green thread.' "

Often when Robbins sang it Lonnie would nod his head knowingly and say, "Yes my brother. Go with what you know."

Bullfrog wasn't singing on that particular morning. He was laughing and dancing around, shouting. "De suits is here! De suits is here! Dem sojer suits is here!"

"What in thunder is all dis carryin on?" Old Eddie Walker demanded. "It ain't even daylight - dey ain't even tooted on dat dern horn yet!" Eddie was an old man, at least in our eyes - he must've been fifty or better - and valued his sleep.

"Outen de way," Chamas said, pushing Eddie aside. "I gots to see dis!"

Chamas rushed outside, and the rest of us hurried to catch up to him. Sure enough, there was several wagons filled with blue uniforms - they must have arrived after dark. They was being handed out to Negro soldiers, still in the tattered civilian clothes which had accompanied them out of slavery. Men was lined up twenty-deep on each side of every wagon, laughing and cheering.

Colonel Wentworth was right up atop one of the wagons, handing out clothes. He seemed to be about as tickled as any one of us was. "Come on, soldiers!" he called out. "Today we're going to drill in uniform!"

The sheer joy of this long-awaited moment far outweighed any concerns for decency. Men was shucking their clothes right out in the open - the first gray hints of dawn exposed hundreds of black backsides, scrambling to get dressed up right.

There was shoes, too. There was all kind of commotion as soldiers passed footwear back and forth amongst themselves until everybody got a pair that pretty much suited them. These uniforms was not custom-made, mind. Every man in the regiment wound up with at least one item that didn't exactly fit - it was either too long, too short, too wide, or too narrow. But it was blue, and it was new, and it marked us as soldiers for all the wide world to see.

We even got some of them little caps like Phillip Moss was wearing the last time I seen him. We tilted them little brims sideways a hair and looked like genuine dandies.

I thought we all stood a little straighter after we signed up; that was nothing compared to how we carried ourselves during drills the day we got outfitted. We did our turns and marches stiff and crisp, with professional pride, and that attitude stayed with us for the whole day – even after we was done and in our tents. All that day, and every day after.

We was men now, not just farm animals. We walked like men. This feeling grew even stronger when we got to shoot our guns in our new uniforms. We had been having a hard time learning about guns before then, and it was causing our regiment to fall behind where it ought to be. When the U.S. Army planned out how to train new recruits, they took for granted that their men was already familiar with firearms. And white men was – even the men from up North.

But most of us colored men had never even held a gun before – and deep down, in spite of everything, we hesitated a little to do it now. In the world we was all raised in, the only difference between a colored man with a gun and a dead colored man was that the dead one didn't have the gun no more.

Once we had our uniforms we all tried a little harder. Nobody could question our right to bear arms now. When they set that target up I blasted it time after time – the deafening crack of the rifle was like music to me. It was the music of power, power over my own life and over anyone who might try to take it.

Then something happened that cut our newfound confidence and pride down a little, at least at first. Some colored troops got transferred in from another regiment. It was a Connecticut regiment, and almost every one of them had been born free. Even the former slaves had been up

North long enough to learn trades and know how to read and write. Some of them was pleasant enough right from the start, but with many it took a good deal of effort for us to put up with them.

They had a lot of advantages over us, and they knowed it. In fact, that was why they was among us – the colonel wanted colored noncommissioned officers, but felt that a good noncom had to be able to read. These Northerners had been brought in as a start, until some of us others caught up.

And we was learning, it was just going to take awhile. Captain Garvey's wife was giving lessons to some of us; I could just about get through writing my name without help.

Until we did get caught up, though, the newcomers was set up over all of us. Most officers, even the colonel, believed they was better equipped than the rest of us was. It turned out that wasn't true, of course. In a lot of ways our experience with slavery gave us an edge over them, especially in battle. When you have been whipped half to death, and when you have picked up the bloody pieces of your friend and buried them in a sack, you are a lot better equipped to handle the sight of bloodletting than any bricklayer from Connecticut is. Educated or not.

But you couldn't tell them that. Some of them new fellows would congratulate each other on their drilling and say, "Of course, you just can't expect those slaves to be able to keep up with us – it ain't fair to them."

Once you looked past all their boasting, though, you had to admire their courage. They could still be safe up yonder, after all, and they was with us. What we didn't know yet, and they did, was that any colored soldier captured by Rebs would be sold into slavery. Whether he was born a slave or not.

Lucky for us, we got a couple of the good ones. They stepped into our tent one evening and stowed their gear. One of them was just a kid, the same age as Josey Layton, who had arrived in camp with me.

This young colored man's name was Maurice Higgins, and he was from Brooklyn. He used to entertain all of us old field hands with stories about New York City, and about working on the docks there. I tried to imagine the big boats he described to us, and the huge town, but it was all beyond me.

The other man was about Lonnie's age. He was average-sized, skinny, and had a thick mustache.

"I'm Robert Graham," he said. "I'm your sergeant now. Once I get to know you fellas a little while, I'll pick one of you to recommend as corporal."

He rummaged through his bag. "If any of you wants some reading material, I've got a Bible here, and some Shakespeare. A couple of novels – *Ivanhoe* and *Oliver Twist.* I'd be happy to lend 'em out – I know it gets a little slow here in the evenings."

Graham held out one of the books – no one moved, or spoke. He was puzzled at first, and then he winced like someone had dropped them books right on his toe.

"I'm sorry," he said. "I wasn't thinking. My father was a slave in Virginia – he was an old man before he learned to read. I didn't mean to embarrass you."

"No, no," Bullfrog said. "We ain't embarrassed. Shoot no. Are we, fellers?" There was a chorus of agreement.

Chamas leaned forward. "Say – sergeant. Do you reckon maybe you could tell us what's in one of dem books? You know – so dat when we do know how to read, we'll know wh'er we want to read dat one or not."

"Well, sure," Graham said. He gestured to the book in his hand. "Now this one, Oliver Twist, was written by an Englishman named Charles Dickens. It's all about how the poor people live in England, see and–" He looked up at us and grinned self-consciously. "Why don't I just read a little of it to you. Just to give you an idea."

"Well," Chamas said. "If you want to, I reckon we don't mind. Long as it's just a little bit." But Chamas leaned forward even more, his eyes wide with anticipation.

"Yeah," Bullfrog agreed. "Long as it's just a little while." As Graham thumbed through the pages, Bullfrog added, "Make sure you start at the beginning, though."

We sat in perfect silence as our new sergeant read to us about Oliver Twist. Afterward we all agreed that the little English boy should have run away a lot sooner.

Chapter Eight

We had our guns and we had our uniforms. We was finally ready to fight.

Didn't seem like being ready was good enough. Nobody else was ready for us to fight, I guess –we just kept right on waiting. There was all manner of fighting going on in Virginia, and over in Tennessee; we expected to get called away to one of them places any time.

We did get a change of scenery. We moved on up and joined with the main body of troops – it was our first march. It was quite a sight. We had been on that one field for so long that I had lost track of how many of us there was. With all the men-slaves our white soldiers had freed, and all the ones that had been sent from up North, we made up a considerable crowd.

We had a lot of camp followers, too – these was mostly women slaves. Some of these was the wives of our soldiers, who ran away from their masters or was abandoned by them and tagged along to serve as cooks and laundresses. There was a few loose women, but at that point there wasn't any whores. That particular job would have been a bad investment of a woman's time, since we hadn't started getting paid yet. As soon as the paymaster caught up with us, though, we all had back pay coming – ten dollars a month, same as white folks, and that wasn't nothing to turn your nose up at. Like a lot of other fellows, I had never possessed any money of my own before.

Civilians straggled out behind us. Some was leading goats and sheep, others was pushing carts – quite a few had young'uns.

One woman was carrying a sick child. The child must've been six or seven, but for some reason he was unable to walk and keep up. You could tell that his weight was a strain on the poor woman, who was none too peppy her own self. A young lieutenant walked up to her. We all kept marching, kind of holding our breath - we figured he was about to tell the woman she was holding us back, and that she needed to head back where she came from. The Rebs would get her if he did; her and that boy would be in chains again in no time.

The lieutenant walked along beside her a few paces. His name was David Newton, and he was from England just like that Dickens fellow. There had been some whispers around camp about his past. It appears that the lieutenant got to feeling right comfortable around one of them loose colored women - comfortable enough that he got to talking. Pretty soon everybody in camp knowed his secrets.

Lieutenant Newton had got a girl pregnant back in England. She wasn't no loose woman, neither - she was one of them high society ladies, higher society than Lieutenant Newton, and there was a big to-do over it. Young Mister Newton slipped off soon as he had the chance. He come to the states to bide his time till the whole thing blowed over, if it ever did, and he wound up in New Jersey when the War broke out. Newton joined the army, figuring he could use a little pocket money. He always planned to desert if things started looking dangerous. Maybe that's how he wound up in a colored regiment; looked like we was gonna be the last to fight and some of us wondered if they was ever gonna let us into combat at all.

Anyways, Lieutenant Newton never said nothing to that woman with the sick child. He just held out his arms for the boy. The mama got a hollow look on her face, like somebody that had just rolled over on a rattlesnake, and she handed the young'un over. I don't think she had meant to do it at all. It looked like her arms took action on their own, out of instinct, not being accustomed to denying a white man anything he should ask for.

Newton took the child - and walked alongside the woman. Everyone was waiting for him to do something else, but that's all he did, just carry that sick little boy. People turned and stared at him, even some of the soldiers that was supposed to be marching with their eyes forward, not able to understand what had just happened.

The lieutenant, seeing their stares, at first seemed to think he had done something wrong. He smiled nervously at us. That action was equally foreign to most of the former slaves - once it sunk in, we all smiled back. Some even chuckled. From that day forward, Lieutenant Newton could do no wrong in the eyes of the troops. And Newton never slipped off from the regiment like he had always planned. Not even when the fighting started, and not even when the Rebs announced that any white officer found serving with niggers would be executed on sight.

I still see that image in my head. The tall lieutenant, with his white face and his blue uniform, carrying that little boy – and the child with his arms around the soldier's neck, holding on to him. When I was a young, bitter man - even on that day – there was a part of me that wanted to say that Newton was just feeling guilty, or wanting to make himself look good by toting around a weak nigger child. But I always knowed that was not really the case. What I seen was nothing more than what there was - a human man doing a simple act of kindness for another human. I could not bring myself to trust that image, but I could not deny it.

Missus Garvey won me over easy enough, though. She was patient and kind, and taught many of us soldiers to read and write even though most folks - even Yankees - did not look with kindness upon a young white woman who consorted with Negro men. She was kind of like Doctor Moss's wife, only she seemed to see us as regular people.

I don't think that her husband, Captain Garvey, was real happy about the arrangement - but there was little he could do or say, since Colonel Wentworth had made it clear he wanted as many literate soldiers as he could get. Garvey was one of those white men who volunteered to serve in a colored regiment just because it was easier to become an officer that way – not many other folks wanted the job.

Colonel Wentworth had wanted the job. He maintained the respectable distance from the private soldiers, which was required of a commander, but he took advantage of every opportunity to watch us when he was off-duty. He was fascinated by us. He spoke to other officers of our "zest for life" and boasted about how quickly we could suppress our enthusiasm and adopt a military manner when the situation called for it.

He especially liked our singing. More than once I seen him, half-hidden by shadow, listening as Lonnie led some of the fellows in singing spirituals around the campfire. Ours was an alien world to him, something to be studied – yet at moments like that, I sensed that maybe he wished he could be accepted into it, just for a little while.

Bivouacking with white troops presented us with a whole new set of problems. Many of them regarded us with distrust. I got a glimpse into how things stood the first night I pulled guard duty in our new camp.

I was standing there at the edge of camp when I heard someone approaching. Two white infantrymen was stumbling through the brush, obviously drunk – they had been into the nearby town, a privilege denied the colored troops in order to avoid trouble with the locals.

The men approached, not seeming to even notice I was present, and started to walk right past me. Looking down a rifle barrel with a bayonet affixed to it made them take notice.

"Who goes there," I said.

"I'm Jim," one said in a slurred voice, "an' this here is Bobby. Now move out of the way."

"Yeah," Bobby said. "Quit monkeyin' around." He broke into uncontrolled laughter. "You get it, Jim? 'Quit monkeyin' around'! There's a monkey around!"

114

They both laughed, until they noticed I had not moved.

"Look here, Sambo," Jim said, pointing a finger at me. "I done told you once to move."

"Cain't do that," I told him, "until you give the password."

"Password?" Jim repeated.

"Oh, yeah," said Bobby.

"Listen," Jim said. "Tell me what the password is, and I'll give it to you."

"You s'posed to tell me dat."

"Why hell, boy, I forgot it! Besides, you ain't even in our regiment. You're supposed to pester your own people, not us."

Jim moved forward. "You take one mo' step, soldier," I told him, "an' I'm gonna have to put you under arrest."

Bobby giggled hysterically. This seemed to be the best joke he had heard yet. Jim was not amused, though. His face reddened. "Ain't no damn nigger arrestin' me!"

He lurched toward me. I raised the muzzle of my rifle; at this point I was within my rights – in fact, was compelled by my duty – to shoot the fool. Duty or not, I knowed that when I pulled the trigger it might as well be pointed at my head, too. I doubted if any amount of regulations could save me from being lynched.

Lucky for me, I was saved from having to do it. Lieutenant Newton arrived, disturbed by the drunken yelling, and called out to us both.

"What's going on here!" he demanded.

"Damn nigger tried to arrest me. A white man!"

"Private Mann, what's this all about?"

"Them two fellers come draggin' in drunk, suh, forgot de password."

"Piss on your password." Bobby giggled. "Pass on your piss-word!"

115

Lieutenant Newton called for guards to shackle the two drunks. The guards was both blacker than me. Jim did not seem able to fathom what was happening to him.

"If I had arrived here two seconds later, private," Newton told him, "your brains would be scattered all over the ground. I doubt if they would have made the grass grow."

"Good job, Private Mann," the lieutenant told me after the two drunks had been hauled away. Then he grinned. "If you think it's bad now, Mann, wait until they have to start taking orders from you."

"Orders, suh?"

"That's right. Sergeant Graham has recommended you for corporal. Congratulations."

Serving as corporal over the other black troops had not seemed like a bad proposal at all. But the idea that incidents like the one I had just gone through might become commonplace - and maybe even more intense - was not a great comfort to me. I forgot to thank the lieutenant.

Fatigue duty became a way of life for us. The old slaves was used to it, of course, but it was a new experience for many of the freemen. Everything we worked at was something that needed doing - picking up garbage, barracks construction - but it didn't take long to figure out that it was always us that did the hard work. Most of our tasks was things the white soldiers would normally have done for themselves - had been doing for themselves, before we arrived. Now that the colored volunteers was on hand, the other regiments took up a life of ease.

White folks have been saying for generations that we're better suited for life in the hot sun -it's a physical thing, they say, it's in our blood. We can labor on in conditions that would endanger the health of delicate white people. It's a very handy way of looking at things - especially if you're white, there's work to be done, and it's hot outside.

These are generally the same people who always complain about how lazy Negroes are. *Lazy, shiftless Sambo.* You have to watch him like a hawk or he won't get any work done. I always wondered why, if we're so lazy and unreliable, do they keep giving us all their work to do? They make it sound like them watching us work is the job that takes all the pep and determination.

A couple of weeks before Christmas we was put to work building a big wooden platform. There was going to be some sort of speechifying, so we had to get it all ready.

I wound up working next to Congo. He could talk near about as good as any of us now, and I enjoyed his company. I especially liked to ask him about Africa. It occurred to me that my grandfather had had to learn to talk regular language just like Congo had.

"Reckon when we're gonna get to fight, Sarge?" Joe Moses asked Graham as we worked.

"Don't know, Mose. It doesn't make any sense to me, either – thousands of Union troops are getting slaughtered, and they keep holding us back."

"Maybe," said Bullfrog, "once't all de white folks gets killed, dey'll let us fight."

Graham laughed. "If all the white folks get killed, we won't have anything left to fight about."

Eddie Walker snorted. "We was crazy to think dat dey would ever let us see any fightin' to start with. Dey got us to dig dey ditches. Dey ain't gonna risk us gettin' in de habit of shootin' at white folks."

"You de onlies' one crazy aroun' here, ole man," Chamas said. I had long been wondering, though, about the very things Eddie said –and I was not the only one who did.

"Go with what you know," said Lonnie, and we all nodded in agreement.

Working together with the other soldiers put me in mind of field work in the old days with Topaz and Sid. I had only been away from the Moss plantation for a few months, but it had already started to feel like a lifetime ago. I hoped that Sid hadn't done nothing foolish and gotten himself killed, and I worried about Roby up there in that big house. What if Mama died while I was gone? Or Uncle Wiley? Frankie and the young'uns I tried not to think about, at least not in the daytime when I was occupied enough to fend their memory away.

I was actually a little homesick for the old place. The very idea made me want to take one of them hammers we was working with and knock myself in the head with it. Missing that hellish life, even for an instant, had to be one of the most foolish notions that had ever crossed through my head. I put it down to boredom, and wished real hard that we had something more exciting to do.

"Dey dress us up like soldiers," Tom Layton was mumbling. "Dey expect us to act like soldiers. But dey won't treat us like soldiers."

I exchanged a glance with Graham. We both suspected that if it ever come down to it, and we really was treated like soldiers – which means getting shot at - Tom would probably be the first one to volunteer for digging ditches.

Bullfrog started singing. "I was down by de river - Lawd, what I seen, what I seen..."

"Tell me 'bout dem big boats, Maurice," I said that night.

I felt Maurice smile in the darkness. "Ships, Alfred. Ships. Call one of 'em a 'big boat' and you'll most likely have sailors and longshoremen both poundin' on your head."

"Anyways," I said. "I bet dey pretty. An dey jest sail around easy as the wind and go wherever dey please. Must be a mighty fine feelin', bein' on one of dem ships."

Congo said something sharply in his native tongue. "Didn't feel so awful fine to me," he said. "Ev'y single one of y'all, he daddy's daddy, or mebbe he daddy, got to take a trip on one dem big boats. It not so damn fine."

I shrugged in the shadows. Such concerns was as distant from me as Adam. I knowed slaves back home that could not be convinced their ancestors had ever been anywhere near Africa, not if you argued with them all day.

"I'd still like to have a look at one of 'em," I said.

We finally finished that big wooden stage a few days after Christmas. Turned out that the main reason they wanted it done was for New Years Day – there was some big plans in the works, and every man on the post was supposed to be there for it.

When the big day come, I couldn't believe how many folks was crowded around that platform. All the colored washerwomen was there, and a lot more civilians besides – colored and white. Some of the visiting folks was reporters, others was fancy types from Washington.

The post chaplain, Reverend Fowler, got up and said a prayer. We all bowed our heads, respectful, as he spoke words from scripture and thanked the Lord in our behalf. Some of the other fellows later told me he done all right at it, but didn't throw in enough feeling – I didn't care to say an opinion, not being much of an expert at it myself.

Then Reverend Fowler introduced Colonel Wentworth. The colonel stood up to the podium with a bunch of papers in his hand.

"This is a momentous day in human history," he said. "I have here a newspaper printing of a document signed by the President – many of you have heard about it, and have an idea what it says. That is no matter – its words still flow into the ear sweet as honey. Listen well, for this is the goal we have striven for so long – one step closer to our final, ultimate goal of a free, restored Union."

The colonel read the words off his newspaper out loud. Some of the words was a little too toilsome for most of us, but the general meaning was clear enough. Mister Lincoln was declaring all slaves in the Confederate states to be free, with all the same rights as white men – the very law Felts and his friend had scornfully anticipated a few months earlier. Wentworth called it a "Emancipation Proclamation", and it was greeted by all manner of cheering. Of course, it had been announced months before, this was just making it official once and for all.

We yelled, hollered, screamed, whistled – all till we was ragged and out of breath, then we turned around and done it again. White folks was yelling and carrying on, too, wearing smiles that split their faces in two. We truly was united.

Wentworth picked out a couple of colored noncoms to come up and say a few words about the occasion. One of these, a sergeant from our regiment named Prince Rogers, offered Wentworth one of the most perfect salutes I've ever seen.

"Dis time last year," Sergeant Rogers said, "I was slave to a Rebel colonel. Today I'm free, and a soldier, and saluting my own colonel!"

When the cheering over that broke down, the Eighth Massachusetts Regimental Band – who was up on stage behind the speaker's box – started to play marching songs. After a little while of that – and by this time the assembly was worked up into a joyful fierce mood – Wentworth stood back up to the box and announced that West Virginia had been accepted as a state in the Union, and was separated from Old Virginia. There was more wild applause. I don't think many of our men was actually from West Virginia, and a few still had no idea where it was. But the way we was that afternoon, after that announcement about the President's new bill, we probably would have cheered at just about anything.

"Praise de Lord," I heard one soldier near me say. "Now we all U.S. citizens. Not just us, but all de folks back home too. We got a country now!"

Somebody up front started singing the Battle Hymn of the Republic. A few others joined in. The band up on stage took the hint, and played along. Everywhere you turned you could see grown men weeping like children. Pretty soon we was all singing, even the colonel – he drawed out his dress saber and whacked at the air with it like it was a baton.

We sang like our hearts was a bellows, pushing the words up out of our lungs to mingle in the air with the words of our brothers. We sang like the power of our voices, and the pure joy in them, was strong enough – if we just kept singing, louder and harder – to pound through the final thin curtain of sadness and injustice in our lives.

We sang.

Glory, glory hallelujah.

Chapter Nine

From then on the number of colored civilians at our post growed – whereas before the only way a slave could free himself was either by running away or joining the army, now every slave in the areas occupied by federal troops was liberated. They had to go somewhere, and quite a few of them came to us. There was more women at our post all of a sudden, and a lot more children.

Many of these new civilians was the families of soldiers in our regiment. Some of the other men got married, courtesy of Reverend Fowler, to girls they had met right there on the post. This made army life a little easier on them –and a lot harder for me. Every time some new freed slaves straggled in looking for a place to stay, I wandered among them looking for Frankie. I never found her there.

Some of the white soldiers decided to take comfort from their coffee-colored laundresses, too – although not through marriage, because that was out of the question. They just wanted themselves a little carnal release. Even some of our own officers was among them.

It's true enough that some of our own soldiers did some carrying on with the colored camp-girls – not as much as white folks seemed to believe, but plenty nonetheless. It's also true that some of them girls took advantage of the situation to get started on the road to self-employment –the government had now got to where they actually paid us every once in a while, although never the complete sum they owed us, and suddenly there was no shortage of whores. I couldn't bring my own self to take such comforts, but I didn't feel like I had the right to look down on them that did, black or white.

The problem lay with a few of the white soldiers who didn't seem to be able to tell the difference between whores and respectable colored women – maybe they thought there was no difference, or maybe they didn't care. The end of it was, they treated both kinds exactly alike. Them men approached the girls a lot different than us colored men did, too – they never asked for nothing, they just took. They acted like some of the old slave-masters.

A fellow in our company name of Joel Stuart was married to one of them laundresses –he had been since before the war, and was only recently reunited with her and their children. Joel was normally a very cool-headed man – even some of the white officers had commended his potential as a combat soldier. He had warmed up some now that his family was close by, but he was still cool-headed.

One evening, me and Lonnie seen Joel come rushing into the barracks. He knelt down by his bunk and rummaged around awhile under the thin mattress – we'd been there at that camp awhile, and no longer slept on the ground – and drawed out a narrow-bladed knife.

"You fixin' to go frog-giggin', Joel?" I asked.

Joel looked up, a little surprised that we was there. He did not look level headed and calm anymore. His face was twisted up, and sweat was beaded all over it.

"I'm gonna do me some giggin', all right," he said, standing up.

"Now hold on, brother," Lonnie said. "What's goin' on here? What's got you so riled up? You don't never get all riled up like this."

"I'll tell you what's got me riled up," Joel answered, his voice a little higher than normal, like some powerful emotion was twisting his throat and wringing the sound out of it. "Dem white sons of bitches from de Fifteenth Maine, dat's what's got me riled up. Dey come into de laundry tent dis mornin' and went pawin' at my wife, squeezin' her titties an ever'thing. I seen 'em, as I was walkin' toward the tent. Seen 'em through the door."

Lonnie and me exchanged a quick look, each hoping the other would know what to say or do. Neither of us got an answer.

"She was cryin' by de time I got dere. Dey had done walked off laughin' an' talkin' dirty. And you know what Lorene told me? She told me it happens like dat almost ever' day. Ever' day it happens like dat! Wid all dem girls! And sometime's dey's officers dat's doin' it!"

"Sounds to me like Lorene knows what she's doin'," I said, "by not tellin' you before. You fixin' to do just what she was afraid of – get yo'self kilt."

Joel shook the knife in the air. "I ain't a-fixin' to get kilt. I'm gonna sneak up on de ones dat was laughin' loudest, and cut dey throats."

Lonnie put a hand on his shoulder. Joel shoved it away – Lonnie put it back up there again. "Den you'll get hung. What good will dat do, Joel? Dem young'uns of your'n won't have no daddy, Lorene won't have no man. What good will dat do?"

Joel was shaking. "What good will dat do?" he repeated. "What good will it do for me to stand here and let dem things happen? What's de good of Lorene havin' a man dat ain't no kind of a man at all?"

I knowed just how he felt. And I never was sure, but I suspected Lonnie must have knowed, too.

"Go with what you know," he said. He made the words sound like they was some kind of magic spell that would blow troubles away like dust

"Dat's just it," Joel said. "I don't know. 'Ceptin dis." He held up the blade. Lonnie, one hand still on the man's shoulder, reached up with the other hand and gently took the knife away.

"Let's go see Sergeant Graham," I said. "We'll tell him all about dis, an he'll see dat de commandin' officers hear about it. Colonel Wentworth, he'll prob'ly take somethin' like dis all de way to de General. You know dat as well as we do, Joel."

Joel did not say anything. His fury was spent. It did not leave him his cool self, though – it left him drained. When we walked away to find the sergeant, Joel followed meekly behind.

Sure enough, the colonel was outraged. There was nothing he could do about de Maine soldiers once he told the brigade commander, but he sure did make life hard on them officers from our own regiment who carried on in such a ungentlemanly manner.

Nobody in the Maine regiment was ever punished, not beyond getting a talking-to. But from then on they generally behaved themselves. They still made crude remarks to decent women who deserved better, but they kept their hands to themselves. Some of them was very resentful, and so was their commanders – everybody knows, they complained, that darkies have no morals. No sense of right and wrong. At least where it concerned lust – we was all just a bunch of rutting animals in their eyes. It was unfair that they not be allowed to join in, and it was unfair that we should complain when they tried. They "wasn't really hurting anything".

As for me, I knowed – like every man in my regiment knowed – that if I was to place my hand on a white woman's bosom, or even talk crude near her, I would be locked up or even dead before morning.

It was on a Saturday afternoon that spring that I received one of the biggest blows to my pride of my army career. It wasn't really a surprise, though, and that was the sad part. I was disappointed, when I heard the words, that the betrayal was not shocking to me. It was like seeing for the first time something you'd always known was there.

Sergeant Graham had sent me to the colonel's tent to deliver a message. I heard his strong voice as I approached the tent flap – he was dictating a letter to his orderly. It sounded like a letter to his family. Wentworth had two young daughters that he adored, and he wrote to them every chance he got.

"Are you girls not afraid," he said out loud, and I could hear the orderly's pen scratching, "that your poor father might 'turn colored'? I have been among the darkies for months now, my dears, and have noticed my skin growing darker, my actions slower, my speech duller. None of this is so alarming as the fact that my nose and lips are beginning to swell – they may soon appear as monstrous as Sambo's!"

Colonel Wentworth had always seemed compassionate toward his men, enough so that I had brushed aside the conversation I had heard between him and another regimental commander – the one in which he bragged about our performance while at the same time calling us his "Sambo." I remembered that conversation now, and his superior bearing, and cursed myself for a fool.

The orderly noticed me standing in the doorway and gestured to the colonel. "Come in," that officer said.

I handed him the envelope. "Thank you, corporal," said Wentworth "You are dismissed." I saluted and marched away.

The colonel must surely have known that I overheard his words, yet there was no hint of shame or apology in his face. He did not seem at all concerned. I did not repeat what I had heard. He may have thought it an innocent, harmless joke, but to me it was too humiliating to speak of out loud, or even to think about.

Colonel Wentworth was a puzzle to me at the time, but the fact is that most officers was like him early in the War. They had heard about colored folks, maybe even seen a few, but they had never really been around us. They had no experience in dealing with us, and did not really know anything about our strengths or abilities. The gap in their knowledge was filled in by things they heard about us – and as wise as these officers believed themselves to be, they was stupid enough to believe almost anything.

"Coloreds are more like animals than men." Only a few officers had views that extreme – though some did – but all of them believed us to be like children, or maybe like half-wits. I heard some say that we must not be very tough mentally, or we would never have allowed ourselves to be enslaved in the first place. Others pointed to the fact that many ex-slaves still had a great fondness for their former masters. This was given as proof that we was feeble-spirited and needed direction.

The fact that some of my brothers could hate an institution which treated us like dogs or worse – without letting that hatred include some of the individuals that had condoned it—was proof to me that my people had strong spirits. That we was human in the very best of ways, even more human than our old masters. The tamest of dogs would know nothing but hatred if it lived as we was forced to live.

That was the situation when our part in the war began. After months and years of fighting together, many officers wised up in their view of us. Their attitudes changed as their knowledge of us growed.

Colonel Wentworth even started a campaign to end the use of the word "nigger," at least among his officers. He encouraged other commanders to do the same, but he was determined to at least accomplish his goal in his own regiment.

He was frustrated, however, that we used the word among ourselves. It was a sore point among the junior officers – "they say it, so it must be all right." Those same officers laughed and called each other bastards while playing cards, but would not have appreciated a colored man applying the same title to them.

Nonetheless, Colonel Wentworth forbade anyone under his command to say the word "nigger". He also forbade anyone under his command to be one.

One evening me and Lonnie was sitting in a barracks tent, talking and comparing the soils and growing conditions of Alabama and South Carolina, when a commotion started up outside. We both rushed out to see what was going on. There was dozens of other fellows out there already, and some was laughing and cheering.

The center of everybody's attention was a couple of soldiers. One was Willie Potts, from our regiment, and the second was from one of the other colored outfits. Willie was bleeding from a cut on his left arm – in his right hand he held a knife, waving it toward his opponent like a playful cat waving its paw. The other man's blade was stained red, and so was his nose.

"Go get 'im, Willie!" a soldier near me called out. The voice was familiar – when I turned I seen it was Chamas.

"Cut dat nigger, Bo!" someone else hollered. "Yeah – cut 'im some mo'!"

"What's dis all about?" I demanded of Chamas.

"Dey bofe been courtin' de same gal. If she lucky, dey'll be enough left of at least one of 'em to court her some mo'."

Willie lunged forward, his knife jabbing for Bo's middle. Bo grabbed the knife hand, and Willie grabbed his, and for a moment it was a contest of strength. Then Bo's knee slammed into his enemy's groin. Willie dropped his own blade and sank to his knees, still holding onto Bo's weapon hand.

I had seen enough. I rushed over, pushing my way through the other soldiers – I felt, more than heard, Lonnie's presence half-a-step behind me. I grabbed ahold of Bo and pulled him back, as Lonnie done the same to Willie. Both men struggled something awful.

"You've had enough for today!" I yelled at them. "You better quit now, while you both still kickin'!"

Several disappointed groans came from the crowd. It sounded like there had been some money riding on the outcome. Chamas looked as disgusted by the turn of events as the other men had, but after a few seconds he pulled himself away from his angry friends and came over to help restrain Bo.

"What is the meaning of this!"

I felt Bo jump at the sound of the voice. It was a major from his regiment, a stern Boston man by the name of Dolan. Our own Captain Garvey was with him.

Dolan walked over to us. "Bleeding," he said. The word wasn't spoken in a caring tone, but as an accusation – it come out no differently than if the major had said "drunk" or "deserting".

"Everyone who was involved in this altercation," Dolan said, "step forward at once." Willie and Bo did as the man had instructed; he stared hard at them.

"Is this it?" he said. "Only the two of you?"

"Yes, suh," Bo said quietly.

"Hm. Well then, what is so important that you two feel compelled to break the peace and endanger government property?"

He received no answer. The major's face reddened. "I asked you a question, soldiers. What were you fighting about?"

"It was – it was over a girl, suh," Willie said.

"What a surprise. Well, this won't do at all."

Sergeant Graham had arrived. "You," Dolan directed. "Go find some shackles for these criminals at once."

Graham disappeared, and was back with the requested items almost immediately. He held them out to the major, who gave Graham an impatient nod. The sergeant placed the shackles on the arms of the offenders.

I felt the chill passing through the soldiers when they seen their brothers in chains. It was a familiar sight, but one which we had dreamed we would never see again.

"I don't know about you South Carolina gentlemen," the major said to Captain Garvey, "but in our Massachusetts regiment such behavior is not tolerated."

Garvey's face reddened more –more upset, probably, at being called a "South Carolina gentleman" than at the implied insult to his regiment. The major noticed his discomfort, and pressed the issue further.

"Punishments for fighting with weapons, in fact, are quite severe. Colonel Callan insists upon it."

Garvey's back straightened. "Any punishment meted out to your men, Major Dolan, will be sufficient for our men as well."

Dolan smiled. "Very well, then. Sergeant, escort the prisoners to the other end of the camp. To the horse." He waved at the rest of us absently. "The rest of you come along as well. It's time for an object lesson."

We fell into ranks and followed the white officers. We could barely hear Dolan and Garvey conversing politely – their voices was obscured by the clanking of the prisoners' chains. Bo and Willie stared straight ahead in mute obedience as we marched. Blood flowed unchecked from Willie's wound.

We arrived at our destination still not knowing what spectacle might await us. Six wooden platforms stuck out of the mud, each one about half as tall as a man, and about half as wide as a man is tall. I had seen these objects before, but never knowed what their purpose was. I assumed they would be used somehow in our training. For such simple devices, they had a vicious look and feel to them. Bo evidently knowed what they was – his eyes widened in terror when he seen them.

"Strap them on," Major Dolan instructed two of the men under his command.

They took Willie first. A soldier grabbed each elbow and led the bound man toward one of the platforms. Willie looked around at us, starting to get scared, too confused to resist.

Willie's feet was tied to the base of the platform with leather straps. Then he was pulled backward so that he was stretched over the device, and his wrists was bound to the opposite base – so that his body was stretched and curled under like a crab, belly up. It fair looked like his back would snap any minute. Bo was given the same treatment. Willie was already letting out cries of pain.

"The horse is an excellent corrective device," the major told Garvey. "When the other troops see the result of their breaking regulations, it will invoke great fear in them. They are very obedient afterwards. I have seen the horse work its miracles on many white soldiers. I can only assume it will bring even greater results in our own charges."

"I'm sure you're right, sir."

"Of course I'm right, Captain! Many of these men were recently slaves, after all, so they are used to such treatment and know what it means. They will soon be eager to please."

We was not eager, nor was we impressed. We wasn't even afraid, especially. The only thing that I felt - and I could tell from looking at the faces of my brothers that they was feeling the same way - was betrayed. A lead weight was in my stomach, pulling me down toward the ground, and the blood and the life felt like it was trickling from my face and my body and spreading into the dirt at my feet, leaving me numb. A tiny spark still lived within me, though - the spark of frustration and anger that had lived within me during my life as a slave. It was a spark which had passed through my father's loins and into me. It had been mostly forgotten for months, but the sight of those officers chattering lightly while they tortured Bo and Willie sent a chilling wind into my soul, and I felt the spark beginning to glow.

"What the hell is going on here!"

Colonel Wentworth was surveying the "corrective devices", his face livid. I had never heard him swear before.

"Garvey!" he thundered. "What is the meaning of this?"

"These men were fighting, sir."

"The horse is a standard punishment in our regiment, Colonel," Major Dolan said. Dolan was as confused now at Wentworth's reaction as Willie had been at the sight of the "horse".

The colonel glanced over the assembled troops. "All of these men do not appear to be in your regiment, Major." He

131

stared down into the frightened face of Willie Potts. "I know this man."

He whirled around and thrust his face toward Dolan. "That is my man you have on that infernal device. Cut him loose at once. Cut them both loose!"

"Colonel Wentworth, I must protest. Discipline is one of the foremost military requirements, surely you must know that."

"Cut them loose, sergeant," the colonel told Graham. Then he returned his attention to Dolan. "Discipline, yes. Savagery, no."

Dolan bristled. "The horse is used often in white regiments, sir. I thought the colored troops were to receive equal treatment."

"You must realize that there are some differences, Major. White troops enter the service with an independent spirit, which must be tamed so that they can work together as a group. Colored troops have no independent spirit – sometimes they have no spirit at all – because all their lives they have been treated like animals instead of men. They need to be treated with respect, so they will learn to respect themselves. We must strive never to act like the men who enslaved them."

"With all due respect, Colonel, what kind of punishment do you recommend?" Dolan's voice carried a hint of sarcasm; it was obvious that his tone was not lost on the colonel.

"All you men of the Fourth South Carolina," Wentworth said, "spread the word to your comrades. If any man of you is caught fighting from henceforth, he will not be punished." Dolan sputtered out loud, but Wentworth ignored him. "No, the entire regiment will be punished, with four extra hours of fatigue duty. Through supper.

"You are brothers-in-arms, and you are men. Your brothers rely on you, and you must rely on them. If you let them down here, how will they ever be able to count on you in battle?" He paused, and walked along the line staring intently at each of us. "How will you ever be men?"

The colonel gave both Dolan and Garvey a withering glance; they returned his gaze for a few seconds, then looked down. The colonel looked back at us, with the faintest hint of a smile.

"Carry on," he said. "Men."

There was no more fighting in the Fourth after that. Even the minor offenses dropped off – little monkeyshines committed by fellows like Sid back home, men who was testing out their boundaries to see just how much they could get away with. It was us, their brother soldiers, that they had to answer to now. Our rest was at stake, and our supper, and their pride.

If Colonel Wentworth went out of his way to instill pride in his men, the United States Congress worked just as hard to take it away. We had been waiting patiently for our pay to be delivered on time and in full; we was told that the pay situation would be ironed out eventually, once the government got settled into the idea of paying for such a big army, and figured out how to get it done.

They figured out how to get it done, all right.

They got it done by paying us – the colored soldiers – seven dollars a month instead of ten. Seven dollars was more than many of us had ever laid hands on all at once in our whole lives, of course, but it was not what we had been promised. It was not the pay received by the white troops.

The paymaster, a white sergeant, grinned at us when we brung that point up.

"You boys wanted to wear those uniforms, didn't ye? Well, they cost money. The government figures about three dollars a month." He grinned even wider, and spoke slowly – like he was talking to a backward child. "Ten take away three is seven. Seven dollars a month."

"We was supposed to get paid the same as the white soldiers," Chamas said coldly.

The sergeant nodded. "And you do. Ten dollars a month, black or white."

"I've talked to some of the fellas over in the white regiments," Lonnie said, his voice soft, his eyes sad but not downcast. "They get a three dollar a month clothing allowance. It's an allowance. That means ever' white soldier gets three dollars extra a month, not three dollars less. Dey gettin' thirteen, we gettin' seven. Ain't right."

"We buyin' dey clothes for 'em," Congo said, laughing. No one else thought it was funny.

"Listen men," the paymaster said. "I ain't the one makes up the rules, I just do my job. It's the U.S. Government decides what you get paid, not me."

Chamas tossed his money back on the table. "I'll take what I'm owed," he said, "or I won't take nothin'."

The sergeant laughed. "You'll change your mind soon enough, once you see all your friends out havin' a good time."

I stepped forward and looked the sergeant direct in the eye, something which made him uncomfortable. "Dis ain't soldier money," I told him as I let my pay drop on the table beside Chamas's. "Dis here ain't nothin' but nigger money. I ain't a nigger no mo', I'm a soldier." I turned away and said – softly, but loud enough for the others to hear – "Don't want no damn nigger money."

I would have walked right away, but Chamas tugged on my shirt sleeve and gestured for me to turn around and look. I did, and saw Lonnie walking behind us, his hands empty. One by one, slowly, all the other men returned their pay and fell into line behind us.

Colonel Wentworth assembled us together later and told us that he sympathized with our "plight". The colonel said that he was going to make entreaties to Washington, and so was some of the other regimental commanders. Until then, he told us, we might as well take what pay we could get.

Sergeant Graham, Prince Rogers, and a couple other black sergeants stepped forward and saluted.

"If you have something to say, say it," the colonel told them.

"Our men are proud to be serving in this uniform," Graham said. "And they are proud to serve under you. But they are proud men, sir – prouder than seven dollars a month. We want to fight like the other soldiers, and we want to get paid like them, too. Until then we'll just not get paid at all."

Wentworth nodded, his mouth solemn. "Does that choice set with all of you?"

He looked out over the assembled soldiers. A few heads nodded slowly, including mine, but no one spoke.

"Very well," said the colonel. "I will see to it that your pay is held for you, in case you change your minds. And be assured, I am doing all that is within my power to remedy this injustice."

The efforts of Colonel Wentworth and officers like them did pay off, months later, and we was given equal pay with the white troops. With all the money we had passed on and had reserved for us, we would all have guaranteed a nice little grubstake after our service was over.

Our money was held by Major Nelson. Everyone agreed that he was as trustworthy a man as we could find. I cast my vote for David Newton, the English lieutenant, but rumors about his shady past made most men trust the more reputable Nelson instead.

Nelson won a transfer to a white regiment, and took all our money with him. Official inquiries was made, but nothing ever come of it

We was plenty mad, but didn't have time to think about it. Our other desire had been granted.

We was on the march, headed toward battle.

Chapter Ten

The sun made the river sparkle like it was made out of diamonds, just like them that Topaz stole from Doctor Moss's mansion. The rolling of the boat under my feet was a funny feeling – I hadn't never been on no boat before, and had never been in no river excepting when I swam for my freedom, I'd only ever swum in lakes and ponds before that. My stomach swayed inside of me, in step with the rolling water. A couple of the other men got sick by the end of the first day, and them that was already used to river travel laughed right hearty at them, but I managed to avoid shaming myself that way.

We was all loaded on flatboats – all seven hundred of us, and the boats traveled one behind another so that the whole thing looked like a chain floating down the river.

Once I got used to the odd feeling of the motion it was a pleasant trip, and was a welcome relief from the marching we had done in order to reach the river.

And it was an enjoyable thing, just standing on them flatboats and watching the world that was on the banks pass slowly by. I would pick a tree and watch it till it went around the bend. For every tree that passed out of sight there was another one to take its place, and another and another, and I knowed it was like that all the way to the ocean which gave that river life. Them trees was like the days of my newfound freedom, stretching ahead of me forever.

But sometimes there was a break in the trees. Then we passed by little towns, and cabins, and lonely shacks. Often we would pass by the manor house of a plantation, standing guard over empty fields once bustling with hard-working slaves. The mansions was shells now, burned or abandoned, but still standing and haunting the river like the h'ants of Topaz's dreams.

A couple of times one or the other of the soldiers on our boat exhaled and pointed limply toward a particular mansion. "Dat yonder was my home," they would say. "Wonder where everybody is now."

"In Hell, where dey belongs at, I hope," Chamas said to one such soldier. "De white folks, anyways. I hope to be sendin' a few to jine up wid 'em dere, pretty soon now."

The soldier shook his head. "Miss Janey, she a kind soul."

"Maybe you wish't you was still back yonder wipin' her kind ass," Chamas said. "Whilst she was busy tallyin' up how much you'd bring at the block if'n de crops was bad next year."

The soldier bristled, but Lonnie restrained him with a hand. "Be easy, my brother," he said. "Dat's jest de whip-scars talkin'."

"What you think, Alfred?" Chamas said. "Was yo' massa a pore, kind soul?"

"It don't matter none," I said. "Anybody I see in Reb gray I aim to kill."

"An' you gonna like it, too, ain't you?"

I didn't answer Chamas. I didn't have to – the flashing of my eyes when the memory of the LaRue boys passed through my mind was enough of a reply. Chamas grinned. Lonnie stared at me sadly, his own eyes imploring me to answer Chamas's question like a Christian would.

I set my jaw. My hand gripped the rifle tighter than before, and I looked down the river for the next tree.

That's when the shooting started. I wasn't even sure it was shooting, not at first. A splinter flew up from the handrail even as I heard the bark of a rifle.

"Rebs on the bank!" Lieutenant Newton said. He pointed, and we seen men scurrying along the edge of the water getting into position to shoot. More bullets whizzed through the air around us, and the Union soldier who once belonged to Miss Janey pitched over the rail. The river was tinged red around his body.

"Present arms," Newton said. "Fire!"

Dozens of Enfield muskets popped at once. My own weapon spat fire toward the riverbank – it was my first shot fired at a human being, but I have no idea if I hit anything. Immediately after the order was given to fire, our little fleet was shrouded in gunsmoke. I rushed to reload, trying to do it with the quickness that the drill sergeants had stressed with such profanity. There was another volley. My eyes stung from the smoke.

I was finally able to make out some of the figures on the bank. They was still moving around, still shooting. They was distant, faceless figures that I knowed nothing about, excepting that they wanted to kill me.

We reloaded yet again, then raised and fired our weapons in a fluid motion, like pieces of a single machine. And that's just what we was, in a way. Flame and lead flowed out from us like all the anger and hate that had been bottled up inside us for so long. And still, I seen little more than smoke.

I heard a gasp beside me. It was a soft sound, but it pierced through my soul. I stole a sideways glance – young Josey Layton had sunk to his knees and dropped his Enfield. The musket slipped into the water without a sound. Josey turned his head and stared at me, slack-jawed. Blood spurted from a hole in his chest. He reached over and grabbed the rail, then leaned against it. His eyes closed peacefully like he had just decided to take a nap. Josey slumped and sagged down – the life had passed out of him and spread into the water like his blood, diluted and swept away.

The shooting stopped. We had floated past the Secesh snipers faster than they could run after us. We had also floated through our own smoke. I could see the Rebs again, more distant than ever, waving their arms and shrieking out their hatred.

The men on our boat was silent. Even the handful of wounded bit their lips and held back any expression of their agony. Tom Layton looked at Josey's dead body – there was fear in his eyes at first, as there had been on every day since I met him, but I was surprised to see the fear melt away. It was replaced by pride. It was a quiet, holy pride that must have showed on all our faces – pride in ourselves, and pride in our brothers.

Chamas' face reflected another feeling, one that struck a chord in my own spirit. It was angry disappointment. Was Chamas disappointed because shooting at Rebs was not as fulfilling as he had expected, or because he was not close enough to see the death-agonies of the enemy? I did not know Chamas' emotions, as I did not know my own. This uncertain feeling about our actions throwed a bitter shadow over my pride in our reactions.

Later that day we disembarked from the riverboats and once more marched toward the south. We was blooded soldiers now, and we walked with the erect pride of men who had faced death and looked past it. But we was all aware of the empty spaces in our ranks – just like your tongue keeps passing over the gap of a missing tooth, our eyes was drawn to them vacant positions. After we had pitched our tents that night we gathered in large groups around the campfires. We was drawn together even more than usual, bound by a chain of shared danger and shared victory. We laughed and talked – though still mindful of those killed and wounded, our laughter was unchecked, maybe even forced. Laughing and singing marked us as living men, and drove the death-ghosts back into the shadows.

Until someone brought them back out again. I was surprised that the someone engaged in gloomy talk of death this evening was Lonnie Blake. Tom Layton, who I would have expected to begin such talk, had in fact been acting no more fearful or grieved than the rest of us.

"You boys hear 'bout the Fifty-Fo'th?" Lonnie said.

"No," I answered. "What about 'em?"

"I heared some of de officers talkin' about it," Lonnie said. He must have had ears like a jackrabbit – he was always picking up mumblings that went unnoticed by the rest of us. "Dey was in a big battle up de coast, at a place called Fort Wagner. 'Bout got wiped out. Dat brave young colonel of their'n, Colonel Shaw, he got kilt. Dey buried him and put him in a common grave right in with his colored men."

Chamas grunted. "White folks'll correct dat mistake soon enough," he said. "Once his fambly finds out who he's sharin' dirt wid, dey'll move him – if'n it means diggin' up every nigger in South Carolina."

"You're forgetting our rule about using that word, private," Sergeant Graham said. He had long ago lost patience with Chamas and his attitude.

"Niggers got short memories," Chamas answered.

"Bunch of colored soldiers got killed over in Tennessee," Lonnie said, ignoring Chamas. "Fort Pillow. De Rebs refused ta accept their surrender, and cut 'em down in cold blood."

"Thought dey was gonna sell Negro prisoners," I said.

"Dat was afore we got uniforms. Now we dressed in blue, dey ain't takin' no prisoners."

I shrugged. "Reckon de best thing for us, den, is not to give up." There was several murmurs of agreement.

"What y'all think 'bout dyin?" Tom Layton said.

"I'd rather not," said Chamas.

"Die," asked Graham, "or think about it?"

"Don't aim to do neither."

"I mean it," said Layton. "All dis trouble to be free, all dis fightin', an' now Josey ain't never even gonna see it. Sorta seem like it was all for nothin', leastways for him."

140

"Bein' free worth fightin' for," said Congo. "Worth gamblin' yo' life – better a gamble like dat, dan livin' life a slave fo' sho'."

"But we ain't got to join de army no more to be free. We ain't got to fight. Sergeant Graham here, he was free to start with."

Chamas leaned forward. "Yes, we does," he said. "We gots to fight to set our own selfs free. If somebody else is makin me free, den I ain't really free, understand. I gots to do it my own self. Besides, dis way I gets to shoot me some crackers – get me some tit for tat, take away dey freedom for a change."

"How 'bout you, Alfred?" Tom said. "You ain't sayin' much. What do you think we fightin' for?"

Lonnie was staring at me again. It was the same disapproving stare that Uncle Wiley used to give us when we drug in hung-over on Sunday mornings. I tried to ignore Lonnie, as I always tried to ignore the old gardener back home.

"Dey's a lot of trufe in what Chamas is sayin'," I told them.

Lonnie's eyes narrowed, like he was trying to see plumb through me. "Maybe some trufe," Lonnie said. "But tell 'em what else, Alfred. Tell 'em what else we fightin' for." His stare grew more intense – not a criticizing stare anymore, but an earnest appeal.

A dozen faces stared at me, expecting, but I did not know what the right answer to Lonnie's question was. I did not know the answer Lonnie wanted me to give, or the answer that the men needed. In an instant my mind opened up like a book, and truths that I had known all along rolled around on my tongue.

I could tell them that we was fighting to prove we was men, free men, just as good and as brave as any well-bred white man. I could tell them that we was fighting for the future – that it didn't matter whether we lived or died, so long as our blood ensured that others of our race would be free, that our children and grandchildren would be owned by no man. I struggled to put these truths into words, but could only shake my head in quiet frustration at the dumbness of my heart.

" 'cause it's right," I finally said. "We fightin''cause it's right." The men all nodded, slowly, and Lonnie nodded too.

"What you know, brother. Go with what you know." Finally even Chamas nodded – barely, but I could see it.

"Yeah," he said. "It's right."

Lonnie placed a hand on my shoulder. "Hate ain't enough to keep us alive," he said. "Pride, and honor, and justice."

"Josey was a good boy," Tom said. "Never complained about nothin'. Never said a bad word 'bout nobody, not even them overseers that whupped him."

"I had a friend once," I said, "that got cut into pieces for running away. He didn't even make it to the next county. Seemed to some folks that he got his self killed for nothin', but I always knowed it wasn't so. He died for his freedom, same as Josey."

"I ain't sure wh'er I wants to die fo' my freedom or not," Tom said. "I ain't sure if I knows what freedom is." He smiled weakly when no one commented on his doubts. "I reckon it'd be worth it, though. To find out."

"I reckon you're right," I told him. "We all got to find out."

"Looks to me," Bullfrog said, "like mo' of dese fool slaves from de plantations we've passed would be j'ining up an' wearin' blue. Dey's free now, ain't dey?"

"Reckon a lot of 'em just don't want to," Willie Potts said.

"Dey scared," said Lonnie.

Chamas snorted. "To hell wid 'em den, if dey's too scared to fight."

"Dey ain't just too scared to fight," said Lonnie. "Dey too scared to be free. Dey never been free befo', an' dey don't know what to expect – dey ain't used to havin' to think and fend for deyselves. Some of 'em probably wish we hadn't never showed up to liberate em."

"Maybe we ought to make 'em j'ine up," Bullfrog said. "So as to help 'em get good sense. We know dat freedom is better'n bein' a slave – if'n dey don't know dat, maybe we ought to take an' learn em."

Sergeant Graham laughed. "We can't do things like that, Robbins. Part of freedom is being able to make decisions. If we go straight from freeing them to impressing them into our own service, we would be little better than the slavemasters."

Chamas shook his head. "You mean we gettin' shot at to save dey black hides, an' dey don't even appreciate it."

Lonnie had lit his pipe, and let out a puff before he answered Chamas. "Jest like Colonel Shaw from de Fifty-Fo'th, dat you was makin' such smart-alecky remarks about while-ago. Nothin' but a pore young boy, left his fancy house up Nawth so's he could come down here and get his self killed tryin' to keep yo' sorry black hide free. Not 'cause you'd appreciate it, but 'cause he knowed it was right. Not just him, but our own colonel too. Dey give up a lot to fight wid us."

"I know dey have," I said. "But de way Colonel Wentworth talks when he thinks we cain't hear – I tole you de things he said. Like he thinks we ignorant chillun."

"He tryin', Alfred. He tryin', an' he learnin'. It don't take away from what he's doin', throwin' in wid us. Don't you boys forget it, neither. An' don't expect white folks to be perfect, or else to be devils. Folks comes in-between too."

There was quiet awhile, then talk turned to other things. I took no part, just stretched out on the ground in front of the fire and went over the things Lonnie had said – and the things he had got me to say, and to think.

"They'll be coming soon, men."

Colonel Wentworth paced back and forth behind us, same as he had with the other companies. We was strung out in a line. Our muskets was at the ready, our palms sweaty, and we all peered so hard into the distant trees – looking for hints of gray – that our eyes hurt.

"This is your first real test," the colonel said. "Stand firm. It is very important that we hold the Rebs here – important tactically, to be sure, but also important to our cause. There are many even on our own side who believe that the Negro is unable to fight, even after Fort Wagner. It stands to us to prove them wrong. If one of you buckles and runs, and others follow, you will have proven them right – and all of our sacrifices will have been in vain."

"Just pretend like you're huntin' coons, boys," a white lieutenant said.

"Dis time it's de coons doin' de huntin'!" a soldier replied, and there was nervous laughter in the ranks. It faded quickly.

An eerie sound came floating out of the timber. It was a high-pitched whine, like a swarm of locusts was approaching. The troopers – me included – all pricked up their ears, unsure what to make of it. Some of the white officers reacted the same way. Colonel Wentworth, though – and Captain Garvey and a few others – stood firm and braced themselves. Their features set into expressions of grim determination. These was the men that had faced Rebs before.

The noise came closer, and got louder – if you listened closely you could make out human voices in amongst the weird cries. There was a thundering noise, too, and the earth pounded. Leaves was shaking on the trees around us, and a wave of fear passed through us all – it felt like we was fixing to try facing down the Coming Judgment, and our doom was being trumpeted to us on the voices of screaming Rebels.

Our enemies appeared out of the timber. Plumes bounced proudly on gray hats, and angry men bounced in their saddles.

"De hoss cavalry!" someone whispered, and the call passed up and down the line. "De hoss cavalry! De hoss cavalry – dey done sent de hoss cavalry agin us!"

"Be firm, men," the colonel said, raising his sword. "Take aim – be steady."

I sighted down the end of my musket barrel, aiming at a red-bearded giant of a man whose grays was mixed with homespun brown. The Rebs' faces showed no fear, not because their hearts was full of courage, but because they believed they had no reason to be afraid – not of us. We was just animals to them, niggers to be run down and scattered. It was something that many of these approaching men had probably done before, to unarmed runaways.

My finger tightened on the trigger, and I thought, today we'll teach *them* to be afraid.

"Fire!"

Our muskets belched smoke and flame and thunder. My red-bearded target pitched backward out of his saddle. Others was falling too, but the woods was still swarming with Rebs. Little puffs appeared as they fired their revolvers at us.

We reloaded frantically, the hollow whining of scores of ramrods was almost as loud in my ears as the gunshots. Bullets whizzed through the air and bit into the trees over our heads. Some bit into men around me. Their cries of pain was vague and distant; the only thing real to me was discharging my weapon, reloading, and discharging it again.

We was kneeling in the middle of a cloud of smoke, created by our own weapons. I could hear the Rebs crashing through the brush, and I could hear their horses, but I could not see them through the gunsmoke. That's the thing I remember the most about war – the smoke. It made you feel like you was dreaming; made you doubt your other senses and wonder if the enemies on the other side of it was real.

Then the Rebs stepped out of the smoke – or into it – and there was no more question about their reality. Most of them was on foot now, with swords and bayonets at the ready. The air rattled when we crashed together.

A Reb on foot ran at me, jabbing with his bayonet. I knocked it aside with my own weapon. I rammed my steel deep into his belly with all my might and jerked upward. The Reb looked at me from behind his loose, dirty hair – his eyes strained and he made a strangling sound. I pushed him away to face the next threat, but I could still feel his eyes upon me. I still do.

I parried another bayonet thrust. I spun on my heel, and the stock of my musket connected with a Rebel's jaw. The stunned man half-turned; I thrust my weapon upward, into his throat, and his blood sprayed onto my face.

I had dreamed of this day for months. It was going to be a day of glory. I had planned to look around me at this moment, searching for a LaRue to exact my vengeance upon. I was going to relive every indignity, feel every stripe all over again, and strike out.

But there was no time. There was time only to fight and kill. Neither was there a chance to consider the things I was doing, or the humanity of my enemies. That would come later.

Yet another Reb charged me, this one on horseback. He swung his saber at my head. I ducked, dropping my musket. I lurched forward, colliding with the horse, and grabbed the man's clothes – I jerked him out of the saddle. The Reb hit the dusty ground hard and lost his grip on the sword. I jumped a-straddle of him and put his own saber into his guts.

Too late, I seen the other Reb. He was running straight at my back, his bayonet lowered. I throwed myself aside, but knowed that the action was coming too late – I expected to feel the cold steel in my flesh.

There was a musket blast. The Reb stopped in mid-stride and looked down in amazement at the bloody exit wound in his abdomen. Then he toppled over.

Tom Layton stood behind him, smoke curling from his gun barrel. Tom flashed a triumphant grin at me, then lowered his bayonet and charged another Confederate. Tom's war-cry was as fierce as any Reb's.

I fumbled for my fallen musket, then stood up. The Rebs had started to run away, even those few still on horseback. A cheer rose up from the ranks.

Chamas appeared at my side, waving an arm. "Let's get the bastards!" he yelled, then ran after the Rebels. Other troops followed after him.

"Dey crazy!" Tom Layton said, laughing. "Dey chargin' de damn hoss cavalry!" He laughed again, and followed the others.

I slid the captured saber into my belt, gripped my musket more tightly, and loped into the woods.

There was still tendrils of smoke in the air, here and yonder, and the forest-floor was littered with bodies. Some was moaning and writhing weakly around. I didn't break stride, just jumped over the ones in my path – the fighting was still going on in the woods ahead of me, and my legs pumped like a steam-engine trying to get me there.

Two Rebs ran at me from around a tree. They was running as furiously as I was, and we almost collided. The first man swung his musket at me like a club – he had either lost his bayonet or never had one. I hopped back to avoid being struck, then stepped in before he could swing again and sunk my bayonet into his chest. The long blade slipped between his upper ribs and pierced his heart. The dying Reb twisted away from me and fell into the brush, taking my weapon with him.

The other Reb charged me, shrieking desperately. This one had a bayonet, and it was pointed at my guts. The Secesh was little more than a boy, and despite his fear-contorted features and dirty face, he looked very familiar.

He made a jab at me. I grabbed his gun-barrel as I stepped aside and jerked him forward, off-balance.

"Phillip!" I yelled. "Calm down, son – it's me, Alfred!" But the boy was not listening to me. He spun around and took another swipe at me. I maneuvered myself behind him and pinned his arms. He dropped the musket. I throwed the boy to the ground hard as I could, hoping to stun him. He rolled over, only to find me standing over him with his own bayonet at his throat. The boy stayed stock-still. His eyes was wide with terror, and his legs dug nervously into the dirt. He whimpered.

I seen now that it was not Phillip Moss. It was some other boy whose dreams of glory and whose family's sense of honor had forced him into a man's uniform and maybe a man's death. I took the bayonet away. "Get up," I said.

The boy whimpered again, looking back and forth in confusion from my face to the wicked blade on the musket.

"Get up!" I repeated. I leaned down and grabbed the boy's arm, jerking him to his feet. I pointed into the woods and said, "Go!" The boy still stood uncertainly before me.

"Don't your ears work, boy? I said go! Get the hell out of here, while you still can!"

"I-I don't... I ain't sure," he said. I knowed now that him and his partner had been running away from the fight, and that fear had took away his senses. They had attacked me only because the suddenness of our meeting gave them no time to think about it. I throwed the musket down in disgust. I grabbed the boy's shirt collar with both hands and drug him deeper into the brush.

"Sweet Jesus," he whispered faintly.

"Shut up," I barked. I looked around for a good spot – I nodded when I seen a large fallen tree. It had fallen across a rock, which kept it from resting flush on the ground. There was just enough room under the log for the boy to hide. I forced him to the ground and shoved him under the tree. Then I thrust my own face close to his and whispered angrily.

"Now you listen to me, boy, and listen good. You're gonna stay right here real quiet until dark, and then you're gonna sneak off and go home. Do you hear me?"

"Yeah," he whispered. "Yes sir." They was words he had surely never said to a black man before.

"If you come crawling out of here, and my regiment catches you, I'll pretend like I ain't never seen you before. I'll rip your guts out then, if I have to. Do you got that?"

He nodded.

"Good," I said as I stood up. "Be careful."

I walked away from the log, back toward the running battle. It seemed to be winding down. There was only a few faint pops of gunfire, only a few yells and screams floating back to me. I paused and looked back toward the boy's hiding place. I could barely make out his form, even knowing where to look, but I felt his gaze. Satisfied, I started walking again.

I looked around quickly to make sure there was no one around who might have seen me helping the young Confederate. I was sure such an action would be unpopular with my comrades, and might even get me shot by some of my officers.

There was no one except the boy's dead comrade. I retrieved my own Enfield from his body and left the boy's captured musket on the ground.

I remember my frustrated disbelief when Uncle Wiley had risked his life to help Phillip Moss. I perceived it then as a weakness. Now I was not so sure. I had spilled blood on this day, had killed men – some was probably slavers, others rednecks who owned neither slaves nor other property. And I had saved one at random, because he reminded me of someone I knowed. If he had been a little fatter, or a little older, I would almost surely have cut his throat.

I did not feel that this action made me weak, or that my other actions made me strong.

All I felt was human, and alive.

Chapter Eleven

When I reached the others, the fighting was over. Colonel Wentworth was walking among the troops, smiling broadly. The men was laughing and cheering – the Rebs was gone, still running except for the casualties they had left behind.

I heard a tortured groan from close behind me. I turned and seen a leg sticking out from behind a nearby tree – the britches was Union blue. I walked around the tree. Joel Stuart was leaned against the trunk, his legs sprawled out, cradling his left arm. Joel's face was pale. His arm was bloody and hung at an odd angle – he still managed a thin smile when he seen me.

"Reckon I should've ducked," he said, then winced.

I knelt beside him and looked more closely at the arm. The skin was ripped plumb open and pieces of bone stuck out.

"I reckon you'll get to go home now."

I turned to see who was speaking. Lonnie stood over me – his shirt was spattered with blood, but none of it seemed to be his own.

"If I wanted to be home, by God, I'd be there already," Joel said. "I ain't leavin' you boys."

"Now ain't no time to be arguin' about who's goin' where," I said. "Bestest thing to worry 'bout right now is gettin' you to a doc, Joel, an' gettin' dat arm fixed. Now come on, I'll help you up."

I extended my hand, but Joel shoved it away. "Don't need no help. I can get up my own self."

He tried to push himself up with his good arm, but fell back with a cry of pain. Me and Lonnie grabbed him and pulled him to his feet. He hollered something awful as his arm was jostled.

"Lean on me, boy," I told him. "I'll help you walk."

"I might not can get up, but I can damn sure walk without no help." He sighed. "Jest let me lean up agin dis tree a minute, to catch my breath."

Lonnie took out his handkerchief and put it on Joel's arm as a tourniquet, then stepped back and motioned me to come closer. Joel closed his eyes.

"De medics'll be here soon," Lonnie whispered, "but dis boy is bleedin' pretty bad."

I looked over at the wounded man, and seen that he had started sliding down the tree. I reached out and steadied him.

Sergeant Graham passed by. "Sergeant," Lonnie called out. "Request permission to take this boy back behind the lines to find a surgeon, suh."

Graham stared at Joel, uncertain. "It's an arm injury – can't he walk?"

I shook my head. "A injury is when you sprain your ankle, sergeant. Joel's arm is blowed all to hell."

"He can't even stand up," Lonnie added. "He's in shock from de pain and from all de blood he's losin'. We patched him up some, but he still might not make it 'till de stretcher bearer gets here."

"I can't spare you both," he said. "The Rebs might still regroup and charge us again." The sergeant gestured toward me. "You're the stronger one, corporal, you go. You might wind up having to pick Stuart up and carry him."

"Yes, suh," I said, and I put Joel's good arm around my neck and shoulder and lifted him up. He mumbled like a man being jostled out of a deep sleep.

"Come on, Joel," I told him. "We got to take a little walk, it ain't far." We made our way slowly through the woods. Every once in a while Joel would take a step or two, but for the most part he hung limp while I half-dragged, half-carried him.

Sometimes we would have to step over dead bodies, and he would cry out in pain as I lifted him over.

I had more time to notice the bodies now than I had earlier, when I was running toward the fighting. I paused sometimes to look into the face of a dead colored soldier – they was all familiar, but I seen none of my friends.

Two fellows lay dead beside the trunk of an old willow tree. One man was white, and a Reb, while the other was black. They was in each other's arms. They had probably died of their wounds while they was grappling together, had maybe even killed one another – and then again maybe, as they lay dying, they just reached out by instinct for the comfort of another human soul. It didn't matter, they was equal now. If they was allowed to go back to the ground in this pose their dust and bones would mingle and no one would be able to tell the difference between them.

Many of the men had rolled onto their backs and died looking up at the sky. Was they looking to find the face of God in the blue expanse, or did they just want their last sight to be of something besides the slaughter around them?

Picking your way through corpses on a battlefield is not as upsetting as you might think it would be. Some of the sights I beheld, had I seen them back home, would have made me sick. But out here, amongst the dead, every body and disfigured form was a reminder that I was still alive – and a cause for a very quiet, very still, secret rejoicing.

I knowed that we was at the field hospital by the sound more than by the sight. There was such a like of moaning and screaming as you would not believe. Men was crying out for mercy or for help or for death – it sounded for all the world like the tortures of hell that the preachers warn you about. The difference was that hellfire was for the wicked, and this damnation was only for today's unlucky.

A officer walked past me. The bloody apron he wore and the saw in his hand identified him as a surgeon, although the same items under different circumstances would have marked the man as a butcher.

"Lay that man down over here," he said, pointing to a table, and I obeyed in silence.

"You look like a strong one," he told me. "That's good. I'm short-handed. Congratulations, corporal, you've been promoted to field nurse. Now, hold your friend down while I take a look at him."

The doctor probed the wound, none too gently, and Joel screamed. He squirmed on the table, but I held him fast. I looked over the crowded area and was surprised to see Chamas at another table nearby, performing a similar task. Chamas had come back to get a flesh wound in his thigh treated – he was still waiting for someone to look at it, and in the meantime he was helping out with the men who needed it more.

The doctor working beside Chamas lifted something up in the air, and his patient thrashed wildly. The article was the bottom half of a leg. He handed it to another assistant, who tossed it onto a pile. Arms and legs was stacked up like cords of wood.

The surgeon who was looking at Joel's wound, Captain Fischer, let out a brief, thoughtful hum. "Hell of a mess," he said. "Has to come off."

Joel's eyes flew open wide. His head spun around to the doctor, frantic. "No! No, doc, please! Put it back together – put it back!" Fischer lifted his saw. "Hold him down tight, corporal." I braced up and leaned in against Joel's body, holding his good arm down. Tears ran down his face. His neck was twitching like crazy, like the cords in it was going to rip themselves right out and thrash around. "Don't let him, Alfred! It'll get better!"

"You still gonna have one good arm, Joel, to hold yo' woman wid. You seen dem pore boys layin' dead out yonder – dey ain't never goin' home at all."

"Don't wanna be half a man!"

Fischer was sawing at the shattered arm. The grinding of the instrument set my jaw on edge, like it was my own limb being cut away. Joel shrieked like a castrated pig.

Then he broke loose from my grip and lunged up – I barely grabbed him in time to keep him from hopping off the table. Fischer dropped his saw in the dirt and fumbled for it while I forced Joel back onto the table. The arm flopped unnaturally – the bone was cut through, and it was held only by a piece of meat.

Captain Fischer struck my face, hard, same as Rupert Moss had slapped my brother the day Roby had carried his umbrella.

"You goddamn ape, I said hold him!"

I bit my lip so hard I could taste the blood.

"Yes, suh," I said, and the words was worse than the metal blood-taste – I was biting back my soul, not just my blood. It wasn't never going to end.

I looked straight ahead, all the while holding Joel down. Chamas was staring at me, his back as straight and his eyes as hot as mine.

Captain Garvey was watching too – he had come to the hospital on some errand or other for the colonel, and his face was flushed with anger. He stalked over to the table.

"I need to have a word with you in private, Captain Fischer."

"I'm a little busy just now, Garvey."

Garvey scowled and hesitated uncertainly for a moment. Then he spoke up. "Such abuse of the enlisted men is unbecoming, Fischer. I would have preferred to point that out in private, but you would not allow me."

"Unbecoming?" Fischer said, his head snapping around. He made the final cut and waved the bloody arm in front of Garvey s face.

"Clean up after yourself, Garvey! You cut the limbs off these men and send them home to their families as cripples! You try to pound the life back into their chests, and then, by

God, you tell me what kind of abuse is unbecoming and what kind is not! Now stand aside, sir – my patients are bleeding to death while you waste my time."

He brushed past Garvey, then paused and looked back at me. "Come along, corporal," he said, almost gently. "Your comrade will be cared for. I still need you."

I took a step forward. Joel clawed at me, mewling like a crazed animal. I shook his remaining hand off my arm and followed after the doctor. Amid all that suffering, I recognized the irony of the episode – my defender, Garvey, cared as little about the colored men under his command as he would about a team of mules. It was Fischer's breach of military etiquette that upset him.

I assisted Captain Fischer in more than a dozen other amputations that afternoon. After awhile I had the same coolness about it all that he had shown at first. But the tragic horror of what we was doing tore up my insides, nonetheless. I knowed then that it was Fischer's very humanity that had made him strike out at me.

"I don't know how long dey think we can take it."

"Take what, Chamas?" I asked him. Rain plopped gently against the canvas roof of the tent.

He shook his head, chewing his lip – he seemed to be unsure of the necessary words to describe his frustration, a feeling I was very familiar with.

"We keep on holdin' it back," he whispered. "Like when dat doctor slapped you and called you a ape. Everything we hold back, everything we swallow, is another piece of mad spite inside of us. One day we gots to bust. We just gots to." I felt his eyes on me in the darkness. "You ever feel like dat, Alfred?"

"Yeah," I said after a moment. "Yeah, I've felt like dat." I said nothing else, because I was never sure anymore what I felt, or what I might be feeling tomorrow.

Lonnie's eyes was on me, too – he said nothing, but I felt them boring into me. Go with what you know, they was telling me, but they did not teach me what it was I needed to know.

Once more I gripped the Enfield, holding it close to my body. The bitter gunpowder smell comforted me – the weapon was an extension of myself, but at the same time it was something more than me. It was power, like no tool on the Moss plantation ever was.

My company was waiting just outside the Wakeman plantation. Lieutenant Newton was with us, and we listened eagerly for him to give the word to attack. We had been chasing bands of Reb regulars, cut off from their main army, for days. The fighting had been house-to-house, and the Rebs was finally cornered at the big Wakeman mansion.

Newton crouched down as yet another volley of musket-balls was sent our way. Little puffs of smoke floated down from the mansion windows. Newton's saber slashed downward through the air, the signal we had been waiting for.

"Use what cover you can find, men," Newton shouted, "and let's take that house!"

We run full-tilt through the big yard, our bayonets jabbing the air ahead of us as our arms pumped. Clods of dirt flew up in front of me as Reb bullets fell short of their mark. I throwed myself behind a tree and paused for a few seconds to catch my breath and wait for a break in the shooting.

No break came, so I swallowed deep and charged the house once more. One of our men, Nickie Johnson, stopped in his tracks just ahead of me and then spun around. Nickie had his hand pressed to his face – blood pumped out of the hole where his eye had been. He toppled over against me. Looking over Nickie's shoulder as he pressed against my body, I seen dust jump from the back of his jacket as another bullet took him. I braced, half-expecting the ball to pass plumb through Nickie and hit me, too – but it must have hit a rib, because it stopped.

I shoved Nickie away with all my strength and closed the distance to the mansion's front porch. I grabbed ahold of a marble column and used it to launch myself against the front door. It cracked, and I half-fell inside.

Two Rebs was in the front entrance, near the door. I discharged my musket into the chest of one. Then I throwed myself aside as the second man fired, barely missing me – the Reb grunted as my bayonet ripped into his belly.

Lonnie and Chamas came in the door, with four or five others close behind them. Sergeant Graham busted in a window with the butt of his rifle and then crawled through. He waved for the men behind him to follow. Together we all bounded up the stairs.

My eyes had taken only a part of a second to scan the fancy decorations inside the house. Crockery and paintings was covered with smoke, pocked or shattered by bullets, but it was still easy to identify as the luxury-world of the slave-owner. It was a world that me and my fellow Negroes in blue had been kept out of all our lives. There was still Rebs upstairs with guns, now making their last stand to keep us out of this special refuge of theirs. It wasn't going to happen today. We was field-niggers no more – we was loyal agents of the federal government, and we would be held out no longer.

At the top of the landing we lunged into a crowd of Rebs. Swords and bayonets flashed, and blood flew, and then we had pushed through. We divided, without words, into four-or-five man squads. Each squad took a separate room of the mansion's upstairs floor. Gunfire and shouts came from all corners of the house as our fight splintered into a dozen smaller skirmishes.

Chamas charged into a lace-filled bedroom and launched himself at the snipers inside, snarling and yelling his anger. He was upon them like a hungry wolf, hacking and slashing, and I rushed in beside him. Lonnie and Congo was close behind. The Rebs paused in the face of our fierceness, like they intended to fight but couldn't quite commit themselves to it, and they died.

Our comrades met with similar success in the other rooms. A handful of Reb prisoners was escorted outside, and we clustered together when we seen Lieutenant Newton approach.

"Secure the rest of the prisoners," he said. "Look for holdouts." Graham nodded. "Yessir," he said, then looked at us and jerked his head back toward the house. "Let's check the cabins out back, fellows," he shouted.

Then, distaste showing on his face, he added, "The slave-quarters."

We all trotted to slave row. Graham indicated that he wanted me to join him; we held our weapons at the ready and throwed open the door to the first shack.

The daylight which poured into the building revealed a colored family huddled in the corner. We stopped short, surprised – we assumed that the Wakeman slaves had already run off.

The shack's occupants was terrified of us. There was a man and woman, three little ones, and two old women – all shivering.

"Y'all come on out, now," I said. "Ain't nobody gonna hurt you." I looked to Sergeant Graham for his approval, hoping I had not spoken out of turn. The sergeant nodded.

"Don't shoot us, marsa," the man said. It dawned on me that, because of the light coming in from behind us, we was nothing but silhouettes to them slaves. They could not see the color of our faces.

"Is we gonna get sold to Cuba, Mama?" a little boy said. His mother's only reply was to pull him closer to her.

"Y'all come on now," I said. They obeyed slowly.

About two dozen more slaves was milling around outside. Our own charges gasped when we stepped into the sunlight and they seen just what kind of men we was.

Chamas laughed. "Dat's right, folks, we jest as black as you is! An' we soldiers for Mister Lincoln, settin' our brothers and sisters free."

Lonnie knelt down beside the fearful little boy and put his long arms around him. The lanky soldier glanced at the boy's parents, reassuring them.

"It's all right, young'un. You don't belong to dese folks around here no mo'."

"Is you takin' us to Cuba, marsa?"

"Naw, chile, we ain't takin' you to no Cuba. Only place we takin' you to is de Promise-Land. De Promise-Land of freedom, boy, and dey ain't no marsa dere but Good God-A-Mighty." He let the boy go and nudged him toward his parents. "You be good now, son."

"My God," Newton said. He had just arrived. "These – these shacks are barely sufficient to keep the rain out, let alone the wind. Do people actually live like this?"

"Dat's how most of us growed up livin', suh," I said.

Newton nodded, a little embarrassed. "Of course, Corporal Mann. I forgot." He squinted at the little courtyard located in front of the shacks. Three posts was set into the ground in a rough circle. "What are those?" Newton said.

"Whippin' posts, suh," I told him.

It took a couple of seconds for the full meaning of my words to sink into Newton's mind. When it did his face turned sort of cold.

"Some of you men find some axes or something and chop those damn things down. Chop them down!"

One of the slaves showed us where the axes was kept. Me, Chamas, and Congo went to work on them posts.

The blade bit deep into wood, sending a shake up my arms. It felt good. I wrenched the ax free and swung it around my body in a circular motion – my next blow went even deeper. Chamas and Congo was grinning as they attacked the offensive stakes. I realized that I was too.

The Wakeman slaves was gathered around us. An old man began to clap - softly at first, then louder - providing a work-beat.

One by one the others joined in. The men in our company started clapping too, keeping time. The people started humming as well: "A-humm, a-humm". The clapping grew faster. The faster they clapped, the faster we worked - woodchips flew in every direction, little pieces of oppression being flung away to be trampled beneath dusty black feet.

Energy coursed through me, driven on by the music. I pumped my arms as fast as I could, biting deep into the torture device, feeling that my actions was holy somehow. It was like them prophets in the Bible who took a notion every once in awhile to cut down the wooden idols of their pagan overlords.

The post started to give a little. I flung the ax down and put my shoulder to the wood. It creaked, and my audience cheered. The post let out a loud crack and fell to the ground - I barely caught my balance in time to avoid going down with it.

Congo's post was felled right about the same time, and we both joined Chamas in pushing the final one over. The Wakeman slaves, who had been fearful and withdrawn just a few minutes before, seemed to come completely alive when the last whipping post fell into the dirt. The old man who had started the clapping went over and kicked one of the posts with his bare toes.

"Let's get ready to clear out, men," Newton said, and we fell into ranks. The former slaves cheered us loudly, pressing forward and grabbing at us to see if we was real, or to see if our confidence could be transferred to them by touch.

"What do we do now?" someone called out as we marched away.

"Whatever you want," I yelled back. "Whatever you want!"

"I deeply resent being manhandled by niggers. Suh."

Colonel Wentworth stared at the Reb major we had captured. The colonel had set up headquarters in the little town whose name I have forgot, if I ever knowed it at all.

"No doubt many - niggers - have resented being manhandled by you, major."

The major shook his head. "I don't believe you understand, Colonel. We are prisoners of war, and have certain rights. You have irresponsibly placed my men and me into the hands of coloreds who have treated us roughly - and will doubtless do worse when they see the opportunity."

"I have seen the stripes on some of my men's backs," Wentworth said. "You are lucky to have been taken prisoner at all. But I assure you, major - upon my word - that you will not be harmed while in my custody."

The colonel gestured to a soldier standing at attention nearby. "This conversation is at an end. Private Foster, escort the major back to his men."

A crowd of local citizens had gathered around us. Most of them had shot venomous glances at my fellow soldiers and me, and many muttered under their breaths about the godless nigger soldiers.

A young white woman stepped forward as Private Foster escorted his prisoner past her. She had fiery red hair and wore a cream-colored dress. "Damn you, you filthy *nigger* bastard," she shrieked. "How dare you lay hands on a white man!" She spat in Foster's face.

Private Foster stiffened, and slowly wiped the spittle from his cheek. "Proceed with your orders, Private," Wentworth said. Foster and the Confederate major resumed their walk to our makeshift stockade. They was followed by the jeers and catcalls of the crowd.

"Everytime you hear foolishness like dat," Lonnie told the rest of us later, "you just remember dem colored folks, and de looks on their faces de very moment dey become free.

Think about dat, an' dis here business don't matter a bit no more."

Lonnie was right. When I thought about it that way, the townspeople's words and actions did not hurt anymore. They stung a little, some, but they didn't hurt. I was joyed at the fact that words was all them folks had left to keep me down. The barbs became stings of pride.

"Come on, Alfred. You a man, not a gelded hoss. Now dat you free to do what you want, why not try livin' a little for a change."

I sighed and shook my head, for what seemed like the hundredth time. "I just can't, Chamas. I got a wife."

Chamas smiled in disbelief. "Why sho', but she ain' t here tonight is she? Dem young ladies is in town right now, just waitin' to make friends wid some well-paid soldier-men."

A two-month wage installment had managed to catch up with us somehow, and the men was anxious to start spending it.

"Leave him be, Chamas," Lonnie said. "Everybody ain't as godless as you."

"Oh hush up, ole man," said Chamas. "One thing I can't stand is a dried-up ole man preachin' at me 'bout how a young man ought to behave."

"Lonnie's just a few years older than you are," Maurice Higgins pointed out. "He's no old man."

"Maybe not, but he sho'nuff is dried up. Now come on, Alfred! Dem gals is waitin'!"

"My Frankie been waitin' longer."

"Good God, boy! You a soldier, ain't you? Hundreds of miles from home, dat's what soldiers do. How long is it been?"

"Dat ain't got nothin to do wid it."

Chamas laughed and nudged Tom in the ribs. "Been a long time, den."

"Dat woman of your'n won't never know," Bullfrog said in a kind voice. I did not answer, or look at him.

Chamas stood up. "Awright den," he said. "You stay here. De rest of us is gonna go live it up. You go on, stay here wid de Reverend Lonnie Blake."

Lonnie stood up as well. "He ain't stayin' wid me, 'cause I won't be here."

Congo laughed heartily. "I thought you was not godless, Lonnie!"

"I never said dat, now. I just said I ain't quite so godless as Chamas North. An' dat it ain't right for him to try an' talk somebody into doin' somethin' dey think is wrong. Me, I don't require much talkin' to when it comes to de ladies."

"How 'bout you, den?" Congo asked me. "You a free man or not?"

I sighed deeply, and pushed myself to my feet. It went against my better judgment, but I couldn't help myself no further. It was just like them Saturday nights with Sid and Raymond down in the holler.

Chamas slapped me on the back. "You'll be glad you came, son. We gonna show dese cinnamon gals what a U.S. soldier can do!"

The little half-sized tent that I wound up sharing with the local girl was not that much worse an accomodation than what I had shared with Frankie, at least not so far as how it looked or how uncomfortable it was. But it was different in a hundred ways you can't see with your eyes, or touch.

It was a cold place.

The girl was young – sixteen or seventeen – and recently freed from slavery. Now she was making her way through life by selling her body her own self, instead of having some white man sell it for her. This was the life she had been liberated to – she acted like she thought it was better than her old one, but surely she must have dreamed of more than this.

I never knowed the girl's name. I was conducted to her tent and practically shoved onto her pallet – clothes was shuffled and we rolled around for a minute or two. There was no loving words, or caresses. There was only mechanical actions, a squeal that might have been real but probably wasn't, sudden release, and the exchange of money.

I laid there a minute, too overcome by a shameful, dirty feeling to move. The girl shoved at me with her feet.

"Keep it movin', big man," she said. "Make room for de next one." I crawled out of the tent and rose to my feet. I walked over to a tree - slowly, because all the breath and all the life seemed to have been drained from me - and leaned against it. I stood there a long time. I listened to the same rustling, the same squealing, the same clink of coins, coming from the tent I had just left, and dozens of others. Every ten minutes or so it would start all over again.

I thought about my first night with Frankie. I had been filled with life that night, not drained of it. I had felt whole for the first time since I was born.

Chamas appeared beside me, smiling broadly in the darkness. "Ain't nothin' like a good woman to make you feel like a real man. Ain't dat right, Alfred?"

I nodded, my head heavy. "Dat's right, Chamas." I looked up at de stars, my eyes lifted above the greasy tents. "You sho' enough right."

Chapter Twelve

Picket duty had never been a real challenging past-time, except for that early incident with the two white soldiers, but I tried to stay as alert as possible anyways. There was no Rebs for miles, but there was other things to watch out for. Local Secesh sympathizers was always trying to stir up trouble. But it was our own sergeants I was most worried about – Sergeant Graham, or Prince Rogers, or especially Sergeant-Major Isaiah Qualls. Sergeant Qualls was a skinny old man from Tennessee, but when somebody riled him he let loose with more meanness than a grizzly bear could handle. And nothing riled him more than a sentry who was anything less than completely alert.

That's why I heard the noise, off in the bushes. It was very faint, sort of a rustling sound, and I could not place what it was. I moved closer. Then I was able to hear other noises – a muffled whimper, suppressed giggling.

I gently parted the bushes and took a few steps inside, aware that I was leaving my post and hoping no one passed by at that moment. Whoever was making the noise could now be no more than a few paces away. I carefully moved the last of the branches that was blocking my view.

I could see them clearly in the bright moonlight. Two colored soldiers was hunched on the ground; one had his britches around his ankles, the other was pulling his own up. A white woman lay before them. Her milky thighs was spread naked and wide-open to the world, and her cream-colored dress hung in tatters on a bush. The soldier who was currently exposing himself to her had one dark hand clamped tight over her mouth, and with the other he held the red hair out of her eyes.

He turned and looked up at me. It was Private Foster, and he was grinning.

"Reckon she knows who de massa is now, don't she?"

The girl whimpered again. Foster took his hand off her mouth and slapped her, hard.

"Shut up, bitch."

"Get away from her, private."

Foster looked back at me. "Come on now, corporal - wait your turn. It'll be worth it - I plan to get her worked up good for you."

I pulled the hammer back on my musket. "Only thing you're gonna do is get away from dat lady and march to de stockade."

Foster's brow furrowed. "You crazy? Dis is de bitch dat done spit in my face. She gettin' what she needs."

"I ain't tellin' you again."

"You can't put me in no stockade wid no Reb prisoners!"

"Watch me."

Foster produced a knife - out of thin air, it seemed like - and lunged at me. I blowed a hole in his chest and he fell back into the brush, clutching at that torn dress. My bayonet was pointed at the other man's throat.

People was crashing through the brush, alerted by the gunshot. Within a minute Graham was staring over my shoulder.

"Merciful Christ," he said. The scene was unchanged since I put my steel at the man's throat - the woman was too upset to even cover herself. All she could do was weep softly. Graham covered her with his coat.

"I never done nothin'," my prisoner said to Graham. "It was all Billy's—"

Graham raised a hand. "Shut the hell up, Private Lawrence. You men milling around back there! One of you, go get the colonel!"

166

When Colonel Wentworth arrived, Lieutenant Newton and Captain Fischer was with him. Fischer bent over the woman and probed her bruises and cuts with his skilled surgeon's fingers.

"Lieutenant Newton," the colonel said softly, raising a finger at Private Lawrence. "That man needs to be hanged at once. See to it."

"Sir?"

Wentworth shook his head. "The fool will be hanged by sunup anyhow. Better that we take care of it, instead of a mob of citizens."

Fischer had managed to get the girl to her feet and was leading her away. "No broken bones," he announced.

"Then she's all right?"

"No, Colonel, she is damn sure not all right."

Wentworth nodded. "No one will be, not when word of this gets out. The locals have been hard enough to deal with up to today."

Newton had walked back up. He saluted the colonel as Fischer led the girl away.

"We don't have any planks on hand, sir. Someone will have to go into town for them."

"Planks? What are you talking about, Lieutenant?"

"To build a scaffold, sir."

"We don't have time for that," the colonel said, irritated at Newton. "There's no shortage of trees around here – tie him to one and let him swing. The most expedient thing would be to shoot the brute, but the locals would not be satisfied with that. We may have to shoot a few of them before the day is over."

The colonel shook his head again. "Brutes," he said. Then he came and stood before me.

"Well done, Corporal. If not for your quick action our position might have been even worse."

"Thank you, suh."

Wentworth paced back and forth, flexing and unflexing his fingers. "Sergeant-Major Qualls!" he called out. When the wiry little man appeared before him, Wentworth said, "If any of the men have managed to sleep through this commotion, see to it they are rousted up and brought here."

The sound of the bugler drowned out the cries of Private Lawrence as he was pushed against a tree trunk and saw the noose being looped over a branch so that it swayed back and forth in front of his face. Private Foster was dragged out of the bushes by his heels and propped against the same tree. His chin rolled over on his chest – his dead eyes bulged out at the bullet-hole as if they was amazed at his bad luck.

The rope was tightened around Lawrence's neck. "Help me! Help me, Jesus!"

"Wait for my word, Lieutenant," Wentworth said calmly. All the troops in our regiment was crowded into the little clearing. Their eyes was bleary with sleep and confusion. Whispers passed through the crowd as the newcomers was informed of the situation. I felt hundreds of eyes upon me as my part become known. Most of them was curious, or sympathetic, a few was approving – but one set of eyes burned into me. It was Chamas, and his jaw was set in anger.

"Do it, Lieutenant."

Newton signaled the four troops who held the end of the rope, and they tugged.

Lawrence was pulled slowly upward. First he was forced to stand on his tiptoes, then he was pulled right up into the air. His feet thrashed and kicked wildly. A terrible hissing, choking sound came from the man, cutting through all our souls. Lawrence's eyes bugged out, and his tongue waved thickly in the air. I was reminded of the last time I seen my father, but realized too that my father had died and lived like a man. Lawrence and Foster had behaved like vicious animals and dishonored us all.

"Hope you happy," said a voice behind me. It was Chamas. Lonnie stood beside him, shaking his head slightly. "What are you sayin', Chamas?" I asked.

Chamas's eyes narrowed. "These crackers around here have their nigger-hangin', thanks to you. What happens if dey ain't satisfied? Are you gonna catch another coon for 'em?"

"You didn't walk up on dem two an' see what dey was doin'."

"No, Alfred, I didn't. But I've walked up an' seen white men doin' de same thing to our women. Even my own mama."

"So you think I should've just looked away. Or joined in?"

"What I think is, we got to stick together. You don't go throwin' yo' brothers to de white man's dogs."

Lonnie spoke up. "You wrong, Chamas. We soldiers, not hooligans – we gots to have pride in ourselfs and do what's right even more dan white soldiers do. If a white man was to do what dem two done, den he's a bad white man. But if one of us does it, why, folks say all niggers is bad. We can't give up and let ourselfs run wild."

"I don't remember sayin' nothin' to you, yaller boy," Chamas said. "You as much a brother to dem white folks as you is to us. Think about dat next time you start wantin' to preach at me."

It was easy to see that Lonnie was hurt by them words, but he didn't say nothing to Chamas. Instead he lifted his face to the sky. "Help 'em, Lawd, dey know not what dey do."

"I know what I'm doin'," Chamas said, "an' I know who I am. I thought you knowed de same thing, Alfred. I thought you was a man."

I bristled. "A real man don't have nothin' to do wid abusin' women."

Chamas sneered. "You heared what she said to Foster, an' how she spit on him. She won't be so bold again."

Chamas started walking off, then paused and looked over his shoulder. "I thought you was my brother."

I said nothing. When Chamas had left, Lonnie placed a hand on my shoulder.

"You done de right thing, Alfred. Right an' wrong ain't got no color, it just is. Go with what you know."

"If I knowed anything for sure, I reckon I'd go with it, all right."

"Don't pay no attention to dat fool, now. Don't let folks like him get you all rattled. He's full of hate and anger – it's got him eat up and rotted inside, like a apple dat's full of worms. It's a good thing dat me an' you ain't like dat. Ain't no way such a bitter man can ever get no joy out of life."

"I reckon you right, Lonnie."

"Of course I'm right. Bein' righteous is its own reward."

I still wasn't convinced, not of anything.

"Fall into ranks! Shoulder arms! March, on the quick-step!" Sergeant Qualls strutted back and forth, issuing orders.

Men reacted with a trained-in instinct, despite our confusion.

Colonel Wentworth charged in on his black horse, reining in right in front of us. His face was sad and furious at the same time. "We're going to town, men," he cried out. "Lieutenant Spears and Private Clanton escorted that young lady to her family this morning – a mob attacked them. Lieutenant Spears was shot and killed, and Clanton was literally ripped to pieces. Be alert!"

We marched, standing straight and with eyes ahead unwincing. We marched on past the hanging tree, where Lawrence still hung swinging in the wind – the branch creaked loudly with every breeze. Foster was still propped against the trunk. He looked stiff enough to break in two if you touched him, and a cloud of flies swarmed around his dried-up wound. His eyes stared after us.

When we reached the edge of town we was greeted by gunfire. A couple of our men dropped – one was dead, the other bad hurt.

"The fools!" Wentworth shouted. "Burn this town to the ground, men – if anyone resists, shoot them down."

"You heard the man," Graham said. "Move out!"

We charged into the town. Women was screaming, and men was shouting – two men ran into the street with pistols, and was cut down before they could fire them.

Rifle shots was still coming from above us. We could see puffs of smoke now, which revealed the town's hotel as the source. Prince Rogers led his company into the building – the shooting intensified, but soon stopped completely.

One of our men was passing out torches. I took one and headed for the general store. I quickly made sure no one was inside, then put the torch to the curtains on the front window and tossed it in. A fat, balding man ran up to the building, his face red with rage. I figured he was probably the owner.

"Animals!" he screamed. "You damned animals! I work all my life to build somethin', only to have a bunch of blue-belly monkeys come around and burn it down – just to prove they can!"

"Step aside, mister," I said. "I got work to do."

Tears welled up in the man's eyes. "You won't be in them blue suits forever, you know! One of these days things'll go back to the way they was. What do you think will happen then?"

I pushed past the store-owner.

"Huh, nigger?" he shouted after me. "What do you think will happen then?"

The whole town was burning. The sun went down while we was herding the citizens into the square, away from the blazing buildings. The fire cracked and danced like it was somebody alive, like it was laughing at us all. It made shadows flicker on all our faces, so that each person seemed to shift back and forth from who they was to some kind of devil.

I could see altogether different faces in the flames of the burning hotel. I imagined I seen the red-headed girl in the cream-colored dress, and Lawrence's contorted features as he strangled to death on the end of a rope, and the grieving storekeeper. If there had been less hating all the way around, the sun would not be coming up tomorrow on ashes and blood.

We was all glad to receive word that we was going to be marching north to battle. No one wanted to remain camped outside the remains of the little town, with all the people around hating us with an intensity we could never have imagined.

It wasn't good news for everybody, though, not completely. Twenty men had to be transferred from our regiment to the Fifty-Fourth Massachusetts, to help fill out their depleted ranks.

Willie Potts was one of the men picked out to be transferred. When the time came to leave, Willie blubbered and took on like a baby. The rest of us was shook up, too – we couldn't stand the thought of our friends going off to face death in the company of strangers. All we had was each other, after all.

The officers did not understand, not even Colonel Wentworth. They had seen many white soldiers get changed around before, without nearly the same commotion. Potts and the others had distinguished themselves in battle, after all, with never a thought of shrinking back. I believe that some officers took Willie's reaction as proof of our childish nature. They just could not comprehend our grief.

The white officers had never had their relatives sold away.

It was July when we reached our destination – just outside of a place called Petersburg. There was men in blue bivouacked as far as the eye could see. I had never even imagined such a concentration of soldiers, almost all of them white. It was a thrilling sight, at first, until I stopped to wonder:

what kind of Reb force could be waiting for us out there, that would require such a huge army to attack it.

In the distance we seen the high barricaded earthworks around Petersburg. Sharpened poles stuck out like teeth on some unearthly monster. There was plenty of Rebs in there, all right—plenty enough to have already repulsed a full-scale charge by the very Union troops we was now joining. Our white brothers-in-arms had taken heavy casualties in that attack, and the Rebs had received reinforcements since then.

We started hearing rumors from soldiers in the other regiments about the possible importance of the upcoming battle. There was all kinds of high-up Union generals coming and going – General Grant himself was in command, and even Mister Lincoln had made an inspection tour. Some said that Robert E. Lee was present behind them earthworks, or at least he had been. We was all a little bedazzled by such big names being bandied around. It was the cannons sticking out over them barricades, though, that really grabbed our attention.

"Gawd-a-mighty," Tom Layton said. "Is we gonna have to charge dat place?"

"If they tells us to, we will," Lonnie said.

Chamas grunted. "If anybody gets sent into de mouf of dem guns," he said, "it'll be us."

"Charging the guns has already been tried," Graham said. "I've been told they have something else planned."

"What dey gonna try?" Bullfrog asked.

"That part I don't know yet. But I'm sure we'll be finding out soon enough."

We found out, all right – it was impossible to miss. Some engineers had come up with the brilliant idea of digging a tunnel. It was a tunnel the like of which you have never seen, and the plan was for it to stretch right under the very feet of the Reb defenders. The idea was to set off a huge bomb and blow a hole in the Confederate fortifications, allowing us to surge through. General Grant was not very happy with the plan, we heard, but his advisors insisted it would work.

We expected that we would be put to work digging the tunnel –we had always done most of the physical labor when we camped with white troops, up to then – but it didn't turn out that way. Instead, our whole regiment started a vigorous set of assault-training exercises.

We was to be the vanguard of the attack.

Every day we climbed over wooden stakes and ran through obstacle courses. Speed, they told us, is the essence. The exercises was made more realistic by the shells exploding over our heads – the Rebs was practicing, too.

A couple of days before the explosion was planned to happen, we was informed of a change of plans. We was not going in first after all – the higher-ups was afraid of bad publicity, claiming that the Union generals was sending colored troops purposely to be slaughtered.

But we was still going to go in, and we knowed it.

"We go out de other side of dat tunnel, boys," Tom Layton said on the night before the attack was to begin, "I'm afraid ain't none of us gonna be comin' back. I been talkin' to some folks dat was in dat other charge – it sounded like hell on earth. One regiment lost almost seven hundred men dead, out of nine hundred. I'm startin' to wish I was back in dem fields, boys, I'm tellin' you." I chuckled. Tom's face darkened. "What you think is so blasted funny, nigger?"

"You funny," I said. "You set around and work yourself all into a frenzy over every little thing. But den, once de shootin' starts, you forget all about your worryin' and go to work fightin' same as anybody."

"So?" Tom said, but his eyes shined a little bit at my compliment of his courage, a quality he constantly doubted in himself.

"So, you make yourself miserable for nothin', wid all yo' worryin'."

"Not to mention makin' our lifes miserable," Bullfrog added. "Look at dem big ole stars just a-shinin' up yonder," Eddie Walker said. "De same stars our folks is lookin' at wherever dey might be right now. Say Congo, is dey got de same stars in Africa?"

Congo kicked at the dirt. "I never looked at 'em much, 'till I come over de big water. When I was home I just looked at de ground beneath my feet. Wasn't till I was in chains dat I started lookin' up, wishin' I was someplace else."

"Dem big boats can tell where dey goin' by lookin' at de stars," I said. "Ain't dat right, Maurice?"

"That's right. I wish I was standing on the docks in New York right now, watching those big ships come floating in."

Sergeant Graham was reading to himself in the dim lamplight.

"What you readin', sarge?" Bullfrog said.

"Shakespeare. Henry the Fifth."

"What's it about?"

"England is about to attack France, you see, on this holiday called Saint Crispin's Day. The English king is giving his soldiers a speech, telling them how proud they should be of what they're about to do."

"You can read it to us," Bullfrog said. "If you want to."

Graham smiled, and started to read.

" 'From this day to the ending of the world,
But we in it shall be remembered,
We few, we happy few, we band of brothers
For he today that sheds his blood with me shall be my brother
Be he ne'er so vile, this day shall gentle his condition.
And gentlemen in England, now a-bed, shall think themselves
accursed they were not here;
And hold their manhoods cheap, whiles any speaks
That fought with us upon Saint Crispin's Day.' "

"What de hell he talkin about?" Chamas said. "Don't dat Shakespeare feller talk no English?"

We all laughed. "We all understand what he sayin'," I said. "Some of his words is funny, but we understand."

"Dat's right," said Lonnie. "He sayin', 'Go with what you know'."

We stood in readiness as the charges was lit. Ledlie's boys from the First Division was more ready than we was, and more nervous – they was going to lead the assault. It was three o'clock in the morning, and the enemy would be at his least alert.

We waited, and we waited some more. There was no explosion. The fuse had gone out. It took the engineers over an hour to re-set their fuse. Once they did, though, it was a remarkable short time before the bomb went off.

I had never seen or heard anything like it. The ground shook so hard I almost fell down – many men did – and my ears felt like they was exploding too. I had stood nearby when cannons went off, firing over the fortifications, but that was nothing compared to the bomb.

A big cloud rose up over the earthen walls, shaped like a mushroom. In amongst the cloud there was flame, spurting a hundred foot tall – and there was other things, blowed just as high. Whole cannons flew into the sky, accompanied by men and parts of men. Dirt rained on us like we was in the middle of a flashflood.

When the dust and debris settled, we found ourselves looking at a giant crater. Somebody later told me that its dimensions was a hundred and seventy feet long, seventy feet wide, and thirty feet deep – it stretched well into the Reb position.

The First Division jumped down into the crater and headed toward the Rebs, moving out of sight in the darkness. Once inside the earthworks they found themselves in a maze of trenches, and faltered. Much quicker than anybody could have guessed, the Rebs gathered their wits and trained their artillery on the fifteen thousand attackers.

The white troops was confused. They had not been taught what to expect, like we was – they floundered in the trenches, and on the stakes, and was ripped to pieces. They neither moved forward nor retreated. Many of their officers was dead, and their commander was behind the lines in a bomb-proof bunker.

Colonel Wentworth trotted past us on that black horse. He shouted to be heard above the cannonfire.

"In my time among you men," he called out, "I have come to believe some of the statements I have heard about race. I have come to believe, as I once heard one of you say, that a white man is 'most as good as a Negro.'"

He pulled out his sword. "If we live or die, we do it together and for the Union. Forward!"

Wentworth half-rode, half-slid his horse into the crater, and we all ran after him.

Shells exploded near us, and among us, kicking up dirt, rock, and men. We screamed our rage and ran so hard our lungs felt like they was on fire.

A shell exploded right at the feet of Jimmy Layton, Tom's "brother" from plantation days. He was tossed into the air like a rag doll, and fell to the ground nothing but a piece of bloody meat. I jumped over an obstacle in my path, and only for half-a-second did my mind dwell on the fact that it was all that remained of Captain Garvey.

We arrived at the position of the First Division. A straight clearing lay between them and the Rebs; it would be a killing field for any group of men who entered it.

Wentworth was waving his saber again, chopping the air furiously, and screaming at the white soldiers.

"Get up!" he shrieked. "Be men – think of how you are going to feel tomorrow!"

None of them moved, except to cringe. Wentworth turned to us. "Let's show them all," he said. "Let's show them, once and for all, that we are men!"

He galloped into that clearing. He rode into the mouth of hell, and we followed him with shouts of pride.

Poor old Mose spun half-around in front of me, his guts splattered on the ground. I slipped on them and almost fell.

The other Layton fell screaming near me, leaving Tom the only one of them four original comrades once owned by a man named Layton.

Wentworth's horse fell with a crash, pinning the colonel to the ground. He kept his hold on the sword, pointing it toward the Reb position.

"Go!" he shouted. "Go, go, dammit, go!"

Lieutenant Newton stooped and took the saber from Wentworth's hand without breaking stride. He urged us forward, setting the example himself.

The shelling got even worse, and was joined now by individual musket-fire. Maurice Higgins took a ball in the temple and fell, never again to see his beloved ships.

And then we was among the Rebs. We collided with them like a steam train, and the ferocity of our attack made them fall back.

Newton swung Wentworth's sword back and forth like a reaping scythe, his arms working like a machine. He was run through by a bayonet, then another, and another –still the sword swung, until he was borne up bodily and tossed away.

Eddie Walker turned to look behind us. "Where's dem damn white boys?" he thundered. "We gots de Rebs distracted – where is dey?"

A crimson blotch exploded out the front of Eddie's chest, and the old man disappeared beneath the feet of the combatants.

Congo received a bayonet through the fleshy part of his arm. He ignored the wound, ripping the arm away so that the muscles was severed. With his good hand he plunged a stolen saber through his attacker's gut.

I was fighting like I had never fought before. For every Reb killed, it seemed like three more stepped in to take his place. Their weight pressing in overwhelmed me, and I knowed I was about to go down.

Then two figures leaped into the crowd of Rebs, swinging their guns like clubs. It was Chamas and Tom. Their fury was like that of mad dogs, and the Rebs hesitated a second. Then more Rebs showed up, and Chamas was separated from us. We had all we could do just to stay alive our own selves, we wasn't able to help him. Like Newton, he was run through but kept fighting. He fell to his knees and dropped his weapon – the last I seen he was lurching forward like he was trying to bite his enemies.

Sergeant Graham fell also, trying to hold his guts in with one hand while he fired a revolver with the other. He emptied the gun and tried to reload with one hand. Frustrated, he dropped the weapon and rolled onto his back.

I heard Sergeant Qualls's thin voice rise over the din.

"Dem white boys ain't comin' to help us!" he said. "Nobody's got de guts to – we have to retreat. Retreat!"

Our men started to run back the way they came. I was reluctant to leave our friends laying dead or dying in the dirt, but seen no other course. We could never take the place alone.

We ran, just as hard as we had run coming there, but with no spirit. A few of the boys paused at the spot where the remains of the First Division huddled, still too scared to even run back to the safety of their own lines.

Congo raised his bloody arm to them. "We men!" he screamed at the top of his lungs. "You hear me! We men!"

Tears streamed down Congo's face and he half-choked as he repeated softly, to us, "We men."

We kept moving, and left the First to follow us if they cared to.

The Rebs had repaired the hole in their fortification within a few hours. No other charges was made that day – not much of anything happened, in fact, for many days. There was several skirmishes about a week after we got slaughtered, and the Rebs fell back a little. A burial detail was chosen to go to the site of our massacre and bury the bodies of our comrades –still within range of the Reb artillery.

It was not the least bit surprising to us that we was chosen for this duty.

The men of the First Division and the Fourth South Carolina had been left by the Rebs to bake in the August sun. The dead Rebs – a fraction the size of our own casualties – had been reclaimed by their fellow Confederates. About half our regiment lay rotting in the crater, along with at least two or three thousand First Division boys.

The stench was overpowering. Even the handkerchiefs over our faces was not able to stop it. It settled down on us like a living thing, trying to choke the life out of us – the spirits of the dead was too heavy to make their way to heaven, and could find no better hell than that crater, so they cloyed to us and twisted our own guts. Topaz would have seen h'ants everywhere.

We started by digging a huge trench, deepening the crater even further. Then we swung the corpses into it, after retrieving such valuable items as weapons, ammunition, and shoes. All the while, shells was exploding near us, trying to find our range. Half-a-dozen Fourth South Carolina men died, not fighting, but digging graves for the victims of a battle already lost.

Me and Lonnie was in the process of prying the shoes off a corpse when we recognized the bloated face as that of Chamas North. Even after decomposing in the hot sun the fierce snarl was visible on Chamas's face. He had died as he had lived, fighting back. Lonnie grimaced, an action that caused him physical pain – a saber cut which he had received down the side of his face in the battle was just starting to knit together.

"He went with what he knowed," Lonnie said, and I nodded. We slid Chamas tenderly into the trench, his musket still clutched in his hand, and his shoes on his feet.

Bullfrog was working a few feet away from us. I realized suddenly that I had not heard him sing in a very long time.

Petersburg stood for eight more months, until the last week of the war. We stayed on hand to have meaningless skirmishes with the Rebs inside every week or two. Colonel Wentworth came back after Christmas to lead us, even though we wasn't actually going anywhere – and that was good, because the colonel could never have kept up with only one leg.

Nobody wrote any newspaper articles about the Fourth South Carolina Volunteer Colored Infantry, and they never sung any songs in our honor.

But we knowed, and the white men who fought beside us knowed, that we fought to free ourselves harder than anybody fought to free us. We was not animals, wild or tame – we was men.

We was men.

Part III: The Emancipated

Chapter Thirteen

General Lee surrendered his army at Appomattox in April of 1865, but for most of us from the Fourth South Carolina Colored Regiment our military service went on for another full year. We had signed on as three-year volunteers, you see, and was obliged to serve out our agreed time. We watched quietly as most all of the white troops headed home.

What we wound up doing was a sort of glorified guard duty. We watched over several little South Carolina towns to make sure they stayed "pacified" while the change of power took place. There was no real confrontations as there had been in the town we'd been forced to burn during the war, just an agonizing period of hateful looks and subtle slurs. White Union troops would have had a bad time of it from the conquered locals, but it was much worse for us.

I had taken Robert Graham's place as sergeant of our company. Lonnie was my corporal. Our regiment was only about half the size it had been throughout the war – none of our casualties was replaced.

There was talk about promoting some of the colored noncoms who had distinguished themselves in the war. Prince Rogers and Isaiah Qualls was the standouts in our own group who was to be considered for officers. There was a big uproar over it, though – especially among some of the white officers. The whole idea was eventually dropped.

The time finally came for us to be mustered out. It wasn't like what I had expected. I hadn't known what to expect, really, but I had thought it would be something dramatic. What we got instead was a little disappointing, sort of like when you're just about to let go of a good cleansing sneeze and nothing happens.

We was basically patted on the back and told we was free to go. Colonel Wentworth made no fancy speeches – he never had, not since the Crater. He just watched us file out and nodded to each man as he passed by.

Many of the men felt set adrift, kind of like the confused freed slaves that Bullfrog had been so critical of. They was not sure where to go, exactly.

I could understand their feelings, to an extent, for the sudden change in circumstances felt odd to me as well. But I had a purpose. The path home was calling to my feet, as it had for three years, and I was finally free to follow it. I said my goodbyes to Congo, Tom, and Bullfrog and then loped off down the road. It felt like the old days, on the Wednesdays when I was allowed to go to the Larue plantation. I had traveled a long way with my battle-comrades, in spirit as well as in flesh, and they would always be my brothers – but it did not grieve me to part company with them, not when I knowed that Frankie and the children was waiting for me. I had three hundred dollars of government bounty money in my pocket to help me start a new life.

There was only one companion that I would be pained to part with. Lonnie Blake had become more than a friend to me; he had become part of my soul. He had always been right there, in his gentle and unassuming way, to whisper the right words at my heart. He had become my conscience. Lonnie served to counteract the burning rage of my other soulmate, Chamas North – they had tugged me in two separate directions, but I owed a part of my humanity to both of them. I seen the irony in the fact that Chamas had spent the last ounce of his fury in combat with his oppressors, dying with a snarl, while Lonnie's quiet wisdom still lived.

As had happened so many times before, I felt Lonnie's presence beside me rather than heard him. I thought at first that feeling him there was just force of habit. I soon realized, though, that he really was walking along the dirt path beside me.

He took a deep breath. "Smell that warm air, Alfred. This here is a good day to be free."

"Any day is a good day to be free."

"Amen to that, my brother."

We walked for most of the day without speaking. People we passed on the road stared quietly at us and at the uniforms we still wore, and the stripes on our sleeves. I grinned at them on the inside. On the outside, though, I stared straight ahead.

We camped that night on the side of the road. Lonnie opened up the pack that had been slung on his shoulder and dug out his pipe, as well as a small kettle and some coffee.

I lit our campfire while my friend smoked on his pipe. "Been a long time," he said between puffs.

"What has?" I said.

"Since I seen that woman of mine, and our chillun. The two littlest ones won't even remember me. I remember them, though. Yes sir. I remember them."

I nodded my understanding.

"Many's the time," he continued, "when I was layin' asleep in some muddy field or barracks tent, that I thought I could smell their sweat – same as when I held 'em in my arms on so many hot Alabama nights. I'd open up my eyes in the dark and expect to hear one of 'em whisper,'Papa!' But it was never so."

We only had one tin cup between us, and took turns sipping out of it. I handed it to Lonnie and he drank, staring over it and into the fire.

"I've done the same," I said. "But them days is past now. We've not just helped to free ourselves, but our families too. Now all we got to do is go home an' scoop 'em up in our arms an' never leave 'em no mo'."

"Hallelujah," Lonnie said, smiling. His eyes shined moist in the firelight. "The Lawd has seen fit to spare us, Alfred. We owe it all to Him."

I felt that I owed my existence to no one except myself, unless it was to my rifle and bayonet, but was polite enough to say nothing. Lonnie swiveled his head slowly to stare at me – he had recognized my silence as an answer to his statement.

"The Lawd is ever'where," he said softly. "He there to guide us to the good things, and to see us through the bad. I hope you learn to see Him one day, same as I have. It'll warm up yo' soul, no matter how cold the nights gets."

"Maybe I will," I said, not wanting to offend him.

Lonnie smiled. "If'n you do," he said, "it won't be because me or anybody else talked you into it."

"Reach me that cup," I said. "I'll fill it back up."

He did, and as I poured he said, "Tomorrow mornin' our paths will be splittin' off. I need to be turnin' south. If you ever near Culman, Alabama, you be sure to look me up."

"You know I will," I told him. "An' if you ever outside of Charleston, at a little town called Hawkins Point, you'll most likely find me there."

"If'n I am, I'll come lookin'." He rummaged through his pack. "I got somethin' for you."

Lonnie lifted out a revolver. It was black, with a brass grip and trigger-guard.

"We was supposed to turn in all our weapons when we left," I said. He nodded. "This here ain't U.S. guv'ment issue. It's Confederate issue – I took it off a dead officer. I got everything you need for it, too – powder, caps, lead balls."

"Why give it to me?"

Lonnie looked into the fire. "'cause I've done decided, Alfred. I'm through wid guns, an' wid killin'. I ain't never pullin' a trigger on a man again, no matter what. I jest don't feel like it's the Lawd's will fo' me to. I might get me a ole bird-gun or somethin' later on, but this here pistol ain't good fo' nothin' but shootin' men."

He tossed it to me. "I was gonna th'ow it away, but it occurred to me that you might have use fo' it. I can trust a man like you to defend yo'-self with a weapon like this instead of usin' it to start trouble. It'll keep my conscience clean."

I turned it over in my hand, and Lonnie tossed me the bag of bullets and such.

"Besides," he added, "I never could hit a dern thing with it nohow."

"Thanks, Lonnie. I'll be careful how I use it."

"Be careful where you keep it, too. Make sure it's always out of sight."

I chuckled. "You don't have to tell me that, no suh." I buried it deep inside my own pack.

I slept lightly on my first night as a free civilian. Even though my friend was taking great pains to be quiet I was awakened by the sounds of him gathering his gear an hour before dawn. I sat up. His form was barely visible against the stars.

"Lonnie," I whispered, and he turned toward me.

"Go with what you know," I said.

I felt his smile in the dark morning air. "Always, my brother. Always."

And then he was on his way, his coffee cup and tin kettle clanking together against his hip. I watched him until he was gone from my sight. Then I rolled back over again in my blanket, completely alone for the first time in my life. The feeling, though new, was familiar nevertheless.

I arrived at the LaRue place early on a rainy afternoon. My shoes was covered with mud.

There wasn't very much activity going on at the plantation – the fields was long neglected.

"Ain't nobody much to work 'em."

I turned around. Old Gus, the feeble stable hand, was staring at me, or maybe at the fields.

"Most of de young field hands run off when freedom come. Massa and Missus LaRue, dey don't care much noways. Not wid two dead sons."

"Which'un's left?" I asked, my voice cold.

"Jest Massa Fred. He livin' in town now. Massa Jesse got his head blowed plumb off - you recollect dat - an' Massa Jake dey say froze to death in a Yankee prison."

"He's warm enough by now, I reckon."

"Lawd, I sholy hope so," Gus said, not fully understanding my words. "Dat po' chile, I hopes his sorrows is over." The old man choked back a sob.

"I come here to get my Frankie." I said, "and little Jenny an Billy. Are they up at the big house?"

"Po' ole Marcus. You'member Marcus, de carriage driver? Always tellin' de white folks' secrets?"

"Yeah, yeah, I remember him - I just don't care. I'm askin' you where my Frankie is."

"Marcus told too many secrets. He got sold off."

"That's a shame," I said, impatient.

"Massa bought a new driver, name of Phil."

I shook my head, frustrated at the old man's apparent senility. "Never mind, Gus. I'll find her my own self."

Gus's claw of a hand gripped my upper arm.

"Frankie run off wid Phil when freedom come. Took de young'uns, said dey was goin' to St. Louis. Said you wasn't never comin' back, an' she didn't much care nohow - she took Massa Jake freezin' pretty hard."

I nodded and tried to speak - but my heart was in my throat, choking me. Another one of Frankie's precious LaRues had died, and she blamed me for it because of my blue uniform.

"She said dat if'n you was to come back, don't trouble yourself to come lookin' fo' her. She said it wouldn't do you no good."

"How could she take them young'uns away from their daddy?" I managed to say.

Gus shook his head. "I done told you. Dey daddy froze to death in a Yankee prison." He looked my uniform up and down, sadly. "Maybe you seen him."

My knees was weak, like I was trying to stand on butter, or like I had leaked half of my lifeblood away. I gave in and allowed myself to fall down. I sat in the mud, blinking away the rain, while old Gus still stared at the empty fields.

"She just left?" I said. "Just like that – with some carriage-driver? Why, damn it, why?"

"Freedom," Gus said. "Dey say we gots freedom now."

"I know. I was there."

There was a couple of minutes of silence. Then Gus turned away from the fields.

"Need to get on up to de house," he said. "See if de Missus needs anything." He walked off and left me alone in the mud.

I leaned forward and plunged my fists into the ground – the mud splashed up into my face. I screamed and snarled like a rabid dog. Even in death, the LaRues had thwarted me.

I trudged my way home to the Moss place. I was unable to take joy in the fact that I was traveling the road in broad daylight, without a pass.

The first thing I seen when I got there was Uncle Wiley. He stood in the rain, with water pouring off his floppy hat like it was a spout, examining the vegetables in his truck garden. The worms always came out in the rain, and so did Uncle Wiley.

He turned and looked at me, with an expression that was puzzled and not entirely friendly. Then a smile started to grow on his face, melting away the cold stare. His eyes brightened up and he ran forward to meet me. He put his gnarled hands on my shoulders and spun me around. "Alfred! Is dat you, boy? Is dat really you?"

"It's me all right, Uncle Wiley." Despite my own recent tragic news, I could not help myself from grinning a little at the old man's enthusiasm.

"It sho' enough is, ain't it. Sweet Jesus be praised, boy! You done come home to us after – after three years. Lawd in heb'm be praised."

"It's good to see you, Uncle Wiley."

"Shoo-ee. I wasn't sure at first whether you was somebody I'd be glad to see. Dem fancy duds of your'n, you looked most like a Yankee."

My grin growed wider. "I been in the army."

"Sho' enough. Has you now?" His eyes widened. "Did you fight'longside of Stonewall Jackson? Ole Massa Edwin – from de Trent plantation – he took his houseboy Jabin to war wid him. I hear dey give Jabin a gun once't, an' he shot at Yankees wid it!"

"I don't reckon I was never nowhere near Stonewall Jackson. Or Jabin from de Trent place."

"Hmm," Wiley grunted. He turned aside briefly to kill a bug he spied. "I tell you true, son, I 'most thought you was a Yankee. Dem no-good Yankees has give us down de road, Alfred, give us down de road hard."

"How's that?"

"How's dat, he say. Where you been? Oh yeah, you done told me – you was in de army. You bound to of been eatin' mo' better dan us here, dat's fo sho! Dem Yankees been burnin' de crops, takin' de food an' stock animals to feed dey own selfs – we might nigh starved, especially de po' young' uns."

"What have you been eatin'?"

"Ash-cakes, mostly. Sometimes molasses made out of may-apples. Our greens is potato-tops an' blackberry leaves. We makes our coffee out of parched corn.

"De Yankees burned down our smokehouse after dey took de meat. We scraped up de ground where de grease had been drippin an' used it to season our greens."

Wiley's face had grown angry, and the pitch of his voice was rising as he recounted the many sins of the occupying Union soldiers.

"Dey stormed into de big house, Alfred. Dey ripped up de mattresses lookin' fo' jewelry – dey found most of it, all dem purties dat belonged to po' dead Missus Moss. We saved some, me an' a few of de others. We hid 'em in our own bodies. Massa Moss at least has dem things left to remember his wife by."

"The jewels that Topaz stole," I said. Uncle Wiley and friends had risked their lives to preserve them for Doctor Moss.

"What about the whippin's?" I said.

Uncle Wiley looked confused again. "What whippin's?"

"Has they been any whippin's since the Yankees come?"

"No – no, I reckon not. Dey's some folks around here dat probably needs a good whippin', though."

"Who you talkin' about?"

He made a distasteful sneer. "Dem house-niggers, for one. Soon as some bluebelly man come an tell em dey free, dey all runs off an leaves Massa Moss to run dat big house all by his self. De field-hands, now, most of dem stayed right here where dey belongs."

"Nobody has to stay nowhere dey don't want to, Uncle Wiley. Everybody free now."

"Free!" Uncle Wiley said, grunting. "I always been free. Ain't never done nothin' I didn't want to, that I didn't need to."

I tried to bite back the harsh words that was my mouth. I could not comprehend the blindness of Wiley and the folks like him – he was starting to stretch to the limit the patience Lonnie had been trying to teach me.

Maybe, I wanted to tell him, the house-hands left because they had lived so long in the big house. They had seen the Mosses up close for years, and knowed that they was human like us. They did not buy into the story the masters peddled, that the fine white gentlemen and ladies was closer to gods than they was to us, and so deserved to be revered.

"Dem Yankees showed up an' said dey was settin' us free. Den dey put us to work fo' dem, cookin' dey food an' cleanin' dey messes. Dey fed de best of de corn to dey hosses, took de best of de Moss hosses fo' dey selfs, and killed and burned ever'thing else.

"Dey grabbed up three strong boys and tied em up – took 'em away to do dey work fo' 'em. Dey said,'we settin' you free wh'er you likes it or not'. Dan'l, de stable-hand's boy, Jimmy, he worked his self loose an' run back in time to help get in de Moss corn crop. Dat Jimmy, he a good boy."

"Goddamn it, Wiley – don't none of you crazy people want to be free?"

Wiley narrowed his eyes at me and spoke in a low voice. "Ain't no call fo' takin' de Lawd's name in vain, boy. You been taught better dan dat."

"I'm sorry."

"Well, anyway. What good is freedom? You can't eat it, can you? Does it keep you warm or keep de rain off yo' head? Dem's de things we needs, an' de Yankees tried to take 'em away from us. Things was fine like dey was."

"Felts was never too awful concerned about how comfortable we was."

"Felts was a no-good cracker."

"Where is he now?"

"You'member Aaron, don't you?"

I nodded – I remembered Aaron well. He was the big slave who assisted the overseer in all his dirty work, the only Negro that Felts talked to like a person – although Felts often demeaned him, not even recognizing the veiled anger in Aaron's eyes.

"After de Yankees come, Aaron cut Felts's throat and run away. We never heared no mo' about him – he must of got away. Felts's cousin Grady Cooper, the slavecatcher, he still around though."

I hoped Aaron did get away. I held the big brute in a different light now – I hoped he got away and was living well.

"Massa Moss, now, he always been good to us," Wiley said.

He was not good to my baby sister, Jenny, who he give away as a Christmas present, but I knowed voicing that opinion to Uncle Wiley would accomplish nothing.

"Look at him yonder."

I had thought I was the only fool standing in the rain, but I was wrong. Doctor Moss stood near the mansion, staring past us – just like he used to stand and watch over his domain, content in his kindness to his colored "children". Now he watched over empty fields, framed by a mansion that was already starting to look run down. Even from such a distance I could tell that Moss's features was as vacant as his fields.

"He been like dat fo' two years now. He comes out ever' day – rain, shine, or snow – and watches de road, waitin' fo' young Phillip to come home. We got a letter sayin' he was kilt, and buried in Tennessee somewheres, but Massa Moss jest won't believe it. At nights he jest sits in de house an talks to hisself."

Wiley had grown misty-eyed. "How dem niggers could leave him now, when he needs 'em de most, is beyond me."

My anger at Uncle Wiley flowed away, replaced by sadness – for I understood now. The Wileys in this slave-world needed the Doctor Mosses, as much as the Doctor Mosses needed them. Just like them slaves we had liberated, Wiley and his kind was afraid to be free. They didn't know how.

They was like the prison inmates you hear of sometimes that have spent almost their whole lives in prison and have forgot how to live in the real world. As soon as they're turned loose from the prison gates they start longing to go back, and set out at once to commit a crime so's they can go home. Such feelings don't make sense to normal folks, but people has them nonetheless – they've never had to take care of themselves.

They've never made decisions. They are like animals that have been kept in captivity for so long that they become completely tame – without a spark of the wild, dignified freedom they once had. Set back loose into the woods, they starve and die. Freedom came too late for them, or maybe too soon - they was like children ripped from the womb and abandoned.

Uncle Wiley was smiling again, and reached out to embrace me. "But enough of dat bad stuff. I'm jest glad you finally home, Alfred - now come on. Dat rain startin' to come down hard, we needs to get in an' dry off."

We walked toward Wiley's cabin.

"I need to go see Mama an' Roby."

He grabbed my shoulder. "Yo' mama died, Alfred. I hates to be de one who has to tell such news, but she died."

"How long ago?"

"A year gone by. When dat woman of your'n run off an' took little Jenny wid her - little Jenny was de only reason yo' mama was stayin' alive."

I nodded slowly - I felt the numbness returning.

"Her mind had been gone fo' a long time anyways, Alfred. She wasn't really yo' mama no mo'."

"I know. I know."

He guided me through the doorway and seated me in his rockingchair. "Now yo' brother Roby, he doin' fine. He lives in town now. He works fo' Rupert Moss - Massa Rupert got him duded up in a fancy suit an' ever'thing."

I leaned forward and put my face in my hands.

"I don't know, Uncle Wiley. I don't know how much more I can stand. All this time I been fightin', an' I come home to find that ever'thing I was fightin' for is gone. I jest don't know if I can stand it."

The tears began to slip out, and once they started I was unable to hold them back, or even slow them down. Wiley was on his bony knees with his arms around me, saying soothing words just like he had with Phillip Moss.

"It's all right, Alfred, you let it out now. You let it out. Ain't nothin wrong wid dat. De Lawd gonna see you through, now, you'll see."

I wept bitterly for the longest time, with Uncle Wiley comforting me just like when I was a little boy and my daddy was hanged. I knowed that he would crawl with me through the mud on his hands and knees, past enemy soldiers, just like he did with Phillip Moss, if he thought it would bring me peace. I was shamed to know that I had thought of his beliefs as cowardly – even if he was too frightened of freedom to take it for himself, he was not afraid to open up his heart. He had love enough in it for everybody, even for someone like me who challenged everything he thought was right and orderly. And even for the men who enslaved him.

Wiley cooked up what pitiful greens he had and shared them with me. The bland imitation coffee he brewed was nowhere near as tasty as what Lonnie had taken from his pack a few days earlier. Still, it was all he had, and he shared it eagerly.

"I know somebody you needs to see," he said, smiling. "I know somebody dat's gonna be wantin' to see you. Yo' friend Sid."

"He's still around?"

"He sure is."

"I thought you didn't like Sid."

"He's a little too much into de monkeyshines, an' too quick to trouble. But he could always make you laugh, an' dat's what you need."

"So Sid's still stayin' aroun' here – helpin' Doctor Moss?"

"Shoo!" Wiley exclaimed. "Dat boy ain't gonna help nobody – not jest from de goodness of his heart. Naw, he livin' in a tarpaper shack over by Raymond's place on de Pine Gate."

"Raymond's place? Raymond the carpenter?'

"Oh yeah, yeah. Ole man Weeks passed on during the War, see, and dis here Federal guv'ment took over his Pine Gate plantation and parceled it out piece by piece to sharecroppers. Most of 'em is white trash like Bill Jardine an'

197

dat patty-roller Grady – folks what ain't got no call to be ownin' nothin'.

"But Raymond an' his fambly got a piece of dat land too. He lets Sid stay on his place, an' Sid helps him out wid de work. Leastways he's s'posed to."

"Are you sayin' that Raymond owns dis land, or that he's sharecroppin' it?"

"A little of both, I reckon. De guv'ment tole him dat if he can hold on to dat land an work it fo' one full year – an' it's jest been a month, so far – it'll be his'n free an' clear."

"Who would of ever thought it," I said. "A colored man ownin' land in Hawkins Point."

"Pure foolishness, if'n you ax' me. But dat's where you'll find Sid. Where dey's foolishness at."

There was no foolishness going on at Raymond's place when I got there. The rain had stopped, and there was an hour or so of daylight left –the whole Carpenter family was in their own muddy field, clearing rocks from it. Baggy-eyed Raymond Carpenter was there; he had dropped the "the" and taken Carpenter as his own last name. His plump wife Annie worked beside him, as did their three young children – and Sid.

Sid whooped like a train when he seen me coming. Raymond tossed the rock he was holding into a rickety cart and walked over to me.

"I declare," Raymond said. "We thought you was dead or somethin', Alfred."

"Hoo-boy!" Sid said. "Alfred is back. Things is gonna light up now, an' dat's fo' sho'!"

"How y'all doin'." I looked around. "I hear dis here place gonna be your'n, Raymond."

"Dat's what dem guv'ment boys in town says." He grinned proudly. "My kids gonna grow up wid de ground under dey feet –widout havin' to be skeered dat it's gonna be whisked out from under 'em."

I nodded my approval, then bent over and pried a rock out of the mud – it came loose with a sucking sound.

"It ain't gonna do you no good less'n it's cleared off," I said, throwing the stone into Raymond's cart. I walked a few steps, looking for another one.

Raymond laughed. "You all heard de man – lets get back to work!"

"What about that big stump yonder, in the middle of the field?" I asked.

Raymond shook his head. "Dat'un won't budge. I gots to save up money to buy a mule. Guv'ment promised us one wid our land, but I ain't seen nary'n. Don't expect to."

Sid was beside me. "Say, Alfred, let me try on dat hat you wearin', why don't you?"

I took off the blue kepi and handed it over.

"It gots a bugle on it!" one of the children said admiringly.

Sid set it on his head at an angle. "How do I look?"

"Like a fool," I said.

"You ever kill anybody while you was in dis here hat?"

"Dey's chillun here, Sid," Annie said, a little angry.

"Well heck, it's just a simple question." He looked straight at me with an eager grin. "Well, Alfred?"

"I been in some big fights," I said. "I wouldn't be standing here right now if'n I hadn't defended myself."

Sid laughed. "I be. You had yo'self a sojer suit and a gun and ever'thing. Dat sholy is somethin'."

I pulled another rock loose. "Raymond has got himself some land," I said. "Now that – *that* is somethin'.

We worked until well past dark, and stumbled our way to the Carpenter cabin by moonlight.

Chapter Fourteen

"What you gonna do now, Alfred?"

I chewed slowly on a mouthful of potatoes while I tried to come up with an answer to Raymond's question.

"I ain't sure no more," I said. "Comin' home was all I been able to think about for three years – but there ain't nothin' to keep me here no more. I reckon I'll be headin' for St. Louis."

Raymond frowned. "Don't sound like there's nothin' for you there, neither."

Sid looked away, embarrassed for me. Annie started to fuss self-consciously with the children.

"It's all I can think of to do," I said.

"Ain't no sense in it," Raymond said through a mouthful of food. "Dat woman done took up wid somebody else, an' dem young'uns weren't yours to start wid."

My knuckles tightened on the knife I was eating with and anger flashed up in my eyes, but the carpenter either never noticed them signs or else decided to ignore them. He continued.

"Besides, you don't even know where St. Louis is."

"It's a big place. I don't see how I could miss it."

Raymond shrugged. "There you go, you said it yo' own self. It's a big place. A place dat big is bound to have a heap of colored folks in it – how would you find one fambly, assumin' dat's even where dey went? An' what would you do if'n you found 'em?"

"Hell, Raymond!" I shouted. The littlest child, three-year-old Davey, about jumped out of his skin. "I'm sorry," I said, more softly, to Annie. "But – hell, Raymond, what in the world do you expect I ought to do?"

The stony look dropped off of his face, and it took on a more kindly cast.

"I didn't mean to step on yo' toes none, Alfred. All I'm sayin' is, there ain't no call for you to go wanderin' off again. Dis plot of land ain't so small we ain't got room for one more. An' I could sure use another hand around here – if you're of a notion."

Sid chuckled. "We needs another worker to make up fo' all de things I don't do."

"What do you say, Alfred? You wanna stay here wid us – at least for awhile?" Raymond gave me an earnest smile, and Annie nodded.

I spread my hands out on the table and stared into my plate. "I don't know," I said. "I hate to impose on y'all."

"Ain't gonna be no imposin'," Sid said. "Dey's room enough in my little shack fo' de bofe of us. It ain't much, but it's better livin' dan what either of us has been used to."

"Y'all are real kind," I said. "But I jest don't know."

"Now you listen here to me," said Raymond. "We gots to stick together, now. You need somethin' to work for. You don't need to go wanderin' across the country widout no home to go to when you're done. An' me an' Annie, we need to get us a decent crop in this first year so's we can get on our feet good."

He reached his hand out to me. "We can't afford to pay you none, but you'll eat good." He paused. "We all needs each other."

I took the offered hand. "I reckon you right," I said. "It's sho' enough good to be home."

"Well, here it is," Sid announced, kicking at a pallet on the dirt floor of his shack. He had another one set up across the room – if you laid on one pallet and stretched your arm out you could just about touch the other one.

"Home sweet home," Sid continued as he dropped onto a blanket.

"I reckon so," I said.

"Not too fancy, though, compared to some of the places you must of seen in yo' travels."

"Hell of a lot fancier than some of them places, actually. I'm surprised you ain't lit out by now to see some new sights yo' own self. Ain't nothin' but the same old mischief to get into around here."

Sid laughed as I settled into my new sleeping spot. "Dem Yankee soldiers showed up one day a-hollerin' 'Freedom, Freedom! You is all free!' Let me tell you, boy, I jumped right up from dem fields and lit out after dem bluebellies. No offense, by de way."

"Where'd you go?"

Sid thought for a moment. "Two days walk to de Nawth. To some fort or other, I done forgot de name. Dey tole me I was a free man, and deserved a free man's wage, so dey put me to work like dey done all de other colored folks dey had set free an' brung there.

"Problem was, dey was too many colored folks and not enough work to do aroun' there. I wound up stackin' logs up on one day, just to unstack 'em de nex' – all for a few pennies, hardly enough to eat on. I had to poach turkeys an' hams. I never got caught at it, but folks there never took kindly to me noways. An' I was sleepin in de rain. Wasn't even many gals aroun', so I figured to hell wid it. I come home."

"I'm glad you did," I said, chuckling. "It's good to have a few familiar faces around."

Sid leaned up on one elbow. "Say Alfred. How 'bout dem yaller stripes on yo' sleeve? You some kind of general or somethin'?"

"Not hardly. I made my way up to sergeant, though. Sergeant Alfred Mann, Fourth South Carolina Volunteer Colored Infantry."

"I declare. Dey lets niggers be sergeants?"

"Sure do – but you gotta earn it. Fact is, though, I would probably have never got the promotion if our old sergeant hadn't of got his self killed."

"Alfred Mann," Sid said. "Sho' does have a ring to it."

"What about you, Sid? What kind of name did you pick out for yo' self?"

"Sid Moss. Most all of de old field hands calls dey selves Moss."

"Why would you want to name yo' self after the man that owned you for? He don't own you no more. I don't see why you should want to wear his name."

"It ain't after Doctor Moss. It's after de Moss plantation 'cause dat's where I'm from."

"They's plenty of good names," I said. "Lots of soldiers I knowed called theyselves Freeman. Or after Mister Lincoln, or Moses – or after a old-time president like George Washington."

"Don't come from no Washington or Lincoln. I come from de Moss plantation. Ain't nothin' wrong wid rememberin' where you from – mo' folks ought to do dat, if'n you ax' me."

"Some folks would rather look to where they goin'."

Sid slapped at me with his blanket. "Boy, all you wants to do anymore is argue, do you know dat? Argue 'bout dis, argue 'bout dat – not just wid me, but it sounds like wid Uncle Wiley too. Me an' you an' Raymond needs to take a trip down to de holler an' drink all de arguin' out of yo' system. If'n we can pry Raymond away from his beloved dirt long enough, dat is."

"I reckon you right, Sid. That sounds like jest exactly what I need. Now shut the hell up and let me get some sleep."

I rolled over. Sid snorted at my back. "Dadgum stubborn, is what you is," he said.

I smiled quietly to myself. I really did feel at home, and it was good.

The next morning I went to town. I hoped that Raymond didn't think I was trying to laze my way out of fulfilling my bargain to work for him, but him and Annie said nothing to make me worry. They seemed to understand my desire to see my brother Roby.

I intended to make it up to them before the day was out, and then some.

I borrowed a set of clothes from Sid, at least until I could buy a civilian outfit of my own. My Army uniform was washed and folded neatly away –the cap, though, remained proudly on my head. Sid's britches was a little too tight, and the sleeves of his shirt too long, but they would do.

It was not hard to find Rupert Moss's office. He was apparently quite a big shot nowadays. The first person I asked was able to direct me to the place.

It wasn't Rupert's office, exactly. It had been solely the law office of Rory Banyon, but was now also the location of the local Democratic party. Rupert and Banyon was high-ups in the organization, and Fred LaRue – Major Fred LaRue, as he was now known – was its chairman.

I walked into the office. There was half-a-dozen white men clustered around; I didn't know any of them. They all stared rudely at me. It was hard to say which they stared harder at, my black face or my blue cap.

"You want something, boy?" one of them said.

"I'm lookin' for Roby."

"Hey, Rupert!" the man called into the other room. "There's a nigger in here looking for your boy."

Rupert hauled his crooked body into the doorway. He stared at me. "I've seen this Negro before," he said, not speaking to anybody in particular.

"I'm Roby's brother."

Rupert hummed. "My boy's got important work to be doing," he said. "But you might be able to help him. He's back yonder." Rupert pointed into the room he had just come from. "Don't waste too much of his time. I've got errands for him."

Rupert brushed roughly past me. I stepped through the doorway.

Roby had done considerable growing since I left. He was twenty-one years old now, and was no longer a boy – his shoulders was all filled out, and he had a neat little mustache.

He was setting at a rickety desk writing something down on a piece of paper with the nub of a pencil. A whole stack of other papers was in the crook of his left arm. Folks had told me true about his clothes, too – he had on a starched white shirt with little bands to keep the upper arms tight, and fancy-looking suspenders, and the foot which stuck out from under the desk wore a shiny black shoe.

It took a second for the light of recognition to come on in his eyes, but when it did he jumped to his feet smiling.

"Alfred! Come over here brother, let me look at you!"

Roby grabbed me by my shoulders, then let go and throwed his arms around me. "We didn't never expect to see you again, brother!" Then, while he stepped back, he added, "I have to say, though, that this ain't the safest place in the world to go wearin' that Yankee hat you've got on."

"I've wore it in places a whole lot more dangerous than this."

"I reckon you have, big brother." Then the smile faded. "Have you been back home yet?"

I nodded.

"So you know then," he said. "What's become of everybody. It's just you an' me now, Alfred."

I chuckled proudly. "You sure has growed up good, boy. What this you doin' with these papers here?"

"Mister Rupert had a teacher come an' show me how to read an' write, and do sums so's I can help him out here in the office."

I whistled. "That don't sound like the doin's of any Moss I ever knowed."

Roby shrugged. "Times are changin'. Important folks like Mister Rupert are smart enough to know that they have to change with them. I could show you your ABC's sometime, Alfred, if you wanted."

"I can read."

"Oh. Well - that's real good, brother. Maybe you could help me out here in the office - and outside, too. We gonna be needin' somebody to do leg-work for us pretty soon."

"I done got a job. I promised Raymond Carpenter I'd help him get his first crop in."

"I'm sure Raymond could find somebody else to help him. I doubt if he's paying you very good."

"He's countin' on me. Besides, I ain't figured out what it is you do around here."

"All right then - I'll explain it all for you. This here is the Democratic Party headquarters in Hawkins Point, you see, and we've got elections coming up soon. That's what these papers are for. They're lists of the different votin' districts, an' who's runnin' for what."

"You really have been learnin' office things," I said.

Roby smiled, proud of himself. "I sure have. Now, about the elections. Mister Rupert, he's running for county assessor. Mister Banyon is tryin' to get elected district attorney, and Fred LaRue is shootin' for state senator."

"Who's runnin' agin 'em on the Republican side?"

Roby's face darkened. "A bunch of Negroes from up North. The Yankees brought 'em down here a few months back."

I grunted. "Shouldn't be much of a election then. This is the wrong part or the country for a colored man to expect white folks to vote for him."

"It ain't the white folks they're countin' on, Alfred. Negroes are full citizens now—we ain't under no special protection no more."

"Special protection?" I said, amazed at my brother's choice of words.

"You know what I mean," Roby countered. "We have to make our own decisions now, even though we don't really know how – and it's easy for these carpetbaggers to fool some of our kind."

"Fool 'em how?"

Roby leaned forward. "Votin'," he half-whispered, like he was repeating the words to some horrible voodoo spell that would unleash evil on the speaker if the wrong spirits heard it.

"There's Yankee soldiers posted all around here still," he continued. "They've made it plain that they aim to make sure that any Negro that wants to can vote. There's no way my bosses can stop that, so they figured the next best thing is to campaign amongst colored folk. Not personally, of course – that wouldn't look right. So I'm their number one campaign man. It's my job to talk sense into all these field hands around here, and make sure they know which side their bread is buttered on."

"So what you sayin' is, you a good colored boy, and most everybody else is niggers. So you gonna change 'em over."

"That ain't the right way to put it, not at all," Roby said, angry. "I'm saying they need to be smart. We can't let these Yankee outsiders pull the wool over everybody's eyes. Suppose these fancy Negroes get elected to public office, Alfred, what do you think would happen? They'd lord it over white folks for a year or two – but eventually South Carolina is gonna be back in the Union, and all these Yankee soldiers will go home. Then these colored politicians would get strung up to the nearest tree, and a good many of the folks that voted for 'em will be there to keep 'em company."

I nodded. "So it's better to just go ahead an' send LaRue to the state capitol, and save everybody a lot of trouble."

Roby's smile returned. "Now you gettin' it!"

I sighed. "Well, you sure has come up in the world, brother Roby."

"A colored man can still go a ways," Roby said, "if he's careful."

"I knowed some Yankee soldiers once – white men – in the First Division. They was real careful, too. They sat back, too scared to come an' help my regiment storm a Reb fort. We could have won that battle had they helped us, but instead we got cut to pieces. I ain't never had much use for careful after that."

"I'm sorry you feel that way, brother."

"Me too." I patted him on the shoulder. "But you're still my little brother, Roby, ain't nothin' ever gonna change that. I hope ever'thing works out all right for you."

Roby stuck out his hand, and I shook it - the first time I had ever shook my brother's hand, like two grown-up men.

"I'm serious about that hat, by the way," Roby said.

"So am I. Take care, Robe."

I walked out, and went back through the front part of the office. The same white fellows was still there; now they was setting in chairs, and had been joined by a couple more.

"Niggers are just children, really," one of them was saying when I entered. I recognized him as the lawyer, Banyon.

They kept talking while I picked my way past them, as if I wasn't there. Or as if it didn't matter whether I was there or not.

"We can't just cast them out on the street," Banyon continued. "It would be cruel. They depend on our hand to guide them, like parents. And remember, a caring parent is strict, and better than a lax one."

As I opened the outer door and stepped through, the other men's mumbles of agreement rattled around in my head.

"If they think they're really free," one high-born gentleman was saying as I shut the door, "they'll get even lazier. Can you imagine that?" I could hear the laughter even through the heavy door as I walked away.

My brother had not changed, or grown, at all.

"Excuse me!"

I kept walking, not suspecting at first that the white man's voice was talking to me. "You there!" he continued. "In the army hat!"

I turned around. A well-dressed white man was rushing toward me -his tall hat bobbed with every step he took.

"Excuse me for saying so, mister," he said, in what I had come to recognize as a Boston accent, "but I must admit that I am taken aback."

I stared at the man, certain that my confusion was showing through on my face. "Say what?"

"I am surprised, is all - that a veteran such as yourself would frequent the offices of men who are determined to keep your race in servitude, one way or another."

"I don't care much for 'em myself," I said. "I was just droppin' in to see Roby."

"Roby Moss? That catamite?'

"I don't know what a catamite is," I told him, "and I don't know what it is you want. But I got things to do, suh, so if'n you'll excuse me I'll be on my way."

"I apologize, private. I have forgotten my manners."

"I ain't a soldier no mo'. An' it's sergeant, anyways."

The man looked around himself, like a thief in a watermelon patch. "If I may prevail upon you, Mister - Mister—"

"Mann. Alfred Mann."

"If I could prevail upon you, Mister Mann, to accompany me to a more private site, I would be happy to explain myself in more detail. If it is true you don't approve of our *noblesse oblige* friends back there, we might be able to help each other."

I reluctantly followed the Boston man down a couple of side streets, until we came to a building with a set of stairs leading up to a bunch of rundown shops and offices. I walked up the steps behind my strange new guide, and paused when he walked through one of the upstairs doors. A sign on the door said "Republican Party Headquarters".

I groaned, then went inside.

My Boston man was already engaged in an excited, whispered conversation with another gentleman. This new gentleman was dressed as fancy as the first one, had a head full of gray hair – and a face as black as mine.

"You gonna tell me who you are an' what this is all about," I said to the white man, "or not."

"Oh, of course, of course. My name is Elmer Carter. My friend here is the esteemed Reverend Ehud Hall."

"At your service, sir," the black preacher said.

"This is Alfred Mann, Reverend – late of the Union Army."

"What's a catamite?" I asked Hall.

"A catamite? Why, that's a boy kept by an older man for – unnatural purposes. Why do you ask?"

Carter smiled. "I made a comment to him about young Roby. What was your business with him, anyhow, Mister Mann?"

"He's my brother," I said, feeling the angry heat rise in my face.

Reverend Hall gave his comrade a withering glance, and Carter stammered an apology.

"It is our hope," Hall then said to me, "that you can assist us. We need campaigners. This is the center of Republican activity in the county."

"I know. I seen the sign."

"Then you can read!" Carter said. "Excellent!"

"I'm glad you think so."

Hall smiled at me – it was a kind smile. "You have given much on behalf of your country, Mister Mann. Now your people need you once more. It is not enough to have set souls free – they must be made to understand what freedom means. That is the calling which the Lord has given me. I hope you will join our crusade."

"I ain't a religious man," I said. "But I know folks around here has already got preachers. Don't know that they'll flock to another one."

"We have more than their spiritual lives to think of. We're going to try to improve their earthly existence, as well."

I nodded. "Well, I ain't much into politics, neither. I got farmin' to do."

"You would leave your friends at the mercy of the Redshirts?" Carter said.

"Who?"

"The Redshirts," he repeated. "You'll see. When LaRue and his friends have a rally, they all wear red shirts."

"An appropriate color," Hall added, "considering their bloody tactics."

"I'll tell y'all the same thing I told my brother," I said. "I hope things turn out all right for you. It sounds like you got yo' selfs a good cause - but like I say, I got farmin' to do."

"You're turning your back on your own people!" Carter said.

Hall raised his hand, quieting his friend. "Nonsense," he said. "Elections are three months away - we'll be talking to Mister Mann again. There is plenty of time for him to think about his position." He held out his hand.

I nodded and took it.

"It is a pleasure to meet you, sir," Hall said. "I hope we will see more of you in the future."

"I'm glad to meet you too, Reverend. You be careful now."

"We did not come down here to be careful," Carter said.

I remembered my earlier words to Roby, and felt the burn of shame on my cheeks.

"I reckon you didn't," I said. "I reckon I'll be seein' more of you folks, at that. I got some thinkin' to do first."

"Of course," said Hall. "Good day to you then."

"Good day," Carter echoed.

I left them then. My footfalls echoed after me down the stairs.

"Lawd have mercy!" Raymond exclaimed. "What has you got Alfred? And where did you get it?"

I swung down onto the ground, and scratched the animal between the ears. "I would've figured you've lived long enough in the country to know a mule when you see one," I told him. "As for where I got it, I picked it up in town."

Sid clapped his hands and laughed. "Alfred's done stole hisself a mule! I cain't believe it!"

"I never stole him, fool, I bought him fair and square. I got the bill of sale right here in my pocket." I grinned. "I made damn sure I got a bill of sale, believe me."

"What did you buy a mule for?" Raymond said as he examined the animal.

"A feller has to get from one place to another, don't he. Besides, I don't aim to do all my work for you on this place by myself, and break my back. I done got me a jackass, settin' right yonder, and he ain't much help – not to mention he snores all night and keeps me awake. I figured a genuine domestic animal couldn't be no worse."

"Dis critter has met his match when it comes to stubborn, dat's fo' sho'," Sid said.

"It takes money to buy a mule," Raymond said.

"That's right. I didn't get my ass shot at fo' three years free of charge, brother. I got me a little grubstake built up."

Sid was grinning widely.

"I see you over yonder," I said, "grinnin' like a drunk 'possum. Don't you even think about diggin' aroun' tryin' to find my money, so's you can drink it all up."

Sid pouted. "You keep talkin' like dat, boy, you gonna hurt my feelin's."

"I'll hurt more'n that if you ain't careful."

Sid made a face, mimicking me. "Next time we go down to de holler, I know who's buyin' – I know dat much."

Raymond squatted down on his haunches and started tracing little thoughtless designs in the dirt. "If'n you all set, like you say, you don't need no job."

"That's where you wrong," I said. "I aim to help you make a go of this place. I can be like a temporary partner – if you need to buy anything else to tide you till things gets goin', I can help out. Then maybe when the property is yours on paper you can set me aside a little corner of it fo' my own."

"I could do that," Raymond said, nodding.

"But first you need to give me some details about what kind of deal they givin' you on this land. How does this whole thing work?"

Raymond stood up and walked around, starting to get excited. His step already seemed lighter than usual.

"Dem Treasury men took de Pine Gate when Old Man Weeks died. Dey took a lot of other places, too – where de owners hadn't died, dey just owed too many taxes. All of dese here places got auctioned off. None of de local folk could afford to buy 'em, not even de rich folks – dey all went to de Yankees. Dey's been a lot of Yankee bidness-men movin' down here lately."

I nodded – it made sense. The LaRues and Mosses, and families like them, was rich in land but had very little access to Federal cash.

"Dis here feller name of Peter Welch – from someplace called Jersey – he bought de Weeks place. Half of it he kept fo' his self, Lawd knows why, an' de other half he parceled out to 'croppers like me. De guv'ment folks said dey was partners wid him an' dat after one year me an' de others would have a claim to buy their forty acres fo' a low price."

"But dey didn't say what dat price is."

"No. But I figure if I raise a cotton crop and sell it, besides de odd jobs I been doin carpenterin', I ought to have de money. Whatever it is."

"I'll be able to help you a little there," I said.

213

Troy D. Smith

Raymond laughed and throwed his hat in the air. "Praise de Lawd," he said. "I do believe we gonna do it!"

"Of course we are."

"Awright, awright," Sid said. "I done had about enough of dis bidness talk. When we goin' to de holler, dat what I wants to know."

"I think we ought to do jest that, Saturday night, to celebrate," I said.

Raymond shook his head. "I cain't do it, boys. I got a table an' chairs to finish, fo' Mister Jarvis. Dat's de onliest free time I got to do it.

"Besides," he added, a little embarrassed. "Annie wants me to be at church dis Sunday. Dey got some kind of special sermon. Did you know we got our own indoor church now, Alfred?"

"No," I said. "Sid never mentioned nothin' about it."

"He wouldn't."

"Hoo boy," Sid said, rubbing his hands together. "Saturday night. An' we can buy de good stuff dis time. I can't hardly wait."

"I'm glad you so happy, Sid," I told him. "Dat'll give you somethin' good to mull around in the back of yo' mind fo' de next few minutes, while we bustin' our hind-ends."

"Bustin' 'em how?"

"Go 'round behind de house an' fetch dat big ole chain, an' you'll find out."

When Sid returned with the chain I started walking toward the middle of the field with my mule. Raymond and Sid followed close behind.

I stopped at the big stump. "It's time fo' this thing to go," I said, and I fastened one end of the long chain around it. The other end I tossed to Sid.

"Hitch this up to Mister Mule yonder," I said. "Me an' Raymond gonna push on this stump, an' you gonna urge Mister Mule onward. Since you a jackass yo' own self, maybe you can communicate with him better'n either one of us could."

"Watch yo' self, Alfred," Sid said with a pleasant laugh. "Jackasses has got a powerful kick."

The mule stretched the chain taut, and me and Raymond throwed all of our strength against the stump. It didn't budge.

"Give it more!" I hollered. "Ain't no stupid piece of wood gonna stand in our way!"

We planted our feet more firmly in the ground – still pretty muddy from the previous day's rain – and pushed.

"Hyah, mule!" Sid was hollering. "Come on now, come on! You ain't earnin no carrots dis way!"

My eyes was squeezed shut tightly. My whole world consisted of that stump and my back straining against it, and the ragged breath coming from both Raymond and me. I thought about Fred LaRue in his fancy office, and about Rupert Moss – and about Felts, and Grady, and everybody that had tried to keep me down.

I could feel the anger gushing out of me and against that stump.

There was a loud creak, and then the stump fell over. Its roots pointed at the sky. Me and Raymond fell over at the same time, into the mud – we rolled over and sat up.

"Yee-ha!" I shouted, waving my fist in the air, and Raymond shouted as well. "We beat it! We beat that son of a bitch!"

We fell back on the ground, laughing and shouting, feeling cleansed somehow even though we was covered in mud.

"Congratulations," Sid told us. "You've outsmarted the bottom of a dead tree. Maybe we ought to throw a picnic or somethin'."

But we had done more than that, and we knowed it. We had outsmarted the whole world.

Our field was ready.

Chapter Fifteen

"Another chicken gone. Damn. That's the third one in two weeks."

Raymond poked at the carcass with his boot. "How many mo' eggs could dat po' hen have laid by de end of de year? Eggs dat we could have eat, an' mo' eggs dat we could have sold."

"Reckon we got us a fox," Sid commented, but I shook my head.

"Them tracks is too big fo' a fox," I said.

"A wolf, den?"

"No. I ain't never heard of any wolfs aroun' here, not in our day anyhow. Somebody hereabouts has got theirselfs a dog who's developed a taste fo' chicken."

"Well," said Raymond, "his appetite is gettin' to be too rich fo' my blood. Dat's one layin' chicken a week ago Sunday, another' n eight days later on a Monday – an' here it is Wednesday an' I'm done already down three hens."

"Maybe we ought to rig up some kind of a trap," Sid said.

"I'll be the trap," I told him. "We cain't have no mo' of dis. De weather is pretty good right now – I'll take my old bedroll an' sleep out behind the henhouse until I can catch the varmint."

"You gonna sleep outside?" Sid asked, astonished.

"It ain't so bad once you get used to it."

"I don't believe I'd be gettin' used to it just so's I could catch some mangy old dog."

"That mangy dog is eatin' into our operation, and I ain't gonna have it."

That night after supper I took my blanket out behind the henhouse and settled in for the evening. Raymond showed up a few minutes later, carrying a shotgun. He held it out to me.

"No thanks," I told him, patting the heavy lump in my pack –which I was using as a pillow. "I got my own artillery, right in here. I'm afraid I'd roll over on that shotgun and blow myself in two."

I slept light. Along about midnight, sure enough, I heard the critter nosing around. I had figured right – every time he had killed a chicken he came back quicker than before.

I reached into the pack and pulled out the .44 Colt Lonnie had given me. I walked softly to the front of the little pen.

It was a dog all right, a lean red coon-hound. He was wriggling around, working his way into the enclosure. When he heard me he jerked his head out and started to run – the pistol boomed, and the hound dropped dead in his tracks.

Sid and Raymond came running toward me. Raymond was carrying the shotgun. Annie stood on the front porch of their cabin, holding the children inside.

"A huntin' dog!" Raymond said. "Shit, Alfred – dat dog is bound to belong to somebody aroun' here, an' dey gonna get mad."

"Somebody done got mad," I said, "over them three chickens this little thief stole. If folks don't want their dogs to be shot, they ought to keep 'em penned up where they cain't bother other folk's animals."

Raymond shook his head. I grabbed the dog's hind legs and drug him across the field, leaving him behind some brush.

"We'll haul him off further tomorrow," I said. "Right now I aim to get me some sleep."

We was working in the fields late the next morning, near to dinnertime, when we heard dogs barking.

"Good land!" I grunted. "What is it this time?

"Why, I do believe it's *dogs*," Sid said sarcastically.

"I'll be right back," I told my friends, and set off for the shack Sid and me shared. Once there I retrieved the revolver again and started outside – I paused in the doorway, the gun in my hand.

I seen the dogs now. There was two of them, and they was perfect matches for the one I had shot the night before. The difference though, this time, was that the dogs was following a man. I reached the pistol behind me and tucked it into my waistband, pulling my shirt-tail out to cover it. I squinted, trying to make out the man's features.

It was Grady Cooper, the former slavecatcher.

I set off at a brisk walk. I reached Raymond and Sid about the same time Grady and his dogs did.

"Hey," Grady said loudly. "Have any of you niggers seen my hound dog? He's a red-bone hound, all ears and feet."

Raymond and Sid stared mutely at him. I was still approaching.

Grady cocked his head. "Are you damn spades deef or somethin'? I ast you if you seen my dog. You better by God start talkin'."

"This here is private property," I said. "You got no call to come orderin' folks around."

"Private property, my ass," Grady said, then spat at my feet. "You ain't nothin' but sharecroppers."

"Same as you," I answered, and managed a cold smile.

"I don't put up with no sass from niggers, boy."

The dogs, meanwhile, was sniffing at the ground where I had drug their partner. They barked and ran toward the brush.

"Easy boys," Grady called out. "Them dogs is goin' crazy – there's somethin' in them bushes over yonder."

"That would be yo' dog," I said.

"What?"

"1 say, that's yo' dog. Or what's left of him. I shot him last night – caught him in our henhouse for the fourth time."

"You killed him?" Grady said, as if the very idea of a colored sharecropper doing such a thing was as amazing as the sun turning green.

"Yeah, I killed him. What would you have done?"

"What I would have done ain't got a thing in the world to do with it. Why didn't you just scare him off, or put some bird-shot in his hind-end?"

"When somethin' comes pokin' around my den," I told him, "I don't waste time just scarin' it."

Raymond and Sid was just as astonished as Grady. Raymond looked like I had just set fire to his children's beds.

"Besides," I added, "that dog of your'n had done tasted blood in that henhouse three times. No amount of scarin' would have kept him away."

"I paid good money for that damn dog," Grady said, ignoring me and turning to Raymond. "I expect you to make good on it."

Raymond nodded a little. "Yes suh. We gonna—"

"We paid good money for them chickens too," I broke in.

"To hell with your chickens. That was a fifty-dollar dog."

"A couple of dollars for a stronger pen would have saved you money in the long run."

Grady was so frustrated and mad he was about to twist right out of his skin, and Raymond was right in there with him.

"I'm goin' to the authorities on this," Grady said.

"This time last year that would've been enough to get me hung," I said. "But whose side do you reckon they'll take now?" With them words I knowed I had crossed a line and committed myself. Elmer Carter's words had gotten to me – I did not want to be careful like Roby.

Grady pulled his hunting knife out. "You an' that mouth of yours has done it now, you nigger sumbitch. I'm gonna take my money right out of your hide, one cent at a time."

I reached behind me and pulled out the Colt in a fluid motion. I shoved the muzzle into his face and cocked the hammer – probably the loudest sound Grady had ever heard. He looked like he was going to wet his britches.

"I got scars on my back that itches ever' time I look at you," I told him. "You better get out of here before I start scratchin' em."

Grady backed slowly away. "You ain't seen the last of me, boy."

"This world has seen the last of you if you don't start movin'."

Grady scurried away, dragging his dogs behind him. We all watched him go in silence – the way you watch a tornado until it's safely over the horizon. Sid had nothing funny to say – a pretty noteworthy event all by itself. Raymond simmered until Grady was good and gone, and then he exploded.

"Dammit to hell! Alfred, dammit to hell!"

I stood and took his words, the anger draining out of my bones and being replaced with embarrassment.

"You gonna get us all killed, you stupid bastard! You ain't in no damned Union army no mo' – we gots to live here, damn it. We gots to *live* here."

"Men like Grady is gonna come after you, Raymond – whether you kiss their ass or not. But you right. I wasn't thinking, I was just red-mad. I didn't think 'bout you an' yo' kids. I gots kids – used to have – I ought to know better."

"Damn it, Alfred."

I nodded. "It's best if I move on, I reckon. I'm the one that opened his big mouth. No sense in puttin' you all in danger from that redneck an' his friends."

Raymond got even madder. "There you go again, fool, bein' stupid. You done give me yo' word you'd help me on dis place. You ain't about to run off on me now."

Sid spoke for the first time since the incident began. "You don't really think Grady is gonna tell any of his friends about dis, do you? Dat he backed down to a nigger?"

"He might not tell nobody about it," I said, "or maybe he might. But he's gonna remember it."

"Hell yeah, he's gonna remember it," Sid said, laughing. "Dat sumbitch was so scared he was pissin' out stuff he drunk last week."

Raymond laughed nervously. "You right," he said. "When he seen dat gun his eyes plumb near popped right out of his head."

I still had the gun in my hand, and it was still cocked. I let the hammer down slowly and put the revolver back in my waistband.

"I truly am sorry, Raymond," I said.

"It's done now. Hell, I ain't never had Grady whuppin' on me an' pourin hot oil on my back. I might of done the same thing. I said it befo' and I meant it - we needs each other.

"Jest - jest go out back an' shoot a squirrel or somethin' next time. My heart cain't take dis kind of excitement again."

We waited everyday for Grady to make a move, but he didn't. Not yet, anyways.

I took a long drink from the bottle, already half-empty. It was genuine store-bought Tennessee whiskey. We had plenty more for when that was gone.

We was half-lying, half-sitting in the grass down in that hollow on the Moss place. There was a full moon - it was bright enough that we could see the tall grass ripple from the wind. It was no longer a matter of us having to come to this site for our getaways.

There was plenty of other, even better spots on Raymond's forty acres, and coming to the Mosses' was actually inconvenient. It required a long walk in the moonlight.

But we went there anyways. We went for old times' sake, and to have a few drinks to the memory of Topaz - the third part of us.

It was just me and Sid. I thought that was appropriate, though I would not have minded Raymond's company had he decided to come along. Sid had come up with some other ideas about company, but I didn't share them.

"It's a little chilly out here!" he said as he reached for the bottle.

"It ain't bad. This stuff'll warm us up."

"We should've brung some women, Alfred, like I said."

"An' like I said, not this time."

"Have you gone and got scared of women agin, Alfred, like you used to be?"

"Shut up, fool. Drink."

"A man's got to have some pud'n ever' once in awhile. How long is it been since you had any pud'n, boy?"

I tried to ignore him.

"Dat stuff gonna build up an' poison yo' bloodstream."

"You don't know what you talkin' about, Sid."

Sid leaned forward. "Did you, uh, did you get wounded in dat war?"

"What's that got to do with anything?"

Sid looked around, acting for all the world like he was embarrassed, and whispered, "Did one of dem Rebs shoot you in de nuts or somethin'?"

I busted out laughing. "Are you serious?"

"Well, shoot, I didn't know. If you had some kind of delicate injury like dat I didn't want to hurt yo' feelin's by talkin' 'bout pud'n all de time."

I was still chuckling. "No, Sid, I didn't get shot in the nuts during the war. That didn't happen till I come home."

Sid passed the bottle back to me. I lifted it up to the moon. "To Topaz," I said. Sid echoed my words. It occurred to me that Topaz never had a chance to choose a last name for himself.

"I kind of miss his foolishness 'bout omens an' signs," Sid said. "An' de way he seen boogers ever' where. He had me convinced of it sometimes, too – 'member how we used to run past the graveyard to get here? I still don't feel right goin' dat way." He took a long swig.

"I've had skeery feelin's sometimes," I said, "but I ain't never actually seen no h'ants. I know they there, though."

"You do?"

I nodded. "Topaz haunts me. I see him everywhere. No matter where I'm at, or what I'm doin', I think about him and wonder what he'd say. He put freedom in my mind. He walks in and out of my dreams, holding them diamonds of Miz Moss's - he holds 'em up an' points to 'em, an' I see that they's actually the stars leadin' Nawth."

"If'n you cain' t hold yo' liquor any better'n dis," Sid commented, "you don't need to be drinkin' no mo' of de stuff."

"I'm holdin' it fine."

"I'm glad I ain't got freedom on the brain, like you an' Topaz. Near as I can figure, freedom is just doin' what you want to - I always done dat. If'n there's somethin' more to it I ain't never figured out what it is."

"A friend of mine in the army was always talkin' about the big ships sailin' into the harbor in New York - just sailin' in, easy as the breeze - that's what freedom is to me. I want to see them ships one day. I'll watch 'em come in an' I'll think of Maurice Higgins, an' Topaz, and everybody else that died to be free."

"If'n you dead, you sure ain't free to do very much," Sid said. "Besides, dey gots ships like dat in Charleston. I've heared folks talk about 'em."

"Not like in New York. There's whole fleets of 'em comes in up there, from all over the world. And the ones in Charleston ain't got nothin' to do with freedom - they've brung God knows how many folks to a life of slavery. For all I know my own grand-daddy stepped off a boat in Charleston, in chains, and set foot into bondage. I don't care to see that place."

"You a strange critter, Alfred Mann," Sid said. Soon he was asleep. I stood up - with some difficulty - and picked up my own blanket. I spread it out over my friend, then fell back to the ground and took another long swallow.

"You sleep easy too, Topaz," I said to the air around me.

Numbness was spreading all through my body. I could feel sleep creeping up on me. I was glad, very glad, to be lying out there under the stars like I was, two miles from our little shack. I knowed I'd be able to sleep easy. I would not have to go through the agony of knowing Raymond was within earshot, with his wife and his children and the life I had thought I'd be coming home to.

I would rest well, too, because the alcohol had fogged my brain and the dreams would not be able to reach me. I would not be troubled by visions of the Rebel with the dirty blond hair, gasping at me as my bayonet ripped the life out of him. I would not see Private Lawrence's bloated face above the noose as he swung from the creaking-branch – I would not be slipping on human guts, or watching as Chamas North's corpse slid – still snarling – into the burial trench.

And I would be spared the other dreams, the ones that was even worse than the horrors of war. The carnage of battle I could handle even in my slumbering mind, but I could not endure the agony of the other dreams that tormented me every night.

Them was the dreams in which I held my babies – knowing they sprung from another man's passion, but loving them anyway. It was the agony of swinging my little Jenny through the air, hearing her laughter, and knowing all the while that I was only dreaming. I would hear little Billy saying "Papa", see him run through the fields – all the things I had never seen at all in my waking mind, and never would.

I would feel Frankie writhing fiercely beneath me once more, feel her nails on my back, and hear her promise to love me completely in the moment – but never promise me anything more than that. And I would see her with LaRue –

224

his face changed from one brother to another while her passion rose.

I jerked out of my half-sleep when I seen a dark figure walking toward us through the waving grass. I stared a moment, to make sure the image was not a trick of my addled brain, then jabbed Sid sharply in the ribs. He sat up, eyes wide, and I put a hand over his mouth.

"Hush!" I whispered. "Somebody's comin'!"

I wished I had brought my gun, and resolved not to be caught without it again. I had decided earlier in the evening – probably with good reason – that drinking with Sid while armed was possibly not a good idea.

The stranger stood at the edge of the holler, looking down at us. It was Doctor Moss. The doctor looked like he had not eaten regularly in a long time. His hair was uncombed, his clothes ragged, and he wore a scraggly white beard.

"Hello, Doctor Moss," I said.

He swayed on his feet unsteadily, like he was the one who had been drinking. "Have you boys seen my son, Phillip? He's supposed to be coming home today."

Sid and me glanced at each other, unsure of what to say.

"You know my boy, Phillip, don't you?" Even in the moonlight I could tell he was smiling. "Such a good boy. His mother's pride and joy – she can't wait to see him again. So proud, in his uniform..."

We looked at the grass, uncomfortable.

"Have you seen him? Someone said he was dead." The doctor's lip quivered. "That can't be right – can it?"

"I seen him, Doctor Moss," I said.

"You did?"

I nodded. "I seen him in a battle. He was real brave, suh, he'd of made you proud. But they was too many of the enemy – I helped him hide in the woods till they left, so's he could get back to his regiment and fight some mo'."

"I knew it!" Moss said, a tear rolling down his cheek. "I knew my boy would be brave. Do you suppose he'll be along, directly?"

"Maybe tomorrow. You go along home an' get some rest, Doctor Moss."

"Yes – yes, of course. Maggie will be wondering where I am." He started to leave, then turned back. "Could –could you boys keep an eye out for him? In case he arrives while I sleep."

"Yes, suh," I said. "We'll watch close."

"Thank you. Thank you very much." He wandered back toward his empty mansion. I watched him until he disappeared.

"Dat was a real good thing you did," Sid told me.

"It wasn't really Phillip Moss. It was just some boy. And he wasn't very brave."

"I don't know 'bout none of dat," Sid said. "You talkin' 'bout war, an' battles. I'm talkin' 'bout a lonely old man, gone out of his mind with grief. It was a good thing you done, even though he'll prob'ly forget he ever even seen us by de time he gets home."

"Jest didn't want to hurt his feelin's, that's all."

"I thought you hated him."

I shook my head. I remembered Uncle Wiley's words from the last night I seen Phillip Moss.

"It's a mean world sometimes."

"You should've been there," Raymond told us when we got up the next afternoon and started stirring around. "I ain't no church-man, myself, but I'm glad I went today."

"I'm glad I went where I did too," Sid said. "You should've been there."

"I mean it, boys. Dey had dis visitin' preacher – name of Ehud Hall. Fanciest-lookin' colored man you ever laid eyes on."

"I've met him," I said.

"He's visitin' all de congregations aroun' here, tryin' to talk folks into votin'."

"He's such a nice man," Annie said.

"How'd folks take to what he was sayin'?" I asked.

Raymond shrugged. "So-so. He stirred us all up real good with his speech."

"Didn't have enough fire, though," Annie interrupted. "Not enough hellfire and damnation."

"But lots of folks," Raymond continued, "is still scared to do anything that would make their old masters mad."

"With good reason," I said. "A wise man considers all the risks befo' he does somethin'."

Sid snorted. "I reckon stickin' a gun in ole Grady's face went a long way toward keepin' things smooth aroun' here."

"I ain't no wise man. Else I wouldn't be livin' wit you."

"I do think de Reverend has got a few good points, though," Raymond said.

"An dat young man wid 'em was so polite," Annie said.

"Young man?"

Raymond nodded. "Reverend Hall's assistant, Andrew. He's comin' fo' supper tonight." Raymond smiled nervously. "I sort of mentioned what happened the other day, with Grady — Andrew wants to meet you."

"I can't wait."

Andrew turned out to be different from what I expected. He was about Roby's age and he was dressed just as good as my brother, but he was very quiet and polite. He smiled shyly at Annie, and played with the kids, and had a hearty appetite. He spoke to Raymond like he thought the carpenter was a distinguished gentleman, and treated Sid like a big brother – and he won them all over before he had even started talking politics.

I was given the war hero treatment. Andrew asked about the many engagements I had been in, awe in his voice – careful not to press for gruesome or otherwise disturbing details. He seemed to genuinely admire my courage in standing up to Grady.

I couldn't help but like the kid, my own self. I was careful though, not to let my guard down – I was stubborn enough not to like the idea of being manipulated into a course of action, even if that action was right.

"You have a lot at stake here, Mister Carpenter," Andrew said. "You stand to be a landowner when the year is up. Now please, do yourself a favor and think about this – if the Red Shirts win the state and local elections, don't you figure they'll change some laws and just plain ignore others? Don't you suppose they'll find a way to take your land away?"

Raymond nodded. "I reckon dey might."

"But if our kind is in office," Andrew continued, "you'll be safe."

"For how long?" I cut in.

"For four years, until the next election."

"All kinds of things could happen in four years," I said. "What happens then?"

"It's impossible to say," Andrew answered. "But I can tell you this much. In four years Mister Carpenter will be well-established on his land – the initial year will be up and he will have his deed. It would be a lot harder for LaRue and his kind to cause him problems then, than it will be now with things up in the air. That is, if the colored community sits back and lets the Red Shirts win this election."

Raymond nodded slowly. "You startin' to make sense, son."

Annie leaned forward over the table. "But what about de white folks?" she said. "Dey gonna be awful mad if we help de Yankees and de carpetbaggers an' all."

"These crackers around here are like snakes," Andrew said. "When you spy a snake in the garden the first thing you do is grab a hoe and try to kill it. If you miss, the snake might bite you. But if you don't do anything to try to defend yourself, that snake *will* bite you. You have to strike first."

"I always jest runs off," Sid said through a mouthful of cornbread. "Or else I stand right still and don't pay attention to it, and figure maybe it'll crawl away."

"What's your point?" Raymond asked.

"My point is, I don't like snakes. They're all slithery an' ever'thing."

"But what does dat have to do wid what we talkin' about?"

"Nothin', I guess. Jest givin' out my opinion on snakes."

"Jest talkin' to hear yourself talk, you mean," I said, grinning.

Andrew pushed himself away from the table and heaved a satisfied sigh. "Wonderful supper, Mrs. Carpenter," he said.

"Why thank you, Andrew," Annie answered, and then she nudged her husband with her eyes.

Taking the hint, Raymond straightened up. "Glad you could come an' eat with us, son. I reckon you need to stay de night –we're a mite crowded here, but we can always find a place for good company."

"Thank you very much for the invitation," Andrew said, "and I hope it'll still stand later. Unfortunately, I can't accept tonight –I hope I don't seem rude. I promised your reverend I'd pay a visit to another member of your congregation this evening. A Mister Wiley Moss."

I chuckled. "You won't get too far with Uncle Wiley, I'm afraid."

"Oh, he's a relative of yours?"

"Wiley's a uncle to ever'body. He'll decide to be your uncle, too, once he's met you."

"I am told he's a fine Christian man."

"Uncle Wiley is de finest Christian man you'll ever hope to meet," Annie said.

"Then I'm confused," said Andrew. "What do you mean I 'won't get far' with Uncle Wiley?"

I sighed. "Uncle Wiley believes we should all be back on the plantation, helpin' the pore old doctor get his crops in. He thinks it's a mortal shame that we all forgettin' our place."

Andrew shook his head. "Sometimes it's hard for old folks to get used to the idea of change – even if it's a change for the better. Maybe all he needs are some kind words of reason."

"Uncle Wiley deserves kind words," I said. "But good luck on the reason part."

"It's worth a try," Andrew said, smiling, as he rose from his chair. "Especially if this Uncle Wiley has as much influence on folks around here as you say. If you could give me directions to his house, I'd appreciate it."

Raymond shook his head. "Dark has done fell, son. It ain't safe for you to go wanderin' around here by yourself – slave-days is over, but de patty-rollers still comes out at night."

"Patty-rollers?"

"Patrollers," I told him.

"They used to look out for runaways. Now they look for 'troublemakers'. Mostly they're just bandits."

Raymond nodded. "Catchin' a free-born Negro like you, out alone after dark, would tickle dem crackers to death. It'd be like Christmas come early."

"Come on, Sid," I said. "Let's walk him over to Uncle Wiley's."

Sid chuckled. "You gonna be in good hands, Andrew – ole Alfred here, he gots plenty of practice findin' his way to de Moss plantation in de dark of night."

"Come on," I said, walking toward the door. "Before Sid starts tellin' things he ought not to."

"What you boys doin' out so late?" Uncle Wiley said. He walked out onto his stoop and looked around. "Folks'll think you're lookin' to get into trouble." The old man shook his head.

"Come on in here," he said, and we obeyed.

"Uncle Wiley," I said, "this here is Andrew. He works with Reverend Hall."

Wiley nodded. "I listened at Reverend Hall today, when he visited our church. He's a mighty good talker – de way he works dem fancy words aroun' an' all, wid his voice all soft an' hard at de same time. He sounds like my daddy used to when he'd catch me sneakin' into his tobacker, or like a angel outen de Good Book. You say you work wid him, son?"

"I'm his assistant."

"Well, I'll be. Den you doin' de Lawd's work, boy – you doin' a good thing. You always welcome here."

"Thank you, Mister Moss. The fact is, Reverend Hall asked me to visit the folks around here and talk to them about the elections coming up."

"Elections? You mean votin'?"

Andrew nodded. "Yes, sir."

Wiley waved the notion away like it was a buzzing fly. "Lawd, boy. I gots no call to go messin' aroun' wid bidness like dat. I'm just a gnarled-up old gardener."

Andrew smiled and offered the old man his hand. Wiley took it in both of his.

"You're more than that, sir," the youth told him. "Everybody counts, you know – and everybody can make a difference."

Uncle Wiley flashed his evasive, dismissive smile. "'Course we do, son, in de Lawd's eyes."

"Well, yes, but we can make a difference here in this world too."

Wiley chuckled. "De Lawd God-A-Mighty is de onliest one can make a difference here, young'uns. You want some coffee? I can brew some up if'n you want. It won't keep you awake, beezun it ain't real coffee. I reckon I ain't tasted no real coffee in a 'coon's age."

Andrew went through all the same arguments he had made earlier with Raymond. The old gardener smiled it all away, shifting attention to kind comments about Andrew and

Ehud Hall, and gentle stories about the hijinks me and Sid got into as children.

We spent the night with him. He sat in his rocking-chair until we was all three bedded down and sound asleep. I pretended to be out just so Uncle Wiley would relent to lower his bones onto a blanket.

Andrew left at the crack of dawn, off to visit some other prospective voter. We seen him off – Sid and me had decided to stay around and tear up some ground for the gardener, and save his back – and Uncle Wiley acted like he was saying goodbye to his own child. Everyone was his child, I guess – I wondered what it was like when Wiley was a younger man. He had probably treated his own elders like they was his children.

"You be careful now, Andrew," Uncle Wiley called after him. "Watch yo' step. Walk wid de Lawd."

We all caught up with Andrew on the way home. Uncle Wiley had decided to walk with us, and see Raymond's piece of land – it was a rare possession, sort of like a two-headed cow.

Andrew was naked. His wrists was lashed to tree limbs – he had been whipped hard, then castrated, then had his throat cut.

Sid took the dead boy's hands loose and gently let him down – tears brimmed out of his eyes. Uncle Wiley just stood and stared like he was numb.

"God damn them crackers," I snarled.

"Yeah, Alfred," Wiley said, then his voice broke for a moment. "Damn them. But God bless this chile – dis po', precious chile. He in God's Kingdom now. He done cast his vote for it."

Me and Sid, we voted. I was a little surprised to see Uncle Wiley there. He offered no explanation as he left the booth, he just nodded at me.

Chapter Sixteen

Lots of colored folks in the county voted – 'most every growed-up man I knowed, in fact. A few of them went over with Roby and that sorry bunch of slavers he was in with, but most of them spoke their intent to vote Republican. They was awed by Ehud Hall, and inspired by him.

I was half-expecting there to be trouble on election day. I remembered how the masters used to send an armed man to our church meetings, just in case we got out of hand, and wondered why no one like that was present at the polls. I finally figured they must be scared of the Federal government. They did not want to draw the army down on them, I told myself.

I soon found out the real reason the Red Shirts didn't show any force on that day. We was all surprised, at least at first, that not a single one of the two dozen or so positions up for grabs went to a Republican, white or black.

The whole election was a sham. The results had been determined long before the first vote was cast.

"Damn it all," Raymond said when we got the news. "I was really hopin' for this votin' thing to go through. My year is up in less dan a month. I ain't seen hide nor hair of no dern guv'ment mule yet, but I don't care about that. Now dem Democrats is gonna cook up some way to steal the land away from me."

Raymond's land was not exactly taken away, but he didn't get it at the end of his year like he was supposed to, neither. He was left hanging in the air by the government folks – not sure exactly when they was going to take his property away, but positive they wasn't going to give it to him. Under them circumstances I felt obliged to stay on past the year I had agreed to. I had no place else to go to, anyhow.

I longed for Frankie, and the thought kept popping into my mind that I should go to St. Louis and look for her and the young'uns – but I knowed that Raymond was right, and there was no future in it. So I learned to walk around with a big chunk missing out of my soul, so big that I supposed people could look right through it and see what was on the other side. Meanwhile I worked Raymond's farm, and we all waited for the ax to fall.

It fell, all right, but not on us. The U.S. government determined that these first post-war elections was nothing more than a mean joke – not just in our county, but all over South Carolina and several other states. The new officials was told to vacate their offices and go out and run again. They was none too happy about it, especially when federal troops came in to supervise the whole thing.

Reverend Ehud Hall got everyone stirred up one more time. He must have stirred himself up some, too, because this time he throwed his own hat into the ring. I was at the local church one Sunday – a rare occurrence – when Hall had been invited to speak. I was not religious, but was starting to become political, so I was seeing the inside of church more often.

The local pastor, a one-time houseboy named Williams, introduced the distinguished visitor. Hall spoke at great length about Moses and the Exodus, and David and Goliath, and then announced that he was running for the state senate.

Roby actually came out to the Carpenter place a few days after that, asking to see me. He rode there in a buggy, so his fancy clothes didn't even get all that dusty.

"I came to warn you, Alfred."

"Warn me about what?"

Roby looked around, to make sure no one else was listening. "To warn you about the company you've been keeping. They're gonna get you in trouble."

I stiffened. "What company is that, exactly?"

"You know just what I'm talking about," Roby answered. "The carpetbaggers and the freeborn niggers and the other Yankees you've been seen with - they're gonna cause this county to get busted wide open, and it's gonna go real hard on anybody that's associated with them. Stay behind your plow, brother, or go out and get drunk with your friend Sid - but don't play with fire."

I stared hard at him for a long moment. "What is Rupert Moss to you?" I said at last.

"I - well," Roby stammered, "he's been like a father to me."

"I got a brother right now, that I don't want the same thing to happen to." I sighed, and put a hand on Roby's shoulder. "It's good to be careful sometimes," I said. "It's good to protect yourself, an' lay plans for what might be comin' up around the next bend. But sometimes you gotta go with what you know is right, Roby, else you ain't livin' for nothin' but the air you breathe. You just livin' to live, like a dumb animal. We more than that."

He lifted my hand slowly and let it drop. "I come to warn you," he said, "and I warned you."

He spun around and walked a few steps, then stopped. He turned back around - his eyes was big and moist and his mouth was being tugged in all directions. He was a little kid again then, the same little kid that used to follow me around and imitate 'most everything I did. "Alfred?"

"Yeah."

He worked his mouth, but the words and the feeling behind them was choking him.

"I know, little brother," I said. "I know."

He nodded. "You take care."

"Dey's a new preacher in town," Raymond told me one afternoon a couple of months later.

"That's nice," I said, casually. I figured we already had enough preachers to go around, and then some.

"He says de Lawd called him to serve here." I continued working.

"He been talkin' to folks aroun' town," Raymond continued. "Axin 'bout you. He's gonna be comin' along later to talk to you."

"Talk to me?" I said. "What was his name?"

Raymond thought a moment. "I don't know that he said."

"What does he look like?"

"A preacher."

"Huh. Probably another one of them fellers workin' with Ehud Hall and Elmer Carter, wantin' to hear war stories."

"I reckon you'll find out soon enough," Raymond said. "Yonder he comes."

Sure enough, there was a man coming down the road, it was a tall gangly man in black clothes riding a white mule. His head was thrown back, and he was singing – the wind carried his distant words up to us.

"Leaning, Leaning, Leaning on the Everlasting Arm
Leaning, Leaning, Leaning on the Everlasting Arm
What a blessedness, what a joy divine,
Leaning on the Everlasting Arm,
Leaning on Jesus, Leaning on Jesus,
Leaning on the Everlasting Arm..."

I dropped my hoe and half-stumbled to the road, unable to take my eyes off the approaching figure long enough to watch where I was going. A grin broke across my face.

"I swear," I said. "I swear."

The stranger reined in his mule a few feet short of me and Raymond, and took off his broad-brimmed hat.

"Go with what you know, my brother," the preacher said.

"Lonnie! Lonnie Blake! What on God's green earth are you doin' here, you ole rascal?" I pumped his hand with all my strength.

"Takin' you up on that offer you made the last time I seen you, 'bout a year ago, partly. You remember? You said I could drop by an' visit with you anytime."

"I remember sayin' it, and I meant it," I said. Then I remembered that I was living on Raymond's property – I gave the carpenter an embarrassed look, and he nodded.

"You welcome to stay in my home if you're of a mind to, Pastor," Raymond said.

"That won't be necessary," Lonnie told him. "I got accommodations in town. If you could give my animal some water though, I'd be obliged."

Raymond nodded. He was grinning and happy almost as much as me and Lonnie was – the feeling must have been contagious.

"Annie!" he called out to the house. "Annie, you an' de young'uns come out here! We got company!"

Soon we was surrounded by the Carpenter family. The children led Lonnie's mule away, while their mother made the ex-soldier feel welcome by asking him all about his journey. Sid showed up, too – scratching his head in confusion.

"Who dis here?" he asked Raymond.

"New preacher moved into the county."

Sid rolled his eyes – I glared at him, and he had the good sense not to say anything.

"A preacher," I said, grinning at Lonnie. "How in the world did that happen?"

He laughed and smacked me playfully on the shoulder. "'How that happen'," he repeated. "How you reckon it happens with ever'body else, boy? I got called, and I answered."

"Where's yo' fam'ly? Is they comin' too?"

Lonnie faltered a moment, and his smile melted. "No, I don't reckon they is, Alfred. I got home to Alabama an' found out that my wife an' all my babies done been dead with the fever, two years gone by."

Annie gasped in sympathy. "Oh, you po' soul!" she said.

"The Lawd has sustained me, sister, but it ain't been no easy road. It helps keep me goin' to know I'm gonna see 'em one day in the promise-land."

"Amen," she muttered, and his smile returned - he looked at me with soft eyes.

"How 'bout yo' fam'ly, Alfred?"

"My woman run off with some other man while I was at war."

Lonnie shook his head. "That's hard, my brother. That's truly hard." He draped a long, bony arm around my shoulders.

"All them nights we spent dreamin' 'bout comin' home to our fam'lies -the only reason we stayed alive - an' then we come home to find we ain't got no fam'lies no mo'. Kinda seem like a mean joke."

He squeezed my shoulder and then let go. "I believe the Lawd has somethin' else in mind for you an' me, Alfred. I believe he got some kind of a job for us to do - no green pastures for us, not yet."

"Maybe you right," I said, although I did not believe he was.

Lonnie was shaking his head. "No green pastures yet."

Annie tried to lighten the mood with a smile. "You come on into de house now, Pastor - you must be tired out. I'll get you some buttermilk."

"I'm greatly obliged, ma'am," Lonnie said. "But it appears as though there is still work to be done out here in this field. I expect I ought to pitch in until it's finished."

Sid grinned. "If'n you got him fo' de rest of de day, Raymond, I don't reckon you need me."

Raymond turned on his helper.

"I was just jokin', Raymond," Sid said. "Cain't you take a joke? Hellfire."

Annie's jaw dropped open and she slapped the back of Sid's head.

"Ow, Annie.'"

Lonnie chuckled. "Don't fret none, ma'am. I've heard worse."

Annie walked back toward the house, mumbling under her breath about Sid.

Lonnie took off his frock coat and draped it over a fence-rail, then placed his hat on top of it. He rolled up his sleeves. "If'n you got a extry hoe, suh," he told Raymond, "I reckon I could make use of it."

We all pitched in and set to hoeing. It was an odd feeling, to have friends from different parts of my life come together at once – sometimes it had felt like my days as a soldier happened in a different world, to some other man. Now Sid was working on one side of me and Lonnie at the other. It felt like they was stitches, drawing the different sides of me together.

And it felt good, too, the work we was doing. Lonnie and me had toiled together so many times to take lives, or to bury the dead, or to build earthworks in hopes they would stop a bullet from cutting us down. Now we was working to help things grow, to bring new life out of the ground and sustain a family.

"*Leaning, Leaning,*" Lonnie sang. "*Leaning on the Everlasting Arm...*"

Raymond joined in, and their rich voices made the air vibrate –they seemed to flow into our tools and make them work faster.

"Come on, brother," Lonnie said to me. "Sing!"

"I'm savin' my breath," I said with a grin.

"The Lawd respects a man when he works," said Lonnie, "but He loves him when he sings. Come on! Sing anything you like."

I started to sing, uncertain at first of my own voice.

"I am bound for the Promise-Land," I sang. *"Bound for the Promise-Land."*

The others joined me, even Sid. The singing loosed our souls, and they poured out through our tools and into the moist earth they had sprung from. When the sun fell on us, and Annie called us in to supper, it was with reluctance that we shouldered our hoes and trudged back toward the house. Its brightly-lit windows shined at us like a beacon, though, and we picked up our pace and marched toward the warm peace that we knowed awaited us inside.

"Are you gonna be startin' up a new church, Pastor?"

"Lonnie," he told Annie over the table. "Y'all jest call me Lonnie."

"All right, Lonnie," Raymond said. "What's yo' plan?"

"I reckon there's plenty of churches around here already."

"Amen, brother," Sid said.

"No," Lonnie said, ignoring Sid – he had caught on that it was what everyone else did when Sid spoke. "No, I got me another idea. Now, if any of the other preachers around here should want an assistant, to help out and maybe fill in on the odd Sunday, I reckon I could pitch in."

He leaned forward. "But I got somethin' else in mind. You all have got a church or two, I reckon – but how many schools do you have?"

"Schools?" Raymond repeated, like it was a foreign word.

"Dey don't let colored chillun in de schools," Annie said. "I would of thought it's de same in Alabama."

"It is. Unless it's a colored school."

Annie cast a nervous look at her husband.

"They ain't no law against colored chillun learnin'," Lonnie assured them. "We people, jest like ever'body else."

Raymond's brow furrowed. "I know dat, an' you know dat. But dese white folks around here, I doubt if'n dey see things de way we do."

"I'd say they don't," Lonnie said. "The devil don't see things the way I do, neither – I'm a pretty polite fellow, for the most part, but I don't aim to give in to Satan just so's I can keep the peace. I doubt if I'll give in to his servants, either."

Annie laughed nervously. "We know things are changin', Lonnie, but you got to remember – it wasn't but a little while ago dat a slave could get hisself in serious trouble if he let on that he could read. He'd get sold off, or worse."

Lonnie nodded. "You can tell a slave he can't learn. But nobody can tell a free man that." He smiled warmly and leaned toward Sid. "How 'bout you, brother? What do you think about it?"

Sid shrugged. "I don't see where not knowin' any letters has ever hurt me. Sounds like a dern lot of work, anyways."

"Think about this, folks," Lonnie said. "White folks around here say that the Lawd his self blessed slavery, an' that the Scriptures said the Negro must be enslaved. You ever hear that read outen the Bible?" No one answered, so he continued. "No, 'cause it ain't in there. If ever'body could read, they'd know that for theirselves – an' Jesus wouldn't be shamed by havin' folks believe he's a slavemaster.

"I been doin some readin' of my own in the past year, an' not just in the scriptures. I been readin' up on history. Did you know that there was folks – white folks – away across the ocean that give up their lives so's we could have the Bible to read? It was agin the law for anybody to read it, 'ceptin in Latin – which hardly anybody knowed how to do anymore— an' you could be put in jail or even kilt for puttin' the scriptures in regular language so regular people could read it.

"But people done it anyway. Some got caught, an' some suffered – an' you know why?"

Sid and Raymond shook their heads, a little confused, but Annie and me was beginning to understand where he was going.

241

"Because," Lonnie said, "to serve the Lawd you gotta read His word. If'n I wanna save somebody's soul, quickest way I can do it is to teach him to save his own."

Raymond still wasn't convinced. "What do you think about all this, Alfred?"

"If Lonnie wants to start a school, I reckon he'll start a school."

Lonnie gave me a warm, proud look.

"It wouldn't be easy," Raymond said. "Especially on de teacher."

"I am prepared," Lonnie said. "The spirit has bore witness to me, an' I have got to answer."

"Don't know about none of that," I said. "But these chillun needs to learn. I'll stand by you."

"It warms my soul to hear you say that, Alfred," Lonnie said. "I can use your help, all right – two people teachin' folks will be a lot quicker'n one."

I put up my hands. "Wait a minute now, Lonnie, let's not go that far – I fo' sho' ain't no teacher."

"You ain't never tried."

Annie's eyes had grown wide, and she looked at me like she had just noticed I had grown a second head out of my shoulders. "Alfred," she said. "You can read?"

I nodded. "Yeah, I can read."

"Good Lawd!" she said. "What you doin' scratchin' aroun' on dis farm, what ain't even yours, when you got book-learnin'?"

"Hush, woman," Raymond said in a low voice. "I reckon de man can decide for hisself what he wants to do next."

"I cain't read a lick," Sid commented, "and I still axes myself what I'm doin' scratchin' aroun' here."

Raymond's mouth twisted in irritation. "You think you funny, Sid, but you ain't."

"My brother, Roby, can read just fine," I told them, "and cipher too, but that don't make him no better person."

"It could if'n he used it right," said Annie.

Lonnie smiled at me. "They plenty of time to talk about such as that. Jest right now, we got catchin' up to do – you 'member dat time, Alfred, when they read Mister Lincoln's proclamation to us? All them folks was there – reporters, and politicians, plus all our regiment and four others. Lawd they was a sea of folks, wasn't there?"

"I never seen the like, all right."

We described the day for our little audience, and other days besides, and they gasped at the proper points.

"To heck wid all dat," Sid said. "We wanna hear 'bout de battles!"

"Yeah," said little Jimmy. "Tell us 'bout de fightin'."

Annie frowned. "You all know dat Alfred don't like talkin' 'bout dat part of it. An' besides, Brother Lonnie is a preacher – he don't wanna tell 'bout no bloodlettin'."

"It wasn't all slaughter," Lonnie said, and he told them about our skirmish on the Wakeman plantation, and how we liberated the slaves and chopped down the whippin' posts.

"Our people is free from the chains now," Lonnie said, "but a-many of them is still enslaved to ignorance. I aim to do my part to chop them posts down too." He nodded sharply, to emphasize that his point was made and the conversation was over.

"That's some mighty fine cobbler you've whipped up, sister," he said then. "I hate to risk gluttin' myself, but yo' cookin' is too much of a temptation for my po' spirit to resist. I'm gonna have to have me some mo'."

He passed his plate to Annie, and she giggled as she spooned in more.

"I gots me a weak spirit too," Sid said as he passed his own plate up, "and I ain't scared to admit it."

I gave her my own dish, requesting more cobbler with a nod – I seen no need to discuss the condition of my spirit, not over a plate of dessert.

"You give any thought to what I ax'd you while-ago?" Lonnie said. The two of us had gone outside and sat under the starlight after the others had gone to bed.

"I done told you, I ain't no teacher."

"Are you a farmer?"

I thought a moment. "I know all about how to be a farmer – but I don't exactly feel like I am, really. I don't reckon I know what I am. Soldierin's about all I've ever done that I really felt comfortable with, but at the same time, I ain't no killer. Not in my nature, noway."

Lonnie put an arm on my shoulder and used it to push himself to his feet.

"What you are don't make no difference, Alfred. Long as you be who you are." With that, he walked away and left me to my own thoughts.

Chapter Seventeen

Lonnie started his school, sure enough. Ehud Hall raised the money to buy a little section of land a few miles from Raymond's place, and we all pitched in and raised a log cabin on it – one big room, with a sleeping area for Lonnie in the back.

"Lawd knows I don't need much space," the new teacher said. "Don't put yo'selfs out none on my account, fellers – save up yo' energy to build that classroom. My chilluns gots to have room to learn in."

Annie made sure all her children was there on the first day of the new school. She stayed herself, becoming the first growed-up student. A handful of other growed folks joined, too, but not many – most folks was occupied with getting their farming done.

I helped Lonnie out in his teaching job. I could never look that man in the eye and tell him "no" on anything. I took two days out of the week to help with "Lonnie's chillun" – a name he applied even to his growed students, but no one took offense. Raymond didn't much like me taking them two days, but there wasn't much he could say about it. I was working his farm for free, after all, and had paid for the mule. He still didn't like it much. Putting learning into a person's mind was pure foolishness, he would say – all a man needs to know is in his hands.

On Sundays, Lonnie served as Pastor Williams's assistant. Sometimes he even preached the sermon. There was plenty of fire when he did, and plenty of heartfelt warnings about damnation, which kept Annie and folks of a like mind happy. But Lonnie seasoned his hollering and Bible-thumping with warm, gentle words. They was kind words. They made you feel like the Lord Hisself longed for the return of your soul just as strongly as Lonnie yearned for his own lost children.

I had taken to going to church – though not regularly – as a favor to Lonnie. When he delivered them sermons it made me feel kind of uncomfortable and confused, like I had missed some key part of the puzzle. I had seen no evidence of God's love on the plantation, or on the battlefield – but Lonnie's words still stirred something up inside me.

"You gonna find it one day, Alfred," Lonnie said to me more than once. "The Lawd gonna guide you to the Promise-Land. Jest go with what you know."

It was no time at all before all the folks for miles around took to loving Lonnie Blake as much as I did.

All the colored folks, that is.

The elections went different, this time. The Republicans took most every office. Fred LaRue, Rory Banyon, and Rupert Moss all got turned out.

And Ehud Hall, the distinguished colored reverend? He was our district's new state senator. The atmosphere around Hawkins Point changed, starting the very day the election results came in. The colored folks was quicker to smile than they had been before, and their laughter came more easily – they no longer glanced around first, to make sure no white man caught them in the act of enjoying life. They held their heads just a fraction higher, and their backs just a little bit straighter. It reminded me of the soldiers in my old regiment, right after we got our rifles and uniforms. We felt like soldiers, then.

My brothers and sisters in Hawkins Point was beginning to feel human.

But there was another change as well, one that was just as obvious –leastwise, it was to me. The eyes of the native-born, southern, white folks had begun to simmer and give off heat like water at a slow boil. There was some quiet mumbling and a lot of hateful looks. Colored men holding public office and exercising authority over whites was an insult added to the injury of defeat in the war, according to some locals – they claimed it was a calculated move by the federal government to make them suffer even more. Ehud Hall and his friends countered that such an idea was ridiculous. The actions of the government was for the benefit of the colored man, not the chastisement of the white Southerner.

I kept silent. I knowed, though, from my experiences with white troops in the war, that a colored man would be a fool to trust entirely to their good nature. Most of them had not really been fighting to free us from slavery – although a blessed few had been – and I doubted if many of them would go to great lengths to preserve our freedom now.

Practically overnight South Carolina, and the rest of the South, had become filled with black officials. The cities up North had plenty of free blacks, too, but if there was any colored congressmen in Boston or Philadelphia, I sure never heard of it.

We was still being used.

But I kept it to myself, knowing few would listen or believe. And it didn't keep me from going to the victory party for Ehud Hall. Sid Moss, alcohol spirits, and a cakewalk – whatever the occasion – was a recipe for a rare good time.

The party was held at the old Thompson manor house. The Thompsons was one of the families that was wiped out by the war, and their property had been bought up by Northern Republicans at a cheap price. Many of the party guests had once been slaves there.

Reverend Hall – now Senator-elect Hall – gave a brief speech. He talked about the changes that was coming on South Carolina and the nation in this new age of freedom. It was more than just a local event. There was a colored man on the state supreme court, another one was now the state postmaster, and a mulatto had been nominated by the controlling Republicans as South Carolina's new secretary of state.

After much cheering and proposing of toasts, the hired band started up and people began to dance. Sid was right out in the middle of them all, full of joyful energy like he usually was. It was not for any particular reason – he didn't know a Democrat from a mud turtle – it was just Sid being his natural self, soaking up the attention like a five-year-old child.

But all eyes was soon turned toward someone else, a slowly shuffling figure who seemed not to notice any of them as he danced the soft shoe with the easy grace of leaves falling in autumn. It was Uncle Wiley. I don't know that I had ever seen him dance before, and I doubted if anyone else in the grand room had either – unless it was some of the other old folks.

Wiley's eyes was closed and his face was relaxed like a man in a gentle dream. His arms swept slow with an easy flourish like wind in the trees. His feet scraped the floor softly – all was silent except for the music and the old gardener's shoes. He moved like a soul without a body. He glided around the room with dignity and ease, as if the blood that coursed through him and directed his limbs could still remember when it flowed free and proud in Africa. We watched him, unable to look off, knowing that we seen our own spirits dancing away the suffering and endurance of three hundred years.

The music ended and Uncle Wiley's dance flowed into a final, deep bow – he held it for a long time. There was no cheering, only respectful silence. Then Wiley stood and moved toward his chair – once more the gardener's body was stiff and crooked like it had always been before. But now we all knowed that music flowed through it.

I felt a touch at my elbow. I turned to find the senator-elect standing behind me, a kind smile on his face.

"I would never have believed that Wiley Moss would one day support our cause so freely," Hall said. "In that sense, at least, poor Andrew's death was not in vain."

"I don't know that it's support so much with Uncle Wiley," I said. "I believe it's mostly that he's a kind man – just like Lonnie."

"Where is Mister Blake?"

"I ain't sure. I expected he would be here."

"Perhaps he is running late. But what about you, Mister Mann? Are you a supporter?"

"I voted for you."

"Many people did. But some of them are afraid to stand with me – and I do not condemn them for that. It is still a dangerous game we play."

"I ain't never been too scared to do what's right."

Hall nodded. "I believe that, Mann. You have proven it many times – perhaps more than any of us know. At the same time you have proven to be a very cautious man when it comes to deciding what is right, a man who weighs matters carefully. This is a valuable trait."

"Thanks," I said with a shrug.

"I propose to you, Alfred Mann, that now is the time to act. We need men like you more than ever. You have not only courage, but more of an education than even many of our white citizens." He placed an arm on my shoulder. "We have gained a foothold in the arena of power. Now we must entrench ourselves deeply. Already some colored men have been appointed as judges. Many of the white judges are Republicans, and our supporters. I have spoken with some of these judges, Alfred, and suggested you as a candidate for magistrate."

I stared at him a moment, unsure of what to say and not completely certain about the meaning of his words.

"A magistrate is like a judge, you see. He handles civil cases where only a small amount of money is disputed. I believe you could provide the community a valuable service – and it could be a stepping-stone to greater things for you."

He removed his hand from my shoulder and clapped once, laughing. "But I have not forgotten your pensive nature, my friend. There is plenty of time for you to make your decision – no positions are vacant as yet. Until then, think well!"

Ehud Hall walked away from me to mingle with his admirers. I was left to mull over the possibilities of his offer.

My concentration was broke by the arrival of Lonnie Blake.

The crowd gasped when he entered the room. The educating preacher had been terribly beaten. He walked among us shakily, stopping when he reached Hall. Lonnie held out his hand.

"My congratulations, Reverend," Lonnie said, "on your great victory."

"Good land," Annie said, grabbing Lonnie's elbow. "What happened?"

Lonnie shook his head. "On my way over here I ran into some white men a-horseback."

"Who was they?" I demanded, and anger overshadowed the concern in my voice.

"Don't know. They was wearin' hoods."

Elmer Carter set a straight-backed chair on the floor right next to the injured man.

"Lonnie, you set down," Annie ordered him, "whilst we check you over."

"What did they say, Brother Lonnie?" Hall asked.

"They spoke the words of Satan, my friends, and I didn't pay 'em much attention. I just rejoiced in the Lawd, that he sees me fit to be persecuted in His name."

A cloud of gloom had settled down on the party guests that had been so festive a few moments before. Their faces betrayed their thoughts – they feared now that they had not really won anything at all.

"Start that music back up," Lonnie said. "Now go on, y'all, this is supposed to be a celebration, ain't it? We cain't let ignorant folks ruin our evenin' now."

The band played again.

"Come on, Brother Sid," Lonnie said. "I know for a fact that you a dancin' fool – get on out there an' show us how it's done."

The celebration continued. Lonnie laughed the loudest of anyone at Sid's antics – the others took courage from him. As for me, I stood in the corner of the room and stared out the window. Lonnie's hooded attackers was out there someplace, waiting, and seething with hatred. I was sure I'd be meeting them soon.

Chapter Eighteen

"The Ku Klux Klan."

"The what?"

"The Ku Klux Klan, Alfred," Ehud Hall said, "is what they call themselves."

The victory party had wound down, and most of the guests had went home. Annie had convinced Lonnie to spend the night with her family – they had all left half-an-hour earlier.

"The Ku Klux Klan," I repeated. "What kind of crazy name is that?"

"No one can say for sure. It's shrouded in secrecy, like most everything else about their movement. What we do know is that it started a few months ago, in Pulaski, Tennessee. The Klan, as they call it, was founded by the Confederate general Nathan Bedford Forrest."

"General Forrest?" I said, my head snapping up. "He's the one ordered the slaughter of them colored prisoners at Fort Pillow."

Hall nodded. "Then you know the kind of man he is – and the kind of men who would be inspired to follow him. Klansmen have been terrorizing colored voters in other districts, in areas with stronger pro-Union sympathies than ours."

"And now they here."

"Now they are here. It seems that our white neighbors have grown desperate. They no doubt believed their position so strong they would not ever have to resort to violence. Now anything is possible."

"Then we ain't got much to be celebratin'," I said. "Not yet."

Hall smiled. "Just think, though, Alfred. If you accept a position as magistrate, you are the one who will be settling these hooded men's financial disputes. What poetic irony that will be, eh?"

The senator-to-be walked, away, and I shook my head as be passed through the door. Men cut from the moral cloth of General Forrest was going to be coming after Hall and his people with guns, and Hall would be answering them with financial problems and poetic ironies. The war I thought I had left behind me, I realized, was still alive and well – and would soon be thriving in Hawkins Point, South Carolina.

The next day they found Uncle Wiley. He had keeled over in his garden while snapping green beans – the old man had toppled out of his rocking chair and into the rich dirt he'd caressed all his life, the dirt which Doctor Moss owned just like he owned Wiley. The gardener's hands had clawed deeply into the soil. Maybe he wanted its soft comfort to be the last thing he touched, or maybe – for all his talk of heaven – he did not want to leave his garden. Uncle Wiley never did like change.

"Brother Wiley was a gentle soul," Lonnie told me at the graveside. Doctor Moss had somehow found the presence of mind to give us permission to bury Wiley right there in his little garden, instead of in the slave cemetery. The doctor stood a long ways off, watching the proceedings – I wasn't sure if he even knowed what was going on. It didn't matter. Even when Doctor Moss was in his right mind he never recognized Wiley, or the love the gardener had for him and his family. The doctor regarded it as no different than the loyalty a dog has for a kind master.

"A gentle soul," Lonnie repeated, running his left hand lightly over the simple headstone the congregation had bought for its most beloved member. "Too kind for this ole world," he added. "Too kind fo' the days I fear are ahead."

Lonnie lifted his eyes to stare into my face. He was bruised and puffy. "They's storm clouds brewin' up, my brother. Gonna be some strong winds, the kind that'll sholy blow some of us away. But it's the kind of storm that soaks the ground and draws new life out of it."

I nodded, staring into the distance. Ehud stood not far away, graciously accepting congratulations for the fine eulogy he had delivered. Many folks was weeping – their sobs and sniffles merged together until their grief seemed like a single living thing.

"This is the time," Lonnie said, "when we all needs to lean on the Lawd, Alfred. When we needs to draw close to him."

If I had leaned on the Lord, it occurred to me, I would never have left the plantation – or if I had, I would most likely have been killed on some battlefield. When a storm rages up the Lord don't do nothing but let it blow. A wise man, I figured, did well to rely on his own good hands and feet to dig in and hold on. But I couldn't say my thoughts out loud to Lonnie.

"Go with what you know," was all I said, and Lonnie nodded.

"A funny thing happened to me yesterday, Alfred – besides getting the tar beat out of me, that is. Wasn't nothin' funny 'bout that."

"What happened?"

"I was over in town to buy my flour an' coffee, an' I seen this chile. He was a little white chile, no more'n eight year old. When I stepped near him the little feller let out a scream that'd break glass and took off jest a-gettin' it down the sidewalk. I didn't hardly know what to do."

I chuckled just a little. "That's pretty funny, all right."

"I didn't mean funny amusin', Alfred. I meant funny strange. Disturbin'."

I shrugged. "Ever'body ain't as tolerant of your looks as we are, Lonnie. You have to admit, you do kind of take after a scarecrow."

Lonnie shook his head. "All the white people turned and looked at me with eyes full of hate."

"Ain't nothin' new 'bout that."

"There is. There is."

"Could've fooled me."

"They's a difference in hate. Back in slave days they hated us the way you hate a bug that's crawlin' near your food. It's somethin' nasty, somethin' beneath you, that you figure might contaminate you or somethin'.

"Now, they hate us like a man hates a hungry wolf or a hydrophoby dog. Somethin' dangerous to him an' his family, that has to be put down quick afore it eats somebody."

"That's silly," I said. "I ain't plannin' to eat no white folks, my own self. They too rich. Prob'ly give me the gout."

"You been hangin' 'round that Sid too much," Lonnie said. His words was a little hard, which was uncommon for him. "You ain't able to talk sense for five minutes without crackin' jokes."

"Sorry," I said.

"It's all right. But we ain't got nothin' to laugh about, I tell you that fo' sho'. I've heared of stories spreadin' aroun' the county."

"What kind of stories?"

"Stories 'bout freed colored folks goin' an killin' they old masters. Stories of rape an' torture."

"I ain't heard no stories like that."

"That's 'cause it ain't true. Nary a bit of it. But people spread them tales anyway, and believe 'em because they scared. Afraid that some of their power has been sapped away an' give to us. An' I expect most of 'em believes, deep down, that if things was turned around – if they'd been treated all their lives the way we have – they would be out for blood if they got the chance. An' it looks like we gettin' the chance – if they let us."

Lonnie put an arm on my shoulder. It was a familiar warmth – he had repeated the gesture so many times in the years I had known him that it seemed like his hand had always been there – trying to gently guide me toward the righteous path.

"But we got 'em fooled, my brother," he said softly. "We ain't gonna fight 'em with sticks or knives or guns. We gonna fight 'em with words, an' ideas. An' you'n me, we trainin' the troops."

Lonnie moved off. I cast one final, longing glance at Wiley's last resting place. I remembered how I felt as a child, sitting on the gardener's knee and floating away on the silky words of his stories. Uncle Wiley knowed everything then. I was almost surprised when I felt a tear burning its way down my cheek – I had been laughing a minute before. I walked away.

I was woke up one night about a week later – it was after midnight. I heard harsh voices outside, and a feeling of danger pressed down on the base of my skull. I stood up and pulled my clothes on. I found my revolver in the dark with no effort and stuck it into the back of my britches. Sid was beginning to stir – I nudged him with a toe. He mumbled.

"What's goin' on?" I sensed him sitting up.

"That's what I'm fixin' to find out."

Sid was close behind me when I stepped outside. Raymond stood in front of his cabin – the firelight cast shadows on his solemn face.

A large cross was planted in the ground a few yards away. It was flaming like a brand from hell. I stared at it, confused – I did not know what the cross was for, but an evil threat rose on the smoke it gave off.

It was several seconds before a movement attracted my attention to the horsemen. They sat so still and silent at the edge of the firelight that I almost didn't notice them. They was dressed in white sheets and hoods.

"Hear me well," one of them said. His sheets was red. He nudged his horse forward a few steps. The mask and the flames combined to make him look like a ghostly demon.

"You niggers," he continued, "are living on a white man's property. A man whose noble family was ruined by the Yankee aggressors.

"Your nigger-loving Yankee carpetbagger friends are not going to be able to help you now. You'll not be bringing crops grown in a white man's soil to town to trade with Yankees.

"You will leave and go back where you belong. Or you will die."

Annie had stepped outside, and was cowering behind her husband. The leader of the Klansmen trotted forward a little further and pointed at her - his hand held a whip. "We ain't joking, boy."

Another of them said, "Your bitch and her little brats will be swinging in the tree right beside you, you damn gorilla." His robes could not hide Rupert Moss's twisted form.

"We'll be back," the leader said, and they rode away. They was about a dozen of them.

"Shit," Sid said, staring at the burning cross.

Annie's tears was shining in the firelight, but her jaw was set in a different position. "De Lawd gonna strike dem down, using his own symbol like dat an' turnin it into somethin' wicked."

"'Go back where you belong', dey says," Raymond shouted. "Where do dey 'spect we gonna go to?"

"We is where we belong," Annie said.

"We'll figure it out in the mawnin'," I said. "They've done their mischief - they won't be back tonight."

We all went back indoors - all except Sid, who lingered in the open air. "Shit," he said.

The next day was Thursday. After breakfast I set out on the road and walked to Lonnie's little schoolhouse, like I done every Thursday. Annie didn't go with me this time - she didn't go to classes every day, not anymore. She was too busy working. She still showed up a couple of days a week, though, to build on what she had learned - and she studied on her own, every night after supper.

By nine o'clock we only had eight children present – instead of the two dozen or so that usually showed up. Three of them – the Baker young'uns – told us that their house had been visited by the Klan the night before, but that their daddy had sent them on to school this morning, anyways. The parents of the other five children had not been called on yet by Rupert Moss's friends – but me and Lonnie both knowed they would be. It was only a matter of time.

"They scared," Lonnie whispered to me. "I reckon anybody would be."

"What do you reckon we ought to do?"

"Teach these little chillun, like always. And later on, when the other families gets tired of hidin' an find their courage, we'll teach their chillun too. We might not be able to do anything 'bout them white-sheeted fools right now, but we givin' these young'uns the power to do it. One day."

The children had been busy writing down the words Lonnie had told them to write a few minutes before. They was all done now, and was growing restless. Lonnie smiled at them.

"We plantin' the seed, my brother," he told me. "Go with what you know."

I still wasn't real comfortable being with the kids. I also wasn't comfortable with teaching other folks how to do something I wasn't all that good at myself—namely writing and ciphering. Still, we got by. I sat down beside the two little Baker brothers and helped them figure out how to spell simple words, like "cat" and "cow", sounding them out one letter at a time, and told them which way to point their *b*'s and *d*'s.

Despite my discomfort, helping out at Lonnie's school gave me a warm feeling. It kind of spread through my bones and took away some of the numbness. It was almost like being with my own young'uns again. In my mind I covered over these kids with the faces of Jenny and Billy, the way I imagined they might look now. I could never dream up a clear image, though – just a muddled, ghostly one. But it was enough to satisfy me a little bit. I pretended like I was teaching my kids to write, just like I sometimes found myself distracted when working the fields by daydreams of teaching them to fish, or whistle, or tie their shoes.

It was after dinner-time, along about two o'clock, that we got our own visit from the Kluxes. They sat on their horses outside the little cabin and called for Lonnie to come out. The men looked a little different in the clear daylight. Fact is, they looked kind of stupid in them outfits. They was hot and itchy, and sweat plastered the sheets to skin in places. I recognized some of the horses this time. Grady Cooper's poor gray mare looked like she was going to sag plumb to the ground from his weight.

"You better stay here fo' now, Alfred," Lonnie said, "an' look after the chillun. In case they's trouble, you can be my ace-in-the-hole."

I nodded and stepped away from the door as he went outside. Lonnie stood in front of the men with his head held high, saying nothing.

"This is your only warning, nigger," the red-sheeted leader said. It was the same voice as the previous night – it was familiar, but I couldn't quite place it.

"Your kind hasn't got any business reading or writing," he continued, "and acting uppity. You'd best remember your place or we'll remind you of it."

I supposed them words didn't apply if you was like Roby, willing to be a lapdog.

Rupert Moss let out a giggle –his laughter was every bit as twisted as his back.

"If you don't close down this miserable excuse for a school," Rupert said, "we will have your yellow ass."

I thought about my brother fawning over such a man, and almost lost hold of the biscuits I had eaten for dinner. I had no doubt that Roby would crawl right into one of them white hoods if they told him to, smiling like an idiot all the while.

Lonnie still didn't speak a word, he just stared at them. It wasn't a defiant stare. It was a look of kindness, probing into their souls – the kind of look Jesus must have give to the Roman soldiers that tormented him.

"Remember, nigger!" the leader said, and they rode away. Lonnie quietly walked back inside and taught the frightened children how to subtract without using their fingers.

It was almost two weeks before we had any more trouble. Then some white men grabbed Raymond off the road on his way back from town and beat him up pretty good, worse than Lonnie that night of the cakewalk. He dropped into a kitchen chair when he got home, and we gathered around as he told us what happened.

"You gots to go, woman," he told his wife.

Annie was crying – more from anger than from fear or sorrow. "You my man, fool! We done took a vow – I'm stickin' wid you no matter what!"

Raymond sighed and put his head in his hands. He was sitting with his elbows resting on the kitchen table. His clothes was still bloody.

"We gots to think of de chillun, Annie," he said, taking her hand. "Go on to yo' sister's, now. If'n somethin' was to happen to you all I wouldn't have no reason to keep goin'." His voice broke for a moment. Raymond was not used to such tender words – I doubt if he had expressed as much emotion when he asked Annie to marry him. I was a little embarrassed for Raymond, not for his words, but for his discomfort in saying them.

"Go on," he repeated. "Me an Alfred can handle things here fo' awhile."

"What about Sid?" Annie asked.

Raymond looked at me, but I said nothing. "Sid can do whatever he wants to do," he told her.

Sid said, "I reckon I'll just stay here." His face was kind of slack and there was a confused look in his eyes, like he wasn't entirely sure why he had said such a thing. He had the shocked, disbelieving look of a man whose world is changing too fast for him to keep up with it. I had seen the same expression many times on my fellow soldiers during combat. "Go on den," Raymond told Annie. She scooted the children out the door without looking back. "Dis is where I belong," she mumbled, voice strained by feeling.

Lonnie showed up soon after. He knocked on the door and Raymond told him to enter - neither him nor Sid looked up when Lonnie walked in.

"Hey, Lonnie," I said.

"Hey, Alfred," he answered softly. "I heard about what happened in town. Thought it might be better if'n we holed up together - at least for the night." He turned to Raymond. "Might be I could help."

Raymond pushed a chair toward Lonnie with his foot "Take a seat, Lonnie."

"Thanks," he answered, and sat down.

The four of us sat around that table, silent and gloomy, while the sun went down. An hour went by without anyone talking or making much of a sound, then two. Raymond was staring down at the tabletop with anguished eyes.

Lonnie stared into the little fire - his expression was calm and peaceful. I had expected him to come in and start singing hymns or leading prayers, but I had been wrong -this was Lonnie Blake the soldier. He was doing his soldiering for the Lord now, sure, but he was still preparing for battle the same way he used to - by relaxing his body and his mind and his spirit much as he could, until the moment they all had to spring into action as one.

Sid was tossing cards into a hat. I don't think he could set still if his life depended on it. Every once in awhile he would make a little grunt when he made an especially good toss.

As for me, I sat stock-still and straight-backed. My every sense was alive. It was just like being on picket duty.

Finally, Raymond stood up with a sigh. He took his old double-barreled shotgun down off the wall and laid it across the table - then he took a box of shells off the mantel, opened it, and placed it beside the weapon. After that, he disappeared for a moment into a darkened corner of the room. He walked back to the table, his footsteps heavy, and set a half-empty bottle of Tennessee whiskey beside the shotgun.

"You been holdin' out on me," Sid muttered, pretending to be hurt. I knowed he wasn't really hurt - just irritated with himself for not discovering the liquid treasure earlier.

"I been savin' it," Raymond said. "Ain't enough there for us to get drunk on, just enough to take off de edge."

"I got de sharpest edge you ever seen," Sid said with a grin. "It ought to take quite a bit of smoothin'." Then he wiped the grin away. "I ain't never held out on you, you know."

"You ain't never give nothin' out, neither, 'ceptin' trouble," Raymond said as he opened the bottle. We passed it around and all took a sip - even Lonnie, though he barely wet his lips.

The talking died back out after that. Everybody took three or four swallows of the whiskey, except Sid. He was drinking it down like water.

"We might all need our wits afore the night is out," I told him.

"You, maybe," Sid replied. "If'n I'm gonna get whupped, I don't wanna feel it."

By midnight Sid had his face flat on the table, snoring like a bear. Raymond's head kept nodding and jerking back up.

"Go on ahead and sleep," I told him. "Ain't nothin' gonna happen tonight."

"You can't know dat."

"Ain't likely to. Them damn rednecks is too lazy to stay up this late and pester niggers. It'd be too much like work, and they ain't got no slaves to do it for 'em. Get some shuteye to last you through tomorrow."

Raymond nodded his acceptance slowly, then folded his arms and rested his head upon them. I nodded off myself, after that. Lonnie was still staring into the fire, leaning forward every once in a while to stoke it up. I knowed that he seen his God in the flames, and was talking to him from behind his heavy-lidded eyes. I wondered if He was talking back.

Chapter Nineteen

"I reckon I'd best push off," Lonnie said the next morning.

"Where do you think you're goin'?" I asked him.

"I sholy wish't Annie was here," Sid said. "To fix us biscuits. I hate to start off a day without no biscuits."

Raymond was still snoring gently.

"You need to stay put awhile," I told Lonnie, ignoring Sid and his wishful mumbling.

"I gots to get on down to the school, Alfred. You know that."

"There probably won't even be anybody there to teach. Ain't been more'n a handful a day all week long."

He shook his head. "Don't matter. It's my school. If any of them chillun shows up, I gots to be there. I always gots to be there."

I sighed, exasperated, and stood up. "I reckon I'd best be goin' with you, then. Sid, when Raymond wakes up tell him we'll most likely be back 'fore long. If'n they ain't no young'uns showed up by the middle of the mawnin' they ain't no sense in us waitin' around there."

We walked to Lonnie's cabin. The birds was all singing, just as joyful as they could be. It must be a happy life, I thought, being a bird. But then again, all that singing just proved they didn't have no more sense than Sid did.

Lonnie ran his hand down that old saber scar on the side of his face. "I was unfaithful to my Thelma, you know," he said absently. "Durin' the war. I consoled myself with whores while she lay dyin', an' the young'uns too. Don't know if I can ever live it down, Alfred. But praise God, He done give me another chance. I cain't fail those chillun. I just cain' t."

264

The hours creeped by and nobody showed up at Lonnie's school.

The soldier-turned-reverend kept walking over and looking out the window, trying to lure the young minds in with the force of his own gentle will. I sat in the opposite corner of the classroom, thumbing through the three beat-up picture books that the school laid claim to. All the little white children in them looked sweet and playful.

Lonnie smiled. "Think I hear somebody comin'," he said, and he walked out the door to check – I heard the rapid hoofbeats and the three gunshots. I sprang to my feet, revolver in my hand almost instantly, and crossed the classroom with giant strides.

Lonnie backed in through the door, then turned around. His face was pale.

"Alfred," he whispered, then sank to his knees. His white shirt was rapidly turning red in the middle. He started to sway forward, and I caught him.

"It's all right, Lonnie," I said. "I got you."

"The chillun," he croaked. "Where's the chillun?"

"Ain't no chillun here, Lonnie."

"I gots to look after the chillun, Alfred. I gots to be here when they comes in."

"You will be."

He coughed, spitting blood on my shoulder. I craned my neck trying to see out the door – the hoofbeats was far away, now. The shooters was gone.

"Alfred?"

"Yeah, Lonnie?"

He tried to lift his head up, but it kept lolling forward. I held his face in my hands and looked into the unfocused eyes. Lonnie smiled.

"I'm fixin' to go see my babies, Alfred. I'm fixin' to see my babies."

I held him closer and tighter, burying his face on my shoulder and rocking. It wasn't long until I felt the breath slip out of him. The pistol was still in my hand. I put it away and laid Lonnie softly onto the floor. I had to get home.

I was running down the road as fast as I could when I met someone going the other way. It was Tobin, another old Moss field hand. He didn't seem to notice the blood that soaked my shirt.

"He dead!" Tobin cried. "Dey done rode by an' shot de reverend an' he dead!"

"How could you know that?"

"'cause I was there! I was there in town when they done it!"

"In town?" I had thought he was talking about Lonnie, but there was something more.

"Reverend Hall," he said. "Ehud Hall! He was comin' out of de Republican office, an dey shot him dead!"

"Ehud Hall," I said, trying to soak it in. Tobin was already going down the road again, shouting it to the world.

"He dead! They kilt him!"

I found the strength from somewhere to run even faster than before.

I approached the house from the rear. I was moving only at a jog – I had been forced to stop twice and catch my breath.

Several figures was milling around in front of the cabin.

There was six Kluxes, including the one dressed in red. They was afoot – their horses was tethered. The Kluxes had a rope around Raymond's neck. The other end was thrown over a stout tree limb, and three of the Klansmen was pulling on it so that Raymond was stretched up in the air and had to stand on his tiptoes.

I went back into a full sprint and hit the back door of the cabin. The men seen me just before I went inside.

I ran to the kitchen table – Raymond's shotgun was still there. He had ventured outside without it. I took a moment to break the thing open and make sure it was loaded, then I snapped it shut and pulled the hammers back. I grabbed a handful of shells and stuffed them into my pocket, then sprinted toward the front door.

It swung open just before I reached it. The Red Klux was standing there like he owned the place, like he was the devil and Hawkins Point was his own personal kingdom of hell. He stood framed in that doorway for a split-second that seemed to last for an eternity. The image was burned into my mind like a brand. Behind him I seen that Raymond was now swinging and kicking in the air. These men had come, in their minds, to whip or kill a few mongrel dogs – and I was no different. But they had cornered a wolf now, and he had teeth.

"You nig—"

Red Klux would have to finish the word in Hell, for I gave him a load of buckshot right in the chest from no more than five feet away. He went sailing through the air, right over the heads of his two comrades on the step below. I took three steps forward and then emptied the second barrel into one of his friends.

"Somebody stop him, by God," the third man said – it was Rupert Moss's voice. He spun around and ran toward his remaining friends. They dropped the rope and let Raymond fall to the ground like a wet sack.

"Stop him! Stop him!" Rupert squealed. I tossed the empty shotgun aside – no time to reload – and drawed my revolver. I put a lead ball between Rupert's shoulder blades, right in his twisted spine.

The other three had finally gathered their wits and taken out their guns. Two of them had pistols, the third had a beat-up old musket. I turned sideways to make a smaller target and took careful aim at a white sheet. Their guns was belching fire already and I felt the bullets cut the air around me – the Kluxes was panicked, and more concerned with shooting first than with shooting straight. I doubted if they had ever been under fire before.

The first man went down clutching his belly. The second man had fired his musket to no use, and now bent and fumbled for his fallen comrade's revolver. There was an explosion from just behind me, and the Klansman went flying backward. Sid was standing with me - it was him that had reloaded and fired the shotgun, and it was still smoking.

The surviving Kluxer swore. His cap-and-ball pistol had jammed - not uncommon with that kind of weapon if you don't clean and grease it properly. He throwed it to the ground, disgusted.

"Where've you been?" I said to Sid, not taking my eyes off the now unarmed Klansman.

"Hidin' my ass, where the hell you think?"

The Klansman sunk to his knees and whimpered. "Please don't hurt me, Mister. I give up."

I reached over and jerked the hood off him. It was Grady Cooper, the slavecatcher. His lips quivered with terror and his eyes was squeezed shut.

"Please mister," he repeated. I knowed that things was going to be bad enough on me and Sid as it was. A witness would only make them even worse. I cocked the revolver.

"No!" Grady squealed. "Jesus, no! Have mercy, oh God have mercy!"

"You done killed 'most all the reverends around here," I told him. "It's yo' bad luck to be left with me. I ain't no preacher."

I blowed his brains out.

"Shit, Alfred," Sid muttered. "You killed him." Now that the rush of fighting for his life was over, Sid was being undone by what had happened.

"I believe you right," I told him. "Now go see to Raymond. Go on, git."

While Sid took the rope off the gasping Raymond, I walked over to the Klansman in the red robes. The shotgun blast had tore him near in two. I took the hood away from his face - as I suspected, it was none other than the honorable Fred LaRue. It didn't feel as good as I had always dreamed to see his dead eyes staring up at me. It didn't exactly feel bad neither, though.

I walked over to the others. "Get up," I told Raymond.

"Choke - I'm chokin'," he croaked. He was leaned up, supported by Sid. I reached down and pulled him roughly to his feet.

"You ain't got the time to choke, dammit. Now listen to me. We got to leave this country, you hear? If we lucky we got a few hours 'fore folks figures out what happened here."

"But my place—"

"You gonna have to find a new place. We got six good hosses here - me an' Sid is gonna take four of em, an' you gonna take two. You gonna say yo' goodbyes to Annie an' the chillun, then you gonna ride west till you can't ride no mo'."

"I cain't leave widout my fam'ly. Alfred, you ought to know dat."

"Take Annie if you gots to, but fo' sho' not the young'uns. You can send for 'em later, when you get away safe - if'n either one of you has got sense, you'll wait an' send fo' Annie too. She'll just slow you down, and keep you from havin' a fresh hoss."

"But I don't—"

"I don't care what you do!" I said. "Jest do it now. Ride!" While Raymond galloped away I hurried into the shack where Sid and I lived and retrieved the little bundle of my belongings. I stuffed it into one of the saddlebags on LaRue's horse.

"You got anything you want to take?" I asked Sid.

"Jest my ass."

"Then plant it in a saddle and let's go."

We each climbed onto a mount and took the reins of our spare horses. I trotted close to Sid and thrust my face near his.

"If you wanna come out of this mess alive, brother, listen to me. You better do what I say, when I say."

"Yessuh, General Alfred. Where we goin'?"

"We need to get to a city. It's always easy fo' a colored man to get lost in a city."

"Charleston ain't far off."

"They'll be lookin' fo' us there. We need to set our sights farther north. I been pinin' to see that New York harbor fo' some time now – this looks like the perfect chance."

We thundered away. We stuck to the woods and to the back roads, riding mostly at night, and did a lot of sleeping under logs and in old barns. But we made it out of the state without no trouble. I had traded my bloody clothes for my old uniform – my sergeant's stripes drawed a few stares in the border states.

Raymond took Annie with him anyway, leaving the kids with Annie's sister. They got away safe to Kansas and settled down. Later on they started a nice big farm in Oklahoma Territory, near to a colored town. I ran into them there years later, long after their young'uns was growed up. It would never be safe for any of us to go back home, but we didn't really have to look over our shoulders in fear once we cleared out. There was so much killing in Hawkins Point – on both sides, Klan and Yankee – that nobody seen fit to bother with looking for a couple of refugees in amongst the haystack of colored folks on the move in America.

I found out that some of the Negroes in Hawkins Point grabbed my brother Roby off the street and beat him to death. Betraying his own people and knuckling under to Rupert Moss turned out not to be as safe a course as Roby thought it was. It hurts when I think about him. Rory Banyon wound up with Ehud's senate seat, and things in Hawkins Point went back to the way they had always been.

Me and Sid, we was free of it all. We was headed North to live out Topaz's dream.

Chapter Twenty

Maurice had been right. Them ships was something to see, sure enough. The way they glided in all soft and easy, full of power and grace, loaded down with treasures from all manner of mysterious, far-off lands. Maybe looking at them ships really was like looking at freedom.

If so, it was the same kind of relation with freedom that I had been having all my life. I was working on the docks, you see –close enough to stare up in wonder at the huge vessels. But I wasn't going to be one of the men going onboard. I wasn't going to be loading or unloading any cargo. That kind of work was reserved for members of the longshoremen's union – and Negroes was not allowed to join.

No, me and a couple of other colored workers – their names was Jack and Earl – we was doing all the mopping and sweeping up and everything else that most folks wouldn't want to do. We was doing the nigger work. And we was being paid nigger wages, barely enough to live on and surely not enough to live well. I had eaten a lot better as a slave – but the food of freedom, if not plentiful, was still a lot easier to digest.

"Psst! Hey Alfred! Get over here!"

Earl was motioning to me from the corner shadows. Jack was a former slave like me, from Georgia, but Earl had been born free – right there in Brooklyn – just like his daddy before him. He lived on the same street as me and Sid.

"What you want?" I asked when I reached him.

"You livin' in another world or somethin'? Don't you see them mick longshoremen walkin' this way?"

I looked. Sure enough, three white men was walking right toward where I had been sweeping a moment before. Their voices made it clear they was Irish.

"If you're smart," Earl whispered to me, "you'll just set still till they pass by."

Only when the Irishmen had turned the corner did Earl begin to stir. "You gotta be more careful," he told me. "One time I seen a bunch of micks - that guy Rourke was one of 'em - grab a colored swamper and chuck him in the river just for the hell of it. Poor fella couldn't even swim or nothin'. Damn micks just stood there and laughed while they watched him drowned."

I stared at the corner that the Irishmen had turned. I had been working for only a week, but I had pretty well figured out where I stood. It was only because I had arrived in summertime that I had a job at all—the bosses had a greater need for help then. Many a family had to go the rest of the year without work; white folks only handed out jobs to us coloreds when it was absolutely necessary - and when the white folks was mostly employed already. Jack told me that he pawned his furniture every winter and did without until the next June.

Sid had managed to get part-time work carrying luggage at a hotel. He spent the rest of his time drinking and gambling; he must have found his calling, because he brung home more money than me.

"You there! Get to work!"

"Yes, suh, Mister Clark," Earl stammered.

Mister Clark was about as fat and sweaty as Grady Cooper had been -and though his accent was Yankee, his attitude was the same.

"Damn nigs," he said, more to himself than to us. "Ya gotta stay right on top of 'em every minute, or they'll never get any work done. I ain't runnin' no charity here, boys - for what I'm payin' you I expect you to work." He chewed on his cigar a second, then added, "Remember, I'm doin' you a favor."

"Some favor," Earl whispered after he was gone. "He probably pays us a third of what he'd pay a white man."

I picked up my first week's pay that evening and started the long walk home. Earl was right, it wasn't much – but then, he had never worked for soldier's wages. Or as a slave. A little bit of change in a man's pocket makes him feel good, makes him feel like a man. It ain't enough to let him do just anything he wants, but it's enough to let him do something.

Like I said, it was a long walk. Three miles worth. All the way to the Eighth Ward, the Negro slums. So far as comfort was concerned, them slums was enough to make any slave row seem like paradise. It was that bad. Let me tell you, folks was packed into them shacks like sardines in a tin – and the shacks was all stacked together close as bricks. There was no outhouses. Folks emptied their chamber pots out into the gutters, and lots of fellows just pissed right out onto the street. It smelled terrible. This was our neighborhood, and it was going to stay our neighborhood whether we liked it or not. No matter how much money a man made he could never live nowheres else. The property-owners in other areas was afraid we would scare away their decent white lodgers if they was to rent to us.

On my way home, I lingered in front of a restaurant. It was called Ropers Inn, and the savory smells that smoked out of its doorway had been luring me toward it every evening when I passed this way – but I had never gone inside, not having the money. I knowed it wasn't a fancy place, like some other restaurants I had heard tell of, because the folks I seen going in and out was just regular working folks, but at the same time I was sure they wasn't just giving food and drink away.

I paused at the doorway longer than usual this time, letting them sweet smells work their way down through my gullet and into my belly, waking up my insides. I jingled the money that was in my pocket for reassurance that it was still there, and walked on inside. I was a little uncertain about what to do. I had never been in a restaurant before, not even a cheap one.

Several white men was lined up at the bar. Quite a few others was clustered at little round tables placed all around the room. I didn't see any Negroes. Tobacco smoke mixed in with smoke from the grill, blanketing the place in an inviting haze.

A fat little man with a sweaty face and slicked-back hair rushed up to me. He was wearing a dirty apron.

"What do you think you're doing, boy? You'll have to go!"

"I come to eat."

He chewed nervously on his huge mustache. "We don't need no trouble. Just move along."

A couple of the white men turned away from the bar. "Is this nigger causin' you problems, Dan?" one of them said.

"I got money," I told them.

"Your money ain't no good in this part of town, nigger," another patron said.

Dan, the waiter, took my elbow in his hand. "Come on," he said. His voice sounded tough, but his eyes was pleading. "Let's go, then."

I let him lead me.to the door, not sure what else to do. Dan's customers was laughing – mixed among the laughter was some angry voices.

"I'd like to know who's been givin' that ape money, makin' him think he can eat with white folks."

"Some damn skinflint, more'n likely – givin' work to niggers when there's white men goin' hungry. It'll be our jobs they'll be after next, mark my word."

The smoke did not seem so inviting anymore. I was glad to pass through the door and get outside. I glanced back into the front window – my face was reflected in it, but the haze obscured my features. It was like having no face at all.

"I can't afford no trouble," Dan was telling me. When he looked up at me his face softened. "Look," he said. "You come back at about nine-thirty, after I've closed up. If I have any grub left I'll dish you some up. That way there won't be anybody around to get mad about it. But don't you ever come around here again in the broad daylight, you hear? I'll have to send for the police."

I walked back down the road, headed for home. I should've knowed better. A colored man leaves his job and don't stop walking or lift his eyes up until he reaches the nigger slums. New York was no different from South Carolina. North was no different than South.

My skin was just as black either place.

I passed by old Rodney on the way to the shack I shared with Sid. Rodney had the consumption - he often sat on the side of the road and coughed up pieces of lung. The old man didn't beg for money, though he would take it if he could get it. He knowed it would be useless to come out and beg - no one in the Eighth Ward had nothing to give him, and no one in the rest of the city cared whether he starved to death or not.

"Hey, Rodney."

"Evenin', Alfred. How you doin'?"

"Same as everybody, I reckon."

I walked on past him. Rodney was seized by a coughing fit and leaned over to retch on the sidewalk, but nothing would come out. I turned and walked back to stand beside him.

"You all right, Pops?"

"I will be, Son, I reckon I will be. Pretty soon de Lawd's gonna scoop me up an' take me to a better place. I'd rather not have anymore lungs noways, than to keep on breathin' de fumes of dis ole world."

I dug into my pocket and took out the money I figured I would've spent at that restaurant, and pressed it into his hand.

"What you doin'?" he said.

"I got it to spare," I told him. "You jest take it."

"No, no, here - you throwin' money away on a man dat's fixin' to be dead soon."

"Don't matter," I told him. "Long as we here, we gots to look out fo' each other."

"Thank you, Alfred. Thank you. De Lawd gonna bless you - if not in dis world, den sholy in de next."

I patted his hand and then walked off.

"De Lawd gonna bless you!" he called out to me. "Blamed if he ain't!"

Our little shack was real similar to the one we had lived in at Hawkins Point. Almost identical, in fact. And we had us a outhouse in the back. We was pretty lucky to have such a place – lots of folks wasn't nearly as well off.

Most of the buildings on our little street was rotted through and falling apart, barely enough left of them to give shelter from the rain.

Our landlords was better than most, though. They was an old German couple, Mister and Missus Schwartz, and they was friendly and kind. They only lived a few blocks away. Missus Schwartz would sometimes come by the house with leftover cake or boiled vegetables, and she would fuss over me and Sid like she thought we was her own young'uns. Sid lapped it all up, enjoying every scrap of attention, but I felt kind of uncomfortable.

"You too dern s'picious," Sid told me once. "You act like all de white folks in de world is out to steal yo' soul."

"If I wasn't suspicious I'd be dead now. So would you, more'n likely."

"You ain't s'picious of de Schwartzes," Sid had said. "You afraid of 'em. You afraid dey'll turn out to be jest as good an' decent as dey seems to be, an' dat you'll have to change yo' way of lookin' at things. You stubborn, Alfred, dat's yo problem. Always has been."

I went into the house. Sid was out, as usual. I checked under my little cot to make sure nobody had stolen my Colt. It was still there. I wished it wasn't so big, so I could hide it on me good and wear it to work without running the risk of being discovered. I felt naked and helpless without it. I wished I had the money to buy a smaller one.

Maybe Sid was right about the Schwartzes after all. From what I'd heard all the colored folks in the neighborhood say, it was the Germans – out of all the different kinds of white people – that was most likely to treat us like they thought we was as human as them. I don't know why that was. I'm given to understand that the Germans was treated bad in their home country by the big shots, almost like they was slaves – but I've heard the same thing said about the Irish, and it seemed like there was more hatred in them than there was in anybody. Maybe they had been trod on for too long to care what happened to anybody else. Maybe all they cared about now was surviving their selves, hungry and wary like a wild animal.

And maybe I was no different. I was afraid to trust to the good hearts of the Schwartzes, much as I had been afraid to trust Colonel Wentworth during the war. Sure, Wentworth and the other white officers in our regiment never really understood us, and some of their notions was wrong without them even knowing it – but they fought and died beside us.

I was like a whipped dog that had been beat so many times it tried to bite any hand that moved to befriend it. I looked into that part of my heart and didn't like what I seen – it was too close to the starving Irishmen or the Kluxers back home – but I feared to let it go. It was that part of me that had kept me alive for so many years. It was the fuel that fired my soul and kept me moving forward instead of sinking down.

I put the Colt back under my bed, with my cap and old uniform. I seen the ranks marching before me in my mind and for a moment felt a twinge of longing to be with them. Despite the unfair pay and rude treatment by the white regiments – and despite the danger – it was in that uniform that I felt honor and glory and dignity.

Sid walked in – his ever-present smile broadened when he seen me.

"Yonder sets de workin' man," he said

"The onliest one I see around here," I said.

Sid laughed. "You needs to loosen up, brother. You ought to come wid me an' see what dis city is all about."

"I'd be scared to travel in yo' circles. You gonna wake up some mawnin' with yo' throat cut, the kind of people you run with."

"Shucks, you say. You crane yo' neck all day long lookin' up at dem sail-boats – but I'm tellin' you, dese streets comes alive at night. Alive in a way you ain't never seen."

"Reckon not."

"Laughin' an' dancin' an' singin'," he continued, not really paying much attention to me anymore, "till it starts to flowin' in yo' veins somehow, makin' em burn. Ever' night is corn-shuckin' time."

He looked at me and shook his head. There was pity in his eyes. "If'n you won't let me educate you, son, den here." He took a roll of bills out of his pocket and throwed it down on my bed. "Take de rent outen dis. Wid what's left over you ought to go find yo'self a nice, soft whore to take some of yo' edges off."

"You must of been awful lucky to come up with that kind of money, Sid."

"I'm de luckiest damn nigger you ever seen in yo' life, boy. If you stick close maybe some of it'll rub off on you."

I held the heavy roll in the palm of my hand. "Could be this ain't all gamblin' money," I said.

"You behave yo'self now, Alfred," he said as he moved toward the door. He tossed a set of dice into the air and snatched them back playfully. "I'm glad you brung me here," he said in a more serious tone. "I wish't you'd come with me an' have some fun – like we used to."

I looked at him and let a smile tug one corner of my mouth up. "I'll go with you next week. When I get paid again."

Sid winked, tossed the dice up one more time, and disappeared out the door.

"Here come those damn micks again," Mister Clark said as he tapped the ash from his cigar. "Probably trying to stir up

278

trouble. They're starting to piss me off – I'm trying to make a living here."

He turned to me. "Hey you, boy. Hide your black ass somewhere. No point in getting them more excited than we have to."

I took my mop and moved into a little tool closet. I sat on an upturned bucket and sighed. I hated being hidden like I was something dirty.

"We ain't happy, Clark." I recognized the voice as that of Rourke – one of the longshoremen's leaders. I peeked out. Rourke had two other Irishmen with him.

"When have you been happy?" Clark grumbled.

"Not since you've been givin' work to nigs, that's for sure. I got my cousin right here, Kevin, just come over from the Isle – is he supposed to starve?"

"He wasn't here last week when I needed somebody."

"We know what you're about," one of the other men said. "Puttin' jigaboos on the payroll dirt cheap. Not only does it keep new fellas from gettin' the jobs they need, it's gonna drive all our salaries down too."

"We can't live on shit, like niggers and other low animals," Rourke added. "And we don't plan to."

"Why don't we send 'em back down South?" Rourke's cousin Kevin said. "We don't want 'em, do we Johnny?"

"South, hell," Johnny said. "Send 'em back to Africa with the other apes. We're sick to death of 'em."

"It's too late for that, gentlemen," Clark said. "Mister Lincoln saw to that. Nigs are everywhere."

"So why not make a buck off it, eh Clark?" Johnny said, voice thick with scorn.

"We can't do nothin' about the rest of the country," Rourke said. "But we can sure as hell run 'em out of Manhattan and Brooklyn. There's more of us than there are of them – we need to act before they outbreed us."

"We've done it before," Johnny said. "In 'sixty-three."

Rourke stepped closer to Clark. "An we can take care of you too, boyo. We can burn this place down around your ears - you'll be blacker than they are, then."

Clark sighed heavily. "I'll put your young man on the payroll, Rourke. It's taken care of."

"It better be. A lot of things better be taken care of around here."

I stepped out into the open once I was sure they was gone. Clark seemed not to notice me at first; when he did see me, the cigar fell plumb out of his mouth.

"Get the hell out of here," he shouted. "Go on, scram."

I stood there, a little confused about his meaning. The mop was still in my hand.

"We don't need you anymore," Clark said. "Go plague somebody else, for Chrissake. God above, my overhead is gonna be chewing a hole right in my pocket." He took out his wallet. "Here's your wages. Go."

I tossed the mop aside, pocketed the money, and started the walk home. I didn't bother stopping at any restaurants and sniffing the air, not anymore.

"You home early," Rodney said when he seen me walking up the sidewalk. "Dey declare some kind of holiday or somethin'?"

"They declared a holiday all right, just for me - a permanent one. I got fired."

"What brung dat on?"

"An Irishman wantin' a job, that's what."

Rodney shook his head and exhaled. "Dem damn Irishers is a heap of meanness. Dey been gettin' dey tails up lately. I sholy hope there ain't no trouble like in sixty-three."

"That's the second time I've heard that year mentioned today. What happened in sixty-three?"

"Where was you at den, boy, hidin' in a hole?"

"In 'sixty-three I run away from my masters. I swum across the river and joined the Union Army."

"So you fit in de war?"

"I did."

"Well, bein' in de middle of a war would've seemed safe compared to what was happenin' here."

"I cain't hardly believe that."

"It's true. The Irishers went plumb crazy on account of the guv'ment started draftin' 'em into de Army."

"A lot of good soldiers I knowed was Irish."

"Maybe, but dat was de ones dat wanted to go. Dese here'uns didn't. Dey didn't want to get shot at to free no niggers – especially since dey was afeared we might get their jobs. It aggravated 'em too dat rich folks didn't get drafted. All dey had to do was pay a little money to get out of it. But dese Irishers, fresh outen de ocean, dey didn't have no money.

"So dey went crazy. Barricaded their selfs up, burned down factories, beat up rich folks. Fought agin de po-lice an' de Army.

"An dey come here, hollerin' an' shootin', burnin' an lootin'. An' killin'. God-a-mighty, at de killin'."

"I never heard about nothin' like that," I said, shocked.

"Dat's jest de biggest one. Dey've rose up two or three times since den, jest not as bad."

"Good Land," I said softly. "What's to keep 'em from doin' it again?"

Rodney just stared at me. He held my gaze a long time, then he turned away to cough.

Sid popped into the shack soon after I got there.

"Awful early for you to show up," I said.

"Had to get some mo' clothes – playboys like me has to look fresh, you know." He cocked his head. "Kinda early yo'self, ain't you?"

"Got fired."

"Prob'ly de best break you ever got, friend. Don't worry about rent an' such – I gots enough to cover it." He grinned. "Now dat don't mean I plan to carry you for de rest of yo' life, you understand."

"It ain't the money so much," I said. "I just like to feel like I'm doin' somethin' worthwhile."

"What is it exactly dat makes sweepin' off dem decks so all-fired worthwhile?"

I shrugged. "It's hard to explain. I just ain't much of a lounger, I reckon."

Sid knelt down beside me on one knee. "All my life I been watchin' men like you, Alfred. Watchin' 'em work dey self right into de ground, strippin' de flesh right offen dey fingers,'till dey've wore theirselfs plumb out. An' den die.

"Well not me, son. Life is for livin', not for throwin' away. If a feller was to take a full whiskey bottle an' bust it over a rock jest to kill a fly – well, I reckon dat would be useful an' worthwhile. But it'd be awful damn stupid."

"I reckon you may have a point."

"You know I do. One thing we got in common, Alfred, you an' me – all these pore folks thumpin' on their Bibles an' dreamin' 'bout de Promise-Land, but we knows better. If'n dey is such a place, we know it ain't gonna help us much. No more'n it did pore old Lonnie. Problem wid you is – you don't believe in de hereafter, an' you afraid to live in de here an' now."

I had no answer for him. Sid stood up, fresh clothes over his arm, and headed for the door.

"I aim to cure you of dat problem, Brother Alfred," he said. "If'n it takes me twenty mo' years." He smiled – wide and clean – then tossed his dice into the air and disappeared.

Chapter Twenty-One

"Alfred!" someone was shouting. "Alfred!"

I was standing outside the shack talking to Rodney. Sid had been gone for two hours – the sky was turning dusky.

Earl was running toward me as fast as he could go, arms beating the air like he was trying to take off and fly.

"What's eatin' you?" I said when he reached me.

"The micks. They got ahold of Jack. They tore him into pieces, man, and dragged him down the street. Now they're comin' this way – gatherin' more and more micks into their crowd as they go."

"I reckon it's about time for 'em," Rodney said. "We overdue." He talked about it with the emotion of a man describing a rain shower.

"What do folks around here usually do when this happens?" I said.

"Go to ground," Rodney said. "Burrow down and hide like a rabbit."

"Don't you fight back?"

They both stared at me like dumb animals. "What good would that do?" Earl said.

"What good? Hell! It would stop them people from doin' whatever they want to us. It would make 'em think twice next time!"

"It'd make 'em mad," Rodney said calmly.

"There must be hundreds of people livin' in this neighborhood. Why the hell don't *we* get mad for a change?"

Rodney shook his head like he was dealing with a young child, and limped off. Earl scampered away too.

I ran into the house and got my revolver. I was ready. I had done been through too much and fought too many men to roll over now, not to satisfy a bunch of drunken thugs.

I went back outside to see that the mob had arrived. They was about four blocks away, smashing windows and torching buildings at random. Women was screaming. A few of the rioters had guns with them – I watched in disbelief as they pulled a colored man right out of his house and blowed him to bloody rags with a shotgun.

I ran in the other direction. There was nothing I could do for these people. I had to find Sid – he didn't have sense enough to take care of himself. I wished now that I had gone with him before on one of his sprees, so I would know where his haunts was.

I didn't get far. The mob had split into factions and was seeping into the neighborhood like floodwater. They had me cut off.

About a dozen of them was coming toward me.

"There's another one, boyos," one of them said. "Kill him too!"

I sped up, running straight at them – which made them pause a bit, unsure of theirselfs. I pulled out my pistol and fired as I ran. The crowd parted, but they left a couple of their members to lie bleeding on the cobblestone. I leaped over the bodies without breaking stride. A thought briefly entered my mind – how many lives have I taken in the last five years? But I pushed it away and concentrated on staying alive.

"After him, boys!" someone cried. "Get him!"

They was pounding on my heels. A few of them had brung guns and I heard bullets smacking into the pavement around me. I would not have thought it possible to run any faster than I already was, but the popping of guns made me pick up steam like you wouldn't believe.

I had run plumb out of the colored neighborhood. I was twisting and turning my way through alleys and around corners, trying to reach the river. I risked a quick glimpse behind me. Some of my pursuers had broke off, in search of easier prey, but about half-a-dozen of them kept up the chase. Maybe they was friends of the men I shot.

I pulled ahead of them a little bit, though I knowed I hadn't lost them – they'd be coming around the corner soon, like they had been for twenty minutes. To make things worse, more white folks was milling together and heading for the Eighth ward to join the fun. But they was ignoring me, maybe considering me the private property of whoever was chasing me – my first enemies was the only ones I had to be directly worried about, at least for the moment.

I had found the river. I vaulted over a handrail and slipped into the water, hoping I didn't leave too many ripples. I stayed under for as long as I could. When I peeped out I seen my pursuers running up and down the street in confusion, so frenzied to find me they was practically foaming at the mouth. More people joined with them in their search.

I decided that the river was my safest bet for awhile yet. I swam beneath a small pier, grabbed hold of a stray rope, and just floated there. Folks in the streets was still in a mad fit – a few other colored people had followed in my path and run straight into the mob. I could do nothing for them, and very little for myself should I be caught. My powder was wet, and the revolver probably useless – I sure didn't want to have to try it.

The sky clouded up, bringing dark more quickly than usual.

Rain was coming down in sheets but it didn't slow up the rioters. I crawled out of the water under the cover of the storm and hid in the shadows – it was dawn, though, before I felt safe enough to venture out.

The police was stirring around too, now that the riot was over and it was safe to keep the peace. Broken glass littered the streets I had run down the evening before.

My neighborhood looked about as bombed out as the Crater in Petersburg. Windows was busted and some houses was burned to the ground – though I could see my little shack, and it seemed to be safe enough.

A few bodies lay in the street. The scared folks who had made their way back to their houses was afraid to draw attention to themselves by touching the corpses.

One dead man grabbed my eye –he was white. I wondered why his comrades had not carried him away when they left, instead of running the risk of angered Negroes dishonoring his body. I found the answer when I got close to him. It was poor Mister Schwartz. The mob had beaten him to death for his kindness to us.

Three men was hanged from the rusty lamp-posts lining our street. I stood beneath one of them, blinking back the rain that pelted my face. I reached up and pried open the fingers of the clenched hand – Sid's dice clattered to the pavement. The once-warm face which had never gone an hour without smiling was now puffed and bruised and unrecognizable. Rain rolled freely over the bulging eyes.

I leaned against the lamp-post and slid slowly to the ground, my face buried in my hands. I took them away and leaped up.

I screamed what was at first a silent scream – it seemed to take forever for the sound to come out of my twisted mouth.

"No more!" I screamed. "No more! No more!"

I raised both shaking fists at the stormy sky. "Promise-Land!" I yelled. "Is this your damn Promise-Land? Is this where you leadin' us to? I cain't stand no more of it, do you hear me?"

I went into the shack and quietly cleaned and reloaded my gun. Then I slung my few belongings over my shoulder and started walking. I was going west to St. Louis, to find my woman whether she wanted to be found or not. I passed by the docks and seen the tall ships coming in. I never had gotten onto the deck of one of them things.

The hell with them anyway.

It took me three months before I reached St. Louis. I worked bussing tables in a fairly nice restaurant - the food was good, and at least I got to set in the kitchen on my lunch break and eat it.

I walked the streets of the colored neighborhoods looking for her face, describing her to everyone I met. I had no idea what I would do if I actually found her, I had never thought that far ahead. I was being pulled along by a deep aching need that ground away at my soul, like a man lost in the desert. It wasn't even Frankie's love that drawed me, because I knowed I had lost that. It was the solidness of her. I wanted something. Something that used to be mine and could be again, something I could anchor my spirit to - I felt like it was on the verge of blowing away.

"I seen that woman," Charley said one day. Charley was a waiter at the restaurant - he was cockeyed, and we all made fun of him every once in awhile. But not to his face. He was too kind of a man to do that to.

"What woman?"

"That'un you're all the time goin' on about. Looks just like you describe her, and I heared another woman pass her on the street and call her Frankie."

I dropped a whole stack of dishes on the table. None of them broke, but I wouldn't have cared if they did.

"Where is she?"

"Across the street, in the butcher shop."

I ripped off my apron and throwed it on the floor, then headed outside.

"Hey," Charley said. "You can't just run off like that. You'll get fired."

I kept walking. I grabbed my cap as I went out the kitchen door - my old army kepi with the infantry insignia still pinned on the front.

I ran into the butcher shop, but the only customer there was an old colored man. "Where's she at?" I shouted at the butcher.

"Who?"

"The woman who was just here."

"I don't know, boy. She just walked out a minute ago."

"Which way'd she go?"

"I don't follow every Negro that comes here out the door."

I rushed outside and scanned the crowd desperately. Then, finally, I seen her – just in time, too, for she turned the far corner. Another minute and I would've lost her.

I followed her at a careful distance. I wanted to rush up to her, but something held me back. Then she turned down a path and went into a little shack, and it was too late for me to just pop up in front of her.

I stood in front of the shack, staring at it, my heart pounding. My mind raced around in circles, trying to find the right words.

"Whatcha doin', Mister?"

A little boy stood next to me, looking up with curious eyes. "Nothin'," I told him.

"Are you lookin' for my daddy?"

"No." I glanced over at him – the wide eyes stood out darkly against his creamy coffee skin. "What's your name, son?"

"Billy."

"Billy." I longed to scoop him up in my arms. "How do you like your daddy, Billy?"

Billy shrugged. "Fine, I reckon. He whups me some, when I'm bad. But he loves me." The little eyes lit up. "He tells me so."

"Hello, Alfred."

She was there, not five feet away from me. Her face was calm and peaceful. Even though she was so close, she was holding her eyes a long ways off from me – just like the last time I seen her.

"Hello, Frankie."

"Go and play, Billy. Mama gonna be on in a minute."

He left.

"Where's Jenny?"

"Jenny gone. De pneumonia took her two year ago."

"Not my little Jenny. Not my baby." I felt my face turn dark. "She might not of caught no pneumonia if you'd kep' her at home where she belonged."

"Maybe not. But I left, an' she gone. What you doin' here, Alfred?'

"I don't know."

"Ain't no use in it. I got a whole 'nother life now, wid a new man an' two mo' young uns. A man dat won't go off an' leave me alone like you done – after I ax'd you not to. Don't wanna remember dat other life no mo'.."

I sighed and looked around – anywhere but at her. I nodded as I bit back the tears.

She stared at my cap. "I see you still playin' sojer."

I shrugged. I thought about telling her how I had blown the last of her precious LaRue brothers clear to hell. But it didn't matter.

"You can't stay here, Alfred."

I nodded again. "It was good though, wasn't it?" My voice broke. "For awhile."

"It was real good. It was real good, Alfred." She touched my face, just for a moment. "You a good man, Alfred. Go on, and find yo' life."

I watched her disappear into the shack. I walked away – I had no notion in the world where I was walking to.

"Hey, sarge!"

I kept going, not sure at first that the words was directed at me.

"I mean you. The colored infantryman."

I turned around. An army sergeant was seated at a little table at the entranceway to a nearby building. He pointed at my own faded stripes.

"You're a veteran, I see."

"Yeah."

"What regiment?"

"Fourth South Carolina Volunteer Colored Infantry."

"I'll be. I see you're still carrying that military pride. Ever thought about joining back up?"

I shook my head, confused. "Nobody invited me to."

"That's changed now, Sergeant. We need men like you. Do you know what this place is?"

"No."

"Recruiting station. Tenth Cavalry. It's a colored outfit – Congress decided to bring 'em back. And we need experienced noncoms."

"But there ain't no war."

"This regiment is going west. There's always a war out there – the Injuns are always scalping somebody. There's the Tenth, the Ninth Cavalry, and the Twenty-Fourth and Twenty-Fifth Infantry. All colored."

I found myself nodding. "What's your name, soldier?" he asked me.

"Mann. Alfred Mann."

"Sign here, Sergeant Mann."

It all made sense now. I had found what I was looking for in St. Louis after all. Solidness. Something to anchor my spirit to.

I was twenty-nine years old, and once more I was a soldier in the United States Army.

Part IV: The Buffalo Soldier

Chapter Twenty-Two

I seen her for the first time at Fort Leavenworth, Kansas. She was the one wearing a purple silk handkerchief on her head. I glimpsed her out of the corner of my eye and, before I knowed it, I was staring at her. There was several brightly-clothed young women standing around the parade ground watching our mounted drill – but there was no one else like this honey-skinned girl.

She watched me with what appeared at first to be a casual interest. After a little while, though I could feel the intensity in her eyes. She did not smile. She seemed to be judging me in some stern way, like I was an animal at an auction that might or might not be worth a small investment.

I called my men to a halt and dismissed them. I was First Sergeant of Company M, Tenth Cavalry, and I was trying to whip my new recruits into something resembling military order. It was not proving to be easy.

I trotted my black mare slowly past the crowd of young women – all the while I studied the honey girl.

"You handle 'em well," she said – her tone was neither friendly nor rude. I could not tell if she meant horses or men or something else.

"Yes, ma'am," I told her. "I do." And I trotted right past her.

"Who is that girl back yonder?" I asked James Jefferson. He was one of the sergeants in my company.

"Isabella somethin'-or-other," Jefferson said. "Farrier, I think. She's Injun."

"Looks colored to me."

"Seminole. Her granddaddy was a runaway slave. Her pa and her brothers are Injun scouts. Why you want to know, anyways? You got somethin' special in mind?"

"Nothin' special," I said. "Just wonderin' who she was."

I had the girl's name and background. I still wondered who she was—especially since she acted like she already knowed me after just a few minutes. I might have to prove her wrong.

The next day I looked for the Seminole girl but she was nowhere to be seen. I was kind of relieved and disappointed, all at the same time. Like before, there was several women clustered around—some was washerwomen, some was soldiers' wives - I took a second to scan their faces, just in case. I realized that my own men was staring at me, waiting on my orders, and I was uncomfortably embarrassed for a moment.

Across the parade ground, where Company G was drilling, stood First Sergeant Abe Armstrong. We was equal in rank, and had become fast friends. Right now he was looking back and forth between me and the crowd of women, snickering behind his hand - Jefferson must have run and told him about my experience the day before. I turned back to my Company M boys and glanced at Jefferson—he shrugged, grinning, and quickly turned his attention to his own platoon. Jefferson might be a sergeant, but I was his First Sergeant—and I could make life difficult for him. I smiled myself, in his direction, and he swallowed.

I paced slowly back and forth in front of the recruits, giving them all an impassive look. None of them moved or looked away, which was good. I drawed all the air into my lungs that I could get, so as to make my voice boom out enough for all the men to hear me. There was about a hundred of them.

"Sergeant Jefferson! Fall out!"

Jefferson stepped forward, whirled around, and repeated the order to his men. A dozen blue-clad troopers stepped out from among their comrades.

"We have already spent time gettin' familiar with our mounts," I said. "Today we're gonna try somethin' a little more advanced than just canterin' around. This is the United States Cavalry, this ain't ridin' ponies on Grandpa's farm."

At my signal a string of black horses was brought forward. It was the tradition of the Tenth for each company to ride horses all the same color. Company A rode white, Company B rode chestnut, Company C rode spotted. Company M's horses was all solid black.

I swung up into the McClellan saddle.

"Mount up," I ordered, and Jefferson's boys obeyed. The other platoons stood motionless and watched.

"Draw sabers," I said, as I drawed my own. There was a loud metal rasp as a dozen men pulled steel from scabbard. One of the men giggled just a little. I trotted my black up to him.

"What is your name, Private?"

"Wilson, suh." He wasn't giggling no more.

"Is somethin' funny, Private Wilson? Am I amusing you in some way?"

"No suh, Sergeant Mann. Suh."

"What are you findin' so damn funny then, Private?"

Wilson's face colored up. "I just always wanted me one of dese pigstickers, sergeant. Jest like de old colonel back home."

"This is not a pig-sticker, and it does not belong to the old colonel back home. It is the saber of the United States Army, the army that whipped the old colonel back home, an' now you have got one. I am fixin' to show you how to use it. Would you like that, Wilson?"

"Yes suh!"

"Good. Just remember, you don't giggle out in the open air unless you're on leave or unless I order you to. I can tell you now, neither one's gonna happen soon."

I turned my horse so that I could face all the mounted men. I saluted them with my saber.

"Go on," Jefferson said. "Salute the sergeant!" They returned the salute. I showed them how to thrust, how to slash, how to parry. Then I spurred my mount and galloped toward a line of poles set into the ground at about the height of a man. I leaned over in the saddle and took a whack at one of them, cutting a chunk out of it. Then I returned to the men.

"Now each of you in turn," I said. The recruits attempted to follow my example. The first one lost his balance when he leaned forward, and almost fell out of the saddle. He missed the pole completely. The next man did a fairly decent job. The third man wasn't holding his saber tight enough, and the pole knocked it out of his hand. I sighed, running my hand over my face and stroking the thick mustache I had grown since returning to the army.

The fourth man hesitated, his eyes a little wide.

"What are you waitin' for, boy?" I demanded.

"I ain't never rode nothin' but a broken-down plowhorse, suh. I ain't so good at this."

"Reckon you should've thought about that before you joined the cavalry."

"I don't think I can do this, sergeant. I'm liable to break my neck."

"I can't do it for you. I ain't yo' mammy. If any of you men tries to go draggin' on my tit, you'll get a mouthful of somethin you didn't bargain on. Now ride!"

The frightened man rode. I was not all that surprised when he fell off the horse just as it reached the pole. I trotted over and looked down at him.

"Get up, soldier. What's yo' name?"

The trooper brushed the dust off himself. "Collins." When he seen the angry glare I was throwing at him he remembered to add the "sir".

"If that post was an Indian, Collins, yo' throat would be cut by now. Reckon you better mount up an' try it again."

"Reckon I had, sir."

Collins tried again, and this time did a passable job.

"Well done, young soldier," I told him.

I couldn't be too critical of Collins. It had taken me a little while to get used to galloping around at breakneck speeds on horseback. After several months, though, it felt almost the same to me as walking. And despite the troopers' fears, there was no widowmakers among our herd. They was all rundown and old, the castoffs of other regiments. White regiments. Our colonel, Benjamin Grierson, had been raising a royal fuss ever since we arrived at Leavenworth for better horses and equipment. So far we had not got it.

Grierson himself, I had been told, had to overcome a lifelong fear of horses. He had first joined the infantry during the Civil War, but had got transferred to the cavalry.

Grierson, a mild-mannered piano teacher, bore an ugly scar on his face from a childhood kick by a horse. He managed his fear of them, though, and led a famous cavalry raid behind Reb lines that made him a hero.

I spent the morning drilling my men – not just Jefferson's but the whole company.

Pretty soon I had them charging forward by platoon to whack the posts, then wheeling back and passing the next wave as they charged. There was more than one near-collision, and more than one resentful trooper snuck a glance in my direction.

Them fellows had been recruited from all over the South, and from several Northern cities. They came from all walks of life, and some of them was probably common criminals. Some wasn't really healthy enough to be in that uniform, and some wasn't really smart enough – but they had all signed on to serve the U.S. Government for five years at thirteen dollars a month plus room and board. They realized that it was the best employment deal they was likely to be offered.

I intended to make men out of them, proud men, before their first year was out.

Captain Jordan, who had been watching the whole time, dismissed the men for mess.

For the first time I noticed the presence of the Seminole girl—she was standing far behind us, and when she seen me she turned slowly away and walked off.

Abe was standing beside me now, grinning.

"Looks like you got yo'self a admirer, Alfred."

"She might just be admirin' my scalp."

"That has to be it. Still, there ain't nothin' better than wedded bliss."

"I don't know about that," I said.

Abe shrugged. "Did yo' boys do any better'n mine did this mornin'?"

"I doubt it. Most of 'em ain't used to ridin'—they startin' to figure out just what it means to be a 'raw recruit'."

Abe laughed. "We gotta take 'em to the firin' range tomorrow. I'm plumb scared of that. Say now, Alfred—I got me some more of that good peach brandy. What say I drop by yo' quarters this evenin' and swap war stories?"

"What'll Jessie say?"

"What Jessie don't know won't hurt me."

I chuckled. "If they ain't nothin' better'n wedded bliss, how come you're always sneakin' off from yo' wife?"

"It's just like them young soldiers is learnin' today, Alfred. You set too long in the saddle an' you'll get chafed. Set longer'n that an' you can get used to it—which might be even worse."

I laughed. "I'll be there," I said. "An' I've got a couple of clean glasses."

"I might bring Dickerson with me. It never hurts to liquor up the Sergeant-Major ever' once in awhile, you know."

Abe walked off. I stayed a couple of minutes, staring at the spot where the Seminole girl had stood.

That evening after supper I trudged toward my tent. The mud came almost to my ankles, and my every step was accompanied by a wet sucking sound. The Tenth was quartered on low ground—the recent rains had turned it into a swamp, and a few of our men was now in the hospital with pneumonia.

It was all because of the Third Cavalry's General Hoffman, who was in command of Fort Leavenworth. Hoffman scorned Negroes and didn't seem to think too highly of white officers who served with them. We wound up with the worst of everything. Colonel Grierson asked for our quarters to be moved to someplace more comfortable and healthy, but his request was denied. Then he asked for wooden walking boards to be laid down so at least we didn't have to slog through the mud, but that was denied too. Meanwhile our men was reprimanded for being "untidy" because their quarters and clothing was often muddy.

Hoffman gave orders that no colored soldier could come within fifteen yards of a white soldier during drill, and we was not allowed to march with the other troops—we had to stand at attention.

Once, on the parade ground, Hoffman had called us - for maybe the hundredth time - the Tenth Colored Cavalry. Grierson walked up to him, his long beard flapping in the breeze, and loudly said, "We are not the Tenth Colored Cavalry, sir, we are the Tenth United States Cavalry."

Hoffman had stared at him dully.

Grierson paid him no mind. He just stood there a minute and slowly scanned our ranks, a look of pride in his face.

"Tenth United States Cavalry," he had repeated. "And they will do."

Grierson was like that, see. He was usually mild and gentle in the way he dealt with us, but he would stand up and scrap like a wildcat in our defense. He had volunteered for the job, too—just like in the Civil War, not many white officers was willing to accept a position in a colored regiment.

George Custer had turned down command of a black outfit and held out instead until he was offered the Seventh Cavalry—probably lucky for us, as it turned out.

Grierson went a step beyond what Wentworth had done in the old Fourth South Carolina Volunteer Colored Infantry. He not only recognized our humanity, but he actually believed in us as men – right from the very start. The way that he looked at a fellow told him that Grierson had no doubts at all that the man would do the exact right thing. The men loved him for it.

I kept on waiting for the colonel to show his true colors. I watched and listened, confident that eventually he would show a superior bearing – more than he would to white soldiers. But he never did. Not in them first few months, and not ever. I still kept my guard up. But as the months wore on – and then the years – my heart softened to him. It was still suspicious toward most white folks, as Sid had said, but I found room in it for the old piano teacher.

I reached my tent just minutes ahead of Abe, as it turned out. I just had time to sit on my hard cot, pull off my boots, and loosen my braces before I heard his voice outside the canvas door-flap.

"You in there, Alfred?"

"Yeah, I'm in here. Come on in."

Abe stepped through the flap, flashed me a conspiring grin, and winked. He held a sack tightly under his arm. Close on his heels, as I suspected, was Sergeant-Major George Dickerson.

I stood up and swept off my white hat.

"Lord have mercy," I said. "I am honored by whatever it is that brings yo' great person into my humble tent."

"Quit smartin' off, son," George said, "and fetch out some glasses."

George had a habit of calling all the first sergeants 'son', even though he was only a few years older than me and Abe.

A faint touch of gray was beginning to show at George's temples, and in his goatee.

I pushed a chair forward with my bare foot and George took it. Abe seated himself in the remaining chair and unwrapped his prize; he twisted the top off and held his hand out for a glass. As he poured the brandy, he let out a long whistle.

"You drink deep of this stuff, Alfred," he said as he handed me the glass. "It'll take yo' tortured mind off that Seminole gal."

My eyes darted toward George – he was smirking. "Abe told me 'bout yo' new friend," George said. "Don't pay him no mind, though. Abe wants ever'body to be as whupped as he is."

"Whupped my foot," Abe said. "I'm a happy married man."

"You just watch yo'self, Sergeant Armstrong," George said. "If you keep pushin' matrimony at us like you do, you ain't gonna have no mo' bachelor friends to hide you out when you wants a little nip of whiskey."

I chuckled. I was reminded a little of the Saturday nights in the hollow, back on the Moss place—just sitting back with friends, drinking and laughing.

There was some big differences, though. I wasn't hiding now. I had nothing to hide from. I was a free man. I didn't have to steal a little bit of freedom here and yonder like I used to, and the uniform I wore meant I could hold my head up anytime I wanted.

Of course, Abe Armstrong did remind me of Sid a little bit. He had the same foolish sense of humor and contagious smile, and the way he was riding me about the Seminole girl put me in mind of the way Sid used to josh me about Frankie.

Abe was very different from Sid, though, in one real important way. He was always willing to buckle down and work, and to take on responsibility. To most folks that would mean he was a much better man than Sid had ever been.

Fond as I had become of Abe, I missed Sid anyhow.

"Looks like we finally gonna be gettin' out of this mudhole," George said, then he took a long sip.

Me and Abe looked at him. "Well?" Abe said after a few seconds. "You talkin', or ain't you?"

George smiled. "You never heard nothin' from me, now. But it seems the Cheyennes is gettin' stirred up somethin' awful."

"Go on," Abe prompted.

"The Cheyennes around here," George said, "and the Comanches and Kiowas to the south, they took advantage of the Civil War to take back some of the land they'd lost before. They settled down an' signed a treaty in 'sixty-five, but neither Kansas or Texas would give up enough land to make a reservation for 'em. So they been wanderin' around without no home all this time. Reckon they got tired of it."

"What've they been doin?" I asked. Indians was still mysterious to me then.

The Tenth had never seen actual combat, and the only Indians I had ever seen was the ones who loafed around the settlements in ratty blankets, begging for food. In fact, nobody I personally knowed had ever actually been in an Indian fight – nobody except the scouts, that is. One scout, Brit Johnson, was a colored man—and I reckon he knowed as much about Indians as just about anybody.

"They been doin' the usual," George said. "Raidin ranches, attackin' stage coaches. Here lately, though, they been focusin' on the railroads. They've hit several rail stations and work crews—the whole Kansas Pacific operation has been brung to a halt."

"And that was the last straw, huh?" Abe said.

George nodded. "Killin' civilians is bad enough, but stoppin' the railroad? The government sho' enough won't put up with that."

"So we're movin' out?" I said.

George nodded again. "A few companies is goin' to Fort Harker, some to Fort Wallace, some to Fort Hays."

He raised a glass. "We've already seen the elephant, my friends," he said, "an' we know what the battlefield means." George and Abe had both served under Colonel Shaw in the Fifty-Fourth Massachusetts. "'Fore long we gonna be leadin' these green boys right into hell. That's what they're payin' us for, though."

Abe poured himself another glass. "I'd still rather have a few dozen Indians shootin' arrows at me than have to face ten thousand Reb muskets."

Me and George both mumbled agreement with our friend's words. We would soon have reason to reconsider our feelings on the subject.

I discovered that fighting Indians was like fighting Rebs, at least in one respect – most of a fellow's time is spent waiting. It wasn't idle waiting, though, we had plenty to do.

We went out on scout patrols, for one—all over the place. We scouted the Arkansas River, and the Saline, and the Solomon, all without seeing a hostile. We pulled guard duty too, escorting stages and watching over rail crews.

And we drilled. Every chance we got, we set them boys to practicing, until they had learned everything they could learn on a parade ground. They was unblooded and untested. We would not know the truth about these men until time—and fire—brung it out of them.

One good thing about Fort Hays, that's where most of the Seminole scouts ended up going. Brit Johnson wound up at Fort Hays, too, but as much as I enjoyed the man's company, news of it didn't excite me quite the same as did news of the Seminoles – and their women.

Soon the honey-girl was watching me. She was sneaky about it, true, but she was watching me nonetheless.

I got to know Isabella's brothers on those many long patrols. Zeke and Pedro Farrier was frequent companions of

Brit, and they stalked silent as hawks. They never spoke much, even when they wasn't hunting or trapping, though. I struggled for a way to ask them about their saucy sister without drawing too much attention to myself and my interest, yet still prying an answer out of them.

Brit Johnson made up for the Farrier brothers in talking. He spun many yarns for me—some of them no doubt true—about his travels and adventures. He also taught me the history of the tribes close by, and how to track a man. He was working on teaching me the Indian sign language, but I was a slow learner in that category.

All the while Brit's little terrier, Jack, sat on the saddle in front of its master, scanning the horizon. I could've sworn old Jack was looking for Indians. Brit was real fond of his tiny dog, and had refused to trade him to many angry Indians who had coveted Jack for a supper dish.

Brit claimed Jack was his partner, not his property, and he could not morally sell him.

I suspected that Brit had been sold like a beast himself, sometime earlier in his life.

We finally got our chance for some real action one hot June day when a frazzled-up railroad worker come tearing into the fort. His horse was lathered up something awful, and he wasn't doing much better. The poor fellow practically fell off his horse and into the arms of several troopers.

"Injuns!" he croaked, barely able to catch breath enough to be able to speak at all.

"I'm the onliest one that got away!"

"Where?" I demanded. From the corner of my eye I seen Sam Jordan, my company's captain, rushing over to us. He paused just long enough to exchange a few words with a corporal. The corporal then ran back toward the officers' quarters, I reckon to fetch Colonel Grierson.

"Carter's Station," the civilian said. I nodded. I knowed the place. It was a temporary work camp about thirteen miles away to the north.

"How many?" Jordan said.

"'Bout a dozen of 'em. They came whoopin' over the rise. They was on us before we could do anything about it. Them other fellas never had a chance – they woulda got me too, only I happened to be on my horse. I was fixin' to head to town for supplies." The man sobbed. "Don't need 'em now, I reckon."

Colonel Grierson had arrived. He stood and watched over us, hands clasped behind his back—his face showed no emotion, but there was a hint of sadness in his shadowed eyes.

"Captain Jordan," he said. "Take the remaining half of your company and overtake the hostiles."

Part of Company M was out on patrol, to the south of Fort Hays – Brit was with them.

That would leave us with thirty-four troopers plus the Farrier brothers as scouts. We would outnumber the hostiles three-to-one—if we could catch them.

Our first stop was to be Carter's Station, to pick up the trail. The camp was silent as midnight, so still that it made my skin itch. Plumes of smoke crawled up to mingle with the clouds. We rode through the charred ruins of the workers' shack—just beyond it the naked bodies was scattered. I imagined I felt eyes trained on my back, though I knowed the Indians was long gone. It felt like the prairie itself was alive and watching us with hatred, knowing we pursued its natural children.

We rode closer to the pale bodies. Now we could see the evidence of Indian slaughter—the bloody skulls, the death wounds. Some had missing eyes or noses or ears or privates.

All of the men had one arm cut, some so deep that it was severed.

"Cheyenne," Zeke Farrier mumbled. His skinny brown face had already turned away from the scene, like it was the most common sight in the world, and searched the skyline like a hungry hawk.

"It's their brand mark," his younger brother, Pedro, explained to me. At least he strung together a sentence every once in awhile. "It's why the Cheyenne are also called the Cut-Arm People." He moved away then to help his brother look for sign.

Our green troopers was still staring at the mutilated railroad workers. Even Jordan, a veteran of Grant's army, was frozen in place. I could feel their terror rising up like the smoke, growing with every second that the gruesome sight pressed in on their mind. I choked back my own fear as best I could, trying to look unconcerned. I found myself wishing the Seminoles would locate the trail quick—too much time spent dwelling on the situation would unnerve the men before the fight even began.

"Northeast," Zeke said, and without another word he nudged his gelding into a trot.

Jordan snapped out of his stupor and urged us all forward.

We had traveled about a dozen miles when the scouts reined up. Zeke half-turned in the saddle to face us. "Another band," he said.

"About ten more," Pedro added. "They've joined the first group, and they've headed for the Saline." He glanced up at the sky. "Only another hour of tracking-light," he said.

"Won't catch 'em today," Zeke commented.

We kept going until the sky was dark gray.

"Better stop," said Zeke. "It's too dark. We might miss something."

"All right," Jordan said, reluctantly. "We'll camp here for the night."

"No fires," Zeke said. "No coffee, and no cigarettes."

We sat hunched in the cold dark, miserable and scared. None of us slept much—we didn't trust the pickets to keep the Cheyennes from cutting our throats while we napped.

I finally managed to doze off for a couple of hours. I was woken at dawn—not by a gentle shake from one of our guards, but by the wild shrieks of furious Cheyenne warriors.

It was hard to tell exactly, they was moving around so fast, but it looked to me like there was seventy-five or eighty of them.

The scout, Pedro, had grabbed his horse by the reins and wrestled it to the ground, until the beast was lying on its side.

"Get them horses down!" Pedro shouted. "If the Cheyennes kill 'em, we're done for!"

I followed Pedro's example. "You heard the man, young soldiers," I hollered. "Move it! 'Less'n you want to walk home through these Injuns!"

The horses went down, and so did we. Arrows thunked into the ground around me.

One man's leg was pinned into the dirt. Our rifle-fire drove them back out of range – I reloaded my weapon and thanked Sweet Jesus that there was now such a thing as a Spencer repeating rifle, instead of the breechloading muskets I had shot at the Rebs with a few years earlier.

It was far from over, though. They'd shoot a few arrows at us to keep us on our toes. Then every once in awhile they'd regroup and charge us from every side. We lost a few horses and had a few more men wounded—Sergeant Bill Christy, a free-born farmer from Pennsylvania, got a arrow through the eye and into the brain. He was the Tenth's first mortality.

It went on like that for six hours.

"We almost out of ammunition, Captain," I finally had to inform Jordan.

The captain took a deep breath, then winced – he had taken an arrow in the hip. I'd had to pull it out of the bone.

"Tell the boys to mount up," he said. "We can't stay here."

I lifted my head so as to be heard better.

"Hit the saddle, soldiers!" I yelled. "We bustin' out!"

Soon, we was mounted up and charging. Them Cheyennes was about as surprised by our move as we had been when they woke us up. We broke through them, but they was on our tail like hornets.

The braves chased us for fifteen miles. Seven or eight of our horses was carrying two riders – here's where all that horseback drilling paid off, as we had to ride and fire our rifles at our pursuers at the same time.

When we came in sight of the fort the Indians broke off—just in time, too, for the horses was about to give out, the doubled-up ones especially.

We dashed into the safety of Fort Hays. The Tenth had survived its first encounter with the enemy—barely. We had one man dead and six wounded, but that was after facing a force twice our size.

It was only a brief taste of what was to come.

Chapter Twenty-Three

"My name is Isabella."

I turned slowly around and looked at her – she stood only a couple of inches shorter than me, and her limbs flowed when she walked like a Carolina willow. She was colored, but she was Indian. Her head was held up, like somebody who had never had to bow it down and her big eyes was afraid to look at no one.

I had just shut the corral door and was headed for the chow hall. Dust still hung in the air, raised by the horses of my returning patrol.

Her name was Isabella.

I nodded. "I know," I said.

"And you're Alfred. My brothers tell me you're a good soldier. They say you done good in that fight the other day."

I shrugged. "Zeke and Pedro are good scouts. We might have took some heavy losses if not for them."

"They're Seminoles," Isabella said, letting that fact alone answer any praise directed at her brothers.

She took a couple of steps forward and tilted her head back a little, so that her gaze locked onto mine.

"You gonna take me to the Fourth of July dance next week," she asked. At least I think she was asking, it was hard to say. She might well have been telling me.

"Well, yeah," I said. "Course."

It was Isabella's turn to nod, and the faintest trace of a smile played at her lips. It was barely enough to notice, but more than enough to pull my heart right up in my throat, like iron going to a magnet.

"Do you know how to dance?" she asked.

"No, ma'am," I answered. I had never thought about that. I felt a moment of panic - I might have talked myself right out of the chance to escort her.

"I can teach you," Isabella said. She took one final bold step, closing the distance between us, and gave my cheek a light kiss. Then she was gone.

I stood there for several seconds, then shook my head in a failed effort to clear it. This girl had set my world to spinning and I had no control over it.

I had been drawn to Isabella since the first time I seen her, but I didn't want to be. I'd had enough of that business with Frankie to last me the rest of my life. But Isabella Farrier, she somehow knowed just which way to tug at me to make me respond. I always considered myself a strong man - why was it that these women kept on taking charge of me? I didn't care to think too much on that one. I chalked it up to shyness and left it at that.

"See them birds flyin' up yonder, boys? That means water is close."

I noticed that the faces of the men nearest me brightened up considerably at my words.

Like most of the huge area we patrolled, the land we was riding through was rough and dry. And there was no trees - that had been one of the hardest things for me to get used to. A man could ride all day without finding any shade.

"Better go light on what you've got," Brit Johnson said. "We're a ways from water yet." The men's faces fell again.

"Them's quail you seen," Brit told me. "Quail can go a long time without no drink. If it was doves, now, it'd be a different story. Doves have to go to water every day."

I nodded, and let that information settle into my brain real good, like I done with all the things Brit told me. The Negro scout never stopped amazing me with the things he knowed. We patrolled all over Indian Territory, West Kansas, and North Texas - and Brit always knowed exactly where he was, just from looking at the land around him. I never seen him read no map.

"Tell your men to put a bullet in their mouth and suck on it," he directed me. "It'll make their mouth water, make it a little easier to bear up under the thirst."

"I thought you was supposed to use a pebble."

"Bullets work better. Copper works even better'n that – but the best thing is prickly pear. 'Pears good for cleanin' up muddy water a mite, as well – you peel it an' let it sink to the bottom of your water, and quite a bit of the dirt will stick to it.

"Wild mustangs can help you find water, too. They need to drink every day – antelopes don't – and what you do is watch how they walk. If they're strung out an' walkin' steady they're goin' to water. If they're scattered and grazing as they go, they're coming back from water."

I chuckled and shook my head. "You heard the man, fellers. He says suck the bullet, we better suck the bullet."

That night when we made camp, Trooper Wilson fished out his corncob pipe. He lifted it up and waved it in my direction.

"Is it all right, Sarge?"

I glanced at Brit, and he nodded.

"Light'er up, trooper," I said.

Wilson looked at the match in his hand warily. "Are you sure it's all right?"

"There's no Indians around for miles," Brit assured him.

"You must have spent a lot of time in this country," I said to the scout, "to know it as good as you do."

"Lived here all my life," Brit said. He tossed a little piece of raw meat to his dog, Jack.

"The fella that owned me was a peddler – a comanchero, really. Spent all my youth traveling through this country, as well as down by the border and in Old Mexico."

"What became of him?"

"Who?"

"The feller that owned you."

"Oh, him. I happened to him. Slit his throat one night and took off."

I stared at him a moment. "Are you tellin' me you a wanted man?"

The scout chuckled. "Wanted? Because of that old buzzard? Nobody missed him, believe me. I'd watched him do the same thing to many a trusting stranger. Some of 'em was whole families."

Brit stared quietly into the little fire Trooper Collins had made. He spoke no further of his past, he just sat cross-legged and absently scratched Jack's head. The ten exhausted troopers needed no urging to turn in for the night – they was soon rolled into their blankets and a few was snoring softly.

"I'll take the first watch," I told Brit. "You get some shuteye."

"Ain't that sleepy. Might as well stay up and keep you company, then take the second watch."

We sat there awhile in silence, then – when I was sure all the other men was asleep –I cleared my throat softly and spoke.

"What about them Seminole Indians? They from around here?"

"They from Florida – they lived in a big swamp called the Everglades. Them folks has got more fight in 'em than a panther with a toothache. The U.S. Army had its hands full tryin' to whip 'em – never could flush 'em all out. What ones they could catch they sent to Indian Territory.

"Turns out a lot of them Indians was colored. Slaves from all over the Deep South would run away to that swamp and get adopted into the tribe. Black Indians was the same as red Indians, in the Seminoles' eyes."

"Imagine that," I said. Maybe I had run in the wrong direction.

"But not in the white man's eyes," Brit continued. "Slavers from Arkansas started making raids into the new Seminole territory and stealing Negroes to sell into slavery.

The government never done nothin 'bout it – what did they care? Then came John Horse."

"Who's that?"

"He was born a Negro slave. He run away and married a Seminole woman, became a chief. He led hundreds of colored Seminoles across Texas and into Mexico – they sold their services to the Mexican government, helpin' guard the border agin Apaches and Comanches. An' Americans. In exchange for this the Mexicans gave 'em protection, refusing to send 'em back across the border to the U.S. government. One of John Horse's lieutenants was the son of another ex-slave – his name was Will Farrier. That was Zeke an' Pedro's pa.

"After the War, with slavery no longer bein' an issue, several dozen of 'em come back an' joined the American army, in the Seminole Negro Scouts. They're a generation or two removed from the swamp – most all of 'em has growed up in these deserts an' mountains. They fight like hell, and can track as good as an Apache."

He winked at me. "One other thing. They're real protective of their women. If anybody was to be the least bit forward with a Seminole girl, why I reckon he'd most likely wake up to find his liver hangin' on a tree limb."

"You don't say."

"I do say." Brit snickered into his hand. "From what I hear, you're prob'ly safer out on patrol in hostile territory than you would be at home."

"You may be right," I said, and smiled broadly. "Then again, I might just wind up bein' a Seminole chief."

The scout chuckled. I heard an owl in the distance – before I realized it I was scanning the darkness all around us, feeling uneasy. I seen Brit grinning at me and the unease turned into embarrassment.

"Hell," I said. "Cain't be too careful out here, can we? For all I know that was a Cheyenne brave out yonder hootin' at his buddies."

"If you listen closely," Brit said, "you can always tell the difference between a animal and a man imitatin' a animal. The human voice has a peculiar sort of echo to it - can't be disguised."

I nodded, then listened closely awhile to the sounds of the desert. I heard no suspicious echoes.

"I reckon I'll be doin' all right," I said, "if'n I can just remember all the things you been teachin' me. Maybe I can get by in this country after all."

"A man has to go on learnin' if he's gonna survive," Brit told me. "And he has to be alert every minute of every day. I've known men that spent a long lifetime on the frontier to wake up one mornin' and get swallowed; up by it, just as easy as any greenhorn."

"That's real comfortin'," I said with a little chuckle.

"You don't master this land," Brit continued, ignoring my attempt at humor. "You respect it. You admire it, and you love it -but you can't ever trust it. It's wild, you see."

He had scooped Jack up and was absently stroking his head. "I knowed a man once," he continued, "that rescued a bear cub and raised it as a pet. That bear growed up to be about as big as a house - followed the man around everywhere, did tricks, like a big dog. Then one day the man turned his back on it and the bear took a swipe at him. Smashed the poor fella's brains out. Then the bear just loped off into the woods like it was nothin' unusual."

"Why would he do that?" I said.

"Because he's a bear. It's nature, son, nature." He looked at me in a peculiar way - the firelight danced on his ebony face and his white eyes stared coldly with a wisdom and a fear and a courage I could not understand.

"A man can live off this land if he knows what he's doin'," Brit said. "But it's always lookin for a way to kill you. Eventually, it'll find one."

"The Indians seem to do all right."

"That's cause they ain't civilized men –they're natural men, with a wild spirit just like that bear. They're a part of all this," he said, waving his arm toward the darkness, "in a way that we can never be. Stupid people back East think that they can put the red man on a reservation and civilize him. It won't happen. The red man just can't live in the white man's civilized world. He'll die first – and take a lot of folks with him."

I thought for a moment, then asked, "What about the black man? Can he live in the white man's world?"

"I can't answer that one," Brit said. "I'll leave it for someone else. It's a good question, though – our ancestors had the same kind of spirit the Indians do. All I know for sure is, I don't even wanna live in the white man's world. I'd rather die out here in this one."

I peered around us, staring into the shadows at the edge of our camp. There was danger there, if not immediate – it was the same danger I had felt when looking at them slaughtered workers, even though the Indians was long gone. It was a natural, pure danger – cleaner than the threats I had faced back East.

Still, I did not believe I could ever feel completely at home in it.

I went to bed. My life I left in the hands of the rough scout and his dog, and the desert.

Off in the distance the regimental band was still playing parade music – they'd had a big day, like everybody else, what with the parade and the troopers' riding display. They played real good, the best band I had I ever heard; Colonel Grierson, the ex-music teacher, would settle for nothing less. He believed that if the Tenth could produce a top-notch band it would bolster our pride. Turned out he was right.

The last light of the late afternoon was starting to fade, and I was standing on the little street where the outpost's

Seminole Negro scouts lived. There was a dozen men altogether, most of them with families.

I was wearing my full-dress uniform, complete with shiny buttons and white gloves, and a bright helmet that had a feather crest. I removed the helmet and cradled it in my left arm. Then, with a deep breath, I stepped forward and knocked on the door of the plain-looking shack.

The door opened and Will Farrier stepped out. At around sixty years he still had a powerful build, and he carried himself with the same self-confident dignity as his daughter, Isabella. The elder Farrier's face showed more of the Negro features inherited from his father the runaway than did his own children. He wore white man's canvas pants and riding boots, but his upper body was wrapped in a wine-colored blanket and a scarf was tied around his white hair. His eyes bored into me. I like to believe that my own grandfather, on the day he stepped out of the African forests, looked like this man.

I had done some more asking around since I returned to the fort. Not only had Will Farrier helped John Horse lead his black Seminole exodus from the Territory to Mexico; in Farrier's youth he had fought as a guerrilla warrior under the legendary Seminole leader Osceola, in his swampland struggle against the very army Farrier now served. Sherman, now the commanding general of the Department of the West, had been a young officer during that war.

"Good evenin', Mister Farrier," I said. "I've come to escort yo' daughter to the dance."

He continued staring at me for several seconds without speaking, which made me uneasy. Then he nodded slightly, looking me up and down.

"I hear that you ran away from your masters to join the army," he finally said. His voice was even deeper than I expected.

"I did, suh."

"My father also made the journey from slave to warrior."
He nodded again. "Wait here."

I spied a woman inside with copper skin and iron-gray hair – I figured it must be Isabella's mother, a full-blooded Seminole.

He disappeared into the house, and a moment later Isabella stood before me. She wore a simple red dress and moccasins, and her only jewelry was a glittering cross at her throat; despite that, she had a glow, which warmed the air around her. She smiled openly, with her eyes as well as her mouth.

"I have been waiting for you," she said, and I took her arm and led her away.

The parade ground was crowded by now with soldiers and their wives and sweethearts. I felt all their eyes upon me as I entered with my Seminole princess—they must have known, as I was finally beginning to know, that there was no more escape for me. The honey girl, with all the skill of her ancestors, was entrenching herself into my heart.

Her hand on my shoulder was warm as sunshine. The directions she whispered as she waltzed and I tried was sweeter music than the band could ever play. I tried to draw up as a protection all the bittersweet memories of Frankie, and our love, and my pain – I had lost it all somehow.

I gave in. We danced.

Chapter Twenty-Four

"I'm starvin'."

The rail worker rubbed sweaty hands down his lap. "Me an' Lack is gonna go see if we can't scare up some game."

"You know how rowdy the Cheyennes an' Comanches has been lately," I told him.

My words was maybe a little sharper than they should have been. The blazing sun had my brains about half-broiled, and the boredom of just sitting in the saddle to guard this rough-mouthed railroad crew was getting to me. I knowed it was getting to the nine troopers under my command, too.

"It's dinner-time," the worker said. His name was Evans, and he acted like he didn't know what bothered him worse – being threatened by Indians or protected by Negroes.

"Maybe we can catch enough for you an' your boys too. We won't go far."

I sighed. "All right," I told him. "Private Randall!"

The young trooper nudged his horse forward. "Yes, sir."

"Escort these men on a hunting party. Make sure they're not gone too long. Jones, go with him."

Randall, Jones, and the two white men trotted away, leaving only three workers under our protection. We was expecting a couple of teamsters to roll in sometime the next day or two with supplies, but Evans just couldn't wait – he had been whining for fresh game all day long.

The hunters was barely out of sight when we heard yells and gunshots – way too many gunshots. We galloped over the rise and right into the sights of about thirty Cheyennes. One of my troopers died at once with a bullet through the throat, and another had an arrow break his collarbone. We fell back to the cover of some nearby rocks, dismounted, and began returning their fire.

Evans and Lack was dead. So was Jones. Randall had reached the safety of an overhanging rock and squeezed into the tight space beneath it. I could hear him screaming – three braves stood beside the overhang, poking spears into it. I dropped one of them, and the others scampered away. We kept up enough covering fire that no one else ventured over to Randall's hiding place, but then again neither could we. The wind carried an occasional moan back to my ears.

The Indians, between gunshots, hooted and yelled at us. One of them was laughing and hollering in our direction in pretty good English. "Come on out of there you son of a bitches," he said. "Give us a fair fight!"

"We can't let 'em flank us," I told my men. "Or they'll be able to reach them three civilians back in camp. I hope they had sense enough to run away an' get help, but we ain't got the time or the chance to go check."

Bullets flattened against the stones and pinged above our heads. Our little rock fortress was covered with gunsmoke.

"How you holdin' up, Millen?" I called out.

"It hurts like crazy, suh," said the man with the broken collarbone, "but I reckon I'll live. An' I can still shoot my pistol."

"Glad to hear it."

"Look yonder, Sarge," another trooper said. "The supply wagon's comin'!"

Sure enough, the teamsters was drivin' that wagon in from the north. About half the warriors broke off and moved to intercept it, grateful that fate had given them some easy prey. The two Cheyennes near Randall's hiding place took advantage of the diversion to move closer to his culvert. Reckon they hated to see a good scalp go to waste.

"I'm fixin' to draw 'em away from that wagon, fellers," I said. "Cover me good."

The troopers opened up with them Spencer repeaters as fast as they could, and I come charging out of the rocks. I broadsided them Cheyennes headed for the wagon - they parted before me, surprised, and I shot a couple of them point-blank. Then I wheeled my black and headed for Randall's spot. An arrow whizzed past my ear - a sound I had never heard before, it was kind of like a bee - and my horse took a bullet. I grabbed for my rifle and started jumping even as I felt him go down. I rolled a couple of times and come up running, pistol in one hand and rifle in the other.

Them braves was in the process of sticking their spears into that hole again when I run up on them. One of them died right in the middle of his little game, a lead ball through his heart, but the second one had time to hurl his spear at me. I twisted to one side and managed to avoid it, then drilled him.

I pumped my legs harder than ever, trying to close the last ten feet to the protection of that overhang. Little puffs of dust raised up all around me, and then a bullet took me in the thigh. I hit the dirt hard but kept rolling, right into that opening and on top of Randall.

He screamed in pain.

"Glad you still with us, Private," I said, and then I raised up to spray Spencer fire at my attackers. They was bearing down on me hard. A couple of arrows thunked into the ground just to the right of me.

Then the Cheyennes scattered. My six remaining troopers had mounted up and followed my lead, and hit the Indians from behind. One Cheyenne, evidently the leader, gestured to the others. The man had a lean hawk-like face - a jagged scar showed through the black paint on his jaw.

The warriors thundered off, having suffered enough upsets for one day. The leader of their party must have been pretty smart, for such a retreat showed good tactics more than it showed cowardice. The Indians couldn't afford to waste any more men - they'd strike again when they had a better chance of an easy victory.

Randall pulled through, despite the fact that he had eleven stab wounds. Me, him, and Millen received purple hearts in recognition of our injuries – Randall insisted that, since the medal is given for being wounded in action, he ought to be awarded eleven purple hearts, but you can't have everything. I was also cited for courage and received the certificate of commendation.

As we all attended the military funeral of Troopers Jones and Adams, though—me with a crutch under my right arm—we realized that such trinkets don't mean much in comparison with the greatest reward: our lives. The regimental band played with the colonel himself on violin, and the young men was lowered into the ground.

Still, the medals did mean a lot in another way—as did all the other medals won by the Ninth and Tenth down through the years. They showed that we was just as willing and able to shed blood and bolster courage for our country as any white man.

The Cheyennes understood, for they had developed a respect for us as fellow warriors. They even had their own name for us. Maybe it was because of our dark skin and wooly black hair, along with our stout hearts, or maybe it was just because in winter our uniforms included thick robes made of buffalo fur, an animal the Indians regarded as the most sacred of all beasts on the Plains. Whatever the reason for it, the nickname stuck with us from then on.

They called us the *Buffalo Soldiers*. We wore the name with pride.

"I sure will be glad when I'm healed up enough to sit in a saddle," I said.

Isabella snorted. She had been waiting on me hand and foot since my injury – I was almost embarrassed in front of my friends, but not quite.

"I suppose you prefer being shot at over being here with me," she said, and I laughed.

"What is so funny?"

"I'd get shot ever' day of the week if'n it meant havin' you to take care of me."

She smiled and leaned closer over my chair. "I would always be here. I can only pray to the Sweet Lord that this wound is the worst you will receive. I know I do not have to pray for you to be brave."

I felt my eyebrow arching up, and my eyes darted to the cross she always wore. "I never realized that Seminoles was such Christians," I said, and then – fearing my words might've offended her – quickly added, "'Course, they's a lot about yo' people I don't know. Yet."

She shrugged. "Some Seminoles are Christian. Most of the Negroes are – my family especially. My grandfather was a very religious man. He always believed that God had guided him through the swamps to my grandmother's people."

She put her soft hands on my shoulders. "You're tense," she said. "Something is troubling you."

"Not really," I lied. "I just hate to think of riding off on another patrol and leavin' you."

She removed her hands and knelt in front of me. "A moment ago you were looking forward to riding again – so that's not it. You must trust me, Alfred. Trust that whatever is on your heart I will take onto mine as well."

I breathed deep, letting the scent of her body fill my chest and give me the courage to speak.

"I ain't no Christian," I said.

"You can be."

"No, darlin', you don't understand. I've killed men, and enjoyed it. And not just when I was in this uniform, neither."

"You're a warrior – so is my father. There's no shame in that."

"But that's all I am – all I know how to be. I've tried other things, but they just fell apart. All my life has been rage an' war, an' I feel like I don't know how to be tender anymore.

I don't know how to do nothin' except kill – there ain't nothin' else for me."

She put a hand on my face. "What you know how to do, Alfred Mann, is survive. That is what you have done all your life, no matter what the odds. And you know how to love, though you try to hold it in. But your heart is too big." She stroked my cheek. "I see into it. I know."

I felt the tears forming in the corner of my eyes. "Why would God lead your grandfather to the Seminoles, only to let the white man take their land away? Why would He let people suffer so much, if He's so full of love?"

"We do not pray for a life without pain. We pray for the strength to endure the pain we have, and for our spirits to rise above it."

"You sound like my friend Lonnie. He was always preachin' at me with words like that – until they murdered him. He died in my arms, Isabella." The tears I'd been holding burst forth, along with deep sobs which wrenched my stomach. I crumpled forward and she caught me in her arms.

"Other people can believe," I said in a high voice, trying to catch my breath. "And it brings 'em peace – but I can't believe! It just ain't in me, no matter how hard I want it. Oh, God," I sobbed to her. "I want to believe."

Her arms was tight around me, and my cheek rested on her heart. "You have found the emptiness," she said, "and that is a start. The faith is on the other side." She whispered, "I'll help you find it."

"Oh 'Bella," I said. "How could you love a man like me – let alone marry him?"

"I can, and I will. I love you." And then, as if to answer my unspoken thought, she added a word – a word that Frankie would never say.

"I'll love you forever, Alfred. I'll love you forever."

I told her about Frankie, and of how I was not able to produce children. She told me she didn't care about none of that. She held me for hours.

I cried softly for much of that time, and was not ashamed.

Much of the next night I spent with my friends. We met at Jefferson's quarters for poker. I had never gambled before joining the Tenth – had never seen any sense in it – but slowly I let myself be drawn into the group of card-playing noncoms, mainly for the company. I never risked much and usually lost it all, but the whiskey kept flowing along with the laughter. I finally realized what Sid had always seen in it.

Abe was winning, as usual.

"If you was wise," George Dickerson said, "you'd let me win a few hands. A broke sergeant-major is a angry sergeant-major."

"I can't help it," said Abe, "I am rollin'. When I get to rollin' I can't stop."

"You know what they say," said James Jefferson. "Lucky at cards, unlucky at love."

"I guess that would explain why Alfred is almost broke already," added George with a chuckle.

"Y'all just hold on now," Abe insisted. "With two young'uns and a third one on the way, I wouldn't exactly say I'm unlucky at love."

"Yo' wife sho' is," retorted James.

Abe ignored him. "Speakin' of young'uns, me an' Jessie has made a decision, Alfred. If this next one is a boy we want to name him after you."

I was at a loss for words. "Well...thanks," I said. "But why would you want to do that?"

"Because you my best friend, fool. And because yo' poker money has done added up to half-enough to buy our own farm. By the time yo' hitch is up I'll be able to buy all of Kansas."

"Thanks, I think," I said. "An I've made a decision too. I want you to be my best man. I'm gettin' married next month."

Everybody patted my back and congratulated me, and Abe gave me a firm handshake.

George grinned. "So you gonna get yo'self whupped too, just like po' Abe here."

"A man's gotta get whupped ever' now an' then," Abe said, "so he'll know he's alive."

I grinned, and nodded my agreement.

Zeke and Pedro Farrier rode up beside me. We was on patrol, almost sixty miles from Fort Hays.

"Reckon you're gonna be family," Zeke said.

"I reckon."

"What Zeke means," said Pedro, "is welcome—and congratulations."

"Thanks, Pedro. I'm honored to think I'll be included in yo' family."

"You're a brave man and a good soldier," said Zeke. "That don't mean you're a good man. You better be good to our sister. Or I'll kill you." He galloped away, over the next rise, to return to his scouting.

"What my brother means," said Pedro, smiling to cover the embarrassment we both felt, "was that we wish you the best."

The wedding was held at the post chapel. It was conducted in full military fashion by our chaplain, an educated black man from Philadelphia named Cashian. It was a far cry from my first wedding, which was nothing more in the eyes of the law than a breeding agreement between human property. There was fancy words, and soldiers in full-dress uniform, and a band. I was even going to be allowed to actually live with my wife this time around.

When I looked into my bride's eyes, I knowed I could see straight down into her heart, and that there'd be room for me there forever.

Troopers was lined up on both sides of the chapel door when we walked out - they raised their sabers to form an arch for us to pass through. Abe winked at me when we turned to face the crowd. Even my new brother-in-law Zeke was smiling.

It occurred to me then that my love for Isabella was different than my love for Frankie had been. It was not a white-hot intense blaze, it was a warm comfortable glow.

It's fires like that which burn the longest.

Chapter Twenty-Five

I looked back on the day, over a year past now, when we was at Carter Station and I got my first look at victims of angry Indians. I had been sickened then. I thought there could be no greater butchery performed on the human body.

I was wrong.

We stood in the middle of what had once been the Graham place. The Grahams was a young family trying to make a go of it in Texas – their neighbors was all real fond of them. I wished one of them neighbors had found them instead of us.

Mister Graham was cut up even worse than the railmen had been, only his arm wasn't slashed. His guts had all been cut out – Brit said they was definitely cut, it wasn't just a case of varmints tearing them out – and his privates was stuffed into his mouth.

"Hard to tell," Brit said, leaning over the body. "Because the birds have eaten his eyes – but I'd be willing to bet the eyelids was cut off."

The woman was worse. Mrs. Graham was shy of thirty and, according to the neighbors, right pretty. It was hard to tell now. Her naked body lay spread-eagled and covered with dry blood and buzzing flies. Her face was sliced up. Her breasts was cut off and her lower body was covered with bruises. Half-a-dozen arrows was in her body. Brit knelt beside her and probed her pelvic area with a surprisingly gentle hand.

"A lot of tearing," he said. "She was raped God knows how many times – then violated by a blunt object." He looked up at me. "The man has been dead for maybe two days. The woman only for a few hours."

I frowned. "What does that mean?"

"It means they did this to her, pinned her to the ground with arrows, and didn't even finish her. They left her here to die - and it took a day and a half.

"These are Comanche arrows - with a couple of Kiowa. They run together a lot these past several years. They was so good at killin' each other I reckon they decided to band up. Seven men altogether."

I was distracted from the terrible scene by the sound of Trooper Millen sobbing. I walked over to him - an infant lay at his feet, its head bashed in.

"I'm sorry, Sarge," the soldier said, with difficulty. "Sorry."

I placed a hand briefly on his shoulder. "It's all right, Private," I said.

Captain Jordan walked over and looked at the child. "Dear Lord," he said, shaking his head.

"The neighbors told us there was three kids," Jefferson said.

"Has anybody seen more bodies?" Jordan demanded.

"There are no more," Brit answered him.

Jordan nodded. "We have to get those children back."

Jack the terrier sniffed at Mrs. Graham and whined.

Finding the little girl was easy. We followed the Comanches' trail for ten miles—it led south - and then we seen her laying near a clump of brush. Five-year-old Sadie Graham was crumpled facedown in a heap. I dismounted and picked her up. Her body was stiff and cold, and her muddy face was streaked by tears now long dry.

Something about her, maybe it was her round little face or the way her dull eyes seemed to stare up at me, put me in mind of my own little Jenny, who died so far from home even while she was still living in my hopes. Hot tears blinded me. I didn't have the strength to blink them back. I felt like somebody had run their fist up into my chest and squeezed my heart.

Any doubts I had was gone. Any tender feelings that might've taken root in me, any suspicions that the Indians who lived on these ranges might have souls that was kindred to mine, disappeared.

I hated these savages. They was monstrous animals, and the sooner we killed them all the better.

Brit gave the child in my arms a quick lookover.

"Lance in the back," he said. "Run her through, then retrieved the weapon."

"She's just a baby," I said softly, though I knowed the words sounded foolish. If they would dash out an infant's brains, why wouldn't they throw a spear at a little girl?

Sam Jordan stood beside me and looked down into the girl's features. The captain's own face, which was starting to become jowly since he'd reached forty and was normally flushed a reddish tint, was pale and slack. He had lost his youngest girl to the fever eight months before, so I knowed that his feelings right now was the same as my own. We shared a bond of hidden grief that set us quietly apart from the other men.

"She gave them some kind of trouble," Brit explained. "Or more likely, she was just too little to keep up."

Jordan took off his hat and ran a hand through dirty blond hair, still unable to tear his eyes from the little girl's face. "They still have the boy," he said. "We can still catch them."

Brit shook his head. "This trail is gettin' cold. They're in Texas by now."

"Then we'll go to Texas."

"What'll we do when we catch them?"

"You said yourself there's only seven."

"They're most likely with the main band by now. We'd have to go back for reinforcements, and that would lose too much time. They'll be across the Mexican border."

"Maybe they won't go for the border. Maybe they'll go to the reservation, thinking one of those damn Quaker Indian agents will protect them from us."

"Not with a captive child," Brit said.

"What are you suggesting, Johnson?" the captain said, with sudden fury. "Do you want me to go back to that little boy's grandparents and tell them we gave up? That we were afraid to rescue him?"

Brit thrust his face forward. "Even if we do close in on those Comanches they'll kill the boy, sure as the world. If he keeps up he'll be safe – they'll put him to work, one of the tribe might even adopt him. We can send word to some of the chiefs and negotiate to get him back."

"Unless they sell him to the comancheros," Jordan said. "He'll wind up as somebody's slave."

"It's a terrible thing when you look at it right in the face this way," Brit said. "But the fact is, Captain, the Comanches steal children all the time. We parley for 'em or take 'em back by force – with one company, we're in no position to do either."

Jordan let out a ragged breath. He stared at the southern horizon, chewing his lip.

Then he shook his head.

"Let's go, men," he finally muttered, defeat in his voice. "Let's go."

"We need to take back this chile," I told him, "and lay her to rest with her folks."

He nodded, than climbed back into the saddle. "I doubt if they'll rest any better than I will, with their boy in the hands of those savages."

The ride back was a long one.

A messenger was at my door soon after we got back to the fort, a young private. He informed me that Captain Jordan desired my presence at his quarters.

"Come in," the captain said when I knocked at his door. I stepped inside – Jordan sat at a little desk in the corner.

"My wife took the children to visit her folk in St. Louis," he told me. "Said she had to get away from forts for awhile – too many bad memories. They won't be back for a couple of weeks. It's been pretty quiet around here." He gestured at a wooden chair. "Have a seat, sergeant."

I took the chair. We both sat quietly for a moment – it made me uncomfortable. It was dark outside and Jordan had lit only a single candle. I could not see his features clearly.

"I apologize for taking you away from your wife after such a long patrol."

"No need, suh."

He cleared his throat. "Do you – do you know what it means to lose a child, sergeant?"

I nodded. "I had a little girl that died of the pneumonia." I didn't tell him she was not really mine, or that her mama had run away from me. I didn't love poor Jenny any less for it.

"I suspected," Jordan said. "I knew, really, from the look on your face, when we found the Graham girl."

"That was bad, Captain," I said. "Awful bad."

"Awful bad," he agreed. Then he reached under his desk and fished out a bottle of whiskey. "I thought you might want to share a drink with me, Mann. There's glasses in the cabinet there, if you don't mind fetching them."

I got up and took down the glasses. I put them on the desk and sat back down.

"I don't make a habit of drinking with enlisted men," he said. I knowed that was especially true of colored ones. "Against military etiquette, actually." He splashed the liquor out into the glasses and nudged one toward me. "Tonight, I don't give a damn."

I nodded my understanding. I sipped my drink slowly – he was well into his third when I finished my first. We continued like that until the bottle was drained. Neither of us spoke the whole time.

Finally, I stood up and told the captain goodnight. He didn't answer. I paused in the doorway and looked back – Jordan's face rested on one hand, and he cast a longing stare at the empty bottle. Maybe he was wishing the bottle was full again. Maybe it reminded him too much of his own soul.

I stepped quietly out the door and made my way home. I slipped under the covers beside Isabella; she was warm, and alive. She moaned softly in her sleep to acknowledge my presence, then rolled over to nestle against me, her face on my chest.

This country will find a way to kill you, Brit had said. It wasn't just this country, I knowed, it was the world. But it wasn't going to take me tonight. I was alive, and my bottle was full.

We hadn't pursued them Comanches that killed the Grahams into Texas, but we wound up going there anyways. Four companies of the Tenth was transferred, at least temporarily, to Fort Davis - there we was quartered with several companies of our sister regiment, the Ninth. Fact is, the whole entire Tenth Cavalry was never assigned to the same post all at once, we always got spread out.

We had patrolled in Texas before, but had never lived there. We soon learned that life in Texas was going to be different from Kansas or Indian Territory.

My first lesson came in connection to the Jacobson brothers. This pair, Perry and Jim - along with their partner, Tommy Siegler - had been stealing horses left and right, like they was just rounding up their own stray cattle. After every raid they would run off to the north and hide out in Indian Territory. Local law couldn't touch them there, only federal authority could - this usually came in the form of U.S. Marshals, but it could also come in the form of us. We was assigned to protect the frontier from any threat, and that included horse thieves.

Brit Johnson tracked the bandits to a rundown shack in a wooded gully. More than twenty horses was grazing in a corral behind the shack.

I motioned to Jefferson - he took six men with him and moved silently into the trees.

The rest of us remained still, watching the thin plume of smoke rising out of the chimney flue and alert for any sign of life around the little building. Occasionally, a patch of blue flashed by among the green of the trees – Jefferson's boys was on the move. When I was certain they had positioned themselves safely on the far side of the Jacobson's hideout, I gestured for the four men with me and Brit to move up.

"Remember to keep a cool head," I whispered to them. "Follow my lead – use the cover." Our horses remained hobbled where they was, with the last two men of our detail staying behind to watch over them.

The six of us, Brit included, eased down the hill. We zigzagged, moving from the cover of one tree to another. I was reminded of the skirmish at that plantation, during the War – only this time no one was shooting at us. At least not yet.

I stood with my back to a tree, rifle in my hands. The front door was only a few yards away. I nodded at my men and took off running. The thin door splintered easily against my shoulder, and my rifle was trained on three very surprised white outlaws.

James Jacobson lunged at me with a frying pan. I was lucky it didn't have no grease in it. I half-spun and brung my rifle butt down on the back of the fool's head. He was sent sprawling into the dirt floor. Two of my troopers had already rushed through the door and wrestled the other Jacobson brother to the floor.

Tommy Siegler had grabbed his Winchester out of the corner and run out the back door. I heard Jefferson's holler of "halt", and Siegler's two rifle shots – then there was a whole volley of gunfire. There was no more shots after that.

I grabbed James Jacobson by the collar and jerked him to his feet. The horse-thief was shaking his head, trying to clear his vision.

"Get your hands off me, you damn nigger."

I backhanded him. "You're under arrest," I informed him then.

When I walked outside I found Siegler. He was stretched out on his back in the dust, with one leg bent beneath him in a way that would torture any living man. His arms was spread wide to heaven. He looked like he was seeking help, or forgiveness - whatever he sought, it was too late. He looked to have at least eight or nine bullets in him.

"He didn't leave us no choice, First Sergeant," Sergeant Jefferson said.

"Don't matter none," I told him. "He'd have hung in a couple of weeks anyway. This'll save somebody the expense of feedin' him."

"You killed my pard!" Perry Jacobson said as we tied him onto one of his stolen horses. Then he laughed - his brother gave him an annoyed stare.

"There's some as suspect y'all have killed a man or two yourselves," I said. "I believe they even got witnesses."

Perry was still laughing. "I won't swing alone," he said. "When folks back home find out you murdered a white man, you'll all be hangin' on a tree-limb like crows."

I could read the worry in some of my men's faces. "Let him have his laughs now," I said. "Once them folks get their horses back and them widows see their husbands' killers, it won't seem so funny."

I was right on that point, anyway - nothing about the whole affair seemed funny. The reception we got in town was not what I had hoped for. I had half-expected it, true, but was nonetheless disappointed when it stared me in the face.

Folks lined up on the streets to gawk as we brung the Jacobsons in—from all I had heard, them shiftless brothers was looked down on by most everybody in the state.

But it was us they stared at. Their hate was aimed at our backs, not the killers'. One scruffy-looking man—in his mid-forties I would guess - sat in a rocking chair on the boardwalk and scowled. From ten yards away I could see his knuckles tighten on the cane he held in his right hand, could see the slight twitching of the stump where his right leg had once been.

A gray kepi was perched on his head, and his left hand held a miniature Rebel battle flag. His eyes bored into me like he was trying to will his gaze to become grapeshot.

"We in Texas now, boys," I muttered.

The sheriff was a fat man—his face was red as a tomato, and the front of his white mustache was stained brown by tobacco. He cocked his head and regarded the captive brothers. "So somebody finally brung you in," he said, and Perry Jacobson giggled.

"If it of been me," the sheriff added, "I'd of accidentally shot you somewhere out on the trail. Reckon you're at the end of your rope now. So to speak."

"They ain't hung, yet,'" I said. The sheriff looked at me with mild surprise, as if he had not noticed me before. "All you got to do, sheriff, is hold 'em in yo' jail until the federal deputy comes for 'em."

The sheriff spit at my feet. Tobacco juice splattered on my boots. My eyes hardened.

"I ain't used to gettin' told what to do by no black boy," he said. "Don't know as I plan to get used to it. They'll stay here if I say so, or else they'll go."

My back straightened like a new-sawed board, and I took a single small step in his direction – just enough that I was looking down on his red face.

"Here's somethin' you better get used to, sheriff. When you look at me you better not see black or white. Onliest thing you better see when you look at me is Union blue."

"Worse yet." He spat again.

"These thieves had best be present and whole when that deputy gets here."

"Or else what, black boy?"

"Union blue," I said, mounting up. "Union blue."

A subdued buzz echoed in the street. The local citizens whispered to each other in alarm over my words. I heard the phrase "sassy nigger" spoken in there somewhere.

They followed their sheriff's lead. As my men and me rode back out of town, the people sent their spittle after us.

I've endured worse.

Their mutual hatred of us did not prevent the citizens from lynching the Jacobson brothers almost as soon as we was out of earshot.

Chapter Twenty-Six

Our next few months was spent chasing Mescalero Apaches down on the border. I say chasing because we never actually caught one in all that time. For that matter, I never even laid eyes on one.

Them Indians could melt into the rocks and the brush so fast you would swear they had just been a mirage. It was scary – just as much to me as to the raw recruits. Apaches is the only thing I have ever encountered on this mortal earth that resembled the h'ants Sid always used to go on about.

They was always one step ahead of us. A couple of times we came upon an abandoned camp, having barely missed the hostiles – both times the campfire ashes was still warm.

But there was no Mescaleros to be seen. The air had a hollow, unnatural feel to it.

It would have helped a lot had Brit Johnson been with us, or maybe the Farrier brothers. Brit had quit the scouting business shortly after we captured the Jacobsons – he got the notion, no doubt correct, that he could make more money as a teamster and with less risk to himself and his dog. Zeke and Pedro, on the other hand, was still scouting. They had been assigned to a different company, though, which didn't help us any.

We was going to have to learn to do our own Apache tracking. And we did learn – but it took time. After years of scrapping with various Apache bands some of our veterans got to be about as cagey as the Indians we fought.

But that was in the future. At this particular time, the Mescaleros outwitted us all the way. At least we managed to stay on their tails close enough that they had to spend their time running from us instead of attacking citizens.

It was on a hot autumn day not far from the Rio Grande that we finally got to cut loose and burn off some of our frustration. Mescalero Apaches didn't turn out to be our target that time, but it was the next best thing – Mexican bandits. Groups of banditos roamed the border in them days making life miserable for the simple folks on both sides, but especially the Americans.

We heard the sound of gunfire from beyond the rise long before we was able to see what was going on. Me and Jefferson exchanged a quick look of concern mixed with triumph. We thought we had finally caught up to our Mescalero friends. Captain Jordan was not patrolling with us that day – he was back at the fort – so I gave the command to move forward and investigate.

What we found was a siege. Three Texans was laying flat in the dirt, trying to make for as small a target as possible, and exchanging fire with eight mounted banditos. The Texans' horses lay dead several yards away, along with what looked like a fourth member of their party. The bandits had apparently surprised them and shot their horses right off.

We charged right into the midst of the Mexicans – it was their turn to be surprised. Three of them had been shot out of the saddle before the others gathered their wits enough to make a run for it.

I waved Jefferson off – he dropped back with two of his men to assist the Texans and find out their story. The rest of us chased them bandits a good ways, dropping another one and suffering one of our own men with a leg wound before the desperadoes got away. Their horses was fresher than ours – plus our rifle fire motivated them a right smart.

We returned to find that the Texans had caught the dead banditos' horses to replace their own. One man, a few years older than the others, was securing his dead comrade to his new mount.

"Wright was a good man," he said as I approached him. "Not much of a picket, unfortunately, but brave."

He finished his task and shook his head, then looked up at me. "Jake Blackwell," he said. "Texas Rangers. Obliged for the save."

I paused for a moment, preparing to choose my words carefully. There had been a lot of friction between the buffalo soldiers and the Texas Rangers since we arrived in Texas – most Rangers was hard men, made even harder by losing the War. They tended to have all the same attitudes as their fellow Texans, both towards colored folks and the U.S. Army, and could be even more violent than most in expressing them.

"Just doin' our job," I said.

"We're obliged just the same. Maybe we can do the same for you one of these days."

"Hope so." My tone was not friendly – the badge pinned to his shirt reminded me of a dozen indignities heaped on us in a dozen Texas towns.

Blackwell gave a big, crooked grin. "Don't be so skittish, amigo. We're on the same side. I wore that blue uniform myself, not so long ago."

My surprise must have showed on my face.

"Yeah, I know," Blackwell said. "That ain't real common around here."

"No, it ain't."

"Just goes to show you shouldn't judge a man by his circumstances, especially when you don't even know him."

Blackwell climbed into the saddle. "Adios," he said, and the Rangers rode away to take their dead comrade home.

"A waste of good bullets," one private said. "Saving the hides of a bunch of Texas Rangers. We'll probably be shootin' at them tomorrow. Damn crackers."

I didn't answer the private.

"Mount up," I said.

We had no sooner returned to Fort Davis than Captain Jordan informed us we was about to head out again. Company M was being transferred north once more, to Fort Leckie. The Mescalero threat was considered under control enough that we could be spared. The Cheyennes and Arapahoes was acting up again from the Indian Territory plumb up to Colorado, and their southern sometimes-partners the Comanches and Kiowas was doing the same in North Texas.

It all started with the coming out of Medicine Wolf. Him and his partner Red Tree, both Cheyenne leaders, decided they didn't much care for the reservation. They lit out on the warpath and started back in at their old pastime of terrorizing white settlers. When the other "settled down" hostiles seen what fun Medicine Wolf and Red Tree was having, they decided to join in on the party.

Most of our time was spent patrolling, and I heard tell of a skirmish here and there, but overall we was not being real effective.

Then General Sheridan—Little Phil himself, Civil War hero and second only to Sherman in the U.S. Army—came up with a plan. Many Indians, especially them north of Texas, ended their raiding season in late fall and then sat back to wait out the bitter cold weather before they got back into the fracas.

This year we was going to take the battle to them - in the dead of winter.

Just about every cavalry regiment on the Plains involved in Sheridan's winter campaign against the Cheyenne and Arapaho, moving in on the hostiles from four different directions at once. Company M and five other companies from the Tenth was assigned to accompany Custer's Seventh on the campaign.

Like usual, like most every other military action from the Civil War up, the colored troops was sent to bring up the rear. A lot of them boys from the Seventh carried an expression on their face that marked them as our superiors, even though we was all freezing our rumps off equally.

Custer wore the same look but on a whole different level. He clearly thought himself to be the natural better not only of us and his own men but even of his own superiors. He was an arrogant bastard. He was brave though, and usually a good hand at tactics when his pride didn't get in his way – Custer was neither the madman some paint him to be, nor the sainted martyr that others sing about.

For most of that winter we slogged through the snow together, worried more about losing our fingers to frostbite than we did about unseen arrows. We pushed the enemy ahead of us all the while – just like the Apaches down on the border, we didn't catch sight of them. What we did manage to do was force the hostiles into the other columns, and into some real fighting. Custer seemed personally offended that he was reduced to delivering glory into some other regimental leader's hands instead of heaping it on himself. Us common soldiers didn't care much about glory – we had been looking forward to a good fight mainly because it would offer us a chance to get warm, at least for awhile.

Finally word began to filter through the ranks that we was going to see some action. I was standing near Captain Jordan when he questioned one of the scouts about it.

"Yep," the bearded scout said – he wore the same type of buckskins that Custer favored, only his was greasy from work and wear. "There's a Cheyenne village up yonder in that draw. By God, we'll get some of them this time."

The scout rushed off, his excitement lengthening his stride. His name was William Cody, but he called himself Buffalo Bill. There was another Bill who did some scouting for Custer, the lawman named Hickock –Cody did not have his dangerous eyes, but he could still be a mean man sometimes despite his good cheer.

We stayed at the perimeters of the village while Custer's boys swept in. Our job was to stop any Indians who made it past the Seventh.

Not many did. It was not a battle – not two military forces meeting each other on the field – it was a slaughter. The Cheyenne men was caught by surprise, while going about their daily routine with their families. Warriors was shot down while trying to get their weapons or after firing only one or two shots.

Old men and women was sabered in the snow—some had been trying to come to the warriors' aid, others was just running for their lives. Their lives, or their children's. Young'uns was trampled underneath the Seventh's hooves.

I sat my mount with my back to the Washita River, my cheeks burning with what at first was discomfort and then became grief and shame. Them same feelings poured out of my comrades—their eyes was shining wet, though their faces showed no emotion—and they soaked over me. I tried to call up into my memory the images of all the butchered women and children settlers I had seen, to use as a shield, but it did not soften the blows being pounded against my soul right now.

We was so caught up in our mixed feelings over the killing that at first we didn't notice the big batch of mounted warriors charging right our way. We had just enough time to steel ourselves for impact when the Indians crashed into us.

It was then that I got my first close-up look at Medicine Wolf. I realized that I knowed him. The white scar on his face identified him as the same Cheyenne who led the raid against that rail camp awhile back, where I was wounded.

Some would call that group of Cheyennes cowards for not fighting and dying beside their brothers, and for that matter beside their own families. Those who would say that did not look into the eyes of Medicine Wolf, like I did, and see the red hatred burned into his face and the faces of his men. All they wanted was to survive long enough to kill even more of us. They lived only to kill. Every decision them warriors made each day was guided by their hatred and their desire to kill white folks as effectively as possible –even if they was black white folks.

The emotion was familiar to me. It had consumed me, too, at an earlier time - though its edges seemed to have dulled a little bit with age - and the hot memory of it surged forth in my throat and I was choked by it.

While them thoughts flitted around at the edge of my mind, my hands operated the weapons they held with the thoughtless instinct of a fighting man. I was killing too; like the Indians, I knowed the most effective ways to do it. We spilled each other's blood on the snow and in the river, red man and black, and we was the same.

I had long ago decided that my red enemies was animals, that they had no souls – and now I seen that we was alike. Ice froze in my belly. Did that mean they was men like me, or did it mean I was as hollow as they were?

A warrior's hand darted toward my throat, the steel of his knife flashing like the sun on the Washita. Our horses collided. I grabbed the Cheyenne's hand before it made contact and jammed my revolver into his belly. He flew backwards off his horse when I pulled the trigger. Behind me, Trooper Collins was being disemboweled by another brave's lance. I turned easily, with no wasted motion, and fired again – the Cheyenne's brains sprayed across the snow.

A handful of warriors had made it through our line – they would live to join up with their kinsmen and continue the circle of red death. My eyes locked briefly with those of Medicine Wolf and seen the recognition in them—not of my face, but of my spirit. Then he was gone.

The fight was over, for today. Buffalo Bill was proudly waving the bloody scalp of a warrior he had grappled with and killed, maybe thinking to himself that the whole thing might make an entertaining show someday. In the village children was crying, but not as many as before.

The snow was soaked with blood, but the morning sun shone on it so brightly that I couldn't bear to look at it for more than a moment. I was forced to look down instead, at the gloved hands that rested on my saddle horn.

Chapter Twenty-Seven

Isabella was a light glowing in the fog. The moments I was able to steal with her while we was campaigning—which was not many at all, as we was mostly in the field covering ground in several states and territories - was a beacon pulling me to the real world. Or maybe she was bringing me out of the real world - either way, Isabella was my anchor to sanity. My moments with Frankie had been moments of desperate madness, and they did not leave me with the peace that Isabelle did.

It troubled me sometimes, though, when I seen her setting on the front stoop playing with her little nieces or nephews or with Abe Armstrong's boy Alfred. I seen the bright smile on her face and the joy in her actions, but every once in awhile I thought I could see a touch of sadness as well. It was a bitter thing to know that I was not whole, and that there was something 'Bella needed for the sake of her own wholeness which I could never give her.

I had sons of my own, of a sort. Sons and little brothers and students in the forms of the young soldiers under my command. They was sons I taught to kill, and sometimes sent out to be scalped and gutted. But I also taught them to have pride in theirselves and in their service, and in their courage. Pride was something that had been denied them as little children in slavery, and which their fathers and grandfathers for the most part had never been allowed to know. There was moments of shame, like at the Washita or when the citizens we fought to protect spit on us, but we weathered them.

We had pride in each other.

One of the most promising young soldiers in my company was named Joe Ferguson. He had replaced Collins.

Ferguson's early youth had been spent on a Georgia plantation.

I recognized in his eyes a fire that had burned in Chamas North's eyes, and to an extent in my own. He was an intelligent man, though not in a book sense - them same eyes took in every detail of the world around him and filed it away.

He was cool under fire, too - remarkably cool for a green recruit. I found this out firsthand when we was scouting just north of the Red River.

There was six of us in all. Trooper Bo Dishman was the only other veteran soldier - the other four, Joe Ferguson included, was new recruits. We scouted out a few miles ahead of the patrol. My aim was to test out these new boys, and try to teach them some of the things that Brit had taught me. There had been no reports of hostile activity in the area for some time, or else I would never have ventured so far out with young soldiers.

Hostile activities has got to start somewheres, I guess.

Before we half-knowed it, about thirty Comanches busted out from over a rise and proceeded to tear into us. Trooper Isaac Green fell to the ground dead, and two other troopers had their horses shot from under them. It was obvious to me we was not going anywheres for a while.

"Dismount!" I yelled, and dropped to the ground.

Trooper Dan Evans hesitated –his eyes was wide with fear. "Are you crazy, Sarge? We gotta get out of here! We gots to!"

I reached up and grabbed Evans by the shirt, then throwed him roughly to the ground. An arrow whizzed through the air where his body had been seconds before. I kicked him sharply in the ribs.

"Get on yo' damn feet an' do what I tell you."

The others had dismounted. I stood behind my horse and fired my rifle across his saddle. He was a cavalry horse, he was used to it. If he had been a civilian animal he might have bolted away, leaving me wide open and in a world of hurt.

Bullets tore into the animal. He died like a good soldier. I jumped back to avoid being caught up in his death thrashings, then crawled forward to take cover behind his body. I did my shooting from a reclining position.

Before long all the horses was dead, and Dishman's left hand had been shattered by a bullet. We was all hunkered down behind our dead mounts, shooting for all we was worth. Ferguson was handling it like an old hand. His shooting was accurate too, which was reassuring – the U.S. government had decided a few years before that excessive target shooting was a waste of taxpayers' bullets. As a result most recruits couldn't hit the broad side of a barn if they was inside with both doors shut.

"What are we gonna do now, Sarge?" Evans hollered.

"Stay alive," I told him. "The rest of the patrol will have heard the shots. They'll be here soon. We just have to hold on till then."

Dishman was balancing his rifle across his useless right arm as he fired.

"Two things you new boys has got to get used to doin' in this here army," he said. "Fightin' Injuns an' buildin' forts." Dishman patted the mound of dead horseflesh before him. "Today you're learnin' the basics of both. Right, Sarge?"

"Right, Dishman. Now shut up and fight. And you better do somethin' about that hand before you bleed to death."

"I ain't got time to bleed to death, suh."

The shooting stopped and suddenly there was not a Comanche to be seen.

"Praise Jesus!" Evans said. "They give up on us!"

Trooper Fred Wilkins, barely eighteen, had not spoken a word throughout the whole affair. He still wasn't talking, but a smile broke onto his face.

"No," Joe Ferguson said. "That's too easy. They gotta be up to somethin'."

They was up to something, all right. Before long we smelled smoke. Evans was confused, and close to panic.

"Grass fire," Dishman said.

"They gonna burn us!" Evans yelled.

"They sho' gonna try," I said.

"They got in behind us," Joe said, nodding toward the horizon. Thick smoke was already floating up toward the sun. A Comanche showed himself briefly, a burning branch in his hands – I jerked my rifle up and dropped him. Then I took a deep breath.

"Boys," I said, "we in some real shit now."

Before long the smoke had reached us, and breathing became a chore.

"We got no choice," I said. "We gonna have to run for it an' hope we can dodge flames an' Injuns both."

"Injuns on hosses," Evans mumbled, uncertain.

"That's just what they want us to do," Joe said. "They'll be waitin' for us."

I nodded slowly.

"Fight to the last breath," Dishman advised the younger men. "Blow your own brains out if you have to. God help anybody that gets took alive."

The sound of gunfire intensified beyond the smoke, and a bugle sounded.

"Lord-a-mighty!" Dishman said. "That horn is the beautifulest sound I ever heard in my life."

Wilkins heaved a relieved sigh.

"We ain't out of this yet," I said. "We still on foot, an' them flames will be here any minute. Let's go."

We stood and moved in the direction of the bugle – all of us except for Evans. He stayed put, knuckles tightened on his rifle.

"Come on, Evans," I said.

He shook his head. "They waitin' on us! They gonna get us fo' sho'!"

"Move yo' ass, Trooper! Now!"

Evans choked on the smoke, but did not move. Joe sprinted to the frightened man and beaned him on the head with his pistol butt. He scooped Evans up in his arms.

"We comin', Sarge," Joe said, and we ran into the flames.

It was like stepping off the edge of the world. Everything was yellow and orange and the heat squeezed the air out of my lungs like a vise – then it was over, and we stood on charred ground breathing real air. My clothes smoked, and I could smell my own scorched hair.

It turned out the Comanches was too busy to pay much attention to us. Jefferson had showed up with the rest of the company and they was laying some wicked fire of their own into them Indians.

At least one of them seen us. No sooner had Joe Ferguson stepped out into the open than an arrow took him in the fleshy part of his right arm. He dropped Evans hard.

Young Fred Wilkins, meanwhile, was screaming just as loud as the Comanches. He had tarried too long in the flames, or else just had some bad luck – either way, his clothes was on fire. Joe, the arrow still in his arm, jumped on Wilkins and knocked him to the ground, rolling him over and beating at his clothes. Me and Dishman turned sideways to our attackers so as to make harder targets – several mounted Comanches had finally took a notion to charge at us – and emptied our revolvers at them. Three Indians fell. The others wheeled around and run off.

"We made it, Dishman," I said – but when I turned, the veteran was lying in the ashes.

I knelt quickly to check him for wounds, but there was no fresh ones. He had passed out from the blood loss of his mangled hand. I reckon he finally decided it was a good time to fall over.

Wilkins' burns was not serious, but they soon would have been. I recommended that Joe Ferguson be cited for courage under fire. Nothing was said about Evans cracking –

the next time he came under attack, he handled it better. He may have learned to be more scared of me and Ferguson than he was of the Indians. He turned into a tolerable good soldier.

As soon as Ferguson healed up, I made it a practice to always take him with me on scouts. I also came to rely heavily on him when patrolling.

It was on one such patrol that we found the wagon. The white man tied naked to the wagon wheel was not anyone I knowed – though his body was burned in so many places I might not have recognized him anyways.

The other man was a different story. Aside from the usual mutilations, his belly had been slit open and a small terrier, its neck broken, stuffed inside.

The wild land had found a way to kill Brit Johnson.

I knelt beside the body and sighed deeply, then sat completely down in the grass. I made a feeble attempt to knock the blowflies away with my hat.

"Somebody you know, Sarge?" Joe Ferguson said.

"Somebody that knowed me," I responded softly. I climbed slowly to my feet.

Sergeant Jefferson stood beside me.

"I reckon we ought to pack these bodies up somehow," Jefferson said, "and tote 'em back to Fort Leckie. Give 'em a decent funeral, with bugles an' guns an' such. We owe old Brit that much, anyway."

I looked slowly around the grasslands that surrounded us. It was a lonely site, where the echoes of a single human voice could be lost forever The sky was as big and blue as an ocean. Hawks wheeled their way gently through it, free as the spirits of the dead cut loose from this earth.

"This is a good place," I said.

We buried them there. When we paused, speechless, at the finished grave, I felt the silence of the site wash over me—I almost envied Brit.

Then I thought of the warm arms that waited for me at home, and I rode away.

"This old army is our master now," Joe Ferguson said one evening. It was yet another patrol, and we was gathered around a small campfire. Most of the others had rolled into their blankets and dropped off to sleep, but I was keeping Joe company for awhile on the first watch. I had found him an easy man to talk to. We was alike in a lot of ways.

I grunted at his comment. "That's pretty plain," I said.

Joe shook his head. "I mean them words to run deeper than you think," he said. "Why are we in the cavalry to begin with? Any of us?"

"You tell me."

" 'cause there was no place else to go, that's why. Why do so many of these men reenlist?"

"Because they proud."

"Hell, no. 'cause they afraid to leave. They say we free now, but have you ever tried to make a livin' out there in the world?"

"Yeah."

"So have we all, an' we know they's nothin' to go back to. The best hope we got is to get shot at defendin' white folks and they freedom, and be grateful we at least got thirteen dollars a month we can count on."

"You could look at it that way, I reckon."

"It's easier if you don't, though, ain't it?" Joe said. We spoke no further that night.

Chapter Twenty-Eight

By the late spring of 1875, what had become known as the Red River War had wound down. Most of the Cheyennes, Comanches, and Kiowas involved in the fighting came in to the reservations – though there was a few notable holdouts, including Medicine Wolf and Red Tree.

Companies D and M of the Tenth was sent to the Cheyenne Agency, on the banks of the Canadian River in Texas, to assist the Fifth Infantry in their efforts to "detain" the ringleaders of the warrior bands. All them braves considered to be bad influences by the U.S. Army was singled out and chained up, to be sent somewhere safe until they learned to be peaceable folk.

The Indians' shame was clear on their faces. They was not a people used to giving up easy – yet here they was, in front of their elders and their women and children, being bound like animals. Some of the women – and old men too – wept at the sight. They must have knowed that it was for their sake that their young men had not only fought and died, but was now subjecting themselves to something even worse.

One Cheyenne brave named Black Horse, legendary among his people for his courage and well-known to us, walked slowly toward the infantrymen. When he seen the shackles he hesitated. We all braced ourselves for resistance.

The moment seemed to pass, and Black Horse stepped forward and held out his hands. Before he could be secured, though, several Cheyenne women in the crowd began to jeer and spit. Their derision was not directed at us, but at Black Horse. I speak no Cheyenne but I could sense the meaning of their words. Black Horse was a traitor and a coward for submitting so easily.

This final indignity was more than Black Horse could endure. His hands shook and clenched into fists – a scream of rage and shame boomed out from his chest. He grabbed the manacles out of the Fifth Infantryman's hands and struck the soldier across the face with it. Black Horse ran toward the river, yelping in Cheyenne as he went.

Before he had taken a dozen steps riflemen from the Fifth opened fire and he was cut to ribbons. The desperate warrior's body jerked and twisted in mid-air like a child's toy as the slugs tore through him.

A lot of other bodies jerked as well. The white soldiers did not notice – or did not care – that the crowd of Cheyenne women and children was directly behind the fleeing Black Horse. Several of them was killed or wounded.

Our own men was getting restless. Captain Jordan gestured at us. "Hold steady," he said.

The Cheyennes was screaming at us in outrage. Several had run into their homes and retrieved what pitiful weapons they had. A few arrows flew toward the riflemen, and a couple of soldiers was struck.

We had no choice but to get involved. I fired into the crowd of Indians, dropping a wrinkled old man just before he released his bowstring –the shaft flew wild. The Cheyennes took advantage of the brief cover their archers gave them to run away – not toward the Canadian, but toward the sand hills behind them. By the time the last of the old bowmen had been cut down the rest of the Indians was gone.

There was a considerable number of warriors in the group, them that had not yet made their surrender when the trouble started. Before long we was being shot at not just by bows but by rifle fire.

"Sly devils," James Jefferson said. "They had weapons hid away up yonder in them sand hills, just in case."

"Jordan!" the Fifth's colonel called out. "You and Holmes take your companies up that hill and soften them up for us."

"Yes, sir," Jordan said.

As easy as that, and companies M and D was racing across the open ground and toward the sand hills. A few men got hit, but the rest of us knowed that we would reach the Indians. What we would do then, with even women and young boys bearing weapons against us, I preferred not to think about until the time came.

But then something happened that none of us had considered. Bullets started tearing into our ranks from behind.

"Dismount!" Jordan yelled to us. "Dismount, by God, and take cover!"

I leaped from the saddle and rolled into the dust. My black mare flopped onto the ground not far from me a few seconds later, tore up by bullets. The infantry had set up a Gatling gun, and it was chewing up them hills like nobody's business – as well as the Indians, not respecting age or sex.

And it was chewing us up. We made the mistake of being in the way.

The Gatling gun paused for a moment.

"Jordan! Holmes!" the infantry colonel hollered. "Get your damn niggers up that hill and pacify those heathens!"

"Yes – yes sir," Jordan yelled back, gritting his teeth.

We stood up and advanced toward the hills on foot. The Cheyennes resumed firing at us. This caused the Gatling gun behind us to start up again –five yards to my right I seen Trooper Wilson's head explode in a spray of red mist.

"Drop, drop!" Jordan screamed, so frustrated that his skin glowed red through his blond hair.

And there we stayed. We hugged the earth, helpless as calves while bullets whizzed all around us from both sides. The Cheyennes was pounded until there was hardly anything left of them – the survivors was easily rounded up and led back to the agency.

The Fifth Infantry was hailed as heroes in the local papers. The buffalo soldiers who fought beside them, meanwhile, was ridiculed as cowards who was afraid to advance on the enemy position.

Sam Jordan resigned his commission and opened a dry goods store in a little town near Kansas City.

I felt Isabella's arms encircle my waist in the middle of the night, heard her breath in my ear. She had no words of comfort for me. I did not need them. The love that dripped from her limbs like easy rain was enough to soothe me.

I slept.

It was not long after that when Medicine Wolf and Red Tree was captured. I was present for the occasion, although the two chiefs did not know it at first.

They had agreed to come into Fort Leckie and parley with the famous General Phil Sheridan himself. The two Indian leaders stepped into Little Phil's big office, accompanied by another four of their prominent comrades. The rest of the warriors waited outside, exchanging nervous and hostile looks with the Fifth Cavalry troopers assigned to watch over them.

Sheridan really was a small fellow. He looked even smaller in the shadow of the two colonels who flanked his desk – the Tenth's own Benjamin Grierson, and the Fifth Cavalry's Ranald MacKenzie. MacKenzie was nicknamed "Bad Hand" by the Indians, on account of the two fingers he had lost at the Siege of Petersburg. They respected and feared him. He was about half-crazy. Not full-of-himself crazy like some folks took Custer to be, but crazy like a rabid wolf. That was something the Indians could understand and identify with.

Besides the three senior officers there was a captain, two lieutenants, and a scout acting as interpreter – all parties on both sides was unarmed. That was part of the truce agreement. Several lamps burned in the big room – Sheridan had heavy velvet drapes along every wall, blocking sunlight out of the windows.

Sheridan said a few polite words of welcome, without seeming to mean them, and the scout translated.

"We don't need him," Medicine Wolf said. "We talk your words."

"Very well then," said Sheridan. "We'll get right to the point. The terms of your surrender."

"Our little ones are hungry," said Red Tree.

"Everyone will be provided for, I assure you," Grierson said. His words, at least, were sincere.

"There will be food," Sheridan agreed, "but there can be no more of this roaming around nonsense. You and your people must stay within the confines of the agency, so that you can be taught the civilized art of agriculture. There will be a daily roll-call to make certain none of you has slipped away."

"We don't want your food," said Medicine Wolf. "Or your farm tools. We want you to leave us alone and let us be free."

Sheridan's face darkened. "There are a lot of white farmers lying in their graves now who wanted the same thing."

Medicine Wolf smiled – it wasn't a pleasant smile. "I know," he said, leaning forward. "Many of them begged me for peace for hours before I gave it to them."

Sheridan slapped the desk hard and jumped to his feet.

Medicine Wolf did not flinch.

"We do not beg, soldier," Medicine Wolf said. His smile was gone.

"Your braves outside will surrender," MacKenzie said. "You six are under arrest."

"This is truce," Red Tree said, his face coloring.

MacKenzie grinned briefly. "You aren't dealing with any damned Quaker Indian agent now, gentlemen."

"There is no truce," Red Tree said sadly. "There is no peace, there is no freedom. There is only empty words." He shook his head. "My father's spirit still walks over these plains – and so does mine. But my spirit only."

I remembered Brit Johnson's long-ago words about the noises of the night. A human voice can always be distinguished from an animal, Brit said, because it has a peculiar echo to it. Red Tree's words echoed inside me.

Medicine Wolf reached behind his back and came out with a huge glittering knife. I don't reckon either side had expected this meeting to be any real truce. He stepped toward Sheridan, moving like a cat. The general's eyes widened. I would say he didn't often encounter problems like this back when all he dealt with was captured Reb officers.

It was at that point when I stepped out from behind the velvet curtains. My rifle was pointed at Medicine Wolf's chest. Eleven other men hand-picked from the Tenth Cavalry stepped out of their hiding places at almost the same time.

Medicine Wolf froze.

"One more step," MacKenzie said, "and you'll be blasted to hell."

"Put down the knife," Grierson said.

Medicine Wolf reluctantly obeyed. We stepped over and searched the six Indians – every one of them had a hidden weapon of some sort.

"First Sergeant," Sheridan called out.

"Yes, suh," I answered him.

"Escort the prisoners to the guardhouse."

"Yes, suh." I looked at Medicine Wolf and gestured toward the door.

"Get movin', chief," I told him. "And step mighty careful."

He paused, studying my face – no doubt figuring all the different ways he would like to kill me. He flashed that black smile of his and headed slowly toward the door.

That's where the real danger began. About three dozen renegade warriors from two or three different tribes stiffened as though struck when they seen us escorting their leaders at gunpoint.

Anything could have happened. Sure, there was enough Army firepower to kill most of the Indians right off, but I knowed that me and my boys would be the first bluebellies to go down. Some of the warriors was already reaching for weapons.

Grierson moved closer to the captives. "Be calm," he said to the Indians all around us.

"Starting trouble won't help your leaders – it will only get them killed." He cast a glance at the scout. "Tell them," Grierson said, and the scout relayed the message in Cheyenne.

There was no trouble. Medicine Wolf and the others was herded safely into the stockade. I could feel the warriors' eyes burning on me – it was the kind of hot, stifled feeling you get just before lightning strikes.

It was the image of Red Tree's eyes that stayed with me, though, long after the cell door was closed on him. They bore a look of betrayal, betrayal by the whole world – expected, maybe, but no less painful. It was the look I had seen on soldiers in the battlefield who ran their hands up into their own bellies and discovered that yes, in fact, they really was gutshot.

It was a look I had worn myself.

A picnic didn't sound like such a bad idea.

"What made you think of it?" I asked Isabella. "And why didn't you think of it sooner?"

I was lying flat on my back on the grass, staring up at the clouds.

"I did think of it sooner," she said. "Only you wasn't here."

I laughed –a deep chuckle that rumbled out of my chest and floated on the air like thunder in springtime.

"I been a busy man, honey," I said. "You don't get to be a beloved hero like myself without puttin' in the time."

"As to what made me think of it to start with—"

"You ignorin' me, ain't you?"

"As to what made me think of this to start with—well. There's clouds up in the sky that needs lookin' at. If'n you don't look at 'em now, while they invitin' you, one day you might look up an' the sky will be empty."

I pursed my lips and nodded, mock-thoughtful. "That makes sense," I said – though it really didn't. It was the way she said it that made sense, I reckon.

We had spread our blanket on the grassy bank of the Red River. My belly was full now. The singing of birds and the chirping of crickets and the easy sound of running water combined to lull my mind into a dreamy state.

"Reckon you gonna be home for awhile now?" Isabella asked.

I nodded. "Medicine Wolf and Red Tree is captured. Quanah Parker hisself has come in – his Kwahadis was the last of the hostile Comanches. The Northern Cheyenne an' the Sioux is still raisin' cain to the north, and there's always the Apaches to the west. It's windin' down, though. At least for a spell."

"Good."

I rolled onto my side, leaning my head on my hand. "I know you get lonely," I said.

She shrugged. "Can't be helped, Alfred. You got your job to do. I'm proud of the way you do it."

"I ain't so proud sometimes." She stared at me, her eyes inviting me to continue. "It just don't feel right sometimes, that's all."

Her fingers brushed over my forehead. "You're a warrior, Alfred. So are my brothers, my father – all my mother's fathers and probably my father's fathers as well. Sometimes warriors have glory. Sometimes they do not. But I will never be ashamed of you for being who you are. I've told you this before."

"How are your brothers doin'?" I asked, hoping she would let me get away with changing the subject. The Farrier boys had been reassigned to Company C months earlier, and had been quartered at Camp Glover.

"Mother says Zeke is coming home for a visit," she said. "He is bringing his new wife with him."

"Wife?" I said. "She must be the most patient woman on the face of the earth, or else a real hellcat."

"Maybe both," Isabella said. "We'll find out soon enough."

I moved closer. "I could give him lessons on how to tame a hellcat," I said, then gave her a kiss deep enough to get lost in. A soft moan escaped her mouth and rolled gently into my own.

The clouds watched us.

"I'll see you a dollar, and raise you another."

I dropped another dollar into the pile in the middle of the table. Abe chuckled.

"You playin' with fire, boy," Abe said. "This young man is hot tonight."

"Hot air an' smoke," said Sergeant-Major George Dickerson. "That's all you got, boy."

I smiled, even though I was on the verge of going a few more dollars into the hole. It was worth it. I had missed our card games – our regular group was finally all stationed at the same fort again.

"How's that new corporal of your'n doin'?" George asked.

"Ferguson's comin' along real fine," I said. "The boy has a lot of promise."

We showed our cards. George took the pot and Remy Golden, one of Abe's sergeants, dealt us out another hand. I always marveled at Remy – he was about the biggest horse soldier I ever seen.

"Promise, huh," Abe said – then added, "Hit me with two more, Remy." When he got his cards, he continued, "I wish young Captain Forster showed some promise."

"He'll be fine," James Jefferson said, "soon as his voice changes an' he has his first shave."

"He ain't no Sam Jordan, that's for sure," I said.

"Here now," said George. "This is the United States Army. Enlisted men never speak ill of commissioned officers."

"Oh no," Abe said. "It's unheard of." We all laughed.

"It feels kind of strange," I said, "takin' orders from somebody that was just a kid when we was fightin' the War."

George nodded. "He's the first officer I've served under that wasn't a Union veteran. There's gonna be more an' more, though—time goes on."

"What it means is," said Abe, "We gonna get shot at for him, but he ain't never been shot at for us."

Abe's words rung true with all of us. There had always been something comforting about the fact that the white men who gave us orders had themselves risked everything for our freedom. Deserved or not, we all felt a little bit of gratitude to them, and gratitude grows into loyalty. These young officers was another matter.

The fact remained, though, that we ultimately fought to free our own selves, just as we now fought to preserve the peace. Nobody seemed too awful grateful to us. A part of me felt a little sick when I realized that even among a bunch of old veterans, and even in some deep pit of my own soul, there should be a revered place for the white man who dirtied his hands to "save" us. We was all grateful, to some extent, that they had taken any notice of us at all.

I bet heavy on a weak hand and tossed back a stiff drink.

Chapter Twenty-Nine

We stopped in at Montreel, Texas, for the sole purpose of buying a drink. A good cold beer sounded like the milk of paradise to men who had worked all day in the hot sun. We had been sent to rebuild Fort McKavett, abandoned since before the War – we could not set up any buildings, though, until we finished the sawmill. We was drained by our day's work, and by the knowledge we had weeks more to go.

Montreel was a small town. There was no colored neighborhood. We had no choice but to go to one of the regular saloons. We didn't think too much of it, though –we was soldiers in the U.S. Cavalry, after all.

At least four of us was. Me, Joe Ferguson, Bo Dishman, and young Boston Henry – the fifth member of our party was a Seminole scout. Lanky Jim was my wife's second cousin. If he had a last name I never heard it. Everybody always just called him Lanky Jim – he stood six-and-a-half feet tall, maybe more. He dressed in a mixture of buckskins and Army uniform castoffs.

We edged up to the bar and I eased my grateful bones down on a stool.

"Beers all around," I said. The bartender was slow to respond, but he finally brought our drinks—all the time eyeing us like we was freaks of nature.

I guzzled the cold foamy brew down, feeling its warmth seep into the cracks of my joints.

"Lawd," Dishman said, "it's gonna take me a-plenty of this stuff to replace all the water I've sweated out today." Lanky Jim answered him with a belch.

Boston Henry was grinning like a kid in a candy store. I decided I'd best keep an eye on him – Henry had not been in the service for very long, and was not used to dealing with the few real temptations which came our way. He'd probably never been off the farm two days in a row his whole life until the time he enlisted. He did know how to read before he put the uniform on, though, which was still rare.

Not as rare as in slave days, true - George was right. Things was changing a little bit anyhow. Being educated put an extra stamp of promise on Henry. He had a head start on fellows like Joe and Dishman, who got their first learning from the post chaplain. It might help make the boy a noncom one day—once he had some experience under his belt.

"I never joined up to build no sawmills," Boston Henry said. "I thought we was supposed to fight Indians. Nobody said nothin' about no constructin'."

Dishman laughed. "You ain't never fit no Injuns yet, young soldier. If'n you had, you would be more than happy if the brass ordered you to build a staircase to the moon. You'd be lookin' fo' ways to make the job last longer."

"I'm half-Indian," Lanky Jim said with a grin. "You wanna fight me?"

Boston eyed the big Seminole up and down. "No, I reckon not," he said.

Lanky Jim shrugged. "Let me know if you change your mind. Bartender, keep that beer flowin'."

"Oh well," Boston said. "It's worth the trip to the sawmill just to walk past the Jackson place an' see that Narcissa gal."

"Damn right it is," Lanky Jim said. "She one fine gal."

"What do you think, Joe?" Boston asked.

Joe smiled. "She is a sweet thing, all right."

Me and Dishman got real quiet. We stared hard at the others.

"You talkin' 'bout a white gal," I said. Dishman nudged me in the ribs and shushed me.

"Keep it down, Sarge!" he whispered. "They's two dozen Texas crackers in here with us!"

"Yeah, you right Alfred, we is," said Joe. "We won't hold that agin her, though." The three younger men laughed.

"You boys don't need to be gulpin' that foam down so quick if'n you cain't handle it like men," I told them. "I believe you've had too much."

"I believe you've all had too much."

I turned around. A tall cowboy stood there staring at us, thumbs in his belt. Three of his friends stood behind him.

"You damn'coons is makin' too much racket," the cowboy said.

"Tell 'em, Horner!" called out one of the many other cowboys who was lounging in the corner.

"You better by God keep it down," Horner continued.

"This is a saloon, Tex," Joe Ferguson told him. "Not a church social."

Horner bristled. "We shouldn't even let your kind in here," he said. "Or anyplace else in Texas. One more peep and I'm gonna come back over here and break some woolly heads."

Horner walked back to his comrades. He was greeted by many a slap on the back.

"Maybe we ought to just leave," Boston said.

"Hell, no," said Joe.

I shook my head. "We'll finish our beers first."

"They done got they dander up now, anyways," Dishman said. "They won't let us just walk out, you can be sure of that."

Dishman fished around in his pocket and took out a handful of metal objects, then hunched close to the bar so the cowboys could not see what he was doing.

"Time to put on the drinking jewelry," he said. "Right Sarge?"

I took a discreet look around. We was outnumbered three-to-one, easy –and that wasn't counting the cowboys who looked too drunk to stand up.

I nodded.

The rest of us took out our "jewelry" as well. What looked at first to be rings was really nails bent into a circle – when you slipped one onto your finger the sharp ends stuck out from your knuckle like spikes I heard spurs being drug across the floor. I turned to find Horner standing over us again. This time most of his friends was with him.

"You're slurpin' on that beer too loud, nigger," he said. "You're gettin' on my nerves."

"Cowboy is just sleepy," Lanky Jim said. "I was too noisy when I visited his mama last night."

I groaned. I was hoping we would at least have the dignity of making them throw down the first glove. I wasn't able to think about it for very long, because a chair was being swung at my head.

The cowboys pressed in on us like dirt filling in a grave. I was swinging my arms like a windmill, my jewelry opening up flesh with every blow. The saloon sounded like a hogpen – grunts and groans and curses, fists smacking meat, air whooshing out of lungs.

"You signed up to fight, boy," Dishman called out to Boston Henry. "Hope you happy!" A chair busted over Dishman's back and he was sent sprawling to the floor. One of the Texans lifted his boot high to smash him in the face – Lanky Jim grabbed the man from behind and tossed him across the room.

No sooner had Dishman climbed back to his feet than someone tripped Joe Ferguson.

Joe sprung up at once, driving an elbow into his attacker's groin.

I had troubles of my own.

I had taken several blows already. My nose was bleeding and my ears rung like Christmas bells. A couple of Texans managed to grab my arms and pin them back – Horner drove a fist into my gut. He grinned wickedly as he drawed back his hand to do it again.

I butted my forehead into his face with all my strength. His grin couldn't bear up under the pressure - it melted into a red mess.

Joe Ferguson drove spiked knuckles into the jaw of one of the men who held me. I knocked the other one over the bar. Me and Joe stood back-to-back - there was plenty more mad-drunk Texans to take the places of the ones we had temporarily dispatched.

Suddenly there was a flash of steel. One of the cowboys had brung a Bowie knife cleaving down through the air - it laid open a horrible gash in Joe's cheek. The corporal bellowed like a wounded bear and launched his self through the air at his attacker. The knife clattered away. Joe's hands was clamped on the man's throat, choking the life out of him.

"For God's sake, Joe," I said. "Don't kill him!" I knowed I couldn't stop him. Too many cowboys was pressing in on me.

Joe kept right on choking the man, screaming in rage and pain.

"We gonna kill you, nigger," Horner yelled at me.

The air exploded in gunshots. I figured this was the end, and resolved to take one or two of them with me if I could.

There was another shot, and a hoarse yell. "Break it up!"

The shots didn't come from the cowboys. They was fired by a man standing in the doorway of the saloon, flanked by two more. A star flashed on his chest. Joe Ferguson finally let his opponent go, and looked to the doorway like the rest of us.

It was Jake Blackwell, the Texas Ranger.

"The next bullet goes to the first son of a bitch that moves."

Blackwell stepped inside. The bruised cowboys moved aside to give him room –all of them except Horner.

"You ain't our marshal," he told Blackwell, "Pepper Cash is. You ain't got no jurisdiction here."

Blackwell's revolver crashed down on Horner's head. The cowboy collapsed in a heap.

"Pepper Cash is hidin' under the kitchen table," Blackwell said. "And my jurisdiction is wherever I say it is."

The other cowboys backed away even further, probably hoping to stay out of the reach of Blackwell's arm just in case they offended him somehow.

"This is over," the Ranger said. "You soldiers pay your bill and be on your way."

One of the cowboys spoke up. "These damn uppity niggers—" Blackwell's gaze fell on him, and the man bowed his head in silence.

I groggily slapped my money on the table, then checked on Joe. The corporal was pressing a handkerchief onto his bloody face – his eyes looked just like Medicine Wolf's had at the Washita.

Hatred and fury.

"Let's go boys," I said, and nodded at the Ranger as I passed by him. "Reckon we even," I told him.

"Reckon we are, Sergeant. For now. But who's keeping score?"

We went outside and mounted up – as bloody, bruised, and mangled-up a bunch as you ever seen. Joe's face healed up, but the scar was ugly. I wondered what kind of scar he carried inside now.

A couple of weeks after the barfight we got a break from sawmill-building. Me and seven of my Company M boys was assigned to escort Medicine Wolf to his new home – a cell at Fort Leavenworth. He had been tried in a military court on a long list of charges, and sentenced to life in prison.

The public didn't know we was leaving, or the route we was going to take. We didn't want a bunch of Medicine Wolf's Indian supporters to swoop down on us somewhere along the trail, Hopefully, them and everybody else would be too caught up in following the news of Red Tree's trial, still going on in Texas, to look for us on the Kansas roads.

James Jefferson drove the wagon team, and Sergeant Moe Hughes sat beside him. Medicine Wolf was in the back, handcuffed –Bo Dishman sat on his right, Jimmy Peeler on his left. I rode my horse a few feet to the left of the wagon, while Joe Ferguson took the other flank. Troopers Green and Ballard brung up the rear. All of us kept our rifles ready.

Medicine Wolf was quiet on the first leg of the journey. He craned his neck in order to see the landscape all around him, eyes wide as he tried to drink in every detail – it was his last look at the land of his fathers. And he looked at the birds. The Cheyenne warrior watched as they floated in the sky, maybe wishing he could float there with them. His eyes was full of peace, and they was full of hatred, contentment and acceptance and bitter fury, all at the same time.

Medicine Wolf chanted. It was a mournful song, the sort of a song a mournful spirit might sing to itself, knowing no one else could hear. Then he buried his face in his hands and appeared to sob for several minutes. This made all of us very uncomfortable.

Finally he removed his face from behind his hands. His fingers snaked out and pulled Bo Dishman's revolver out of its holster. Blood covered the Indian's arm – in that split second I realized that Medicine Wolf had not been sobbing at all. He had been chewing big chunks off his very wrists so as to slip off the handcuffs. He sent a bullet into Dishman's face point-blank, and the back of the veteran's head exploded. Medicine Wolf leaped up and sent a second bullet down into Trooper Jimmy Peeler.

"Free!" Medicine Wolf yelled at the top of his lungs. "I am free!" He pointed the weapon at me, and I pumped two bullets into his chest. Hughes jumped clear of the wagon while Jefferson struggled to control the team.

Medicine Wolf did not drop his weapon or fall, although he did pause in his actions. Troopers Green and Ballard fired a volley into him. The stolen gun slipped from his ringers then, and he sunk to his knees.

"Free," Medicine Wolf whispered, and then pitched forward on his face.

Joe Ferguson had stood frozen the whole time, rifle at the ready but unfired. It was unlike Joe to let himself be ruled by fear, but I seen no other explanation for it.

We later found that the trial of Red Tree was cut short. Red Tree throwed himself out the second-story window of the courthouse, breaking his neck. Everybody was full of questions when we returned to the fort. All the troopers in our company, and all the others for that matter, wanted to hear about the deaths of Medicine Wolf and our brothers Dishman and Peeler. I let Jefferson tell the boys all the details; I made my report to Colonel Grierson and then slipped off by myself.

Joe Ferguson was right behind me, a silent shadow. I slumped down in a wicker chair in front of the post barber shop – I knowed Isabella was waiting for me, but my legs was too heavy to carry me to her just yet. Joe stood beside me.

Soon I sensed the presence of someone else. Jefferson had broken away from the other men – Hughes, Green, and Ballard was now giving the curious soldiers their own take on events. I seen them clustered down the street, a big mob of them. Jefferson put a hand briefly on my shoulder without looking at me. Before long Abe showed up too.

"Your man Bo was a good soldier," Abe said. "Probably would've made sergeant someday."

I nodded.

"So your boys took out Medicine Wolf," Abe continued, in a tone that suggested he didn't know what else to say.

"Yes suh," said Joe. "We tamin' the West." No one missed the sarcasm in his voice.

"Medicine Wolf took his self out," I said. "He just took Dishman and Peeler with him."

"I couldn't shoot him," Joe said. There was uncomfortable silence from everybody else.

"Things happen quick sometimes," Jefferson said.

"No," Joe responded. "No, it ain't that." He laughed – it was a bitter sound. "Don't you see? We killin' the last free people."

"Everybody free," Abe said. His words was defensive.

"We ain't free an' you know it," Joe said. "We used to be the white man's beast of burden, and now we his attack dogs. Ain't no difference."

"They's a world of difference," said Abe. "For one thing, we defendin' people. You ain't seen near as many burnt-up, cut-up farmers as the rest of us, boy. Raped women. Tortured young'uns."

"I seen somethin' damn near like it when I was growin' up the son of a field-slave," Joe said. "These Texas crackers would do the same thing to us that the Indians do to them, if they could get away with it."

Abe ignored him. "Number two," he said, "we gots a choice."

"Do this or starve. That ain't much of a choice."

Me and Jefferson had remained quiet, not even looking at the other two men as they argued.

Joe knelt beside me, thrusting his face up close to my own, his ugly scar level with my eyes.

"How 'bout you, Alfred Mann?" my student said. "Ever' time somebody starts a conversation like this you jest set there like a rock or a tree. I never know if you keepin' yo' opinions to yo'self, or if you jest don't got any."

Only my eyes moved, to stare into his. My face remained impassive.

"Which is it?" he demanded.

"You tired, Joe," I said. "It's been a rough day on all of us."

"Which is it," Joe repeated, his voice calmer.

I sighed. "You got a point in some ways," I told him, "an' it ain't easy to sleep nights sometimes. But we got our own people to think of."

"He's right, Corporal," Abe said. "We ain't slaves no mo' - if'n we wants to be citizens, we gotta carry our share of the load an' do our duty. I got three kids - I gotta build fo' the future. Gotta build them a better life."

"What does that have to do with takin' freedom from the Indians?"

"It's gonna happen anyways," Jefferson said. "They's no stoppin' that."

"We got pride," I said, straightening up in my chair. "We ain't property no mo'—we fightin' men. *Men.* An' if we prove we can do that job as good as any white man - better, even - then we've proved that we men. We've proved that we can do anything."

Joe shook his head. "The world ain't even payin' attention."

"Maybe they will someday," I said, "an' maybe they won't. But we'll know."

"Our sons will know," Abe added.

I said, "An' all the dignity an' pride an' manhood that was beat out of us in Carolina and Georgia and Alabama, we'll have it back. We are men - and we will know. So will ever'body else, too, whether they admit it or not."

Joe stroked his jaw, absently tracing the outline of the scar. "You a bunch of old men," he said. "You been chained up so long you don't even know what it means to think yo' own thoughts. You too scared of change to ever make any. I expected more."

Joe Ferguson walked away.

His words sounded familiar to me. A few years ago I had said them myself, to Uncle Wiley. I had loved that old man, but I had pitied him too - and looked down on him. I wondered what had happened to me. My own anger and hatred had kept me going for years. If it was burned out now, did I have anything left inside? I wasn't young anymore, I suddenly realized. I was approaching forty - truths that was obvious to me when I was twenty had somehow grown foggy along the way. I still didn't know exactly what freedom was.

"That boy is gonna come to a bad end,"Abe said. "'Less'n he calms down some."

"A man carries that much anger around inside him," Jefferson said, "he bound to burn his self out."

"We all full of anger," I said.

"Yeah," Jefferson agreed. "An' we ain't burned out, are we?"

None of us answered Jefferson's question. Not even Jefferson.

Chapter Thirty

"There's that gal again," Lanky Jim said.

"Sho'ly it ain't no accident she stands out here ever' day at this time," Boston Henry said with a grin.

The sawmill was long since completed and Fort McKavett was back up and running. There was still a handful of buildings to put up, though, so every day we trudged down to the mill and turned out more lumber.

And every day we passed by the Jackson place. And every day Narcissa was standing there in the yard watching us, fascinated. She was a pretty girl, that much is truth – seventeen years old and firmed up in all the right places. Sometimes one of the men would sneak a smile at her, or even a wave. Narcissa always responded in kind, giggling behind her hand – I made sure to dress down them men extra good afterwards, for the sake of their own well-being.

"I think she likes you, Jim," Boston said to the tall scout on that particular summer morning.

"You reckon?" Lanky Jim said. Then he blowed the girl a kiss. She giggled.

"Get movin', boys," I said, "double-time!"

Once we was safely out of sight I grabbed Lanky Jim by the shirt collar. "You idiot," I said. "I better not ever catch you doin' nothin' like that again, if I do I'll break yo' arm! That goes for you too, Henry."

"Sorry Sarge," Boston said.

"I'm sorry too, Alfred," Lanky Jim said. "I can't help it if the gals love me. Lanky Jim knows what the gals need."

"You crazy anyway, Seminole," Boston said. "A nice gal like that, you write her a letter – tell her that her face shines like the sun, stuff like that. That's the kind of thing that gets 'em." I gave Boston my meanest stare.

"I don't mean us, Sarge," he said. "I mean a fella that happened to court her. A white fella."

"I can't write no-way," Lanky Jim said. " 'Ceptin' for my name. Not the 'Lanky' part – just the 'Jim'."

"Good," I said. "Then you should be able to stay out of trouble." No more was said about Narcissa Jackson the rest of the morning. Once, though, Lanky Jim passed close by Boston and said, "You sure do know a lot about that poetry an' such. Where'd you learn that stuff at?"

"School, Lanky Jim. I'm a educated man."

"Get back to work," I said, "before I educate yo' ass."

"Shines like the sun," Lanky Jim said under his breath. "I declare. I like that."

Ain't nothing like having company for supper. A little pleasant talk, a few shared memories—it kind of helps a man to wind down after a hard day's work. It calms his nerves. Sometimes the company comes in the form of old friends, or maybe folks you've just met and taken a shine to.

In my case the company came in the form of my two brothers-in-law, Zeke and Pedro – a couple of smelly, horse-wrangling Indian scouts. For added measure they brung along their cousin Lanky Jim – last name unknown – who was every bit as wild as them.

Don't misunderstand me. I've had plenty of times out on the trail when I was lucky to find enough water for me and my horse to drink, for weeks on end sometimes. During trips like that I stunk worse than a three-legged mule with the runs. Point is, once I got back to my post, and well before I invited myself to somebody's house for supper, I would make the acquaintance of a bar of soap. That's where a little thing called "being civilized" comes into play.

And oh, I forgot to mention. Zeke brung his new wife, Emma. It seems I was right in my first estimate of what her character must be. Hellcat through and through. And a very well-fed hellcat.

"Zeke, you ignorant son of a bitch," she said, slapping the back of her husband's head. "Leave some beans fo' somebody else to eat! Idiot."

"Yes, dear," Zeke said absently, then snarled at her when her head was turned. Pedro giggled, and Zeke snarled at him, too.

Yes, sir. Nothing like having company for supper.

"Would you like some more beans, Emma?" Isabella said, forcing a smile.

"Hell no," Emma replied, showering cornbread crumbs onto the table. "Gimme some'a dat deer meat. We didn't never have no deer meat on the plantation back in Miss'ippi."

"It must be a terrible thing to be a slave," Pedro said.

"It is," said Zeke.

"I was better off than I am now," said Emma.

Lanky Jim reached over and took the bowl of beans out of Isabella's hands.

"Lanky Jim loves the beans," he said. Lanky Jim was so big that he often had to refer to himself in the third person.

"So, um, how did you two hook up, Zeke?" I asked.

Zeke shook his head. "It was all sort of like a dream."

Emma laughed. "De dumb son of a bitch got drunk an' woke up wid mo' dan jest a hangover." She punched his arm. "Right, dummy?"

Zeke nodded sadly.

"He ain't hardly got enough equipment to handle a big ol' woman like me. But I knowed a voodoo witch doctor back in Miss'ippi had some potions and exercises to cure up such as dat."

"I reckon I'll just skip dessert, Isabella, honey," I told my wife. "I got some reports..."

Isabella smiled through gritted teeth. "But Alfred. It's your favorite."

"Oh. What is it?"

"It don't matter. It's your favorite."

"Oh. I reckon I can stay."

Isabella nodded, her eyes bulging with the effort of maintaining the smile.

"You didn't write no letters to her or nothin'?" Lanky Jim asked Zeke.

"God, no." Emma punched him in the side and Zeke added, "On account of I can't write."

"If you was to of wrote a letter," said Lanky Jim, "what would you of said?"

Zeke smiled as he thought of the message he would like to have sent.

"Well?" Emma demanded. "Spit it out!"

"There just ain't no words for how I feel," said Zeke.

"Now, that is sweet," said Pedro.

"Hey, Zeke," I said. "Remember when I was about to marry Isabella, and you said if I didn't treat her right you'd kill me?"

"Yeah, I remember."

"Zeke!" Isabella exclaimed. "You didn't!"

"Oh, yeah," I said. "He did."

"He sure did," said Pedro.

"Anyway, Zeke," I said, leaning forward. "Does Emma have any brothers that's keepin' an eye on you?"

"Emma's brothers laugh whenever they see me," Zeke said.

"Real hard," added Pedro.

"You shoulda wrote a letter," said Lanky Jim.

I shook my head in frustration. "You gonna have to get over that letter-writin' business, Jim," I told him. "You got no idea how much trouble you liable to stir up."

Lanky Jim shrugged. He had grown up a free man out on the prairie – he had never really had to worry about what kind of reactions he might cause in white folks.

Emma belched loudly, then giggled. I looked at her, then I looked at Zeke, then back at her.

She was the strongest living argument against strong drink that I had ever seen.

Humpy Jackson was a hard man. When he lit down off his mule that bright sunny morning at the sawmill I knowed there was going to be trouble.

John Jackson had been one of the first white men to settle the area around Montreel. He was a hunchback –hence the nickname –and at fifty or sixty years old was wrinkled and white-headed. He was still a strong, powerful-built man despite all that, and his eyes was like two lumps of smoking coal. His neighbors liked and respected him but knowed enough to stay out of his way.

He had a whole passel of kids. His favorites was his daughters Henrietta, aged eighteen –and her little sister Narcissa.

Humpy stomped his way over to me, leading the mule. A white piece of paper was crumpled in his left hand.

"You, boy," he said. "You got a great big yaller-skinned nigger name of Lanky Jim workin' over here?"

"Jim ain't here today. He's on a scout. He ain't regular cavalry."

"I don't give a good gol'damn what he is," the old man said, then he hopped nimbly onto his mule.

"You over yonder," he said. "Step up here."

Boston Henry stepped forward. He looked at me, wanting to know what to do.

"I've seen you around my place," Humpy told him. Then he held up the scrap of paper. "You dropped this off with my daughter." He spit a thick stream of tobacco at Boston's feet.

"Reckon you'll do for now," Humpy said.

Quick as a snake, the old man pulled his rifle out of its saddle-boot and swung it around at Boston. I was too far away to stop what was going to happen. Our rifles was stacked inside the building, and I had seen no reason to wear my sidearm while sawing boards.

The rifle thundered twice and Boston Henry collapsed in the dust. Another young soldier, Cornelius Drake, fell next. Henry throwed the wad of paper at Boston.

I dove rolling into the dust. "Cover!" I yelled. "Get to cover and arm yo'selves!"

It was too late for that. Humpy galloped away, disappearing into the tall grass – the old man was a local legend, everybody knowed that he had evaded the Comanches here in their own territory for twenty years. He knowed the hills and the caves around the San Saba River better than God did.

Catching him and bringing him in would not be easy.

I dusted myself off with my hat as I jogged toward the corral. "Get yo' rifles an' mount up!" I hollered.

I paused a second to look at the bodies pumping blood into the dust. Jefferson, who knelt beside them, nodded sadly to confirm it – they was dead. He tossed me the paper. I opened it up.

Your face shines like the sun, Narcissa, it said. *You fill my heart with sunshine. Signed—JIM.* The name was written in a different, cruder hand than the letter.

"We gonna have a hard time catchin' him, Alfred," Jefferson said, echoing my own thoughts.

"By God," I answered, "he's gonna have a hard time gettin' away."

Chapter Thirty-One

We didn't catch Humpy Jackson that day. We didn't catch him the next day, neither.

Nor that week, nor that month. We had our best scouts on his trail – Seminoles, a couple of Lipans, several white Texas frontiersmen. Buffalo soldiers from the Ninth and Tenth Cavalry patrolled along with white troopers from the Fifth. Humpy Jackson avoided us all.

"It's these people around here," Sergeant-Major George Dickerson said. "They're all on his side – they probably would've done the same thing, if they'd had the guts. Now they're supplyin' the old coot, probably feedin' him as well."

"Ain't gonna help," I said. "We gonna find him."

Colonel MacKenzie felt the same way I did. Old Bad Hand was furious that someone could assault U.S. soldiers at their own sawmill. He was even more furious that the murderer could be protected from the army's wrath. MacKenzie posted warnings all over the surrounding towns that anybody caught harboring the fugitive would be dealt with severely.

People smiled at us when they seen us combing the hills for Humpy Jackson. Their smiles made me sick.

One day we was riding through the San Saba Hills, looking for any sign of the outlaw. I had about two dozen men with me. All of a sudden, I seen something that churned my guts up. I raised my hand and the other troopers reined in short.

"What is it, Sarge?" One young soldier said.

I trotted over to the side of the trail and examined the object which hung from the limb of a cottonwood tree.

"Don't look like nothin' but a ham," said the same soldier.

"It is a ham, Williams, you fool," said Ferguson.

I took out my knife and cut the ham down, then secured it to my saddle. There was a young washerwoman back at Fort McKavett named Marthie – her and the late Cornelius Drake was supposed to get married soon. Drake was the second trooper Humpy Jackson had shot down. I figured this ham rightly belonged to Marthie.

"How did a ham get all the way out here?" Williams said.

"Somebody left it here," Joe said, irritated. "They left it here for old Humpy. We ought to take ever' damn speck of food they've got."

"No way of knowin' who it was," I said. "Could've come from any house around here."

"Hell, we know who it is," Ferguson said. "It's ever'body in this whole damn county."

"We'd have to catch 'em in the act before we could take any action."

"We know where Humpy's house is," said Joe. "We know where all they houses is."

There was a couple of murmurs of agreement. "Answerin' hate with hate will only make things worse," I said.

"Ain't that what you used to do, Sergeant, before you become a old woman?"

I had come to feel real close to Joe Ferguson in the few years we had served together, and I had let slip to him a few things about my past. I regretted that now. And I already regretted what was going to have to happen.

I thought back to my old friend from the War, Chamas North. I found a lot to admire in Chamas when we was fighting Rebs together every day. But what might have happened, I wondered now, if he had lived to see the peace. It might be he could never have seen no peace.

Joe was right about me, though. I had changed, somewhere along the line - I don't know exactly when it happened, or why. But I changed.

I still got just as mad at the injustice around me. But I was tired of hating. I didn't have the strength for it anymore. Young men like Joe might think me weak for it, like some folks may have thought Lonnie weak.

Me, I feel like it made me stronger.

I rode up next to Joe. "I'm about sick of yo' whinin'," I told him. "You better learn to keep yo' opinions to yo'self, or else learn to love havin yo' ass kicked. 'cause that's what it's fixin' to come to."

Joe's scarred cheek twitched, and his hand moved to his holstered gun. Then he seen my eyes, and the cold steel in them - his hand relaxed and then moved back up to his saddle horn.

"Save it for Humpy Jackson," I said. "The same goes for you other boys! I don't care if these white folks around here loves us or not. I don't care if they make voodoo dolls of us to stoke they fires with.

"Only thing I want is Humpy Jackson in chains. Now, move out. You wastin' my time."

My first thought, when we finally did catch Humpy, was how glad I was that Joe Ferguson wasn't with us. Something ugly might have happened.

There was only me, four privates - Marner, Galle, Browning, and Sailors - and Lieutenant Lewis. Lewis was only a few weeks out of West Point - from which he barely graduated - and was already regretting his acceptance in a colored regiment. News of Custer's massacre had come to us about the same time Lewis arrived. He made it clear to everyone he would rather be fighting Sioux and Cheyenne in the north than chasing around after a half-crippled old farmer.

We could have got by fine without young Lieutenant Lewis.

It was pure luck that we happened upon Humpy Jackson that afternoon – we turned a corner in the road and came face-to-face with him. It was hard to tell who was more surprised, him or us. We wasn't even particularly looking for him that day; we had been sent into Montreel to requisition some supplies.

Humpy whipped that mule of his around and took off down the road fast as he could.

"Hyah!" I hollered at my black gelding, and spurred him into a gallop – I had not even waited for an order from the fresh-faced lieutenant.

Trying to save his dignity, Lieutenant Lewis belatedly yelled, "After him, men!"

I was hot on Humpy's heels, and the rest of the boys was right behind me. The gray-bearded fugitive twisted his neck around to see how close I was.

An instant later Humpy rode full-speed into a thick, low-hanging branch. He sailed backwards through the air while his mule continued to run – I almost trampled the old man beneath my horse's hooves.

I hopped out of the saddle. I landed with the reins in my left hand and my right hand holding a cocked pistol in Humpy's face.

"Hold still," I ordered him. The other troopers had reined in and now held their weapons trained on him.

Humpy squirmed around on the ground and squealed like a stuck pig. He thrashed like a man being stung to death by bees.

"I cain't hold still!" he hollered. "I've broke my back! God Almighty, I've broke my back!"

"Don't get too close to him, boys," I ordered.

The troopers was uncertain and nervous. "What if he's really hurt?" Trooper Browning said.

"That'd be a damn shame, now, wouldn't it," I replied.

"Sweet Jesus!" Humpy shouted. "The pain! Get me to a doctor, please – I need morphine. I need somethin'!"

It was these circumstances that made me grateful Joe wasn't there. He would have been tempted to give the old bastard something for his pain. "It sure looks broke," Lewis said.

"He has a hump, suh. It would be hard to tell."

"My house ain't far from here," Humpy said, breathless. "Take me home an' fetch me a doctor. You wouldn't drag a man with a broke back all the way to Fort McKavett just to put him in the stockade, would you?" He winced again from the pain. "For Christ's sake, Lieutenant, I ain't goin' nowhere!"

Lewis nodded. "We'll roll him onto a blanket and carry him to his house."

I looked up at the officer. "Are you sure that's what you want to do, suh? He could be fakin', an' this could be a trap."

"I am aware of the possibilities, Sergeant," Lewis said sharply. "I am also aware of this - if the public perceives that we have mistreated this man, things will get even worse for us around here." He snarled. "Everyone hates us as it is—you'd think we had horns and a tail."

"You learn to expect that, suh," I said. The poor fool probably never even stopped to think that the five troopers under his command wore a second uniform underneath their blues, one that was even more hated and which they could never strip off.

"I'll go after the doctor," Lieutenant Lewis said. "He probably wouldn't come if one of you asked him. Trooper Sailors, you're with me. The rest of you take the prisoner to his home and stand guard until I get there."

I sighed. "Yes, suh," I said. I took the blanket off my horse and laid it on the ground next to the moaning killer. I hated to think that his sweat would mingle with that of a noble animal like my gelding.

"Come on, boys," I said. "Browning, give me a hand with the prisoner."

"It ain't but a mile down the road," Humpy said, panting. "A easy walk."

Me and Browning carried him on foot while Marner and Galle led our horses.

"Take it easy, dammit," Humpy said.

"Shut up, you son of a bitch," Browning told him. "Cornelius Drake was my best friend."

Humpy lapsed into a sullen silence. I doubt if any black man had ever spoke to him like that before.

When we arrived at the Jackson cabin, two of his children was playing out in the yard. The San Saba River gurgled not far away. When we walked past the young'uns and they seen their daddy, they ran into the house.

"Mama, Mama, come quick!" said one little girl, not more than seven years old. "A bunch of niggers is here, an' they've got Pa!" The other little girl started crying.

Mrs. Jackson appeared at the door. Two little boys peeked out from around her – behind her stood the town beauties, Narcissa and Henrietta. Narcissa smiled at me. It chilled my blood.

"What have you done to my husband, damn you," Mrs. Jackson said in a solemn voice.

"He fell off his mule, ma'am," I told her. "He says his back pains him."

"Pains me hell, it's broke," he said.

"Bring him in the house and set him in bed," she told us.

We went inside the house. Browning and me eased him onto a soft-matressed bed set up in the front room – I reckon with a family that big people sleeps everywhere.

Mrs. Jackson placed a quilt over her husband, then leaned over and embraced him. None of us seen what else happened during that embrace. We learned about it before the whole thing was over, though.

Mrs. Jackson had slipped a revolver under her husband's quilt.

The four of us stood there in sight of the bed, cradling our rifles for the longest time.

"Excuse me, ma'am," I finally said. "I believe that my colonel will expect me to search yo' premises."

Her face reddened and the breath went out of her. "Yo' cabin, ma'am," I said. "I mean yo' cabin."

"Oh," she said. "Well I reckon I cain't stop you, now, can I?"

"I reckon not," I said. "You boys stay alert. I'll be right back." I found nothing unusual inside the actual house. Down in the root cellar was a different story. Underneath some old boards was a hole. I looked around to make sure none of the Jackson children was spying on me, then I pushed the boards aside and climbed down into the opening.

It was a tunnel. I fumbled around inside it awhile, but decided it would be best to explore the thing further later on when I had a light with me. But at least I knowed one reason why we'd had such a hard time catching the old weasel all these months. He had been hiding in his own house, at least part of the time, approaching it unseen by means of a hidden tunnel.

I went back to the Jacksons' front room. It was dark outside now, and Lieutenant Lewis still had not arrived with a doctor. "Everything's quiet, Sarge," Marner said.

I nodded. "That's the way I like it."

Narcissa smiled at me again, an open, inviting smile—I wondered if she was touched in the head, childish innocent, or just plain mean.

My spine stiffened. "Henrietta," I whispered.

"No, I'm Narcissa."

My head jerked around, eyes searching the dim room. "Where's the other girl?" I demanded.

"What other girl, Sarge?" Browning said.

"They was two growed girls when we got here, dammit. Now one of 'em's gone."

I tore through them other rooms, but no one was there.

"Where's Henrietta, ma'am?" I said sternly.

Mrs. Jackson shrugged. "She run away, I reckon. Niggers scare her. I don't know why."

I sighed, and leveled a finger at my men. "No one else leaves this room. Nobody."

The troopers nodded obediently.

The minutes dragged by with no words spoken to break the stillness. After about two hours I felt a tug at my sleeve. It was Narcissa, but she was staring straight ahead. "I gotta talk to you, Mister Sergeant," she whispered.

"Why?"

"In the back room. It's a secret."

I ignored her.

"It's about the letter. It's about Lanky Jim."

I nodded. I stepped away from the girl and walked toward the back room. I heard her small steps following me.

"What is it, chile," I said.

"Lanky Jim, he's a big fella," she said. "He always used to smile at me."

"What's your secret?"

"I liked it when he smiled at me. Ain't you never gonna smile at me, Sergeant?" She ran a finger lightly up my sleeve.

A whippoorwill called outside. The bird's song had a strange echo to it. It had an echo.

I brushed the girl's arm away and ran toward the front room. "Browning!" I hollered. "Watch out!"

But it was too late. Humpy Jackson sat bolt upright in bed and opened fire with his revolver. At that instant the front door flew open and four cowboys rushed in—I had seen them around town before, and believed I knowed their names. They had guns drawed, too, and blasted a volley into my men. The gunshots was deafening in the little cabin, especially when mixed with the screams of frightened children and dying men.

Even as I seen these things, the killer seen me. I throwed myself through the front window. I didn't quite make it in time, though – I felt a bullet plow its way into my side.

As soon as I hit the ground, showered by broken glass, I clasped my hand to my side and started running. I jumped down into the root cellar; seconds later I heard feet running past.

"We hit him good, boys," I heard a voice say. "He's prob'ly halfway to being as dead as his partners."

I moved them boards aside, and was struck by a sobering thought - if them cowboys had light to see by, they could follow my blood trail into the cellar. I bumbled my way through Humpy Jackson's tunnel. I felt the life draining out of me with every step.

Humpy's tunnel led to the riverbank. I slipped softly into the water, until I was hid by it from the shoulders down. I held my revolver out of the river, letting the hand which held it rest on the bank.

"He's gotta be around here somewheres," a distant voice said. "He seen our faces, we have to make sure of him."

It occurred to me that I have had this tune sung to me before. The last time was in New York City. It was getting old quick. My blood flowed away with the San Saba River, and before long my thoughts flowed away with it.

I woke up in a hospital bed, bright sunlight shining in my face. Even before I opened my eyes, I felt Isabella's hand in mine - I smiled when I actually seen her.

"Mornin' honey," I said. "What's fo' breakfast?"

She squeezed my hand.

Then other faces hove into view. The post surgeon was there, and so was Abe, and George Dickerson.

And Colonel Ranald MacKenzie was there. I wondered briefly where good old Colonel Grierson was - then I remembered that him and half the regiment had been reassigned to Arizona.

"Did you see their faces, Mann?" MacKenzie said. His eyes smoldered with barely suppressed fury. "Did you recognize them?"

"This soldier needs his rest, Colonel," the doctor said.

"Three soldiers lie in their graves today, doctor," said MacKenzie. "They need their rest too. They'll rest better if they know they're about to have some company."

I coughed. "Whitey Nelson," I said. "Bobby Steele. Wash Lane." I coughed again. "And there was one fat fella, with a red beard. He works at the Crazy T - cain't remember his name..."

"Nash?" Abe volunteered.

"No," I said, "older..."

"Jorgenson," George said.

"Yeah, that's him."

MacKenzie put a hand on my shoulder, a rare display of affection. "Relax now, soldier. You did a good job."

"I lost three men."

"You were lucky to get out yourself," Abe said. "It's a good thing we found you when we did."

"Where's - Lieutenant Lewis?"

MacKenzie chuckled. "Hiding, probably. That doctor led him on a wild goose chase all night long."

"Lewis didn't know his way back to the Jackson place," Abe explained.

"Rest now," MacKenzie said again. "We have work to do."

MacKenzie rode out to the Jackson place personally, at the head of a company of Fifth Cavalry troops. They burned down the cabin, and then arrested Mrs. Jackson and the two older girls, letting them stew in jail for several days.

Local citizens was outraged. Bad Hand MacKenzie didn't care.

Chapter Thirty-Two

I understood MacKenzie's order to burn the Jacksons' home. The best way to get rid of vermin was to destroy its hiding place. Now, weeks after my release from the hospital, I watched another group of rundown shacks burn. It gave me a sense of deep satisfaction. The bitter smoke that stung my eyes and blackened the sky would bring some cleanness back to the border canyon. Here were some killers who wouldn't escape justice the way Humpy Jackson had.

"They give us a good run," Joe Ferguson said.

I nodded, watching as the last of the bandits was loaded onto the wagon. The chains that weighted down their hands seemed to drag their souls down into the ground.

Good, I thought. *That's where they belong.* I wished I could chain them with a conscience. I wished that the memories of their many victims would one day reach out of the grave and squeeze their darkened hearts.

They had once been comancheros. They was men - and women - from all walks of life, with only two things in common: greed and contempt for humanity. For years they had made a living for themselves by selling guns and whiskey to the Comanches, and from buying the Indian raiders' stolen goods. This included livestock; cattle, horses—and people. Innocent women and children taken from their homes by Apaches and Comanches was delivered to this human refuse, who then sold them into Mexico as slaves.

The Comanches was all gone now. Even the fiercest of them was on the reservation.

Colonel MacKenzie had been waging a smaller war since Quanah Parker's surrender - his goal had been to wipe out the comancheros. He had finally succeeded.

The group which we had arrested that day had been a last holdout. Unable to survive as middlemen, they had turned to raiding themselves. The bandits struck just like Indians. They stole, robbed, plundered...murdered with savage indifference. They struck at Mexicans and Americans alike. They even raided the reservations of their former partners.

Their vicious ride was over now. They had taken two of my troopers down with them. If it was left up to me I ain't even sure if I would have buried the half-dozen renegades we had shot dead for resisting arrest. Captain Forster insisted on a burial, though.

"They was a mean bunch," Joe Ferguson said – I thought his voice carried a hint of admiration. "They was smart, too, but not smart enough." He waved an arm at the canyon floor. "They didn't need to keep using this pathetic little village. It was a holdover from the days when the Indians had to know where to find 'em.

"They should've kept on the move, like a pack of wolves. A smart man could keep operating in these mountains and canyons forever."

"They was evil," I said.

"You sound like a preacher, Alfred. A lot of things is evil. It depends on how you look at 'em."

I walked away – I had to see to the burial of the renegade dead. I looked over my shoulder to find that Joe Ferguson had not moved.

He was staring intently at the canyon walls. I don't know what he hoped to find.

I scouted out ahead of the company, on my own, looking for signs of renegade stragglers. I knowed I wouldn't find any. All the bandits had been accounted for.

I was looking for something else on that mountain. It was something just out of reach, like a common word or the name of an old friend which you can't quite formulate in your mind.

Maybe I was looking for God. Maybe I was looking for myself. Maybe I wasn't sure if I believed in either one. It was a high mountain. I was closer to the sky than I had ever been, I reckon. The air was clean.

I had seen something familiar in Joe Ferguson's eyes that day at the comanchero village. It was a burning. The man was full of rage and didn't know where to send it. I remembered the feeling. Joe reminded me so much of myself – that's why I kept cutting him slack, and had never reported his outbursts and insubordination. I felt kinship with his anger.

And what about me? My own fury had faded quite a bit since I rejoined the army – I don't know where it went to. Somewhere along the line I had become comfortable. I had never thought that would happen.

The real problem was that I had nothing to take the place of the rage. Sure, I had Isabella's love to make me whole when I was with her –but I still wasn't equipped to deal with the rest of the world.

Isabella had something that I was missing, as had Lonnie Blake. Even Uncle Wiley – I realized now that I understood him much better since I had growed older.

They had a dignity about them. They had a sense that there was something more. They had faith.

Without my sustaining hatred I was only a shell. Maybe, I thought, maybe I am not really free. Not yet.

I looked up at the stars – they seemed close enough to breathe on. I picked out the North Star, which had pulled gentle Topaz along like a magnet. I took some comfort in knowing I was closer to it than before.

"Oh Lawd," I said, "I come to You now—" I stopped, uncomfortable. The echo of my own words made me feel silly.

"Show me how," I said simply.

The next morning I went down the mountain, back to my own company. I had not found God. Then again, I was only there scouting for sign – maybe I had stumbled across some, but failed to read it in the darkness. The big sky was whispering to me. I felt like I'd had a brief taste of something, and then it was gone.

I was not as lonely riding down the mountain, though, as I had been when riding up.

Joe Ferguson left a couple of weeks later. He just disappeared one night, with no word to anyone.

"I never figured Joe for no deserter," James Jefferson said.

"You never know 'bout folks," I said. I knowed, but didn't say, that Joe had to run. He didn't know what he was running from, or what he was running to – he only knowed that he had to run. Running was his freedom.

I hoped that Joe could find God, if I could not. Or a good woman. Anything to bring him a measure of peace. I hoped that one day he would understand that, at least to some people, freedom is standing still.

In the fall of '79, we was sent west to be reunited with Colonel Grierson at Fort Apache. It was not to be a joyful reunion –the Tenth was one of several regiments under General Pope's command assigned to comb Arizona, New Mexico, and West Texas for a band of Apache marauders.

Their leader was named Victorio. He made Medicine Wolf look like a Quaker.

The Apaches was upset because the government had decided to remove them from their ancestral home in the Mogollon Mountains and settle them on the San Carlos reservation. Victorio swore he would die free – no one doubted he would take a lot of folks with him.

"Capture seems unlikely," I heard Pope tell Colonel Grierson. "We can kill them all, but it will take awhile."

Within a few weeks after Victorio's war started, dozens of settlers had died horribly. We all growed more and more frustrated—the Apaches struck at will, and we never even got a glimpse of them.

That changed soon, though not in our favor.

About a hundred Apaches swooped down on Company E's corral, only a mile from the fort. By the time the rest of us heard the racket and rushed to our comrades' aid, Victorio had taken off with about fifty horses and left a dozen troopers dead or dying in the dust.

"They ain't human," Jefferson said. "They're ghosts."

"With thinkin' like that," I said, "we'll wind up the ghosts. We'll get 'em."

That was easier said than done. It was two months before we got another shot at them.

Our scouts picked up their trail in the mountains— Captain Forster ordered us to charge in their general direction.

"Their position is too strong, suh," I told him. "We need to get reinforcements."

"Then we'll just knock them out of that position, sergeant," the captain said. "Move them out."

I took a deep breath. "Yes, suh," I said.

It was like the sand hills fight at the Cheyenne agency all over again. Victorio's Apaches pinned us down before we got halfway to them. We lost four men right off the bat, with several others wounded. We lay there and shot at them throughout the whole afternoon; about every half-hour or so we lost another man.

Jefferson crawled over to me, keeping his head down.

"Ain't no way we're ever gonna knock them out of there, Alfred," he said.

"I know it."

"We're wastin' bullets," he said. "An' blood."

I risked a quick look behind us. Captain Forster was hunkered down in back of some rocks, looking completely confused.

"Hold the boys, Jeff," I told Jefferson. "Keep up a cover fire."

"You goin' somewhere?"

I nodded. "I'm fixin' to go have a word with the captain."

I jumped up and ran fast as I could to the back of the line. The noise of bullets pinging around me made my legs pump harder.

I jumped behind Forster's protective rocks.

"Captain," I said.

"What is it, sergeant?"

"We've bit off more than we can chew, Captain. We're gettin' shot up bad, an' I doubt if we've managed to hit a single Apache."

"We have to keep trying," Forster said. He sounded uncertain.

"We're gonna run out of ammunition, Captain," I said. "Once that happens them Apaches can just come down here an' knock us in the head with rocks, if'n they want to."

Forster bit his lip. "We'll retreat then, for now. We know where the bastards are. We can come back in force."

But of course, there was no Apaches there when we came back. We had throwed seven lives away for nothing. Forster was ridiculed in the papers and among the other officers as an idiot.

It wasn't long until Forster retired his commission and we had yet another new captain.

Victorio, on the other hand, did not retire his commission. He just kept right on killing people. He killed just as many south of the border as he did on our side, inflaming the Mexicans against him. The fact that two armies was on his trail did not seem to bother him.

It was February, and I was hunched down beside the campfire having my morning coffee and hardtack. Grierson himself was in the field with us. We believed we was closing in on Victorio.

Fact is, he was closing in on us.

Our breakfast was disturbed by a single gunshot. Trooper Jurgens, our picket, pitched forward dead.

"We're under fire, men," Grierson said. "Take cover!"

We all scrambled for whatever protection we could find. About a half-a-dozen men from company G was not able to find cover from the sniper attack, though – they had been caught out in the open, on foot. Within seconds they had all fallen. A couple of them was still moving. One was First Sergeant Abe Armstrong.

"I'm hit, Sweet Jesus," the other survivor said, and he tried to climb to his feet. I was able to trace the path of the Apaches' next bullet as it entered the top of the man's chest and came out the small of his back, taking bloody bowels with it.

Abe stayed still.

Our enemies kept spraying rifle fire at us from the rocks.

"Shit," I said.

"I'm startin' to get tired of this," Jefferson said. "If this keeps up *I'm* movin' onto the damn reservation."

"Cover me, Jeff," I told him. I ran for my horse – once more bullets kicked up dust all around me. Jefferson and the boys raised up and fired back, distracting the Apaches a little. A bullet ripped a new crease in the top of my white hat.

I jumped into the saddle and jabbed my spurs hard. I was leaned sideways against the neck of my horse, trying to imitate the trick I'd seen the Comanches use so many times. I fired my revolver at the rocks as I rode.

When I reached Abe, I hopped to the ground, holding the reins in one hand and crouching beside my friend.

"Alfred, you damn fool," Abe said – tears of pain in his eyes. The bullet had entered his chest just below the right shoulder. "Get your ass out of here!" he rasped.

"Believe me, that's my plan. Now, come on!" I reached under his left shoulder and pulled him up. A bullet hit close by.

I shoved Abe onto the horse and climbed up behind him. Abe grunted as a shot took him in the arm. I felt hot pressure as another one got me in the fleshy part of the thigh.

I spurred the black gelding's flanks harder. We leaped over some low rocks and was back among our comrades – we both fell out of the saddle. Jefferson was there to catch me. My hand was locked in Abe's.

"My God, Sergeant," Grierson said. "That was magnificent. Simply magnificent."

"It hurt," I said.

The rifle fire finally stopped. The Apaches decided to do us a favor and leave.

Chapter Thirty-Three

The thigh-wound wasn't serious enough to keep me out of action for long. Abe's chest injury was more serious, of course – it looked for awhile like he might have to go back to the civilian life. As it was, all he had to suffer through was several months of undivided attention from Jamie and the kids.

We, on the other hand, was receiving the undivided attention of Victorio.

I had twenty-five men from Company M with me at the old Barrows stage station in New Mexico territory. We was just getting ready to bed down for the night – at first light we was going to mount up and join the rest of the battalion in Arizona. They once more had Victorio on the run, and we had been called off our patrol.

Everything changed when the courier arrived. He thundered his horse into the station and ran from the lathered-up beast without even securing it. The private was breathless and pale.

"What is it, son?" I asked him. I was in my undershirt, and still pulling on my suspenders.

"Victorio," the private said, which somehow did not surprise me. "He slipped past us – he's doubled back to New Mexico territory. He's headed right for a little town called Ageeville. Somebody's got to warn 'em, if he ain't burned the place down already!"

"Mount up, men," I ordered. "Private, you rest up a few minutes, get a bite to eat, an' take a fresh horse back to the General.

"Tell him Company M is in Ageeville."

We arrived at the town at about three o'clock in the morning. We had beat the Apaches there, but had no way of knowing by how much. Victorio could show up at any minute.

Ageeville was sleeping peacefully. I ordered a dismount, than drawed out my revolver. Its familiar weight was a comfort to me in the darkness. It was not the old cap-and-ball given to me by Lonnie – that one had been packed safely away in my foot locker for years, made obsolete by the cartridge pistol – but it felt like an extension of me anyways.

I fired it into the air – then a second time, and a third.

"Wake up people!" I hollered. I waved my arms as a signal for the other men to make as much racket as they could.

Folks slowly started to fill the streets. Quite a few of the men was bare-chested or in their nightshirts – several was carrying guns, not sure what to expect. I took a quick glance around the moonlit town. It was bordered by open ground on three sides – the north side was nestled against a stand of trees.

There was nothing to stop a few dozen Apaches—maybe a couple of hundred – from riding right in.

A red-faced little man in a night-dress stomped up to me. "I demand an explanation for this!" he said.

"Who are you?"

"I'm the mayor of this town, that's who I am!"

"Pleased to meet you, Mister Mayor," I said, and then I brushed past him. "Quieten down, people!" I said. "Listen to me!"

Their curious murmurs faded away.

"I am First Sergeant Alfred Mann, Tenth Cavalry, Company M. Yo' town is in the direct path of Victorio an' his Apache warriors. We got to get ready for 'em, an' we got to do it now."

A sick feeling of dread hovered in the air around the crowd. A couple of women was crying.

"I reckon y'all got some kind of general store or somethin' in this town," I said.

"We – we've got two, actually," said the mayor.

"Good. We gonna need axes an' saws, an' lots of 'em. Anybody that gots them things at home, fetch 'em now."

"Why?" the mayor asked.

"We gonna cut down them trees yonder an' stack 'em up in a barricade all around this town." I raised my voice up a notch. "An' we gonna do it now! Come on, get movin'!"

Some of the citizens hesitated. "Ain't no damn niggers can come in here and start tellin' us what to do!" one man said.

"Get to work on them trees," I told my own men. Then I turned to the citizen who had spoke.

"I been fightin' Indians fo' twelve years," I told him. "An' I got the scars to prove it. Have you ever seen what Apaches does to women and kids when they get ahold of 'em?"

The man shook his head.

"Well, I'm here to make sure you don't see them sights today." I stepped back and faced the whole crowd. "So you all gonna do what I say, when I say it. Next one that argues with me gets his skull cracked, 'cause I ain't got time for it. Move, people!"

The people moved.

We all attacked them trees like we was swinging our axes at Victorio himself. We shouldered the logs side-by-side, black man and white, and set them in place on Ageeville's perimeter.

While I worked I hollered out encouragement.

"Faster—move faster!" I said.

In five hours we had a crude barricade. There was plenty of trees left, and we could easily have spent two or three more hours on our project, but we suddenly had more pressing matters to attend to.

The Apaches was in sight now. They was riding in from the west.

An unnatural silence settled in on us all when we seen them. I found myself wishing - not for the first time - that

Jefferson was with me to watch my back, instead of in Arizona territory with the rest of the company.

"You civilians will fire when I say to fire," I said, "and not before. Anybody that jumps the gun, or that tries to run away, I will shoot down myself."

I sent the women and kids indoors. Then I stepped up to the barricade and aimed my rifle.

"Get ready," I shouted.

The Apaches was close enough now to pick out individual targets. "Fire at will," I said, and we punched a volley of bullets into them.

Them Indians was mighty surprised – except for a handful that never had a chance to be. Apaches started dropping like ripe apples.

I always respected the Apaches, and understood why they would fight us. But when you are staring at a hundred Apaches who are barreling down on you, eager to take your life and cut you in pieces if possible, and take their revenge on women and little kids and old folks – when you are in that situation, your heart leaps at the sight of every dead Apache that hits the ground. Every dying Indian adds a few minutes of life to your own self, and dead Indians become beautiful to you.

Later on, when your blood stops racing and your life is securely your own once more, you might take time to dwell on the injustice of it. You can reflect on the tragedy and wish it could have all been handled differently.

But in the thick of the fight you want only two things: to kill and to stay alive. There is room for nothing else in the universe.

The Apaches was falling back.

"Cease fire!" I yelled. "Cease fire! They're leaving our range. Save yo' bullets in case they come back!"

They came back in less than half-an-hour – I guess to see if we was really serious about this staying alive business. We showed them how serious we was.

"Fire!"

More Apaches died, and the rest finally decided to give it up and ride away. We watched the horizon for several minutes to make sure they was really gone.

"We did it," a citizen muttered. He seemed to be having trouble believing his own words. "We did it!"

A cheer erupted from the throats of every man present. It was the most heartfelt cheer I've ever heard.

The women and kids came running out of their houses. People was embracing their families right there on the barricade. Women was hugging me – not even stopping to think that it might be improper – and white men was pumping my hand and clapping my shoulder. We was all laughing and grinning. The man who called me a "damn nigger" a few hours before shook my hand.

Us soldiers took turns standing watch at the barricades, just in case Victorio decided to test his luck with Ageeville again, but he never did. The town would live. It had come within a hairsbreadth of being a slaughterhouse, but it would live.

The women of the town prepared a feast. We all ate together, sitting on the logs we had cut together—the only color that mattered to anyone was the red of the blood that was still in all of our veins. It was a very sweet day. I opened up all my senses and drunk in every precious scrap of it, for I knowed that such things are rare in this world.

"Hey Alfred—did you know that we've been trailin' Victorio for almost a year now?"

I paused, weighing Jefferson's words, swirling the coffee around in my tin cup. "It *has* been that long, ain't it?"

"It's about as frustratin' as when we hunted Humpy Jackson," Jefferson said, leaning closer to the fire.

"At least now we've got an enemy we can respect."

"Yeah, it's a shame, ain't it. Victorio's gonna wind up either dead or in chains. Humpy Jackson is prob'ly the mayor of Montreel by now."

I chuckled. "That's life in these United States, I reckon."

"I've got two years left till my third hitch is up," Jefferson said. "I'm thinkin' about pitchin' it in."

"Why would you wanna do that?" I asked him.

He shrugged. "I'm about ready for somethin' different, I guess."

"Gettin' shot at by Indians beginnin' to bore you, is it? 'cause if it is, shoot, we about out of Indians. They'll have to find somebody new to shoot at us before long. It'll be a change of pace, anyways."

Jeff laughed softly. "No, no. There's gotta be somethin' more than this."

"You got two years to come to your senses."

"Yeah," he said. "I don't wanna go Joe Ferguson's route."

"Seems like I'm the onliest one crazy enough to want to stay here."

"You a born soldier, Alfred. You make it look easy."

"I've never heard that before."

"Everybody knows it." Jeff nodded for emphasis, then pulled out his pipe. He stared into the fire while he drawed on it.

I felt like a born soldier, but I wasn't sure that's what I wanted to feel like. I had to admit to myself, though never to anyone else, that I was afraid. I wasn't scared of Indians, especially. I was afraid to take off this uniform.

The Apache snipers was at us again. We had been on patrol -thirty of us, including our new captain—when they opened fire on us. We was hot and dusty. The waterhole we had been headed for was only a couple of hundred yards away, but it was suddenly out of reach.

The first bullet dropped Captain Rieburger. The second took Trooper Charlie Wilkins in the shoulder; the third found its way to Trooper Garvey Hayes's throat.

"Fall back to them rocks!" I hollered. We drug the injured men with us. A fourth trooper was hit in the back before he found cover – he died instantly. Garvey Hayes thrashed madly, trying to suck in breath through his destroyed windpipe. His last minute of life seemed to take hours. Listening to him die shook up even the veterans. Bullets smacked and whined off the stones around us. We could find no targets to shoot at.

"Looks like we're gonna be here awhile," I said.

"I've always heard that Injuns was bad shots," one young soldier said.

"I wish somebody would tell them that," said Jefferson.

"I'm thirsty," another man said.

"You'll get thirstier 'fore it's over," I told him. "Jeff, how's the captain?"

Jefferson shook his head. He was kneeling beside the young officer. Rieburger was conscious – blood was caked on his mouth.

"I think it missed his lungs," said Jefferson, "but I ain't sure. It's bound to have tore up some organs. I just don't know which ones."

Rieburger could not speak. He looked up at me like a helpless child.

"You gonna be all right, Captain," I said gently. "Wilkins, how's that shoulder?'

"It hurts like hell, Sarge," the man said between clenched teeth.

I sighed. "If any of you boys sees an Apache, by all means shoot him. But don't shoot just to hear the sound of your own guns."

We got through the afternoon with no more major injuries. One man got his face cut up from rock chips when a bullet struck right next to his head.

"Stay alert," I told the men once the sun went down. "They might try to rush us in the dark." There was no moon in the sky, but I doubted if blindness would stop an Apache.

The night wore on. Every once in awhile a rifle sounded – the Apaches' way of letting us know they was still at home.

"Damn," Jefferson whispered. "That water is so close. I can smell it." We had been planning on filling our canteens at the natural water tank. What little water we had left was gone now, and our lips cried out for more.

"I sure could use a good drink," Trooper Thompson said.

"These wounded men needs it a lot more than we do," I reminded him. "If we had any."

I sensed Jeff's nod in the darkness. "They need water bad, Alfred."

"Maybe we could make a dash for the tank?" Thompson said.

"They're expecting us to do that. Half of us would die afore we got our feet wet."

"It's dark," Thompson said.

"Thirty men moving make a lot of noise," I said. "All they'd have to do is shoot at the sound."

I took a deep breath. "Jeff–give me your canteen. Some of you other boys too. I figure I can carry about half-a-dozen."

"What you up to, Alfred?" Jefferson said.

"One man might can slip by 'em. If he's quiet."

"But you in command now, with the captain out. We needs you right here."

"You in charge now, Jeff. Till I get back." I paused. "It ain't my idea of a good time, but I figure I stand the best chance."

"Yeah," Jefferson said, "you prob'ly do. But you be careful, Alfred."

"I will." I grabbed his arm briefly. "This ain't the first time I've snuck my way to water, you know."

Crouching, I moved into the darkness. I flopped onto my belly and crawled, staying as close to the hard-packed soil as possible, for fear the faint glow of the starlight would outline me.

I moved one inch at a time. I forced my breath to come shallow - I wanted nothing to give me away. I heard nothing, but I could sense the Apache eyes probing the darkness.

It seemed to take forever, but I finally reached the water hole. I uncapped the first canteen and lowered it in, letting the water slip in naturally, not gurgling.

I heard voices not far away. They spoke Apache. I flattened myself even closer to the ground, willing myself to melt into it, become one with it. When my task was complete I started crawling back toward the rocks. I was over halfway there when I bumped into the leg of an Apache.

He was a lot more surprised than I was, fortunately. I grabbed his leg and pulled hard - when he hit the ground I hopped on him, my knees knocking his wind out and my left hand clamping around his throat. I had my knife out and was bringing it down when he grabbed my right hand with both of his. He was weak from no air, though, and the blade slipped between his ribs and found his heart.

Someone noticed the noise, for a voice rang out - probably calling the dead Indian's name. I jumped to my feet and started running. Shots barked out all around me, but they had no clear target and I escaped.

The wounded men got their water. The rest of it went to our horses—they was going crazy, thirsty as they was and this close to the tank.

They'd have to do the rest of their drinking somewheres else. Just before dawn we mounted up and broke for it— several of our horses died before we reached the next waterhole, but the soldiers made it through all right. Once again, we had faced the Apaches and barely escaped with our command intact.

I was starting to get mad.

Chapter Thirty-Four

It finally happened at a place called Rattlesnake Springs. There the Tenth Cavalry paid Victorio back, in spades.

We had been moving forward, to reinforce the First, Fifth and Sixth Cavalries in their pursuit of the Apache renegades. Our scouts informed us, though, that Victorio and his band—two or three hundred strong, more than half of them able-bodied warriors—had ditched the U.S. Cavalry near the Mexican border and slipped back through. They was traveling due north.

"They'll be headed for water," Colonel Grierson said, a gleam in his eye. "Rattlesnake Springs is the closest site. If we can beat them there and lay a proper trap, we'll have them. We'll give them a taste of their own medicine."

"But Colonel," said Captain Vaughn, of Company E. "That's sixty-five miles away. We'll never beat them with the head start they got—it's impossible."

Grierson looked directly at me. "How about you, First Sergeant? What is your opinion?"

The question took me by surprise. "With all due respect, suh," I said after a brief pause. "My opinion is that me and my men want Victorio's ass. Suh."

Grierson chuckled. "Sergeant Mann has delivered the most persuasive argument, gentlemen. Mount up. We're riding hard."

Grierson knowed that his objective was possible. He had done something very similar years before, during the Civil War –he'd caught the Rebs completely by surprise.

We moved at a frantic pace. Grierson always kept the mountains between us and our enemies, just to make double sure they never seen us.

Rattlesnake Canyon, and the spring inside it, was calm when we got there. We had done it. We knowed that Victorio could not be far behind. So far as I know, no other army unit ever outmarched any Apaches, before or since.

Grierson assigned Companies M and E to station themselves at the spring, under cover. The other nine companies would hide their selves deeper inside the canyon.

The colonel walked over to me a few moments before he joined the main body in the canyon shadows.

"Sergeant," Grierson said, "we have served together a long time."

"Yes, suh," I said.

"You have shown yourself to be a capable soldier," he said. "Your foray for water while under fire was most impressive. I thought you should know that I've put you in for the Medal of Honor."

"Thank you, suh."

The colonel smiled. "You're proving them all wrong, you know, Alfred." The colonel moved away, and we took up our positions at the stream.

Three hours later the Apaches arrived. I stared at them through my field glasses—Victorio was in the forefront of the group. In over a year of fighting and chasing and killing, this was the first glimpse I had ever caught of the man.

Victorio's appearance surprised me. He did not look like a cruel, ruthless killer. He did not look like a noble warrior. He looked like - a man, just a common everyday plain-faced man.

It's common men, I suppose, who hunger the most for freedom. Victorio reined his horse in sharply and held up a hand. His followers stopped as well. Victorio's horse cantered back and forth in front of the group, its rider staring intently at the spring. The canny Apache sensed a trap.

Now we put Colonel Grierson's plan into action. Both companies left their hiding places and charged directly at the hostiles, shooting as we went. The alert Indians returned our fire immediately. A handful of troopers dropped from their saddles. The Apaches surged forward, threatening to overwhelm us with their numbers.

Captain Vaughan ordered the bugler to signal retreat.

"Fall back," the captain hollered. "Deeper into the canyon!"

We high-tailed it, the Indians close behind us. Some of our fallen men had not received fatal wounds, and was still alive when overtaken – I heard their shrill screams over the thunder of our hooves.

We wheeled suddenly around and dismounted. The other nine companies of buffalo soldiers stood and fired into the mass of charging Indians. The Apaches was punched from all sides. It was just the sort of trick Victorio himself liked to pull. I'm surprised he fell for it – I reckon he didn't think we could ever be as clever as him.

Victorio had half the United States Army combing the desert looking for him, and he slipped past them like they was blind children. And now we had him. The Tenth Cavalry had done put him in a stranglehold, and we wasn't about to let go.

Apaches died by the dozens. They still stood there and fought, though, and quite a few of our boys went down too. A young trooper standing five feet away from me suddenly found an arrow growing out of his eye socket. The horrible sight made some of the newer soldiers pause.

"Don't let up!" I hollered. "Keep poundin 'em 'til they quit!"

The Apaches did not quit easy, but neither was they foolish. They ran away, leaving well more than half their number dead or dying in the canyon. The waters of Rattlesnake Spring ran red. A cheer rose up from our ranks, but there was no time to celebrate.

We chased after them.

Victorio slipped away from us one last time, just over the Mexican border. His people was bruised and tired – they could run no further, and we almost had them. That's when the Mexican army stepped in.

The Mexican force was twice our size. Their commander informed us that we was violating international law by our presence, and would we please withdraw to the border.

Grierson had no choice but to comply.

We was still close enough to see what happened. The Mexicans closed in on the weakened Victorio from all sides and began the slaughter – even the women and children who traveled with the warriors. No quarter was given. They all died. Long after the killing stopped there was still Mexican soldiers stalking among the dead, hacking and chopping – many of them had no doubt lost relatives to the Apaches.

"We have done our job, men," Grierson said. "It needed doing."

He was right, of course. We could take pride in the fact that, even though the Mexicans delivered the killing blow, it was the buffalo soldiers who caught and crippled Victorio – something no one else was able to do.

Or we could take shame, I reckon. It didn't matter. We had done what needed doing.

And we done it well.

The Medal of Honor ceremony took place about six months later. It happened at Fort Apache. Every regiment posted in the area turned out – the only soldiers missing was the cooks. Everybody was in their finest dress uniforms.

There was two other recipients besides me. There was Private Earl Summers from the Twenty-fourth Infantry – he was a guard on a payroll shipment attacked by bandits. He stayed at his post, engaging the enemy, until help arrived. This was despite being wounded five times. Also standing beside me was Lieutenant Adam DaCrosta: the lieutenant had led a charge against a far superior Apache force, dispersing them and thus rescuing the passengers of the stagecoach the Indians had been attacking.

The three of us stood on a big wooden platform that had been set up in the center of the parade grounds. All the regiments was in formation around it, and I seen several folks that I took to be reporters. Several colonels and lieutenant-colonels stood on the platform with us, and even three generals—Sheridan among them. Sheridan gave a little speech about honor and valor and outlined our achievements.

Then the medals was passed out. Under normal conditions the whole ceremony would have been held in Washington, and the President himself would hang the medals around our necks, but the Indian Wars presented a few problems. There was a lot of fighting going on, spread over a whole continent, and there would be too much traveling involved.

The President had a country to run, after all, and we had a war to fight.

So instead of President Garfield we got the Secretary of War. The Secretary was a tall man, with dark piercing eyes and a thick black beard. He gave a speech of his own, telling all the assembled troops they should strive to be just like us, and saying how proud his father would have been of such fine soldiers.

He lifted the first Medal of Honor by its powder-blue ribbon and draped it around Lieutenant DaCrosta's neck.

"Congratulations, Lieutenant," he said, "you make us proud."

"Thank you, sir," DaCrosta said.

Then he moved over and stood before me – I looked into the deep eyes of the Secretary of War, Robert Todd Lincoln. He was the son of Abraham Lincoln, the Great Emancipator.

"You make us all proud, First Sergeant," he said.

It was a great day for me. The medal itself was fine, of course – but it was a heartmoving thing to be able to look into them dark eyes and see the reflection there of another man, now just a memory—a man who risked all and gave all for a people not his own, as did some of my old officers in the War.

"Thank you, Mister Lincoln," I was able to say. They was some of the deepest words I have ever spoke, much deeper than the events of that day, and the Secretary seemed to see and to understand. I was thanking his father through him, and not just for making me free—I felt I had some hand in that my own self—but for seeing that I *was* free, and deserved to be.

"You're welcome," Mister Lincoln said, and then he moved down the line to the other colored soldier, where the experience was repeated.

I spent almost the whole of my growed life in the U.S. Army, and in that time I received a lot of medals and commendations. I won four Purple Hearts - each one of them represented my spilled blood - as well as two certificates of commendation and the Distinguished Service Medal. I also wear campaign medals from the Civil War, the Indian Wars, and the War with Spain.

But when I lift up the medal which Robert Todd Lincoln presented to me that day, when I look upon the white stars against the soft blue of the ribbon, it makes me feel different from all the others. It is the highest honor that can be given to a citizen of the United States, and the neck around which it hangs was once yoked with the chains of slavery. It stirs my soul.

The comancheros was gone, but the border was still haunted by a few holdouts - bandits and outlaws of every stripe, who robbed banks and trains and plundered whatever isolated settlements that they found unprotected.

One of the worst of these groups was the Rio Bravo gang, named for the area where they had pulled their first several holdups—they had spread out quite a bit since then.

Their leader was a vicious killer called the Cherokee. His skin was dark, and he was believed to be the result of a union between Indian and Negro, like the family I myself had married into. The Cherokee was every bit as skilled a scout and tracker as my brothers-in-law, but he was a lot quicker to draw blood. There was rumors that him and his gang was keeping the slave trade alive, selling whatever isolated folks they could capture. Them poor souls wound up deeper in Mexico, or even South America. Young white girls was especially popular. The Cherokee was a rabid wolf. He killed for pleasure; making money was just a side benefit.

The Rio Bravo gang had struck a little town in New Mexico Territory called Dry Creek. They killed the bank teller and struck out for the border with the town's savings. The sole peace officer present got up a posse at once—most of the town's men climbed into the saddle to reclaim what was theirs. A clerk telegraphed Fort Apache for help – in turn the army sent a wire to the Durham stage station with a message for me. I was on patrol with thirty men and scheduled to stop at the station. The lieutenant who had been leading us had broken off with the rest of the command to track what he took to be renegade Apaches, and left me in charge. His renegades turned out to be Mexican farmers.

The telegram ordered me to head south and join up with the posse. The outlaw gang had got their names into the paper a lot lately, and the brass decided it was time the bandits stopped humiliating the government.

We joined up with the posse, all right. What was left of them. They was on their way back to Dry Creek. They carried their dead and wounded with them – almost half their number. The Cherokee had doubled back on them and struck at the amateurs without mercy.

I let the ragged citizens continue their journey. We rode at top speed in the direction the outlaws had taken. I knowed we would have to slow down once we reached the ambush site, to look for sign, but I wanted to gain as much time and distance early on as I could. It was my hope that the killers, believing the pursuit to be abandoned, would slow down a little bit. Maybe even become careless.

My hopes was fulfilled. A bunch of desperadoes like the Rio Bravo gang might make for some pretty good killers, but they tended to lack quite a bit where discipline was concerned.

Their trail was fairly easy to follow. It was not too easy – I had been fighting Indians for fifteen years, and I knowed the signs to look for on an obvious trail which proved to be bait for a trap. This was no trap, just the tracks of relaxed men.

I missed having James Jefferson beside me. I knowed I could always fall back on him if need be—we had served together for so long that he was able to read my mind in battle. Jeff was busting dirt on some Kansas farm now, with a wife half his age. I wished him well, and wondered if he was weaker than me or stronger.

We found the outlaws camped by the banks of the Pecos River. The sun was just setting—me and the two men I had brung with me to scout ahead of the main group stayed still until it was good and dark. Then I sent one trooper back to alert the rest of our command.

The gang had posted one sentry, but he was half-drunk. The other twenty or so seemed fast asleep. It was an easy task for my troopers and me to gallop down into the camp and meet the enemy—no one offered to surrender, and I ain't a patient man, so we engaged them at once.

Our fight took place in starlight and firelight. Shadows flickered all around, and men on both sides screamed as they was hit by bullets or steel blades. It was very much like the scenes of Hell described by that energetic little preacher back home in Carolina.

My horse had been shot out from under me - which made me mad - and I had quickly reloaded my revolver and run toward the river's edge to head off three men trying to slip into the water.

"Hold it right there," I hollered. The man lagging in rear swung toward me, rifle pointed in my direction, and I dropped him with a bullet in the chest. The second man tripped in the darkness and went sprawling into the dirt. I ignored the clumsy outlaw, leaving him for one of my men to get—hopefully—and kept running. It was the lead man I wanted, and he had already reached the water. His dark skin identified him as the Cherokee. He was already knee-deep in river.

"Stop or you're dead," I hollered. He turned around, pistol in hand, and I was face-to-face with the Cherokee.

Only he wasn't no half-breed. He wasn't even no Cherokee. I knowed that scar, even in the dim light. He was the deserter, Joe Ferguson. "Howdy, Alfred," he said.

"Joe?" I said. Then, in a sterner voice, "Drop that gun, Joe."

"Cain't do that."

"What the hell are you doin' here, Joe? Are you crazy? Have you really done all the things people are sayin'?"

"I ain't never harmed no Negroes, Alfred."

"But you've sold white folks an' Mexicans as slaves. Young'uns even."

"Yeah," he said with a big smile. "Ain't that a turn, though?"

I heard a noise behind me. The outlaw I had left laying in the dirt was sneaking up on me, trying to get close enough in the darkness for a guaranteed kill-shot. It was a big mistake, but he didn't have much chance to dwell on it between the time I shot him and the time he died.

When I turned back in Joe's direction I found that he had raised his weapon. We both stood motionless with our arms straight out, pistols pointed at each other's hearts. The seconds slid slowly by. I was trying hard not to blink back the sweat that was running into my eyes. Still we stared at each other.

"Don't, Joe."

"You could let me go, Alfred. It sounds like yo' men is winnin' – if I don't start swimmin' now it'll be too late."

"You know I cain't do that," I told him, and he nodded. I seen the tiny jerk in his eyes that told me he was about to squeeze the trigger.

I fired my own weapon and throwed myself to the side – I felt the wind of Joe's bullet.

I put another shot in him, and then a third. The gun dropped from his hand and fell with a splash. Joe fell slowly backwards, the river taking him, and his sightless eyes peered up at the stars as his blood mixed slowly with the water.

The stars kept on shining, the river kept on flowing – the things that once led me to freedom. They could not save Joe Ferguson. The hate he tried to carry across with him drug him down.

I knelt down on the bank. I put the pistol in my lap, resting my grip –my fingers was tired. I hoped that my own men arrived before any of the surviving outlaws did. I didn't know if I had the energy left within me to kill anyone else, at least not tonight.

"We gots 'em under control, suh." I recognized the voice as belonging to a young corporal. "What you want us to do now, Sergeant?"

I didn't turn around. "How many still alive, Parkins?"

The corporal hesitated. "Us or them, suh?"

"Both."

"We just lost fo' men. A couple of others has got torso wounds. They's eight bandits left, suh." He looked at the floating body. "You got the Cherokee?"

"I got him."

I sighed. "All right then, Corporal. Bind the prisoners securely and post four men as guards for the first watch. Then settle in for the night."

"Here, suh?"

"There's already a fire."

"Just...settle in, suh?"

Joe's body turned slowly on the surface of the water, moving with the river current. "Just settle in."

After Corporal Parkins had left I waded in and retrieved the body – if I put it off much longer it would be carried downstream. I drug Joe onto the bank and closed his eyes.

I slept fitfully that night.

"These poor children," Isabella said.

Company M had been posted near the Apache agency at the San Carlos reservation. There was very little Indian fighting going on anymore – Geronimo was the last Apache leader still running loose, and it was only a matter of time until either us or the Mexicans caught him.

Isabella's heart was moved at the sight of the Apache young'uns—and I have to admit, they was a pitiful sight.

"They have to learn to live in the white man's world if they are going to survive," she said. "And there is no one to teach them."

The sight of the scrawny kids and the defeated elders, I'm sure, must have reminded my wife of her own people and the hard times they had when they went through the same thing two generations earlier.

"They must learn to read, and they must find God," she said. "Then maybe they'll survive."

"Government says they got to learn how to farm, too."

She snorted. "The government always says that Indians have to learn how to farm like white men. Then they stick them on land no white man would have, land where even the grass won't grow. They will wither and die here."

She stepped in front of me.

"You've been a teacher before, Alfred. You could help me start a school."

"The agency has already set up a school for Indians."

"But not a school by Indians. These children must also be taught about their own people. Their pride must be kindled and kept alive."

"The white folks around here wouldn't like that. The last thing they want is a proud Indian. Besides, the last time I tried schoolin' anybody a bunch of folks shot at me."

Isabella shrugged. "I'm not afraid. Between the two of us, we could handle them."

I chuckled. "We could at that, honey. But what about that other part - findin' God? I ain't found Him my own self."

"He is always close at hand."

"That's what Lonnie said. I reckon God is close by to folks like Lonnie and you, but He keeps His distance from me."

"He is there," she said, "you just refuse to see Him. You have to forgive God, Alfred."

"Forgive God?" I said. It was a peculiar notion.

"You don't trust Him—because you was born a slave. Because of the suffering and hurt you have seen. God is not the cause of it all, Alfred, He is the solution. When the time comes, wouldn't you rather die with a peaceful heart like Lonnie did, instead of being twisted by anger like your friends Chamas and Joe Ferguson?"

"I reckon so," I said, unsure. "But I don't know how. It don't come natural to me."

"You're nearly there," she said with a smile. "Helping me find a way to teach the children will bring you even closer."

She turned and looked at the Indian kids playing in the mud. Her smile did not fade away - her eyes looked beyond them. They was the children she would never have. She had found the missing piece to her heart. I would fight a hundred Klansmen to make sure it was put into place.

Isabella got her school. It was a very informal arrangement, and some of the government agents was not real happy about it - but nobody shot at us. I gave my spare time to her as I once had to Lonnie. I was posted elsewhere from time to time, but it was never for long - Isabella would leave the kids in the charge of her helpers until she could return.

We always went back to Arizona. With the constant flow of young'uns passing through our care, it began to feel like home to me.

One of my temporary absences was due to the Oklahoma land rush. On the assigned date the government was going to take a whole bunch of land they had took back from the Indian reservations and put it up for grabs. Anybody would be free to stake a claim, until the land ran out.

The Boomers didn't want to risk waiting. They was settlers who tried to sneak in and stake their claims early. Our job was to comb the countryside looking for them, and evict any we caught. Some of them was reluctant to go – until we threatened to arrest them. The Boomers would slink off then, waiting for a good time to come back and try it again.

Quite a few other folks just camped out near the strip and waited for word that they was all clear to move in legally. One day I was passing by a bunch of them settlers when I seen a couple of familiar faces. I trotted my mount closer to them. The couple looked nervous at first, probably because of my uniform, but they brightened up when they seen my face.

"Alfred!" Raymond Carpenter said. "Lawd-a-mercy is dat really you?"

I dismounted and shook my old friend's hand. "It sho' enough is," I told him. "How are you, Annie?"

Annie hugged me briefly. "I never expected to see you again, dat's fo' sho'!"

"You soldierin' again, Alfred?" Raymond said. "You been soldierin' all dis time?"

"Pretty much, yeah."

"Where's Sid at?" Raymond asked.

"Sid is dead. He got lynched up North – in a riot."

"Huh," Raymond said. "Reckon Up Nawth ain't all it's cracked up to be."

"Reckon it ain't," I said.

Troy D. Smith

"Po' Sid," Annie said, her eyes misting. "He was jest a big harmless chile. Never done nobody no harm – never done nothin' but make folks laugh."

I shifted my weight. "Where's the young'uns?"

"Lawd," Annie said, smiling again. "Dey all growed up now. Lawd, yes."

"We came to Oklahoma to make a new start," Raymond said.

"Lot of folks are," I said.

"Dey's plenty of colored folk around here," Annie said. "We been talkin' 'bout maybe stakin' all our land close together an' startin' our own little town."

"Wouldn't that be a sight," I said.

"You still always got a room in our house, Alfred," she said. "You know dat."

"Thanks, Annie. I might stop in some day."

"Ain't you never put down no roots, Alfred?" Raymond said. "You gettin' up yonder in years, boy – you need you some kind of home besides the U.S. Army." He said "U.S. Army" like it was a cuss word. I smiled – same old Raymond.

"I got a wife," I told him. "Her name is Isabella."

"They Lawd!" Annie said. "We gots to meet her!"

"I wish you could. She's back home in Arizona – I'll be goin' back to her once this Boomer business has passed over."

"You ought to stake out some land of yo' own," Raymond said.

"I got some, down on the border," I told him. "Isabella inherited it from her daddy – he was a scout for the Army, and they paid him in land. We thinkin' about sellin' it all and buyin' a little lot in Arizona. We're kind of settled in there."

Raymond grinned and jabbed my ribs. "You sly, all right Alfred, you sly! Got yo'self a rich woman!"

"In more ways than one."

"Say," said Annie, her eyes widening. "You one of dem 'buffalo soldiers', ain't you!"

"Yeah."

418

"You fight any Indians?" said Raymond.

"Near about every kind there is, I reckon. I'd rather fight them than Kluxers - they more civilized."

Raymond chuckled. "I reckon you an' me still better stay away from South Carolina."

"Fine by me," I said.

"We all heard about what happened to dat po' Lieutenant Flipper," Annie said. "Now dat was a pure shame!"

Henry Ossian Flipper was a lieutenant in the Tenth Cavalry—the first colored man to be an officer in the U.S. Army. He was a good fellow. Rumor had it he got a little too friendly with the white ladies, though, and the other officers brung him up on some trumped-up embezzling charges. They never proved nothing, but he was drummed out anyway.

"Flipper is a brave man," I said. "He'll make his way."

"White folks ain't never gonna let no colored man be nothin' important," Raymond said.

"We'll all make our way, one of these days," I said. "I gotta be movin' on now, folks. If I don't help hold them cheaters out of the Strip, they won't leave you any land to claim. You all take care - maybe I'll find that town of yours one day."

There was more handshakes and embraces. I never found that town, nor heard of it, but I know it existed. I know Raymond and Annie Carpenter.

Chapter Thirty-Five

The Indian Wars came to their shameful end on Christmas week of 1890, at a place called Wounded Knee. The winter had been mighty hard on the proud Sioux Indians, now confined to four different reservations in the Dakotas. They was half-starved and desperate.

Then a prophet named Wovoka brung new meaning to their lives. It was a ceremony called the ghost dance. He gave them a new religious truth—if all the Indians of the Plains would only do that dance long enough and hard enough, a new age would dawn upon them. The ghosts of their ancestors would return from the spirit world. The buffalo would come back. The whites would be swept into the sea, never to return. The Indians would have pride once more.

The Sioux confined to the Pine Ridge reservation embraced the new religion with open arms. So did the ones at the Rosebud, the Cheyenne River, and the Standing Rock reservations. They defied government orders to quit their new rebellious practices - many Sioux warriors armed themselves. The government growed very nervous.

So nervous that fully half the U.S. Army was stationed in the Northern Plains, around them four reservations. General Nelson Miles, the man who had brung in Geronimo, was in command. It was no surprise that we was among the regiments called up.

Government agents at Pine Ridge singled out a particular Indian to blame for the sudden resurgence of Sioux pride— Sitting Bull. Whether he was really behind it or not I don't know, but the Army and the public never forgave him for slaughtering their fairhaired boy Custer fourteen years before. Eighth Cavalry troopers combined with Indian police went to the old chief's home by the Grand River and took him into custody. About a hundred of Sitting Bull's outraged followers attacked, trying to free their hero, and the fighting was begun. Several Indians and soldiers was killed in that skirmish, including Sitting Bull.

The rest of Sitting Bull's followers took refuge in the band of the chief Big Foot.

Soldiers closed in on the area. Big Foot convinced his people to surrender, probably hoping to avoid further bloodshed – they came into the Army encampment on Wounded Knee Creek.

Colonel James Forsyth was in charge of that camp. Aside from his own regiment – the very Seventh Cavalry that had been defeated by Sitting Bull so long ago – he had several pieces of artillery and two companies of the Tenth Cavalry—M and B.

Big Foot was a very nervous man. He acted like a grandfather whose children and grandchildren was feuding, and he wanted to calm them all down.

"Tell them that they must be disarmed," Colonel Forsyth told his interpreter. "All weapons must be turned over to us immediately."

This got a real cold response from the Sioux. They didn't want to be completely at our mercy. Maybe they feared we would massacre them, or maybe it was just pride – either way, it took Big Foot awhile to convince them to go along with the colonel's command.

A small rusty pile of beat-up, wore-out old guns was dropped into the middle of the camp. Several warriors was openly sneering their displeasure. The women and children of the band simply stared straight ahead with empty eyes.

"This isn't all of them," Forsyth said. "They're playing us for fools. Search their belongings."

One company of the Seventh moved toward the blankets and bundles belonging to the assembled Sioux. A puny old medicine man was stomping back and forth among the warriors, hollering and waving his arms angrily at them. Several Indians sat cross-legged in the deep snow, covered with blankets, and started to sing – it was their death chant.

I had seen this kind of thing before. At the sand hills. The Indians had been pushed as far as they would go – they was on the verge of choosing death over this indignity. My hand tightened on my rifle. I wished we was mounted, like cavalry was supposed to be.

"Stand ready, men," I said in a voice just loud enough for my own company to hear me. The new lieutenant in command of Company M give me a rude look, probably wondering where on earth a simple non-com got the brass to speak out like that in the presence of his superior.

I didn't care. I had been facing enemy fire since before that young lieutenant was born. This was one simple noncom who planned on keeping his self and his men alive.

Forsyth was right, as it turned out – the Sioux had held onto their real weapons. Many of the warriors had rifles concealed under their blankets. One old man, though, refused to let go of his beat-up old rifle when ordered to, and when a white soldier moved to take it he raised up the barrel—two or three soldiers shot him at once. Later we found out the old man had been deaf. His death spurred the Sioux to action. One leaped to his feet and pumped two bullets into a Seventh Cavalry private. The Indian was immediately cut down, and all hell busted loose.

"Fire!" Forsyth hollered. The Indians had come up with the very same plan. We surged forward, white, black, and red sending deadly fire into each other at almost pointblank range. A few troopers died. A lot of Indians did. Them artillery shells tore through the crowd of Sioux like a tornado, sending women and young'uns flying through the air like bloody rags.

Big Foot raced around among the combatants – pleading with his own people, pleading with the soldiers, pleading with the Good Lord. Bullets from half-a-dozen unknown riflemen provided the old chief with the only answer to his pleas that he could honestly have expected.

The fighting was over in a few minutes. We suffered a couple of dozen dead. There was about a hundred and fifty dead Indians – almost the whole of Big Foot's band. The snow, so clean when the sun came up, was stained red.

Most all of the soldiers was shaken by the sight. Here and there a little child moaned for his mama, or a bleeding woman cradled her dead baby. There would be a few more skirmishes in the days to come, we knowed – there was other Indian bands on these reservations, and their tempers would be up when they got word of Wounded Knee.

But them skirmishes would not matter. They was already decided. We all knowed, when we looked out at the corpses littering the white banks of Wounded Knee, that it was over. It was all over.

I felt like a man who had just killed the world's last buck antelope, so as to keep from starving. I would live on. But I would never see that antelope running again. I wasn't sure how I ought to feel.

We picked our way through the battlefield, looking for injured comrades. I knelt down beside the twisted bodies of a mother and her children. A warrior's corpse lay beneath the mother – they had both been killed by the same artillery shell.

"I got a mother who is waitin' fo' me in the Promise-Land," I whispered. "I am bound for the Promise-Land...bound for the Promise-Land."

I looked up in the sky, following the gaze of the dead warrior. The winter air was cold.

There was no hawks flying among the clouds.

I tipped my glass against Abe's and took a long swallow. I set it back down on the rickety card table. Abe sighed.

"I wish you hadn't of done it, Abe," I said.

Abe shrugged. "Lord have mercy, Alfred. I gotta retire sometime. So do you."

I looked around the empty tent. "Just us left," I said. "Us and a bunch of ignorant kids."

"I'm a granddaddy now," Abe continued. "I cain't just keep on totin' around guns and bugles."

I nodded. I took another drink and waved my glass at the empty seat that had held George Dickerson in so many card games. George had stayed in till the end – one day he just slumped out of his saddle, dead from a heart attack. His passing had left me to fill his job – Sergeant-Major of the Tenth Cavalry. The most fresh-faced white second lieutenant to arrive from West Point, though well over thirty years my junior, would still outrank me.

Abe must have sensed my thoughts. "You still a nigger," he said. "But you the top nigger."

I chuckled. I had another drink in honor of all the top niggers that had went before me. My brother would have been proud.

I stayed there at the empty card table long after Abe had gone home to his grandchildren.

It sounds funny, I know, but everything came together for me in the jungles of Cuba. I was fifty-eight years old at the time – old enough that if I didn't retire soon they'd probably force me out at bayonet point. I knowed this would be my last campaign.

The Spaniards had been mistreating their Cuban subjects, you see, or at least the newspapers said so, and a lot of Americans was outraged by it. Others thought we should mind our own business. Still others wondered how all this was going to affect the price of sugar.

Then an American ship called the *Maine* blowed up in Havana in 1898, and everybody figured the Spaniards done it, so naturally we went to war. I kissed Isabella goodbye and boarded a train for Florida. We trained in them swamps to prepare us for Cuba – it made me feel even more connected to Isabella, for it was in these very swamps that her people had fought for their freedom against the U.S. Army.

Once we landed in Cuba and started marching inland, and we seen all the Cuban refugees, a familiar feeling come over me. Them civilians was half-starved and miserable, and confusion was branded into their eyes. They reminded me of the displaced slaves I had seen during the Civil War.

Our first fight came just a few days later, at Las Guasimas. There was some colorful folks fighting on our side, I can tell you that. The cavalry was commanded by General Joe Wheeler -an old man who had once been a Reb general. I don't know for sure if it was senility, malaria, or just plain craziness - but in the heat of battle General Wheeler completely forgot where we was at and what year it was.

At one point in the fighting, he reined in his horse beside me and pointed at the Spanish position with his saber.

"Them damn Yankees is cuttin' us to pieces, boy," he said. "We got to stop them bluebellies now!"

I looked down at my uniform. It was a new design -the hat and trousers was khaki, but the jacket was still the familiar Union blue. If Wheeler noticed that - or the color of my skin - he didn't show it.

"I wish I had some of my good scouts from the old days," Wheeler said. "If I could send Champ Ferguson and his guerillas into that brush yonder, why, he'd find out what's what. Probably do a murder or two, but he can't help himself."

The general shook his head. "Damn Yankees hanged him, you know. But we'll get 'em, boy, we'll get 'em! Come on!"

The lieutenant who distinguished himself the most in our regiment - and who seemed to naturally step forward and take the lead when other officers faltered—was John Pershing. He was a regular bulldog, a born commander. His friends and fellow officers in other regiments had given him the nickname *Black Jack* because he was willing to serve with Negroes - Pershing defied them by wearing the nickname with pride.

I ran through the dirt, machine-gun fire chewing up the ground all around me, and fell to the earth behind a log. Pershing was already there -I gave him a message that a runner had brung me from the general.

"You're still pretty spry, there, Alfred," Pershing said, after he had read the message and folded it away.

"When somebody is shootin' at me, yes suh, I am." I ducked down as a shell whistled overhead.

"Damn," I said. "I'm gettin' too old for this shit."

"You don't look old," said Pershing. "I've noticed that black men don't seem to age as quickly as white men. Can you explain that?"

"We don't lay awake at night worryin' about a white uprisin'," I said.

The lieutenant laughed, then we both jumped to our feet and moved forward.

Among the Arizona volunteers I found an old acquaintance. I recognized him at once, despite the fact that his hair and mustache was frosty white. He was a few years older than me. Like the other Arizona men, he somehow managed to look more like a cowboy than a soldier.

"Howdy, Captain," I said as I settled in next to him.

Jake Blackwell, retired Texas Ranger, looked at me twice. "I know you," he said. "You used to be a cavalry sergeant - still are, I see."

I nodded. "Not much career advancement for a buffalo soldier," I said.

"Reckon not. And if you notice, I'm still just a captain. I reckon fellows like you an' me is put here to fight the Indians while somebody else fills out the paperwork, huh, Sarge?"

"Reckon so, Cap," I replied. We fought side by side throughout the rest of the afternoon. We had watched each other's backs before, after all.

By far the most unusual fellow on our side, though, was the leader of the volunteer cavalry regiment, known as the "Rough Riders" - Colonel Teddy Roosevelt. With his great big teeth and his tiny spectacles, and his way of strutting around like a rooster, yet clumsy as a child, he made fellows snigger almost out loud yet still want to follow him most anywhere.

I stayed in the forefront of the fighting in the following days, close beside Lieutenant Pershing, as we made our way through the jungle. There was always several of our Tenth Cavalry boys close up behind us –I could feel their eyes upon me, watching my every move to see what they was supposed to do. The bullets from them German-made rifles whistled through the trees around us, cutting a path through the branches, and sometimes finding flesh and bone. The sound was like the approaching footsteps of an angry death-angel.

"I miss the old days," I told Pershing, "when I only had arrows and muskets shot at me."

We sat around the campfire after the fighting at El Caney. Pershing squatted in the dust, looking into the flames; he normally spent his time with us regular troops instead of with his officer friends.

"How long you reckon dis war gonna last?" Private Dibrell asked. Dibrell was a fresh recruit – he probably hadn't seen his twentieth birthday yet.

"Things is movin' along," I said. "This looks to be a short war. I been in battles that took longer – the siege of Petersburg went on for months."

"You been in a lot of battles, ain't you, Alfred," Sergeant Vinnie Coslette said.

Coslette was First Sergeant of M Troop, my old company. He was twenty-five years my junior, but still closer in age to me than most of the others was, so we had become friends. I was more of a teacher than a friend to him, really, I reckon. He was of a different generation. Coslette was born the year the Civil War ended, and had risen to the rank of First Sergeant without ever being shot at by an Apache.

And most all of the boys was younger than him. The chains of slavery had never weighed down their souls, though they carried the same scars inside as if they had. Still, they was not like my old comrades in the Fourth South Carolina—they was not driven by a fire to prove their humanity and their worth. Most did not respect the army the deep way I did, for it had been the instrument of their parents' freedom and not their own.

"Yeah," I answered Coslette. "More'n I can count."

"How many men have you killed?" Trooper Dibrell asked, and the other young faces turned toward me eagerly. Pershing listened closer, too.

"Don't rightly know," I said. "But it ain't about killin'. It's about stayin' alive."

I seen the uncertainty in their faces. They was each wondering how he would do in the next day's fighting.

"I'll tell you one thing that ain't changed," I said. "Before a battle my stomach gets all churned up and I feel like I'm gonna puke."

"Really?" Trooper Harris asked, running a hand over his smooth-shaved head. "You get nervous?"

"Scared," I corrected him. "I get scared. Everybody gets scared –but once the shootin' starts I don't have time to notice it. Concentrate on stayin' alive—and on keepin' yo' brothers alive an' safe - an' you'll do all right. It don't matter if them Spaniards eat babies or if they're saints headed right for heaven. Just remember that they're shootin' at you an' yo' brothers, an' you have to stop them. You'll forget to be afraid."

"Way I been hearin' it," Harris said, "the onliest reason we here is so dem big shots back home can keep dey hands in dis Cuban sugar bidness."

"I don't know about none of that," I said. "I know I ain't fightin' over no sugar, though. I takes my coffee black. I don't care 'bout no sugar bidness."

"Why are we here den?" Harris said.

"We here to set these people free," Sergeant Coslette said. "Same as the Army set our people free."

Now maybe that was true and maybe not. We fought just as hard to keep freedom away from the Indians, though it is true that we protected civilian lives in the process. It was a pleasant thought that we could be in Cuba to bring liberty to the Cubans, and it gave me a good feeling despite the nagging doubts I had about our real purpose, but there was something more.

"We are here," I said, "to prove one more time, once and for all, that the Tenth United States Cavalry is the best regiment in this whole army – of any color. We are the men. We can stand beside anybody and outfight 'em."

"Dem Rough Riders is gonna wind up takin' all de glory," Harris said. "Dey white."

"They can take the glory," I answered. "But we are citizens of the United States same as anybody, and we got a duty to defend it. We got a right to defend it. Other folks might take the glory, but cain't nobody take away our honor. Cain't nobody take away our pride."

"Well said," Pershing commented.

I nodded my thanks. "We got a hill that we supposed to take tomorrow – us and the Rough Riders. It's called San Juan Hill. We gonna take that hill, brothers. We gonna show 'em what men can do. And people is gonna remember."

I looked around the assembled faces. "You gonna remember. You ain't no man's slave, and you ain't no common soldier sent to do the dirty work. You are fightin' men, and you the best there is."

I fished out my pipe and lit it. It was a habit I had picked up in earnest only in recent years – partly as a private memorial to all the pipe-smoking comrades it reminded me of.

And partly it was because the smoke curling around my graying head made me seem like even more of a wise man to these soldiers in my charge – more like a father. I believe it made them feel better, somehow. I decided to lighten the mood.

"Well, boys," I said with a chuckle. "Mama always said we'd end up in Cuba if we wasn't good - and here we are."

Nobody laughed. I don't think they knowed what I was talking about.

"You see, suh," I explained to Pershing - and, through him, to the others - "when I was little the scariest thing a slave could be threatened with was bein' sold away to Cuba. The stories we heard about this place was enough to curdle your juices."

Pershing nodded. "And what do you think now, Sergeant-Major?"

"I think they better be scared of us, suh."

In the schoolbooks you see pictures of Roosevelt's Rough Riders charging their way on horseback up San Juan Hill. The fact is, us and the Rough Riders together ran up that hill - without benefit of horses—while machine-gun fire chewed at us.

A sudden burst knocked down three men who had been running to the right of me. One of them was Sergeant Coslette. I dropped to one knee beside him.

Vinnie's guts had spilled onto the ground. He was trying to scoop them back into the hollow bloody pit of his stomach. His eyes bugged out in confusion and disbelief. He tried to hold himself in with both hands - his guts had gotten dirt on them.

"Oh shit, Alfred," he sobbed. "Oh shit..."

I held a hand on Vinnie's shoulder until he died a few seconds later. Then I was running again.

We broke through the lines and engaged the Spaniards in close quarters. I was bayoneting, clubbing, kicking - I caught sight of a Spaniard drawing a bead on Lieutenant Pershing, and I shot him at once. Pershing didn't have time to thank me, but I seen the recognition and gratitude on his face.

Trooper Dibrell was fighting like a pain-mad bear. He cut a path through the enemy and fell on a machine gunner, jabbing his bayonet into the man's throat. Dibrell was terrified, and it made him fight all the harder.

The Mauser bullet took me hard in the left shoulder, spinning me around two or three times before I collapsed onto the ground. I seen the legs of the Spaniard running to finish me while I was down. Then I seen that same Spaniard fall down dead, a Bowie knife ripping into his chest, and I felt strong arms lifting me to my feet.

It was Blackwell again.

"You better hunker down safe till the fightin's over, Sarge," he said.

I shook my head, trying to clear it, and drawed out my revolver.

"The hell with that," I said. "Let's go."

Me and Blackwell rushed into a machine-gun nest, spitting fire at them until they was all dead. Blackwell sat down behind the gun, pushing a corpse out of his way.

"Feed that cartridge belt in, Sarge," he hollered. "There's gonna be a hot time in the old town tonight!"

The machine-gun leaped in his hand, churning out shells. "Keep 'em coming, Mann!"

I kept them coming, right up until another Mauser bullet knocked Blackwell back into the dust. It didn't prove to be a fatal wound, but it was enough to knock the tough old Texan out of the fight. I took his place behind the machine-gun and manned it myself. I hardly noticed Dibrell beside me, feeding the belt in as I sprayed bullets at the enemy. Somewhere along the line we ran out of ammo, I passed out, and the battle was won. I could never remember what order it happened in.

Chapter Thirty-Six

You'll remember I said that everything came together for me in Cuba. When I stepped off that train in Arizona and seen Isabella waiting for me, the whole world looked different somehow.

I swept her up into my arms, wincing and almost dropping her when she touched my shoulder. It had been shattered good. The wound might have healed back right had I been a younger man – though I doubt it. I would not be breaking anymore horses. My retirement was no longer a matter of choice. It was just as well – I was finally ready to make that move.

"I ain't never leavin' again, honey," I said.

"Damn right," she said, smiling through her tears.

I saddled my horse early the next morning and rode out into the desert. Isabella lay sleeping in the little house we had bought near the San Carlos reservation and her school.

The smell of her body still clung to me and mixed with the scent of the desert air.

There was many things I wanted to say to her, but I felt the need to first search the Arizona sky for the right words. The things I had needed to say my first night home had not required words.

I had learned something about myself in Cuba. Not while the bullets was whizzing around, of course, I was too busy – though when I was fighting side-by-side with my own troopers and with Pershing and Blackwell and the others, an understanding started to take form in the back of my mind.

I had plenty of time to think when I was laying in that field hospital. And later, on the deck of the ship which brought me home; I leaned against the railing and drunk in the sight of the ocean as it fell over the edge of the world, and of the white birds floating overhead. I had been cramped below-decks on the voyage over. Now I was able to savor it. I wished I could tell Maurice Higgins that I had finally made it onto a ship. The deck rolled gently beneath my feet, a peaceful feeling. It lulled my mind into opening all the way up.

All my life I had made my way on my own. I had never relied on anyone else, except for the two women I had loved, and never really trusted no one who offered me help. I never bent - it kept a fire stoked within me. It kept me alive.

And it kept me in control.

San Juan Hill showed me I didn't have to fight against the whole world. I freely put my life into the hands of other men - white men - and they put theirs in mine. We was equals. We was the same.

Blackwell was not better than me -and I was not better than him. The rest of the world might not recognize that, but it didn't matter. It didn't matter if Blackwell recognized it, or even if I did—it was still the truth. A truth that just *was* - and I knowed finally that I did not need to prove it to anyone, not even myself.

I didn't have to fight anymore.

After all these years I had finally found peace. And I found freedom and knowed what it was. I was ready to help 'Bella with her school, to help teach them Indian children to have pride in themselves and their people - to teach them to be free.

Freedom is not a place you run to. It's something no one can give to you, and no one can take away - unless you give it to them. I thought back on all the folks I have knowed in my life. Some of them was really free, and some of them was not.

Freedom is a place in your soul. It is a voice whispering in your dreams, telling you who you are. It is the dignity and pride of being a human man or woman. It belongs to us all.

I look up at the birds in the sky, as I have always done, as my father done before me, and I know the truth.

Freedom.
Freedom is the Promise-Land.

The End

About the Author:

Troy D. Smith was born in the Upper Cumberland region of Tennessee in 1968. He has waxed floors, moved furniture, been a lay preacher, and taught high school and college. He writes in a variety of genres, achieving his earliest successes with westerns -his first published short story appeared in 1995 in *Louis L'Amour Western Magazine,* and he won the Spur Award in 2001 for the novel *Bound for the Promise-Land* and the Peacemaker Award in 2011 (being a finalist for both awards on two other occasions.) A founding member and past president of Western Fictioneers, he edits and co-writes that organization's western series *Wolf Creek.* He earned his Ph.D at the University of Illinois, and is currently teaching American history at Tennessee Tech.

"To some he was a brutal thug, a heartless murderer - a monster.
To others he was a protector, a beloved martyr to the Confederate cause - a hero.
To a few he was a family man, a good old boy caught up in passions beyond his control - a man.
He was all these things, and more.
He was an American tragedy.
He was Champ Ferguson." ~ Troy D. Smith

"Troy Smith is a superb writer. The life of Champ Ferguson is a powerful story. Put the two together and you have a wonderful read. I highly recommend *Good Rebel Soil*." ~ Frank Roderus

The legendary days of the cattle drive era come to vivid life in THE TRAIL BROTHERS by award-winning Western author Troy D. Smith. This classic novel follows a group of cowboys, young and old, as they push a thousand head of stubborn cattle north from Texas to the railhead in Kansas, encountering Indians, outlaws, and a vengeful lynch mob along the way. If they manage to survive the dangers that dog their trail, by the time they return to Texas they truly will be brothers for as long as they live.

Troy D. Smith is a past winner of the Peacemaker and Spur Awards, and current president of Western Fictioneers. He teaches American Indian history at Tennessee Tech University. Smith is one of the most highly regarded young authors of Western fiction, and this compelling, action-packed novel is a good example of why he has that reputation. For a great yarn, saddle up and ride with THE TRAIL BROTHERS.

"This is one of the best cattle drive novels you'll ever read, folks. Highly recommended." -James Reasoner

Roy Carpenter, harmonica-playing bluesman in 1957 Nashville, knows great music when he hears it. He also knows a dangerous woman when he looks at her . . . and finds her looking back. Beautiful Sallymae has a brutal husband--just the sort of guy to end up dead, with Roy taking the fall. Prize-winning western writer Troy Smith turns to the crime novel with dazzling results. A tough, passionate, honestly written tale.

"CROSS ROAD BLUES isn't just one of the best crime novels I've read recently, it's one of the best crime novels I've read in a long time. Roy is a great character, very human, very flawed, but at the same time someone the reader can't help but root for. The other characters are very well-developed, too, and the setting is the sort of flawless recreation of a time and place that makes you think you've been there, even though you really haven't. You need to read this one, and I recommend it very highly."   -James Reasoner

"Troy Smith's *Cross Road Blues* has a great setting (both time and place), and his characters are a match for it. He takes a little blues, a little voodo, and a little mystery and mixes up a winning concoction. Check it out!" -Bill Crider

www.ingramcontent.com/pod-product-compliance
Lightning Source LLC
Chambersburg PA
CBHW061508020726
47502CB00006B/1981